The Nordic Translation Series

Sponsored by the Nordic Cultural Commission of the governments of Denmark, Finland, Iceland, Norway, and Sweden

Advisory Committee: Einar I. Haugen, Harald S. Næss, and Richard B. Vowles, Chairman

The
Fourth
Night
Watch

Johan Falkberget

The Fourth Night Watch

Den fjerde nattevakt

Translated from
the Norwegian by

Ronald G. Popperwell

The University of
Wisconsin Press

Madison, Milwaukee,

and London, 1968

Published by
The University of Wisconsin Press
Box 1379
Madison, Wisconsin 53701
The University of
Wisconsin Press, Ltd.
27-29 Whitfield Street
London, W. 1
Copyright © 1968 by the
Regents of the University
of Wisconsin
All rights reserved
Originally published by
H. Aschehoug & Co. (W. Nygaard)
Oslo, Norway
Copyright © 1923 by
H. Aschehoug & Co.
Printed in the United States
of America by
The Colonial Press, Inc.
Clinton, Massachusetts
Library of Congress Catalog
Card Number 68-9016

Introduction

It is sometimes said that the foreign reader finds it difficult to identify himself with the very localized settings of some Norwegian fiction, and that this has hindered a wider appreciation of much valuable literature. There is probably some truth in this, and it might seem to apply especially to the present author, whose work is little known outside Norway and is extremely localized both in place and time. However, though this aspect of Norwegian literature may create some difficulties, it is really only a relatively unimportant part of the total process of identification which any worthwhile piece of literature requires of the reader; identification with life in its wider and deeper aspects, which literature ought to call for, is much more important and much more exciting. In these respects the reader will find that *The Fourth Night Watch* is rich in scope.

In many respects the life and literary work of Johan Petter Falkberget are inextricably mixed. He was born in the copper-mining community of Røros in the province of Sør-Trøndelag in 1879, where he also died in 1967, having lived there for most of his life. The historical Røros also provided him with a setting for the majority of his novels, including the most important of them. Known as *Bergstaden* (*the* mining town), Røros was in its heyday the most important and lucrative mining center in Norway. It was founded in 1644 when a German, Lorentz Lossius, was granted the right to exploit a find of copper ore there, and the economic potential of this hitherto practically uninhabited region attracted a mixed population of Norwegians, Germans, and Swedes, who combined in a racial amalgam which lent a distinctive flavor to the other special characteristics of the mining community they created. This in itself gave Røros a special potential as a setting for historical novels. In addition, its mountainous situation as the highest township in Norway, its dramatic contrasts in climate, its proximity to the Swedish border and involvement in the wars with Sweden, its great church which soars over the low wooden cottages of the town —all these things provided Falkberget with an inherently dramatic background for his historical novels.

Falkberget was of part farming and part mining stock. His father was a mine foreman who, like many other miners, had his own smallholding which he looked after in his spare time. Falkberget himself, from the time he was eight, worked full time for several months of the year at the mines, washing and sorting ore, an occupation which, at times, shortened still further the scanty amount of schooling which the educational system of the day provided. He was a bright boy and, on leaving school, he had thoughts of training to become a teacher, but instead he continued to work in the mines until 1906, when he became the editor of a new newspaper in Ålesund on the west coast. This was not an entirely new departure. Falkberget had, since he was fourteen, been a contributor to the Røros newspaper *Fjell-Ljom*, where he had also published a number of feuilletons and short-stories; he had also contributed items to the press of the capital. However, though these early stories showed talent and attracted attention locally, they are mainly derivative and must be regarded as juvenilia. He made his real debut as a writer with the short story *Black Mountains* (*Svarte Fjelde*), which appeared in 1907 after he had moved to the capital, Christiania (now Oslo); the Ålesund newspaper had failed.

With *Black Mountains,* and with *In Eternal Snows* (*Ved den evige Sne,* 1908) and its continuation, *Primeval Night* (*Urtidsnatt,* 1909), Falkberget's work revealed for the first time some of those features of his literary physiognomy which later were to develop into distinctive traits. They establish the mine worker and his milieu as his proper province and the individual fate as his highest priority. Stylistically, they inaugurate the sharply focussed and strongly illuminated impressionism of Falkberget's literary method which later became such a marked feature of his work. However, although the voice of the protesting humanist is invariably heard in Falkberget, the contemporary settings of these works, with their deep social conscience and revolt against oppression, place them in these respects within the tradition of the novel of social criticism, to which *Ice-Age Winter* (*Fimbulvinter*, 1911) and *Burnt Offering* (*Brennoffer*, 1917) also belong. In fact, in its sociological aspects, *Burnt Offering* is Falkberget's most significant contribution to this particular genre. It is a story of grinding poverty, social and physical deprivation, fitfully illuminated by aspirations, dreams, and faith, and set first in the country and then in the town. It was clearly intended as a comment on peasant migration to the towns, a social phenomenon which was one of the most pressing human and sociological problems confronting Norwegians in the first decades of the present century, and one of which Falkberget had firsthand experience during his continued residence in the capital.

In 1913 Falkberget published *Eli Sjursdotter,* the first of the long series of novels set in the Røros of the seventeenth, eighteenth, and nineteenth centuries on which his reputation as a novelist chiefly rests. *Eli Sjursdotter* is set in the early part of the eighteenth century, but the action in it is preceded, chronologically, in *The Bear Hunter* (*Bjørne-Skyttern*) which was published in 1919, although it had been written some five years earlier. *The Bear Hunter,* which is set in the years from 1679 onwards and has Eli Sjursdotter's father, Sjur, as its chief personage, is not one of Falkberget's more important works, but in his characterization, especially of the violent, wayward, and fanciful Sjur, he evokes, often dramatically, the half-pagan ethos of seventeenth-century rural Norwegian life which, with its violence and ironic life-style, still contained much that was reminiscent of the ethos of the Saga Age. Its sequel, *Eli Sjursdotter,* has a firm historical anchorage (though points of historical detail were criticized) in the aftermath of the defeat of the forces of the Swedish general, Armfelt, in 1719, and their decimation in a blizzard during a retreat over the mountains from Norway to Sweden. A young Swedish deserter, Pelle Jønsa, meets Eli, and from then on the book becomes a tale, realized in monumental terms, of the

couple's passion for each other and of the hatred of Eli's father
for the young Swede. The couple flee to the mountains where
their love, tribulations, and starvation are depicted in similarly
larger-than-life terms: Pelle is killed by Eli's father; Eli's child
is stillborn; and her father eventually finds her lying dead out
in the mountains. It is a book with great dramatic potential,
and it has been both dramatized and filmed. It also represented
a big advance in Falkberget's work. Never before had he
focussed the elemental forces in human nature so sharply, or
depicted the environment in which they erupt with such
persuasiveness.

   The setting of *Lisbet of Iron Mountain* (*Lisbet paa Jarnfjeld,* 1915)* is historical in a sociological rather than a chrono-
logical sense. Its first short chapter takes place three hundred
years before the rest of the book (probably in the sixteenth
century), but it introduces the theme which was to be the
leitmotiv throughout: the incompatibility in psyche, outlook
and habit between the dweller on the high plateau and the
dweller in the valley. The story which then follows of Lisbet
and her dalesman husband Bjørn, whom she has only married
to spite another man, derives its dramatic thrust both from
the couple's inbred environmental incompatibility and from the
hate which a loveless marriage generates. These hindrances are
as elemental as the harsh plateau of Iron Mountain itself, and
are projected starkly and forbiddingly as the products of the
frustration of primal impulses, and from which disaster inexorably flows: Lisbet causes her husband's death to save her
family home on Iron Mountain from being sold; her children
are weaklings; and her lover (who is the father of one of her
children), whom she had spited by her marriage to Bjørn,
becomes an object of indifference to her. She glimpses the
Cross as a way to redemption, but her nature is too stubborn
to bend. It is the clash of characters that provides the drama in
Lisbet of Iron Mountain, but it is a clash that is rooted in tradition and environment, and as such it gives insights into

   * Tr. as *Lisbeth of Jarnfjeld* by R. Gjelsness, 1930.

Norwegian folk psychology which are admirably conveyed by the terse, harsh style of the book.

A clash of cultures, this time between Lapp and Norwegian, also provides the background of the short novel *Sun* (*Sol,* 1918), which is subtitled *A Story from the Seventeenth Century* (*En historie fra 1600-tallet*). The Lapp girl, Siri, and the miner, Brodd-Sølle, fall in love, but in spite of the difficulties caused by their disparate social and cultural backgrounds, and the hatred and violence of Siri's pagan father, all ends happily for them. In this book, too, love and hate are depicted almost as if they were autonomous forces; the one fruitful and the other destructive; and they provide the work (it has been dramatized) with its dramatic mainspring. Though *Sun* is primarily a love story, the cultural and mining backgrounds are firmly sketched in. In fact, Falkberget makes an important digression from the main story to depict an uprising of Røros mine workers, led by Brodd-Sølle, which looks forward to his *Christianus Sextus* series of novels (1927–35), and also reflects the anticapitalistic views which, partly prompted by World War I, he expressed in a tract published in the same year as *Sun.*

In the autumn of 1922 Falkberget gave up residence in Christiania and returned to Røros to live; both his parents were dead and as only son he had inherited the family farm. Apart from a short period as an editor in Fredrikstad (a town on the Oslo fjord), he had lived in or near the capital since 1907, deriving his most regular income from journalism. In particular, he had contributed to left-wing newspapers and to the magazine *The Wasp* (*Hvepsen*), where he had published many feuilletons, some of which (like *Sun*) were later published in book form. Most notable of these was *Bør Børson, jr.* which, though untypical of Falkberget's work, became his greatest popular success when it was published as a novel in 1920. The rollicking story of the peasant lad who gets caught up in the speculative boom period in Norway towards the end of World War I and becomes a millionaire was filmed and dramatized, and Bør himself became for the Norwegians a concept, rather like Peer Gynt before him, as the embodiment of a specifically Norwegian type, at least of the period.

Falkberget's return to his native region was a homecoming in every respect. Not only did he return to traditional avocations—he broke new land on his farmstead and built himself a smithy—but he was now lapped on every side by the history and traditions which had been the stuff of his imaginative work. It stimulated him to a deep study of the history of Bergstaden and to the writing of the great series of novels, *The Fourth Night Watch* (*Den fjerde nattevakt*, 1923), the three-volume *Christianus Sextus* (1927–35), and the four-volume *Bread of Night* (*Nattens brød*, 1940–59), which together are his crowning achievement.

The Fourth Night Watch, which will be discussed later in this introduction, showed that Falkberget's work had entered into a new and rich phase, strongly characterized by the imaginative use of history and local color. This is especially true of the three volumes of *Christianus Sextus*. In them Falkberget covers the period immediately after the end of the Great Northern War (the 1720's) in which Norway and Sweden had been on opposing sides, and uses the Christianus Sextus mine at Røros as a geographical pivot to which he relates his characters, and, at the same time, places them in the context of the aftermath of the war on both sides of the border. It was a setting and a period rich in possibilities for the depiction of character, conflict, and drama, and Falkberget exploits it to the full. Bergstaden had, by this time, been a mining center long enough for it to have developed its own character, self-awareness, and social complexity, and the war had left a legacy of economic misery and of bitterness and hatred between Norwegian and Swede. Also occupying a pivotal position in the work is the *déclassé* Adam Salamon Dopp (a character based on a real person). At the beginning of the book he is a bookkeeper and the local organist, and a dreamer who establishes a claim to an ore strike, knowing that another man had discovered it first. His fluid social position (his wife is a mem-

ber of the Bergstaden aristocracy) makes him a central point
of contact with the rest of the characters in *Christianus Sextus,* especially with the thirteen Swedes from the Swedish
province of Jämtland who come to Bergstaden looking for
work, and find it at his mine, Christianus Sextus. Also, Dopp's
feeling of guilt at having deprived another man of his rights,
and which leads him to seek reconciliation with him, points
to a central theme in the work. In fact it is the resolution of
antagonisms, between individuals, between Norwegian and
Swede, and between the individual and life, which gives the
book its direction. As elsewhere in his work, the harshness
of the environment in *Christianus Sextus* permits Falkberget to
depict individuals who are desperately close to the naked facts
of existence and whose human qualities are equally barely
exposed. It is the feature of Falkberget's work that he sharply
focusses these human fates—as in the love story of the Swede
Jöns and the Norwegian girl Dråka, the relationship between
the broken-down Brodde and the young girl Gölin, and others
—while at the same time correlating them with their social and
climatic environment and their collective experience of hunger,
danger, and the struggle for existence in all its precariousness.

The action in the four volumes of *Bread of Night* takes place
in the second half of the seventeenth century. Thus they pre-
cede *Christianus Sextus* in the period they cover, and complete
the historical picture of the Røros mining area which had
begun with *The Fourth Night Watch.* It is clear that part of
Falkberget's purpose in writing these novels was to document
the early history of the community from which he himself had
sprung, and to this end he had thrown himself into a detailed
study of the source material. Nevertheless, although the *Bread
of Night* series is impressive in the vividness of its realization
of historical and sociological material, all four volumes are
sharply focussed on the central character An-Magritt, a Norwegian girl who from the most unpromising beginnings grows
up to become the most influential force for good and positive
action in the community. And, although in depicting her Falkberget clearly intends that she shall transcend her immediate

role in the book and become a symbol of the best qualities of her race in her tenacity, enterprise, and invincible spirit (the first volume of *Bread of Night* appeared in 1940 after the occupation of Norway by the Germans), he always keeps her in a specifically human context, especially through her unfailing devotion to her German husband, Johannes. Otherwise, *Bread of Night* maintains much of its purely literary grip by the tensions generated by disparities in character, in race and class, in custom and belief, and in attitudes to tilling the soil and serving industry and Mammon. And there is the overriding tension of life lived with a very narrow margin for survival, which may at any time be breached by famine, disaster, or war.

Apart from these major works, Falkberget wrote numbers of short stories and a collection of verse, *Poems from Rugelsjøen* (*Vers fra Rugelsjøen,* 1925), which often throw illuminating sidelights on the author and his work; especially the poems, which not only allow full expression of the lyric gift which frequently shows itself in his prose work, but also voice the dream, the sun-dream (*soldrøm*) which, also in his prose work, symbolizes hard-pressed humanity's longing for a new era and a freer life. Falkberget also wrote a number of volumes of essays.

The Fourth Night Watch

shares many of the features of the works discussed above. It is set in Røros during the first decades of the nineteenth century, and both the incident in it and the individuality of its characters are very much rooted in this period; the principal character, Benjamin Sigismund, is supposed to be based on an actual person, a certain Svend Aschenberg, who lived from 1769 to 1845. Here, too, the action moves against a background of life lived with a very narrow survival margin, and always fraught with the possibility of sudden disaster, famine, and warlike incursions from over the border. However, it is not an undifferentiated social picture Falkberget gives. The whole spectrum of the mining community is sketched in, and is made relevant to the human fates with which the novel is principally concerned.

The problem, which was mentioned at the beginning of this introduction, that the reader may find it difficult to identify himself with a milieu that is geographically and historically remote, ought to be resolved, if it exists, by the essentially dramatic method Falkberget uses in *The Fourth Night Watch* (it has been dramatized), by which conflict and tension are generated by the juxtaposing of opposites on practically every level. Geographically, the North and South are juxtaposed in the person of Kathryn Sigismund; the cold North where she is to end her days and the South whither she longs to return in the wake of migrating birds. The story of the bell of Arvedal also brings out the same point: once it had rung out over the blithe shores of Zealand to a gaily attired assembly; now it rings in the new shift of miners on a bare Norwegian mountain. The seasons, too, contrast dramatically. Thus *The Fourth Night Watch* presents the common experience of habitat, not in a different but in a more vivid and crucial manner than it may be experienced in other regions.

From the historical point of view, all that is antithetical in *The Fourth Night Watch,* including the character of Sigismund, serves to endow it with a baroque quality which gives the book an appropriate period flavor. At the same time such antithesis is part of the drama which makes the setting come alive for the modern reader. In another respect, too, the historical situation in *The Fourth Night Watch* has a two-way dimension. The Bergstaden community was on the edge of important historical happenings in the outside world, over which it had no control, but which might involve it. It is one of the threats which, in the background, lends urgency to the novel. At the same time it is a threat which parallels the threats to which Norway had been recently exposed in World War I, and of any community or country exposed to the depredations of external forces.

But the main focus of drama in the novel is to be found in the characters. Here, too, it is generated by antithesis, though

not as *between* characters in their personal relations. The two
sets of personal triangles in the book—Sigismund, Gunhild,
Kathryn, and Sigismund, Gunhild, David—connect only very
loosely; even the relationship between Sigismund and Gunhild is, on the whole, adumbrated rather than described. Instead, drama arises from tensions and contradictions *within*
characters. They reveal themselves most of all when they are
alone. However, in a wider sense, characters in *The Fourth
Night Watch* are antithetical to each other, in the degree to
which they embody human types. Seen in this way, Sigismund
is the idealist with a streak of the quixotic; Ol-Kanelesa is a
northern Sancho embodying the common sense and life experience of the race; Dopp is an onlooker operating on the surface of life; Jon Haraldsen is of the race of Antaeus, unshake-
able, with his feet firmly on the soil. And interwoven in this
pattern of antithesis are, on the one hand, the tensions generated by the social organism itself, with its defensive attitude
to outsiders, its norms, speech differences, prejudices, and class
structure; and, on the other, the compulsive workings of sub-
conscious forces in the shape of Eros, belief, and heredity.

The basic patterns of existence emerge strongly in *The
Fourth Night Watch:* the drama of religious belief, love, and
jealousy; man in his libidinous aspect; man in his oscillation
between God and the world; in his relation to society; man
caught between volition and fate. It may be that there is
something peculiarly Norwegian in the antithetical vigor of
the book. Structurally, too, it may at times seem episodic. But
there is no lack of cohesiveness. The author's use of interior
monologue induces a close rapport between fictional character
and reader; his use of light as a pervading symbol has a unify-
ing effect; and, as commonly occurs in Falkberget's work, there
is a final resolution of antithesis in self-knowledge (the fourth
night watch) and ethical demand. *The Fourth Night Watch,*
though not on the monumental scale of *Christianus Sextus* and
Bread of Night, is in many ways his most successful work.

From the translator's point of view, *The Fourth Night Watch*
poses a number of problems which derive from the peculiari-

ties of the language situation in Norway. Until well on in the nineteenth century, and even later, the literary language of the country was, in general, practically indistinguishable from Danish. There were also considerable speech differences, especially between the official classes and the peasantry, but also between the dialects of the different areas of the country. In *The Fourth Night Watch,* Benjamin Sigismund speaks a stiff, bookish *Riksmål;* Ol-Kanelesa (the *Riksmål* version of his name is Ole Korneliusen) the clipped, pithy dialect of the region. The proximity of Bergstaden to Sweden and the use of German mining terms also gave an individual character to the speech of its common people. In English translation, since the use of dialect seemed to be excluded, these special speech characteristics have had to be rendered by turn of phrase and oral style.

In general terms, Falkberget's work lies within the "documentary" tradition in Norwegian literature. Historically, this stems from the situation of the Norwegians after 1814 when, following several centuries of Danish overlordship, they found themselves comparatively free, though joined in an unwanted union with Sweden. This new freedom gave enormous impetus to the national life, and in the renaissance that followed writers played, and were expected to play, an important part. This, together with the advent of literary realism, tended to give much of the literature written in Norway in the second half of the nineteenth century the character of social debate and documentation. An important function of literature at this period was to help establish the identity of the new Norway after the long period of Danish cultural and political domination. Just before 1900 and during the decades that immediately followed, this documentation took on a regional form called *hjemstavnsdiktning.* Writers used their native region (*hjemstavn*) as the setting for their work, and thus they gave a closer look at regional life in Norway than had been given before. Generally speaking,

Falkberget's work comes within this category, though with its historical settings and its close scrutiny and testing of the individual, it has special affinities with the historical novels of Sigrid Undset (1882–1949) and the "Juvik" series of novels by Olav Duun (1876–1939); and, with its contribution to the saga of the workingman in Norway, it has a link with the work of Kristofer Uppdal (1878–1961) and others.

Falkberget himself lived very much in the tradition that expected writers to be prominent in public debate. He was not only active as a journalist, but he was in demand as a public speaker, and he also participated in local and national politics; for a time he was a member of the Norwegian parliament (*Stortinget*). His literary work, in revealing the Norwegians to themselves and in heightening their awareness of their true identity, belongs to the great tradition in Norwegian literature. Few countries can, in this respect, have been so well served by their writers; Norwegians rightly regard Falkberget's work as both springing from and constituting part of their national heritage. But this specifically Norwegian aspect of Falkberget's achievement is not something which stands in the way of the proper concerns of literature. It is invariably seen operating in the context of individual human beings, and within a network of temporal, spiritual, and psychological relationships. And it is the management of these levels so that they seem both embedded in their age and currently valid, coupled with an individuality of style, tone of voice, and point of view, which entitle Falkberget to be regarded as one of the most important Norwegian novelists of the twentieth century.

RONALD G. POPPERWELL

Cambridge, England
May, 1968

Bibliography

Works by Johan Falkberget

IN NORWEGIAN

Hytten ved Vesle-Klætten (*The Hut under Vesle-Klætten*). First printed in the newspaper *Fjeld-Ljom*, Røros. Pp. 63–66 in *Det første jeg fikk trykt* (*My First Publication*), edited by Eli Krog. Oslo: Aschehoug, 1950.

Naar livskvelden kjem. Forteljing (*When the Evening of Life Comes. Short Story*). Røros: Amneus boghandel, 1902.

Bjarne. Et billede fra en fjeldbygd (*Bjarne. A Picture from a Mountain Parish*). Røros: Fjeld-Ljoms trykkeri, 1903.

Moseflyer. Skitser og sagn fra Dovrefjeld (*Mossy Heights. Sketches and Legends from the Dovre Mountains*). Trondhjem: Ingv. Scheide, 1905.

Vaarsus. Fortælling (*Rustle of Spring. Short Story*). Trondhjem: Ingv. Scheide, 1905.

Hauk Uglevatn. Fortælling fra Dovrefjeld (*Hauk Uglevatn. Short Story from the Dovre Mountains*). Larvik: M. Andersen, 1906.

Svarte fjelde. Fortælling (*Black Mountains. Short Story*). Christiania: J. Aass, 1907.

Mineskud (*Blasting Shot*). Christiania: J. Aass, 1908.

Ved den evige sne. Fortælling (*In Eternal Snows. Short Story*). Christiania: J. Aass, 1908.

Fakkelbrand (*Torch-Flame*). Christiania: J. Aass, 1909.

Urtidsnatt (*Primeval Night*). Christiania: J. Aass, 1909.

Nord i haugene. Eventyr (*North Amongst the Hills. Fairy Stories*). Christiania: J. Aass, 1910.

Vargfjeldet. Smaa fortællinger (*Wolf Mountain. Short Stories*). Christiania: J. Aass, 1910.

Fimbulvinter (*Ice-Age Winter*). Christiania: J. Aass, 1911.

En finnejentes kjærlighetshistorie (*A Lapp Girl's Love Story*). Christiania: Kioskernes 50 øres Bibliotek, 1912.

Eli Sjursdotter. Christiania: Aschehoug, 1913.

Jutul-historier (*Tales of Giants*). Christiania: Aschehoug, 1913.

Av jarleæt (*Of the Race of Earls*). Christiania: Aschehoug, 1914.

Lisbet paa Jarnfjeld (*Lisbet of Iron Mountain*). Christiania: Aschehoug, 1915.

Eventyrfjeld. Historier for barn. (*Fairy Tale Mountain. Stories for Children*). Christiania: Aschehoug, 1916. New, enlarged ed., 1925.

Helleristninger (*Rock Carvings*). Christiania: Aschehoug, 1916.

Brændoffer (*Burnt Offering*). Christiania: Aschehoug, 1917.

Rott jer sammen! (*Gang Up!*). Christiania: Arbeiderpartiet, 1918. Article.

Sol. En historie fra 1600 tallet (*Sun. A Story from the Seventeenth Century*). Christiania: Aschehoug, 1918.

Barkebrødstider. Nye fortællinger (*Bark-Bread Days. New Short Stories*). Christiania: Aschehoug, 1919.

Bjørne-Skyttern (*The Bear Hunter*). Christiania: Aschehoug, 1919.

Vidden. Fortællinger (*The Mountain Plateau. Short Stories*). Christiania: Aschehoug, 1919.

Bør Børson, jr. Christiania: Aschehoug, 1920.

Naglerne eller Jernet fra Norden og andre fortællinger (*The Nails or the Iron from the North and Other Short Stories*). Christiania: Aschehoug, 1921.

Den fjerde nattevakt (*The Fourth Night Watch*). Christiania: Aschehoug, 1923. There are later editions, including a shortened version for school use, edited by R. Førsund, 1939.*

I nordenvindens land (*In the Land of the North Wind*). Christiania: Aschehoug, 1924.

Vers fra Rugelsjøen (*Poems from Rugelsjøen*). Oslo: Aschehoug, 1925.

* This translation has been made from the first (1923) edition of *Den fjerde nattevakt*. In the second (1925) edition and in subsequent editions of the work a few minor cuts were made, and in one place two entirely new paragraphs were substituted for the original version (see p. 283 of this translation). In the shortened edition of the work for school use, first published in 1939, six of the chapters of the original were omitted.

1826–1926. Anders Reitan, liv og virke (1826–1926. The Life and Work of Anders Reitan). By Johan Falkberget and Elisabeth Wexelsen Jahn. Trondhjem: Trondhjems adresseavis boktr., 1926.

Christianus Sextus. De første Geseller (Christianus Sextus. The First Mine Workers). Oslo: Aschehoug, 1927. First volume of the Christianus Sextus trilogy.

Det høie fjeld (The High Mountain). Oslo: Aschehoug, 1928.

Solfrid i Bjønstu og de syv svende (Solfrid of Bjønstu and the Seven Swains). Trondhjem: Nidaros og Trøndelagens tr., 1928.

I forbifarten (In Passing). Oslo: Aschehoug, 1929. Articles.

Prolog ved Museumsutstillingens åpning på Røros 22. juni 1930 (Prologue for the Opening of the Museum's Exhibition at Røros on June 22, 1930). Røros: Dovres tr., 1930.

Christianus Sextus. I hammerens tegn (Christianus Sextus. The Sign of the Hammer). Oslo: Aschehoug, 1931. Second volume of the Christianus Sextus trilogy.

Der stenene taler– (Where the Stones Speak–). Oslo: Aschehoug, 1933. Essays.

Christianus Sextus. Tårnvekteren (Christianus Sextus. The Tower Watchman). Oslo: Aschehoug, 1935. Third volume of the Christianus Sextus trilogy.*

I vakttårnet– (In the Watch Tower–) Oslo: Aschehoug, 1936. Articles.

Nattens brød. An-Magritt (Bread of Night. An-Magritt). Oslo: Aschehoug, 1940. First volume of the Nattens brød tetralogy.

Runer på fjellveggen. Sagn og fortellinger (Runes on the Mountain Wall. Legends and Short Stories). Oslo: Aschehoug, 1944.

Ved Rolf Midttømmes båre (At Rolf Midttømme's grave). Røros: Fjell-ljom, 1944.

* In the edition of Christianus Sextus published in 1938, and in subsequent editions, the trilogy was divided into six parts, as follows: 1. De første geseller (The First Mine Workers); 2. Bergløitnanten (The Mine Engineer); 3. Over Kjølen (Over the Kjølen Mountain); 4. I hammerens tegn (The Sign of the Hammer); 5. Arbeidets riddere (Knights of Work); 6. Tårnvekteren (The Tower Watchman).

Nattens brød. Plogjernet (*Bread of Night. The Plowshare*). Oslo: Aschehoug, 1946. Second volume of the *Nattens brød* tetralogy.

I lyset fra min bergmannslampe (*In the Light from My Miner's Lamp*). Oslo: Aschehoug, 1948. Articles.

Ex Animo. Rugeldalen-Bergstaden. Røros: Fjell-ljom, 1949. Thanks for greetings to the author on his seventieth birthday.

Klippen som vil holde (*A Firm Rock*). Trondheim: Nidaros boktr., 1950. Speech to the Swedish-Norwegian Society in Stockholm, May 31, 1950.

Nattens brød. Johannes (*Bread of Night. Johannes*). Oslo: Aschehoug, 1952. Third volume of the *Nattens brød* tetralogy.

Nattens brød. Kjærlighets veier (*Bread of Night. The Paths of Love*). Oslo: Aschehoug, 1959. Final volume of the *Nattens brød* tetralogy.

Verker (*Works*). 12 vols. Oslo: Aschehoug, 1959. A collected edition of Falkberget's most important works.

Den gamle bergstad. Fører gjennom Røros og omegn (*The Old Bergstad. Guide to Røros and District*). With contributions by Johan Falkberget and Olav Kvikne. Oslo: Aschehoug, 1960.

Bergstaden Røros og residensstaden Trondheim (*The Bergstad Røros and the Capital Town Trondheim*). Trondheim: Aktietr., 1963. Privately printed. It also contains some of Falkberget's short stories.

Jeg så dem— (*I Saw Them—*). Oslo: Aschehoug, 1963. Biographies.

IN ENGLISH TRANSLATION

"Röros, the Copper Town of Norway," in *The American-Scandinavian Review*, 13: 412–21. New York, 1925.

"Petrus: The Silent Mountain Priest," trans. Anders Orbeck, in *The American-Scandinavian Review*, 14: 750–58. New York, 1926.

"Old Heggeli's Last Polka," trans. Anders Orbeck (from *Runer på fjellveggen*), in *Norway's Best Stories*. New York: The American-Scandinavian Foundation, [1929].

Lisbeth of Jarnfjeld (*Lisbet paa Jarnfjeld*), trans. Rudolph Gjelsness. New York: Norton, 1930.

Broomstick and Snowflake, trans. Tekla Welhaven (from *Eventyrfjeld*). New York: Macmillan, 1933.

"Miners Courageous. The Story of Bergman Ole Johnsen Jamt of the Røros Copper Mines," trans. Anne Tjomsland (from *Der stenene taler*), in *The American-Scandinavian Review*, 46: 363–71. New York, 1958.

Books and Articles on Johan Falkberget

Aas, Lars. *Trønderne i moderne norsk diktning*, pp. 127–60, 246–47. Trondheim: Brun, 1942.

Amdam, Per. "Fra modell til symbol. En studie i *Nattens brød*," in *Edda*, 65: 193–207. Oslo, 1965.

Beck, Richard. "Johan Falkberget," in *Scandinavian Studies*, 16: 304–16. Menasha, Wis. 1941.

———. "Johan Falkberget. A Great Social Novelist," in *The American-Scandinavian Review*, 38: 248–51. New York, 1950.

Berggrav, Jan. "Johan Falkberget," in *Kirke og kultur*, 59: 391–98. Oslo: Grøndahl, 1954.

Beyer, Harald. *A History of Norwegian Literature*, trans. and ed. by Einar Haugen, pp. 295–97. New York University Press, 1956.

———. *Norsk litteraturhistorie*, revised and enlarged edition by Edvard Beyer, pp. 385–89, 513–14. Oslo: Aschehoug, 1963.

Borgen, Johan. "Johan Falkberget," in *Samtiden*, 58: 424–28. Oslo: Aschehoug, 1949.

———. "Unge Johan Falkberget," in *Vinduet*, 11: 208–10. Oslo, 1957.

———. "Runer på fjellveggen. Til minne om Johan Falkberget," in *Samtiden*, 76: 243–50. Oslo, 1967.

Bukdahl, Jørgen. *Det skjulte Norge,* pp. 195–209. Copenhagen: Aschehoug, 1926.

Døhl, Einar. *Bergstadens dikter Johan Falkberget.* Oslo: Aschehoug, 1936. Revised and enlarged edition, 1949.

Freding, Thyra. "Johan Falkberget," in *The American-Scandinavian Review,* 21: 401–6. New York, 1933.

Hauge, Ingard. "Predikeren Falkberget i *Nattens brød,*" in *Norsk litterær årbok,* pp. 101–10. Oslo: Det Norske Samlaget, 1967.

Hedenvind-Eriksson, Gustav. "Lång väg till en diktare," in *Ord och bild,* 56: 56–61. Stockholm, 1947.

Houm, Philip. *Norsk litteratur efter 1900,* pp. 98–104. Stockholm: Forum, 1951.

"Johan Falkberget 80 år," *Universitetsforlagets Kronikktjeneste,* Oslo, No. 97, Sept. 25, 1959.

Johnsen, Egil Eiken. "Om Johan Falkberget og *Christianus Sextus,*" in *Edda,* 53: 275–307. Oslo, 1953.

Kojen, Jon. *Dikteren fra gruvene.* Bergen: Ansgar, 1949.

———. "En dikter stiger fram. Betraktninger omkring Johan Falkbergets første små skrifter," in *Samtiden,* 68: 113–25. Oslo: 1959.

———. "Grand Old Man of Literature Johan Falkberget," in *The Norseman,* No. 6: 10–13. Oslo: 1962.

Kommandantvold, Kristian Magnus. *Nabo i speilet. Sverige i norsk litterært perspektiv,* pp. 186–200. Oslo: Gyldendal, 1958.

———. "Skriftstedet 'Den fjerde nattevakt' som dikterisk og kunstnerisk motiv," in *Kirke og kultur,* 64: 632–37. Oslo: 1959.

Krogvig, Anders. *Bøker og mennesker,* pp. 119–23. Christiania: Aschehoug, 1919.

Kvikne, Olav. *Bergstaden,* especially pp. 113–25. Oslo: Aschehoug, 1949.

Larsen, Alf. "Det nye brød," in *I kunstens tjeneste,* pp. 132–48. Oslo: Dreyer, [1964]. On *Nattens brød. An-Magritt.*

———. "Med barnekjelke i korketrekkeren," in *I kunstens tjeneste,* pp. 149–66. Oslo: Dreyer, [1964]. On *I lyset fra min bergmannslampe.*

Midbøe, Hans. "Johan Falkberget," in *Det kongelige Videns-kabers Selskabs Forhandlinger*, 40: 90–95. Trondheim: 1967.

Paasche, Fredrik. "Johan Falkberget og *Christianus Sextus*," in *Samtiden*, 47: 155–62. Oslo: 1936.

———. (ed.). *Til Johan Falkberget på 60-årsdagen*, Oslo: Asche-houg, 1939. Contributions from many hands on Falkberget's sixtieth birthday.

Ramløv, Preben. "Johan Falkberget. Arbejdets og Drømmernes Digter," in *Ord och bild*, 55: 142–47. Stockholm: 1946.

Rogstad, Kaare Granøyen. *Johan Falkberget*. Trondheim: Rune, 1964.

Sørlie, Mikjel. "Johan Falkberget og fornorskningen," in *Den Høgre Skolen*, pp. 141–44. Oslo, 1968.

Thesen, Rolv. "Johan Falkberget seksti år," in *Mennesket i oss*, pp. 76–85. Oslo: Aschehoug, 1951.

———. *Diktaren og bygda. Natta og draumen*, pp. 143–46, 149–55, 196–206. Oslo: Aschehoug, 1955.

———. *Johan Falkberget og hans rike*. Oslo: Aschehoug, 1959.

———. "Humoren hos Falkberget," in *Syn og segn*, 65: 291–98. Oslo: 1959.

———. "Livsbelysning i Johan Falkbergets diktning," in *Ord och bild*, 69: 388–94. Stockholm, 1960.

Welle Strand, Edward. "Johan Falkbergets kampår," in *Gads Danske Magasin*, pp. 562–73. Copenhagen, 1950.

Winsnes, A. H. *Norsk litteraturhistorie*, 5: 549–66. Oslo: Asche-houg, 1961.

Contents

The
Fourth
Night
Watch

Benjamin Sigismund and the Old Charcoal Wagoner

The old charcoal wagoner walked in front of his horse and tested the ice with a long, yellowish juniper stick. It wasn't without danger to travel along the frozen river now. Today was already the 25th of April. Even though there hadn't been any appreciable warmth in the air yet, the ice was melting underneath all the same.

The ice re-echoed hollowly under the blows of the stick. And the sway-backed horse struggled and tugged at the heavy load of charcoal.

Charcoal! Was it a load of charcoal he had? The wagoner had to laugh. No, today he had, sure enough, something which was both finer and dearer than charcoal in his wagon. He shifted his stick over to the other hand and tried once more to take on a serious expression. He was driving the pastor, of course! The new pastor of Bergstaden. His name: Sigismund! Benjamin Sigismund! And the pastor's wife and two boys were also sitting up there. The woman was miserably grey and thin; but the pastor himself, well, he looked like a soldier; like a Swedish dragoon.

At this point the wagoner suddenly grasped the bridle and halted. There was open water in the river, and it foamed green against the edge of the ice.

The pastor, Benjamin Sigismund, stuck his head out of the sooty wagon.

"Well!" he said, and cleared his throat with great authority. "Is the ice thin?"

"Hm! Thin as it can be."

"Then drive around it, man!"

"That we must, if we're going to move from here."

And pastor and wagoner glared at each other, the one reprimandingly, the other with concealed contempt.

The pastor pulled his cap down over his ears and looked away. He had never seen such a wolf-like face on a man before. If that was the sort up here, he was in for a hard time.

He pursed his lips. He intended to give as good as he got. Above all, these rough and ignorant people must not be allowed to get their pastor on his knees.

Now his wife began to stir herself amongst all the sheepskin blankets they had borrowed at posting stations on the way up the Østerdal.

"What is it, Benjamin?"

Her voice was thin. Her teeth chattered and she had difficulty in speaking. Her thin, bloodless lips were almost frozen.

"Sit still, Kathryn!"

She heard from her husband's voice that he was out of humor, and she tried to remain calm. If only she wasn't so cold.

Whew! Actually the air was not so cold just now, but the frost was still in her body . . . from a time far back in the past. Once a poor creature was thoroughly frozen, it was surely no use trying to get really warm again. Yes, if all the sun in the world shone on her it wouldn't help. She closed her eyes—slowly, tiredly, and indifferently. No, for her it was no use ever trying to be warm again.

Sigismund jumped up off the wagon. He was an active man with powerful movements.

"What is happening, Tøllef?"

"It looks as if we'll have to drive round."

And Tøllef gripped the horse more firmly by the bridle and led it slowly and carefully in a big circle past the open water.

Sigismund climbed up into the wagon again and spread a hairy horse-rug carelessly over his long, dubbined boots. Now he was really put out. The wagoner's last answer hadn't pleased him at all. On the whole, this beginning augured nothing good. This dirty wagoner had given him a feeling of what the people up here were like. A blast from their soul had touched him; it was cold, icy cold! It was a question of getting the upper hand from the start, a question of being firm! Above all, no vacillation! By virtue of his high and holy office, his will should be stronger than theirs. . . . Hadn't God plainly promised that? Yes, of course! He felt a growing inner strength; he had taken on the full armor of God.

And yet! From the first moment he had crossed the frontiers of this mountain landscape a peculiar steely, cold quiet had met him. Something immoveable. All these silent lips, all these cold grey eyes, spoke a hard language. The further north he came, the closer the mountains, the harder and more stony the minds of the people seemed to be. Neither sorrow nor joy seemed to affect them. . . . Or was that just a shell, an outer husk which had congealed in this harsh landscape?

He was somewhat in doubt. He still couldn't be certain about anything. Nevertheless, he would go ahead, break ground and make way for a really deep and true Christianity. Once the eternal sun shone right into their souls, the outer man would change on its own. He had much past experience to support him in this view.

His wife, Kathryn, glanced furtively at her husband. Once again Sigismund had a wicked expression in his eyes. No, not exactly wicked. She didn't mean that; but a hard, imperious expression. A minister of the church, she supposed, had to look like that, but sometimes it could affect her as something cruel—something boundlessly unmerciful. She suppressed a sigh. Sigismund mustn't be disturbed now. Perhaps he sat there thinking of his inaugural sermon. That was always a very important sermon. It was decisive for a clergyman's reputation. Well. That was almost a worldly thought. She remembered what Benjamin had said about his inaugural sermon in his last parish: "The inaugural sermon is the banner!" he said. "It is a pennant in the breeze!" Benjamin Sigismund's banner would be seen as a red sign over the great snow-covered moors. She had heard that there were such enormous snow-covered moors around this northerly Bergstaden.

Every day, yes, many times a day and at night too, she had prayed to God that her husband might be given the grace and strength to concentrate on one thing alone: the further-

ance of the kingdom of God on earth. Then everything would
be well—first of all for himself—and then for her and the
children.

She forced a fresh sigh down into her sunken chest. And
the cold fingers of her thin hands grasped each other in pain,
in despair, under her homespun coat.

The wagoner was still leading his horse by the bridle. He
was thinking about the pastor. He looked like a handsome,
a real sturdy fellow, but sure to be hard and self-righteous,
wasn't he? He was probably the same as the rest of the bigwigs. Had no idea what the working man had to contend with.
People said he was a good preacher and not lost for words
in the pulpit. Yes, that's what they said, anyway—but it would
have been just as well and more comforting for a wage-slave
if the pastor had had a little understanding of what it meant
to slog night and day for daily bread. And holding the sheriff
at bay at Elgsjøen; that was the worst of all. What did the
pastor know of being out on the roads with a worn-out nag
year in and year out in all sorts of weather and conditions?
No, thank you very much! He certainly didn't know that.

The wagoner blew his nose with his fingers. There he was
again thinking of everything that was wrong; hadn't he promised himself many a time that he would never think in that
way again about the powers-that-be? And yet! All these
wicked thoughts were over him again, all at the same time, before he could so much as turn around—they came rushing at
him like a pack of wolves.

It was queer, this wagoner's job. One was so much alone.
One just thought of the bad things. And about one's debts! But
when he was with others, it wasn't much better either. Then,
everything he said was wrong and blasphemous. No, no one
should be a charcoal wagoner. Charcoal was black, and black
was he who transported it too, both in body and soul.

"Gee-up," he said to the horse. "Gee-up, will you!"

Today he couldn't exactly say that he had a load of charcoal,
and he ought therefore to have thought better thoughts; but

these bigwigs! They were scum. No! No! Again his thoughts
were all wrong.

"Gee-up! Gee-up!" He wasn't speaking to the horse now but
to his own stubborn thoughts.

The slow and monotonous movements of the horse and the
wagon made Sigismund sleepy. There was something grey and
lifeless about the whole journey. A snail's pace which dulled
the senses.

In any case he hadn't slept much during the last two months.
He wasn't at any time one of the Seven Sleepers. When he was
a student in Copenhagen almost weeks could go by without
his closing his eyes. At the most he would take a little nap at
the table with an empty tankard beside him in the early morning hours.

"When are we going to arrive at Bergstaden, Tøllef?"

The wagoner went on for a while without answering. He
was going to say that it depended on whether the ice on the
river and the iron chains on the shafts would hold—but since
it was the pastor who asked, perhaps he'd better answer more
or less politely.

"About seven o'clock." He half turned his head. "The road
is so damned mucky!"

Perhaps the pastor would give him a tip as well, when he
heard that the road surface was so bad? Parsons were usually
pretty tight when it came to paying for transport. The worst
of the scoundrels just said thank you for the trip.

Sigismund didn't understand the wagoner's brogue very
well, but he possessed himself with patience. The man's tone
was happy and friendly; it told him something of the temperament of the people here, that it had a bright side.

To the east the trees on the hillside began to sough in the
rain-laden wind from the south—the warm wind that would
melt the snow! The wagoner heard it and looked up. He knew
what it meant, and it was as if something in him changed
from dark to light. Now the spring winds were blowing over
the Elgsjø Lake and its slopes. Every spring when he heard

that wind he thanked God. And now the sun was coming out.
. . . "Praise and thanks be to God for sun and wind," he
mumbled.

Sigismund hadn't heard the south wind in the forest. He and
the wind were still strangers, but he saw the sun, and a great
joy leaped in his mind. The sun! The light! "Let there be light!"
God's first and most glorious command to this earth. The watch-
word of God's children should be, "Let there be light!" The
earth was once again sailing into darkness, as when the Spirit
of God moved upon the face of the waters. But it was a darkness a thousand times worse: the darkness of hate and discord!
Brother fought against brother, son against father. The whole
world still stood under the Sign of War. Now it was the year
of our Lord 1807. And the sword dripped with fraternal blood
as never before. But the life, death, and resurrection of Christ
was a renewal of God's first word. The lives of His servants,
too, ought to bear that device, "Let there be light!"

"Kathryn!"

She looked up slowly, almost fearfully.

"Yes, Benjamin?"

"Have you ever thought how eternally much there is in
those words, 'Let there be light'? What a sum of the living life!"

His wife blinked up at the sun. It flooded with light. Now
light shone both from the sun and from the snow. She had
heard that in the mountains the snow shone so piercingly.

"Yes, yes. It's lovely."

"Lovely?" Benjamin Sigismund repeated. "That word is quite
inadequate; Ah, it is something much more! Something infinitely much more!"

He sat there, his eyes closed, and let the sun shine on his
face. Worlds rose up, worlds of brilliance and glory; millions
of beings sprang out.

But Kathryn disappointed him. She lacked that inner, intensely burning flame. Why didn't she cry out, "Oh, they're
wonderful, those words! Wonderful!"

The horse stopped again. They had met a long line of ore

wagons coming from the mines. And at once the drivers and
Tøllef began to abuse each other.

"Out of the road!" a driver in an ankle-length sheepskin coat
shouted. "Get packing!" And he swung his crook over Tøllef's
head.

"Watch yourself, Stæffa," Tøllef said, and tried to calm the
angry driver. "I'm driving our new parson, Pastor Sigismund."

"Oh, go to hell!" the ore wagoner said. "D'you think I'm getting off the road for a dog-collar!"

"What's this?" Sigismund shouted in a mighty voice, making
the driver start. "Will you move out of the way, this very
instant!"

He braced his hands on the side of the wagon and with one
jump landed out on the ice.

"Benjamin!" his wife wailed. "Take care, Benjamin!"

The people up here at the mines were almost savages, she
had heard.

"Over to the right with you!" Sigismund bawled.

He shook his fist at those standing nearest him.

"We're not driving our loads out into the river!" came the
defiant reply from a lame man at the back of the crowd. "It's
worse for the load to get wet than the parson; he's always got
time to dry himself!"

Now nearly everybody began to laugh, and spat out brown
tobacco spit over the snow. Their faces became better humored.

Kathryn was greatly upset and looked paler than ever; it was
frightening how dirty these people were, they looked like robbers. She had time and again to clutch at her heart.

Sigismund became even more infuriated that they stood
there laughing at him to his very face. All these wild and in-
solent peasants were presumably his future parishioners. That
they could really have the impertinence! He seized one of
them standing nearest resolutely by the collar of his sheepskin
coat and gave him a good shaking.

Now everybody laughed; they roared with laughter! Even the man who was being shaken laughed.

Kathryn had got up on her knees in the wagon.

"Benjamin!" she shouted. "They'll kill you! For our sake, Benjamin!"

Robbery and violence were no doubt almost daily occurrences here in the mountains. She had also advised Benjamin against accepting this parish. Now he could see for himself. If only he had said no, firmly and decisively, when he received instructions from the Danish chancellery to set off up here without delay, the authorities would certainly have given in.

Sigismund's rage got completely out of hand. He would soon turn their impudent laughter to weeping. He pushed the man and he fell back sprawling on the edge of the road.

"You're depraved, I tell you! Depraved, the lot of you!"

In the meantime Tøllef had got his horse and wagon up on to the upper side of the road. And then the ore wagoners began to drive past, one by one. They sat there with faces like blackamoors, laughing and showing their white teeth at the pastor.

"You will all pay for this!"

He had the greatest difficulty in controlling himself. Most of all he wanted to lash out at them, wanted to mete out corporal punishment to them.

Slowly, at a monotonous pace, they continued up towards Bergstaden. Tøllef tried to explain and make the pastor and his wife understand that the ore wagoners weren't anything to bother about, it was nothing but tomfoolery. Kathryn still trembled with terror. And Sigismund sat with his hands clenched in his grey woollen mittens. When Tøllef saw that all his explanations and reassurances were only adding fuel to fire, he kept quiet. They could sit there; to be sure they could! Was it his business to calm them?

Kathryn still had to clutch at her heart, her terror wouldn't leave her.

"How could you dare, Benjamin?"

"Dare? Dare?" he repeated. "It would be a fine thing if I

didn't dare! I'll teach these vulgarians manners; be certain of that!"

Kathryn didn't answer. The very fact that Benjamin dared so much was so terrifying. She had always wished that he would dare a little less.

And the day went on; it was approaching evening. And Sigismund asked Tøllef what time it was. He hadn't a watch now, Sigismund. Shame to say, he'd had to pawn it to get money for the long and expensive journey.

The wagoner pulled a face, and with one eye half open he looked inquiringly at the sky and said he thought it was nearly seven o'clock.

"And where are we now, Tøllef?"

"We're soon up by Sjaafram."

"What! What did you call it?"

"Sjaafram."

The pastor and his wife looked at each other. Neither of them understood what the peasant had said. The peasants in these parts spoke so indistinctly—they swallowed the ends of their words.*

"What is that smoke over there to the east?" Sigismund then asked.

A strong, acrid smell of sulphur seared their nose and throat. And now Kathryn began to cough. She felt as if she was going to be suffocated. She gasped for breath.

"Smelting smoke," Tøllef answered.

"What?"

"Smelting smoke!"

"Speak so I can understand you," Sigismund said harshly. The driver was silent.

"Can't you speak so we can understand what you are saying?"

The driver still said nothing. He had no difficulty in holding his peace. He wasn't going to talk like the bigwigs. And if the parson couldn't understand what people up here said, then he had no business to be here at all. Then Tøllef remembered

* *Sjaafram* is a farm name meaning "Look Out" or "Look Forward."

that he would soon be getting paid for the journey. And an
extra penny or two wasn't unimportant for a poor charcoal
wagoner from Elgsjøen. But was it worth buttering up the parson for an extra copper? No, he could do without that! He
would be ashamed to have that sort of money in his purse.

Benjamin Sigismund sat there and wondered about the thick
smoke. It forced him to think of Hell. Quite frankly, he felt
that he was now on his way to the land of the damned. The
smell of sulphur penetrated into his soul. Was it a blast from
the fiery furnace?

That, too, should remind him of the task he had before him
here: to fight the world, the Devil, and his own flesh. The
flaming sword of zeal and faith, which he already held in his
hand, must never rest.

He breathed deeply. Now he knew what it was: the smoke
came from the smelting works at Bergstaden. It was supposed
to be a very healthy smoke. It even protected one against the
plague.

"Kathryn," he said. "I am certain that the smoke here will
do your poor chest good."

"Are you sure of that, Benjamin?"

"Quite sure!"

He shut his eyes and took some really deep breaths, so as
to demonstrate the great curative properties which lay in this
smoke.

"Ah! Sulphur is, of course, one of the most important things
in the whole of medicine."

"Yes, you studied medicine for a while in your first student
years, didn't you, Benjamin?"

"Have you forgotten that, Kathryn?"

"Yes, but now I remember. Didn't you write something
about it in a letter from Copenhagen?"

"In two letters," he said. "I even asked your advice as to
whether I should become a doctor or a parson."

She nodded.

"You must forgive me, Benjamin."

Sigismund found it difficult to forgive her just that—for the

truth was that Kathryn really had forgotten a matter which at
one time had been extraordinarily important to him. After a
great struggle with himself, he had finally decided to become
a clergyman. He had written in great detail in two letters to
Kathryn about it. Had it not been those two letters she had
forgotten, but two others, he would have said nothing about
it—then it would have been excusable.

He turned away from her moodily, and sat there peering
northwards, towards Bergstaden.

The town lay under a cloud of yellow-grey smoke. Only the
uppermost part of the church, with its gilded cherub with
trumpet on the spire, stood out.

In this high spire Benjamin Sigismund saw the flagpole
under which he was to battle; for a short or a long time, that
rested in the hand of Almighty God.

His thoughts were filled with a deep solemnity at the sight
of the church to which he had been appointed. He was now
driving through the gateway to a new land. And to a new
and unknown people! Even so, one thing would remain the
same wherever he went: *God's law and the gospel of Christ!*

As he sat there he wondered why everything was so quiet.
Towns usually have their own unmelodious sound. Perhaps
the people of Bergstaden had already gone to bed?

High over the town and the sulphurous smoke he saw that
a star had come out. A pale star with a bluish hue.

Hark! The song of many bells rose suddenly out of the heavy
quiet. It sounded like a carillon from a church tower in southern lands. Like a hymn of praise, it rose over the heathland.

He seemed to recognize its tune. He sat there, his gaze
turned towards the pale blue star, and hummed:

Now my star is burning
Lit by thee O Lord,
O'er this earthly state.
At thy bidding word
Now through grace is turning
The page of my sick fate,

The bright turned up,
The black turned down,
Blest and signed
By love divine.

Yes, it was of His love that he had been called to bear witness. And in this desert of snow and ice. He, the most unworthy
of all the Master's disciples.

"I say, Tøllef! What are those bells we can hear?"

Tøllef pretended not to hear. He wasn't going to be delayed
by talk. He was eternally glad they would soon be there. And
he gave the reins an imperceptible jerk.

"Tøllef!" Sigismund shouted.

His voice was kind; very kind.

Tøllef stopped unwillingly.

"Tell us, my good Tøllef, what is this wondrous sound of
bells we hear over Bergstaden?"

"Bells? What does the pastor mean?"

Tøllef looked uncomprehendingly at the pastor and his wife.
What in heaven's name was it he meant?

"Come here," Sigismund said, still kindly. "Come here at
once."

The wagoner put his stick under his arm and came bent-
backed and with long steps up to the wagon.

"Do you not hear that strange sound of bells in the air?"

All three listened.

"It's the Works' bell," Tøllef said. "They're ringing in the
nightshift up there."

"Are they not the church bells we are hearing then?"

Kathryn had thought that she, too, must ask about something.

"Oh, far from it," Tøllef said. "No one's going to take it into
his head to ring the church bells now."

Tøllef couldn't help smiling a little out of one side of his
mouth. The pastor asked stupid questions, but the questions
his missus asked were so nonsensical that they weren't worth
an answer.

Shortly afterwards they drove into a cloud of sulphur smoke. In there a crowd of people and horses met them, and Sigismund and his wife noticed with a feeling of terror that all the people were black in the face and on their hands.

Now there was a song not only from the Works' bell but also from hundreds of bells round about them. Every single horse pulling the charcoal and ore wagons had a bell, either on its wooden collar or on the shafts. And these bells had their own rhythm—their own sad melody.

After the Long Winter Sleep

Night. Bright night.

The fire was burning down on the hearth. Now everyone was dreaming on his straw couch with eyes open and senses awakened, dreaming of past joys and future happiness.

The Lapp in his twig hut, the miner in his stone cottage, and the peasant under his low rafters, all of them lay there and listened: Was the spring coming now? A dripping from the roof, the high-pitched note of a bird, ay, it was a miracle of God.

In Bergstaden there was excitement and a swarm of travellers coming and going. In the lodging houses doors opened and shut day and night—in the outbuildings as well as in the main building. The closer spring came, the greater the excitement. The light nights, with blue sky and stars that were almost white, kept both young and old from their beds. They walked along side by side, thinking, No, you're not asleep, are you? Now, when they had just awakened from their long winter sleep? Now life was beginning again at the beginning.

And out in the stables which the travellers used, there was a strong smell of horses and tarred harness. Ice and snow were melting in the yards. Hay which had fallen from the hayracks lay floating like yellow mats on the mud. Sledges stood on end with their shining runners turned outwards, glittering like silver in the light of the night.

Avalanches of snow, black earth, and withered straw fell from the house roofs. And the magpie was busy building its nest under the eaves from dried twigs fetched from afar; it was so far to the nearest forest from Bergstaden. Laughing and chattering they put one twig on the other in the morning sun. "Skarr! Rarr! Arr!" they said. "Skarr! Rarr! Arr!"

In one of the stable doorways Tøllef Elgsjøen stood counting some coins he held in the hollow of his right hand. The light from the clear spring sky in the north fell on their silver. And it seemed to the wagoner that they shone with such luster that it almost hurt his eyes. Yes, now he had to see how much money he had got from Sigismund for the journey. And Tøllef counted and counted, over and over again. He'd got too much, for sure, hadn't he? A whole crown too much, at least. That Sigismund was a queer chap. When he got out of the wagon outside Leich's house, he took out his purse, laughed, and rattled it close up to Tøllef's ears. And then he said something which Tøllef hadn't understood, sounded like Greek to him. And then both he and his wife laughed. "Cup your hand and hold it up, my good Tøllef!" he said. Then he took his purse and emptied it into Tøllef's hand. When Tøllef wanted to count the money, he just closed his hand and said, "We'll count it later." "He's cheating me!" Tøllef thought. "Downright cheating me!" He must count the money once again. He got down on one knee, cleaned the doorstep carefully with his elbow, and laid one coin beside the other. . . . He tried to work it out, tugged at his hair, and counted! He couldn't exactly say that he had a head for figures, but there was a crown too much, that there was. God bless the pastor! Now he repented all the bad things he had thought about Sigismund. Wasn't it just what he had always said to himself, that one should never say or think anything bad about a person one didn't know? The wagoner put the money remorsefully into his purse and snapped the lock. "Click!" it said. And then he put it, slender though it was, into the inside pocket in his waistcoat, and buttoned up each brass button thoughtfully and seriously.

He stood there wondering whether he should go into the house and sit down for a while on a stool; he wouldn't get any sleep tonight anyway—it was queer with sleep in the spring, it was as if it disappeared with the snow and the ice. But what if he just went into the stable and sat down there on a hayrack? He could let the stable door stay open; then he could see the pale, beautiful spring light.

He reached out for his food bag and took it with him. His swallow was dry; he had an empty feeling in his stomach. He hadn't eaten any real food today. But then he remembered that his bag was empty. Well, it was no good complaining about that! Tomorrow he could buy enough to fill both his knapsack and his metal food container. That was easy when one had the money.

Tøllef slapped himself proudly over his chest where the purse lay.

Yes, that old sheriff wasn't going to get his hands on *this* money. He seldom saw any cash for the charcoal and the transport; all he got for his hard work went straight to the provision store. And to the sheriff!

He tottered, exhausted, the empty food bag over his shoulder, in through the door, and threw himself down on the straw put out for the horses.

When the church bell struck one shortly afterwards, the wagoner was asleep. He tossed in his sleep. He dreamt that he ate and ate and was never satisfied. And then he dreamt about the big gold nugget.

The First Night in Bergstaden

The new pastor had taken lodgings with Mr. Morton Leich, the biggest merchant in the town. Here Sigismund and his wife had been given a tiny, poverty-stricken room with small lattice-windows and yellow whorls in the panes.

Kathryn was standing in her travelling clothes out in the passage, and peeped into the half-dark room. A ghastly hole! It smelled of dry rot and dirty furniture. There were no curtains at the windows. No carpet on the floor. She could have cried out—it was as if she was looking down into a grave. So this was where they were to live. . . . Or perhaps it was here she was to die? It seemed to her that she could see herself, lying there pale and lifeless, in a bed away by one of the walls.

"Benjamin!"

Kathryn wanted to say something more but words escaped her. She groped for her children's hands—for their precious small hands.

Sigismund went into the room and stopped in the middle, his hands at his side. He stood there like a giant in a doll's house. And he turned round on his heel a couple of times, so that the thin, worn floorboards gave under him. He cleared his throat ominously and gave Leich, who stood there bareheaded and with a bunch of keys in his hand, a forbidding look.

"Haven't you any worse accommodation for your pastor, Mr. Leich?"

"I have nothing worse and nothing better, your Reverence." And added, after he had made a characteristic movement with the keys: "We're not, I'm afraid, used to anything better here in Bergstaden."

"Come, children!" Kathryn said to her two small boys, who stood there blue in the face, their arms dangling in adult coats. "It's impossible to stay here."

"Kathryn!" Sigismund shouted. "We and the children can't spend the night in the street."

"If that happens it won't be my fault, Mr. Sigismund,"
Leich remarked.

"We'll come back to that subject later," Sigismund said.

He tried to give the merchant another of his forbidding
looks, but it bounced off him. And then, to their great astonishment, Leich asked them in a most friendly tone if they
wouldn't be good enough to make the best of the accommodation. In the meantime Gerhard could put some fuel into the
stove and light the fire, so that it would be more comfortable
in here. He would also tell the maid, Anne-Sofie, to bring in
some water so that the pastor and his lady could wash. And
Leich smiled sweetly, as if completing a business deal, first
to Kathryn and then to the pastor.

"Thank you very much," Kathryn said, and bowed con-
descendingly.

"Thank you," Sigismund said curtly.

At table in Leich's sitting room, Sigismund and Kathryn and
their hosts avoided conversation on anything other than the
journey up through the Østerdal. It was a bad time of the year
to undertake long journeys. The pastor and his wife hadn't
been too cold, had they? No, not too bad. Indeed. Well, that
was good to hear. It was worse for the children, naturally.
But with children one should never travel so far except on a
summer's day, when the sun was shining and there was
warmth in the air. According to the calendar it ought, true
enough, to be spring, but this year it had kept one waiting.
As a matter of fact, it seemed that spring came later and later
for every year that passed, and on top of that there was this
war which never ended. And to make the time pass further
at table, Morten Leich told them about a number of exhaust-
ing journeys he had had to make to Christiania. On one of
them he had developed pneumonia on the way down and had
lain ill for three weeks at the sheriff's in Eidsvold. He'd had
to get a German surgeon from Akershus Fort in Christiania.
He had bled him. Well, well. The whole time he was away,
his wife had had to manage the business alone. Yes, they

would never forget that time; on the whole, it had been a very difficult year.

"Mrs. dean, may I have the honor of drinking your health?"

The merchant again smiled sweetly and bowed deeply to Kathryn. There was almost nothing left in his glass, a drop or two. Mr. Leich was a very careful gentleman.

"Your health, Mr. Lig!"*

"Leich," Sigismund said.

"Oh, I'm terribly sorry," Kathryn stammered.

"Your health," Morten Leich said. "Thank you! Thank you!"

It was always difficult, to begin with, with strange names, Leich maintained; many of his business friends, even some of his old ones, both in Trondhjem and Christiania, had often confused Lig with Leich, it was so easy to mix them up.

Nevertheless, Kathryn felt embarrassed and put down her glass unnecessarily near the center of the table. She didn't even know if the name Lig existed.

Leich then took out his gold snuff-box and passed it over the table to the pastor. Both gentlemen took a pinch of snuff and then sneezed. Leich sneezed very violently today; he wasn't in the habit of sneezing, but in order that his Reverence shouldn't sit there and sneeze alone, he followed suit and sneezed repeatedly.

And, meanwhile, he sized up the pastor and his wife: What vain people! He had on purpose called Mrs. Sigismund "Mrs. dean," but neither she nor her husband had corrected him.

Kathryn lay and shivered with the cold during the night. Cold came off the walls. And the bedclothes, too, were icy cold. Now the cold froze her both from within and without. And the darkness between these walls was colder and blacker than any other darkness; a darkness of past ages, full of poison! She could almost grasp it with her hands—slimy and cold as a serpent it felt. And it spread itself heavily over her chest and her face.

And she lay there for a long time listening to the breathing

* *Lig* (Norwegian) and *Leich* (German) both mean corpse.

of the boys. Just as if she was afraid this darkness would
smother them. But they slept; Sigismund was asleep too,
wasn't he? The whole world had fallen asleep. Only she lay
awake and listened, not with her ears but with her heart. But
however terrible all this around her was, that was not the
worst of all. Inside her there was something which was even
more terrible: an eternal terror in her mind and soul. But for
what? For all the evil she couldn't see with her eyes or hear
with her ears, but which she knew existed. It was a terror
that had eaten into her soul. In everything that was, and in
everything that would be, there was terror. Oh, this boundless terror accompanied her thoughts as the shadow accom-
panies the body. She couldn't escape from it. Even though
she fled to the ends of the earth, it would hurry along beside
her the whole way.

Finally her eyes slowly closed. Even in her sleep she felt
terror, but finally sleep became the stronger—beautiful, deep
sleep.

But sleep fled after a while. And terror was there again. In
her distress she folded her hands and tried to force her
thoughts to prayer. She didn't pray very much for herself.
And not for the children either.

Yes, there were others to pray for. . . . She lay there listening to Benjamin Sigismund's breathing. She couldn't decide
whether he was asleep or awake.

"Benjamin."

"Yes, what is it, Kathryn?"

"Can't you sleep either?"

"Not yet."

She wondered that his warm body couldn't warm hers. In
her imagination it seemed that someone lay between her and
her husband. And this someone took all the warmth that was
due to her.

"Lord! Lord! Thou who knowest everything, thou knowest,
too, if this is so, or if I'm wrong."

No, this was madness. No one lay here except them, she

and Benjamin. . . . She felt more secure now. And with security
came sleep. Beautiful sleep.

Sigismund spread the sheepskin blanket better over her.

"In the name of the Father!"

He felt relieved when he heard she was asleep. Poor Kathryn! He lifted his arm to stroke her hair, but it fell back pow-
erlessly onto the coverlet. He might only wake her.

Was that why he hadn't stroked her hair? Yes, of course.
She was tired and worn out after the long journey. She needed
rest.

Yes, so here he lay. Here in the desert! Perhaps he ought
to have listened to Kathryn's advice and said a firm no to this
appointment. He would have done so, too, had he not believed
so intensely that God needed him just here. Here in the ice
and snow. "There!" an inner voice had said. "There *you* have
a task to perform. Woe to him who having put his hand to
the plow, looks back." Here, in any case, no memory of the
past would lead him to turn his face towards Sodom and
Gomorrah. He had said goodbye to his scholarship for the
sake of the only sort of knowledge: knowledge of the Word.
The Word which was like a fire, and like a hammer which
could cleave mountains.

During the time immediately after he had been ordained,
and while his days in Copenhagen and the all-too-many festive occasions were still close to him, his inner self had been
changed to a pillar of salt. his voluptuousness died looking back.

With God's support and counsel he had once again turned
his face towards the east, towards the cross of Calvary.

And the First Morning

Benjamin Sigismund opened his eyes and was almost blinded by a strong white light.

Where was he? In a strange land, in Copenhagen again? No, that time was long gone! He raised himself up on his elbows and stared with sleepy eyes at the walls, at the windows, and up at the ceiling. Yes, of course, he was in Bergstaden.

He felt completely rested. In spite of the hard bed, he had had a deep and refreshing sleep. Sleep had lightened his mind. Now he burned to get started.

Supposing he went for a walk in this early morning hour. There was no one here who knew him yet. It would give him the opportunity to make his own observations. Yes, up! up! The early bird catches the worm!

Half-dressed, he stood in front of the bed and looked at Kathryn. She was asleep. She slept more than she thought. Sometimes, in his heart, he could reproach her for sleeping so much. But he who slept sinned not! Good! But to sleep was not to live completely. The blood moved too slowly; it didn't pulse back to the heart often enough. Too much sleep made the human spirit burn with a low flame, it gave out too little light and warmth—there was always something barren and desolate about someone who slept too much.

Well! Well! He wasn't only thinking of Kathryn. He thought, too, of other people he had met.

He tried to force himself to think about completely different things. Thoughts of that sort were not good. They were worldly.

Impatient with himself in the extreme, he pulled on his clothes in a flash. It was just as if he was trying to escape from something.

Then he noticed that he had put his waistcoat on inside out; that wasn't a good sign. Bah! Only superstition! He tore off his coat and put his waistcoat on the right way round. And then he pulled his cap well down over his ears so that nobody should see his face—when he showed himself to his parishioners and the citizens of the town for the first time, he would have to have on his cassock.

He glanced at the wall where his priestly robe hung—it was still a little too crumpled to wear. And he stroked himself under the chin with the back of his hand. Actually, he ought to have shaved before he went out, but he hadn't time, not now. He had first to get a glimpse of the town and its life.

Sigismund was very excited. Both the architecture and the life of this northern Bergstaden were supposed to be very unusual. Some years ago he had read a description of it, and even then it had interested him greatly. But then he hadn't suspected that he would become the parish priest of the place.

As Sigismund went out of the entrance to the Leich house a strangely clear, cold air struck his face. The sulphur smoke from yesterday had gone. Everything around him glowed. Even the black walls of the houses had a bluish sheen. There had been a dawn frost and the ice cracked under the far too thin soles of his boots. Although it was still early in the morning—the clock in the church tower had just struck six —there was already a lively traffic in the streets of the town. It surprised him that almost everybody was driving loads, most of them with horses, but also some with oxen. Here and there a woman was driving, too. And they looked like men: big-limbed, weather-beaten, and freckled.

A little man in a pointed cap as tall as a tower, and wearing a shaggy sheepskin coat, came lurching towards him thrashing the air with a long stick; a mannikin who moved mechanically, lifting his feet in a comic manner high in the air.

"Stop!" Sigismund said. "Stop, my man!"

The man stopped.

"Be you the big boss!" he shouted. "Or what sort of bigwig be you?"

Sigismund realized that the man was a Lapp. The Lapps were a half-heathen tribe who lived with their herds of reindeer around in the mountains. He had thought that these people kept themselves exclusively to the northernmost parts of the country.

"What's your name, my man?"

"And yours?" the Lapp said. His pronunciation of Norwegian was almost incomprehensible.

Sigismund thought that the Lapp had said his name. Never before had he seen such a stunted figure.

It seemed, too, that the Lapp found Sigismund somewhat peculiar. As he moved away he shouted at the top of his voice: "Be you the fire chief?"

And when the Lapp didn't get any answer, he began to laugh. He laughed until his laughter became a howl.

"Ho! Ho! Ho! What a comic of a bigwig!"

Sigismund was about to go back and reprimand the man for his impudent behavior—people couldn't stand there screaming at their parish priest in that way—but then he remembered: Of course, the man couldn't know he was a clergyman. He would remember him for a later occasion.

The colorful and varied attire of the people made Sigismund stop suddenly in the greatest amazement. There was something reminiscent of southern climes in all this color. Up through the Østerdal dress was more uniform. Their faces, too, were livelier, more mobile, than down there; but then, of course, the mining community here was of German extraction. Most of them had brown eyes. There was something coarsely sensuous in their gaze, especially the women who were driving wagons.

Sigismund made his way towards the church. "Bergstaden's Crowning Glory." The light increased in intensity all around him as he walked, it leapt forth over roofs and through side streets, and was reflected in the shining windows and in the quivering ice which had formed overnight on pools of water. When he got to the churchyard he stopped. There he stood for a long time, staring up at the great magnificent church. Here was the House of God and the Gates of Heaven! His going in was in the clear light of morning; in the radiant light from the East! But perhaps God in his omniscience had ordained that his going out from this temple should be in the shadows of the evening, in the shadows of eternal night?

The clock in the tower struck seven just then and a young woman dressed in red passed him. He felt the blood leave his face. He became quite cold. A memory from a long-forgotten spring night in Copenhagen suddenly stood vividly before his inner eye. A bonfire and a dirty gypsy woman talking to him in Low German.

"Noble Sir," she had mumbled. "I can see you early one morning going towards a church and a churchyard. Here you will meet a woman, that is certain. Beware! She will lead you to downfall and misfortune. Her dress is the color of blood; let that be a sign to you."

What could that old hag know of his future after a quick glance into the hollow of his hand? "Fiction! Nothing but fiction!" It was not granted to any mortal to read the tablet of fate; that was kept, sealed with God's seal, in our eternal home.

He walked quickly up towards the church. Whatever happened was predestined by God. "His will be done! His name be praised!" And Sigismund mounted the stone steps to the church door with firm step. The key was in the door. He turned it and went in. Reverently, he removed his cap and remained standing by the back row of pews, gazing up at the altar. The magnificence of the church amazed him. He had hardly seen the like. Then he walked slowly and quietly, with head bowed, up towards the altar and knelt at the altar rail. The penitent's bench, the place of the seeker after grace— that was his place too.

A great joy flooded his mind. He felt himself in God's presence, the everloving God.

He began to pray that He in his mercy might never leave him. Then he remembered Peter's words: "Depart from me; for I am a sinful man, O Lord." No, he dared not in this place repeat the prayer of the holy apostle. Indeed, he needed far too sorely the presence of the Lord.

"Breathe Thou on my countenance, Thou Son of God, and vouchsafe me, as Thou vouchsafed Thy disciples after Thy blessed resurrection, Thy Holy Spirit." After which he said the Lord's Prayer aloud. And when he came to, "For thine is the kingdom, and the power, and the glory," tears began to drip down on to the red covering of the altar rail. And it was as if he heard a voice say, "Here, in this house, shall your task begin. Here, shall your day dawn." And sobbing, he exclaimed, "That I have sworn to Jehovah, with a holy eternal oath!"

Yes, might he always be given strength to keep that promise, that oath sworn in the face of God. His own strength was of no avail.

He got up, strengthened. And he walked through the church, looking at the pictures on the walls, reading the inscriptions under them quickly, and taking a brief look at the ornamentation. Only when he reached the altar piece, which depicted the Last Supper, did he really notice what he was seeing: the Master, the Son of God, who in that night had been betrayed. The night atmosphere was so grippingly depicted in this old painting that he could well understand how people could throw themselves down on their knees in humbleness and prayer before pictures from the Holy Scriptures. Art vivified the Word.

Benjamin Sigismund was torn out of his reveries by the church clock striking again; eight heavy strokes. Now the sun broke in through the windows. The whole church lay bathed in a pale golden light. The reflection from the white spring snow outside and from the newly whitewashed church walls burned and glowed between the rows of pillars. And the two candlesticks up on the altar were like two flames which rose out of the white altar cloth.

Sigismund covered his eyes. All this light quite dazed him. And it was in this position that the mines' secretary, Sigurd Olaus Dopp, found him.

Dopp had come shuffling down from the vestry. As he came he was polishing his spectacles with a green cloth.

"Who are you?" he asked, and stared impudently straight at Sigismund.

"Who am I!" Sigismund repeated angrily. "May I ask you, Sir, what right you have to know that?"

"What! What!" Dopp stammered, confused, and rubbed his spectacles with the green cloth. He heard that the man's speech was educated.

"Are you on a visit here?"

"My name is Sigismund, the Reverend Benjamin Sigismund."

Dopp started back a little. This was his habit when something astonished him.

"Dopp," he said. "Secretary to the mines."

They shook hands quickly and without any warmth.

Dopp apologized profusely for his rude questions. He didn't see very well. And since he had been of the opinion that an unauthorized person had penetrated into the church, he had thought that he had to——

"Of course," Sigismund interrupted him. "No doubt the church plate and holy vessels are kept here?"

"Not here. They are in Mrs. Blom's keeping. She is a very reliable person. One can trust her."

And Dopp went on talking, while incessantly polishing and breathing on his spectacles, about a distant relation of his, Mrs. von Knagen, who was here on a visit to Bergstaden, and who last Sunday had lost a gold brooch. A very valuable heirloom it was. Mrs. von Knagen had only missed it yesterday evening. And as one might expect she was very upset about it.

Dopp looked up and smiled wryly. And half jokingly, half seriously, he said that a noble Danish lady was supposed to have given this brooch, at some time, to a Miss von Knagen for some service or the other she had rendered. But he had talked enough about it. Nevertheless the Danish lady, who was supposed to have been a rather remarkable person, had said that the day the brooch left the possession of the von Knagen family, misfortune was at hand. At that both Sigismund and Dopp laughed, their chuckles reverberating through the church.

"Superstition," Sigismund said. "Inherited blindness."

"Yes, of course," Dopp said. He twirled his spectacles round on one of the sidepieces. "The old lady is, as you understand, a little odd."

Finally, Dopp put on his spectacles and stuck the green cloth in a pocket of his tail coat. With an affected smile in the corner of his twisted mouth he trotted up to his pew in the church and groped along the worn floor with his hand. Sigismund followed him good-humoredly and also peered down at the floor for the brooch. In his mind he was still turning over what had happened just now outside the church gates. Was it chance that it was just there he had met this woman in the red dress?

The rasping sound of the witch's voice again jarred in his ear.

Sigismund made a gesture with his hand. What that pagan gypsy had prophesied must be warded off. Kathryn had her faults. Yes, yes. That she had. She, like everyone else. He would never deceive her—with someone else; that was unthinkable. And Sigismund looked with all his might for the brooch.

"A blind hen will also find a grain of corn, Mr. Sigismund."

Dopp held up the gold brooch in triumph. And then he moved his glasses right up onto his head, as was his habit when he wanted to look really closely at something. He held the brooch right up to his eyes. Yes, it was all there. Just a little dust on it which he tried to blow off—but he blew past it—for his breath, like his smile, came out of the corner of his twisted mouth. He handed it to Sigismund. And Sigismund looked at it carefully.

"Yes, yes. It's certainly in the best order."

It was scarcely a valuable piece of jewelry, but then it had its own little romantic secret. But— He wondered how the half-blind Dopp could have found it. He himself should have been able to see it on the floor. There was something odd here. Could it be that Dopp had had the brooch concealed in his hand? He couldn't make the man out.

Sigismund and Dopp went out together. And Dopp turned the key in the lock.

When they were outside the churchyard gates he said a polite but cool farewell to the pastor and hurried away down one of the narrow streets; Sigismund made his way down Church Street.

He was annoyed at his meeting Dopp. There was some trickery connected with the brooch. Perhaps he had seen him enter the church and knew who he was. And— Oh, well! He couldn't be bothered to think about it any more.

Outside Leich's store in the main street they met each other again. This time they only nodded as they passed.

No Red Carpet or Bed of Roses for Kings and Princes

Kathryn was still asleep when Sigismund came back. He did not awake her. She slept deeply and heavily. Except that now and then her breathing was as if hacked through the middle. Her pale face lay like a shadow across the snow white pillow case; her long brown plaits of hair seemed to be quite black. There was something about her figure which made one think of a corpse—the corpse of a young woman who had just been laid out.

At this sight Sigismund felt a touch of sorrow and of melancholy. He turned away. The air here was foul, too. A stench came off the old walls. He went over to the window to open it but it was without hasps, he couldn't open it. Quite uncivilized! Angrily he banged against the frame so the glass rattled in the leaden cames.

Kathryn heard it in her sleep, but she didn't awake, she was sleeping so heavily.

In his excitement he was going to give the frame another

blow, but he let it be. After all, the house wasn't his property. The house? A ramshackle hovel! In any case they wouldn't stay here any longer than necessary. Sigismund sank down in a green-painted spindlebacked chair and stretched out his long legs over the floor. Ridiculous! His legs stretched nearly to the other side of the room. Completely ridiculous! He glanced up at his cassock which was still hanging there, badly creased. When Kathryn got up she must go at once to Mrs. Leich and borrow an iron. He intended this very day to go out dressed in his clerical attire. And impatiently he pulled off his cap and put it up on the windowsill. Then he sat there looking out over the turf-covered roofs of Bergstaden.

Yes, it had to be admitted, the town was a strange pile; it witnessed more to poverty than to taste. None of the houses were of the same height, most of them had only one story, and all of them had one or more disproportionately high granite chimney stacks. High above it all loomed the church. It was as if he sat looking out over a giant churchyard—the chimney stacks became gravestones and the houses graves.

All these low hovels spoke in a loud voice of slavery. Nevertheless, the whole place had its own strange attraction. Everything from the most ordinary to the most grandiose had a strange atmosphere of its own. Even the round, worn pavingstones everyone trod and spat on had it. Well, it was all only a question of whether our eyes were open and our minds receptive.

The meeting, the brief meeting with her, the stranger at the church gates, had also evoked a mood. He had not seen her face, not quite. But he had met her at a moment when his eyes were not bound and the portals of his mind were open. Once he had read something of the light and the dark of humankind and the power which radiates from them—some people radiate so much light that it shines on one as they pass—others can be so dark that they cast shadows on everything they approach. This woman in red whom he had met today had cast a bright light on him. He felt it. He had carried her light with him, in his body, into the church.

Who was she? Well, indeed! That was going too far, it was no concern of his who she was. Princess or beggar, it was the same to him.

His thoughts now turned again to that odd man, Dopp. Perhaps even now that wizened man was sitting in his office, telling the story of his first meeting with Bergstaden's new pastor. "I won't absolutely maintain that he made an altogether pleasant impression," he no doubt was saying, that dried-up man. And round about him there sat, no doubt, a crowd of long-haired clerks, shaking their ignorant heads in dismay.

Benjamin Sigismund gave his cap on the windowsill a shove. Why hadn't Dopp asked him to walk down the street with him? Yes, indeed, for it turned out, when they met again, that they were going the same way. Dopp was, no doubt, informed as to where Sigismund was staying. Perhaps he was one of those who had decided that this house was to be their pastor's lodging? The mining company, very likely, had a right to have a say in church matters up here; it was the company which had built the church.

Sigismund sat there and worked himself up. He began to have hateful thoughts about this—this Dopp. In any case, he, Benjamin Sigismund, hadn't come here to please people. No! He had come with a scourge. He had it well concealed; but it was there.

He jumped up.

"Kathryn!" he called. "A new day has dawned."

Kathryn started up. She sat up in bed and looked around with half-open eyes. It seemed now as if she had come back from a bright world somewhere a long way away.

"Do you know, Benjamin, what I have just dreamt?"

"No, how can I know."

He smiled a little contemptuously, but she didn't see that. The dream was still so vivid that she was completely absorbed by it.

"I dreamt we were somewhere where there was sun and flowers, roses. Yellow and red roses! And I thought I saw trees that I had never seen before; I heard birds singing too. It was so beautiful, Benjamin."

"Then there will be a storm, Kathryn."

"Are you so certain of that?"

"Quite certain."

He turned away so that Kathryn could put on some clothes, but suddenly he became impatient and asked:

"Can I turn round now?"

"Not yet, Benjamin."

Sigismund remained standing over by the window. His broad back kept out the light—the room was made almost dark because of it. He kept out so much light, she thought—kept out the sun. No, she didn't really think that. She just thought that Benjamin Sigismund was so broad and the window so narrow.

Sigismund was now very impatient, she could hear. He was drumming on the window pane. And she hurried with her dressing.

"Now you can turn round." She hurried over to him. "Good morning, Benjamin."

"Good morning, Kathryn."

And contrary to his custom, he kissed her. Normally it was just two or three routine pats on the back. His kiss was like a torch which flamed up in her face. He was a handsome man. In her eyes the most handsome man in the world. His kiss breathed the breath of life into her love. She became hot and blushed.

He released her quickly. And then she stood there groping out into the air. Her hands were seeking for something to hang on to.

Sigismund began to smooth out his cassock. He fully intended to show himself amongst his parishioners this very day. With a little careful pressing his cassock would look as good as new. The collar was new. But what about his dubbined boots? He looked them over. No, one couldn't say they were new—but if he trod carefully they, too, would do all right for the time being.

"Benjamin!"

"What do you want?"

"Nothing . . ." She grasped her head with both hands. "I only thought that . . ."

"What did you think?"

"I just thought that, after all, it's quite nice here in this old room."

"Well. Yes, yes." He was intensely preoccupied with his own thoughts. "We will, in any case, have to make ourselves at home here for the time being."

She could hear that he was thinking about quite different things. He hadn't understood that she thought the room was nice—for his sake; yes, solely for his sake. Her cheeks again took on a sallow appearance. And the room which she had just found so attractive, now it was nothing of the sort. It was hideous! To hide her disappointment she went over to the boys' bed and looked over their shoes and clothes. Stealthily, she stroked the older boy, Laurentius, over his mop of hair. She'd have to find an outlet for her tenderness here; now, as so many times before. Benjamin had no time for her caresses. When she first had to transfer her feelings to her son, when Laurentius was younger, it was even harder for her.

"Yes, it was the room, wasn't it?" Sigismund began again. "It's not as bad as all that. You were quite right, Kathryn."

"Isn't it?"

"Yes, weren't you standing here just now saying you liked it?"

"Benjamin." She shivered, it was so cold. "I almost thought you knew what I meant."

"No, how could I know it?" And he added mockingly, "Did you know what you yourself meant, Kathryn?"

"Yes! Yes, I did know!" She was almost in tears. "I just didn't say it. Not with words, anyway."

"Well! well!" He could hear that she was upset. "We won't talk about it any more now."

"No, we don't have to."

Sigismund pretended he was preoccupied with inspecting

the hook on the collar of his cassock. Several hooks, as it happened, were quite loose. There was no doubt that he badly needed a new one, but the heavy moving expenses had quite emptied his purse. And he didn't intend to become a mendicant monk.

Yes, but was that in accordance with Christ's teaching? He who had sent His disciples out into the world without gold and silver in their belts. Yes and no! He remembered the Master's words: "When I sent you without purse, and scrip, and shoes, lacked ye anything?" And they said, "Nothing." Then said he unto them: "But now, ye that hath a purse, let him take it, and he that hath no sword, let him sell his garment and buy one." Now, as then, light struggled against darkness. . . . And it was darkness which pressed the sword into the hand of light. The sword *now*. Yes, but that was capital, gold, worldly goods. Today no sword was as active as just those things; they were more than double-edged. But in spite of that—the Master's words did not bar the way which Sigismund had so often dreamt of taking: the way to power, honor, and influence. The way the word of Christ pointed to was not carpeted and strewn with roses, a way for kings and princes, for the arrogant and power-ridden. . . . Oh no, it was the narrow path which led to the dwellings of the blessed. He would pray for strength to take the narrow path. And for strength to seat himself at the bottom of the table. Not on the assumption that the last shall be first, but from the conviction that a seat at the very bottom of the table was really his.

But the world, the accursed world! That stood at the top of the table and beckoned: Your place is up here, Mr. Sigismund! Make your way up here! Push everything aside which stands in the way! Here is a gold-covered chair waiting for your Reverence. Please be seated, your Eminence! And his Lordship Bishop Benjamin Sigismund let himself sink comfortably into the gold-covered chair. Into the gold-covered chair of this accursed world.

At that moment Morten Leich's maidservant, Anne-Sofie, came in without knocking.

Sigismund awoke from his dreams and looked at the girl. He started. Was it she? Her profile was the same. His hands turned blood-red. A strangely mild intoxication filled his heart. . . . He noticed a white patch of grease from a dripping altar candle on his cassock. Half embarrassed he began to scrape it off with his nail. And there was a voice inside him which asked repeatedly, "Is it she? Do you recognize her?" But then another voice came and answered, "No, it is not she! Had it been she the light in the window would have been much brighter than it is. And the walls, these dirty, black walls, would have gleamed."

He took a turn across the room and pretended he had not seen the girl. Phantasies and dreams! Then he stopped in the middle of the room and looked the girl in the face.

"What is your name, child?"

He tried to put on a severe clerical look—but his face didn't want to look like that now. He looked almost benevolent.

She answered in an impudent tone, "Anne-Sofie."

"Anne-Sofie," Benjamin Sigismund repeated. "So, you're Anne-Sofie. Hm! Well, well." He had to collect himself. "Oh, will you ask your mistress if she has an iron she can lend us?"

"Eh! An iron! You mean a clothes iron?"

"Yes, a clothes iron.

Sigismund nodded.

Anne-Sofie lowered her eyes. The pastor was staring so hard at her. Kathryn got up from the edge of the bed. It seemed to her there was something which got hold of her and lifted her up. She stared with her large protruding eyes—first at her husband and then at the girl. Something hung in the air. Something which frightened her. She couldn't understand what it was.

"Was there anything else you wanted, Anne? And what was your other name?"

"Anne-Sofie."

Her tone was not quite so impudent now. And that reassured Kathryn somewhat.

Sigismund was on the point of asking if it was she he had met at the church gates at dawn, but out of consideration for Kathryn he refrained—that would only add fuel to the fire of her suspicions. He would ask the girl some other time.

He put his thumbs into the pockets of his waistcoat and forced himself to look calm and indifferent.

"Yes, was there anything else, Anne-Sofie?"

He had to put an end to this; they couldn't go on standing there, the three of them, staring at each other as if they were mad.

"Yes. There were something besides. I were to ask you from Madam to come and eat at once."

She babbled it out in one agitated breath.

"What are we supposed to do?" Sigismund said. Neither he nor Kathryn had understood a word of what the girl had said.

"Eat!" Anne-Sofie shouted. "Eat, of course."

She wanted nothing better than to be on the other side of the door again. It was a pest having these fancy people in the house the whole time, standing there gaping; asking you to repeat every word you said to them. One should do what Leich's hired man, Gerhard, did: give a shake of the head and make out you were stone deaf.

"Breakfast, you mean?" Kathryn said.

"Yes," Anne-Sofie said.

She couldn't help grinning. As long as she could get them down to the parlor, they could do what they liked as far as she was concerned—eat or breakfast.

Kathryn stared sharply at her. This impudent hussy made her angry. Her speech and gestures were terribly uncultivated. She was also angry with Benjamin. And there was another thing which always angered her: the barrier which rank and education had in the past placed between them and the com-

mon people was no longer there. No, not as in the past!
Both sides would have gained if that barrier had been maintained. Every time she saw that Benjamin was about to stride
over to the other side she became angry. And then she thought
and wished evil things. Afterwards she repented. Repentance
aways stood out on the doorstep and waited until her evil
wishes had gone out again; then it came in. And it took its
time once it had come in under her roof. She had once been
so wicked that she had wished to see Benjamin Sigismund
dead, laid out! Benjamin Sigismund, her husband! Madness!

"Convey our thanks to Mrs. Leich," Sigismund said. "We
will come at once."

And Anne-Sofie left without curtseying and without looking at the pastor or his wife. She bent her back and crept out.

It seemed to Kathryn that Anne-Sofie looked like an animal
as she went out of the door. Yes, so wicked she was now, that
she could think such a thing.

But Sigismund took the opportunity of observing her movements—the way she walked and carried her head. No, there
was no doubt, it was someone else he had met. And this made
him happy.

"Benjamin," Kathryn said. "Do you remember that you once
told me that you were with your father in a boat out in the
fjord. You were going to shoot great auks—and that you were
seized with an inexplicable madness—you wanted to raise your
gun and shoot your own splendid father?"

"Yes. What about it?"

He didn't want to discuss that just now.

"Did you hate him at the moment you were going to do
this?"

"Hate Father?"

Kathryn didn't dare ask anything more—but the thought that
she once had wished Benjamin Sigismund dead had pursued
her, laid traps for her, taken her by surprise; it had taken on
the hideous face of mortal sin. Every time it came to her, her
peace of mind was torn asunder. Now she caught a glimpse

of it again. She didn't dare approach anyone and ask for protection when it appeared, least of all Benjamin. . . . But perhaps she should seek out God? But for all she knew it was
God himself who caused her to see it?

"Get dressed, my dear! I'm hungry!"

He tied his silk neckerchief under his jabot, and then
squinted down, trying to see how the ends of the neckerchief
lay on his chest.

"Will this do, Kathryn?"

He folded the ends of the neckerchief carefully—they were
old and worn out after the thousands of times he had tied
them. Everything he had on was old and worn. It was not
easy to conceal poverty under one's cloak.

After breakfast Sigismund was in great spirits. He had,
quite honestly, been tremendously hungry. And it must be
said to Mrs. Leich's everlasting credit that her table was well-
stocked and appetizing. There could be no doubt, too, that
Mr. Leich was a good and honorable man. Today he had received the best impression of him.

"But his speech is not very grammatical," Kathryn protested.

"Well, well," Sigismund said. "Remember that he is not an
academic. Behind the counter his grammar is more than good
enough. Besides, I can tell you that he is the son of a clergyman."

"Is he? Well, well. Perhaps it is best to use the local dialect
behind the counter."

"Behind the counter and in the pulpit," Sigismund said.

"What?" Kathryn asked. "What did you say, Benjamin
Sigismund?"

"Yes, that is what I said."

He furrowed his bushy eyebrows and Kathryn knew well
enough that that was a sign of stormy weather. She decided
to say nothing.

"Did you remember to ask Mrs. Leich for the loan of a
clothes iron?"

"Do you want it right now?"

"Yes, for my cassock." He lifted it down from the wall. "I can't scrape off these drops of grease from the altar candles, they will have to be steamed."

"You know that I can hardly ask for that sort of thing myself. . . . We must wait until we get a maid who can take a message."

"Wait?" Benjamin Sigismund shouted. "There's no question of waiting!"

. . . She took and dipped a white linen cloth into the wash-basin, fished out a red-hot coal from the fire, and wrapped the wet cloth around it. And with the cassock over her knees she began to steam it. . . . At times Benjamin could ask the most unreasonable things. She went on dabbing the spluttering coal on to the cassock. An unpleasant smell of rancid fat and old cloth filled the room.

Sigismund now began to explain how he had thought they should arrange themselves. Morten Leich had let them have a small room at the side where there was a good open fire-place for cooking and room for the boys' bed. This room here would have to be both his study and their sitting room. When he had to attend to parochial business and at other times when he needed quiet, she and the boys would have to stay in the small room and keep quiet there. He would have his desk here by the window. From there he could see the church. He intended to accustom himself to all these rooftops, with their turf and grey slate and their clay-decked chimney stacks. As long as one was careful to look at things at good moments, when one's soul was turned towards God, then they would take on some of God's glory.

"Beautiful visions give rise to beautiful pictures, my dear. And for the inner eye these pictures adorn a place, a land-scape, in the same way that real pictures adorn a wall for our outer eye."

"But the other pictures, Benjamin, the hateful ones, won't they also appear to the inner eye?"

"Not in the same way. Our memory discards pretty quickly

that which is evil." His good spirits made him grandiloquent. "Have you not felt, Kathryn, how pleasant memories hurry along in front of you, dancing like friendly spirits with roses in their hair along the road you go, whilst bad memories only come sluggishly behind you—and that the distance between you and them constantly becomes bigger and bigger?"

"Do you always feel like that, Husband?"

"Yes, of course."

"Then you were born into the world under a lucky star, Benjamin."

She remained sitting there with his cassock on her lap, staring straight ahead with a fixed look. The hot coal in the cloth burnt through but she didn't notice it. Her white hand became even whiter.

"Yes, and may God rejoice my lovely mother as she lies there in her deep grave, for bearing me into this world under that star. God's own star!"

Benjamin Sigismund went over to the window and stood there looking up at the gilded angel; the sun was shining on it just then, and it looked like a real angel on its way down to earth, blowing its trumpet.

And he repeated, "May God rejoice my dear mother as she lies there in her deep grave."

Ol-Kanelesa, Smith and Sacristan

It was four in the morning; Sigismund was already at his desk. He sat resting his cheek on his hand, waiting for the sun.

Full of zeal he had wakened while it was still almost dark. He had got up at once and done his usual morning exercises.

Then he had lit a candle and started work. He would soon
have his inaugural sermon ready.

For two days he had walked around the streets of Bergstaden in his clerical attire. He had called on all the most
important people in the town. And yesterday he had ordered
two intoxicated smelters to come to his office today. Not later
than 9 o'clock! He had nothing against a modest glass at home
in the bosom of one's family or amongst friends—but drunkenness on the streets, he intended to put a stop to that! He
would give these two smelters a severe reprimand. And in
addition he would summon them to the vestry on the first
Sunday after his installation, so that they could do penance.
He wished to give them a distaste for any future drunkenness.

Now that the daylight began to increase around him and
the smoky candle burned down in the candlestick, he began
to feel sleepy. There was deep peace, there was an increase in
security in the first light of morning; it was an hour for beautiful dreams! Night was the time for sleep, not for dreams.

The pastor nodded. A couple of times his head slipped out
of his hand. He straightened himself up. It seemed to him
that just then a hand, not a strange hand but a young woman's
hand, was stroking his hair. He had seen the pale face of a
girl, not a strange one either; but what her name was he
couldn't say, for he didn't know it, did he?

"Well!" he said to himself. "This is not the time for pretty
visions but for work!"

He began to work again on his inaugural sermon. He based
it on the words of Jeremiah concerning the fearful tenacity
of evil of this earth: "The bellows are burned, the lead is
consumed of the fire; the founder melteth in vain: for the
wicked are not plucked away."

Sigismund's quill pen scratched. He struggled with weighty
words. He forced out images of violent power. He became
gripped by them himself. He, Benjamin Sigismund, was de-
livering a new Sermon on the Mount.

Then the door opened. A thickset man with a strong face
and bushy eyebrows came in. He looked to be something

over fifty. He was dressed in his Sunday best—a suit of yellow, tawed elk-skin, a jabot, and a yellow-red silk neckerchief.

Sigismund turned round in his chair and stared back at the man.

"Are you the sacristan?"

"Yes."

Sigismund looked him up and down sharply. His face and head were as if carved in stone, there was something distinguished about his features, something aristocratic, which at once attracted Sigismund.

"I sent for you yesterday."

"I was up at Aursunna."

"Aur— Aur— Where's that?"

"Doesn't the pastor know, then?"

"No."

"No. No. That's like, that is."

Sigismund started in his chair. He heard some of the same cold contempt in the sacristan's voice as he had heard in the charcoal wagoner's. It occurred to him that it was very strange that the man had come to his office so early, long before most people were up. He jumped up and put some high-backed gilt, leather chairs as a screen in front of the bed where Kathryn still lay sleeping. It wasn't really necessary, Kathryn slept like a stone; but out of regard for the sacristan. . . . Not that it was really necessary on his account either. The common people had no sense of modesty. Not the slightest!

And Sigismund peered out of the window and up at the church tower. Soon the clock would strike five.

It was only then that he noticed the street was already full of traffic. He had been so preoccupied with his inaugural sermon that he hadn't even heard the carilloning from the bells of the hundreds of horses which were on their way up to the Works, with charcoal and ore.

He held out his hand to the sacristan.

"Good morning, I am glad to see you."

"Yes, morning. You're welcome here."

The sacristan glanced shyly in the direction of the bed.

"I'd best be coming back later; the mistress is asleep, I see."

He spoke quietly as if he was afraid of waking her, and made sure he stood with his back to her. Sigismund was taken aback. He was astonished at the man's tact.

"Now, now!" Sigismund said, and patted him on the back. "We can sit down here by the door and talk quietly."

He pointed with his quill pen to an old chair with a broken back and a red-painted seat.

"Honor to him who honor deserves!" The sacristan sat down on the doorstep. "It's more than good enough for me here."

"He that shall humble himself shall be exalted, sacristan." Sigismund sat down carefully on the chair. "So your name is Ole Korneliusen?"

"Ol-Kanelesa, yes."

"What?" Sigismund said, and got up again. "Isn't your name Ole Korneliusen?"

He went over to the table and picked up the church register. "Sacristan Ole Korneliusen, parents Kornelius Olsen Bonde and his wife Gunhild Erlingsdatter, born—" Sigismund held the book closer to his eyes. "Is it Hjulmager?"

"Right!

"Right?"

Sigismund didn't quite understand.

"I mean you've read it right."

Sigismund threw the book down over on the table. Was he another one of them who spoke with a cloven tongue? He would break these mountain dwellers of their irritating double talk. He felt like giving the sacristan a warning now at once, but as this was the first time they had met he had better keep his tongue between his teeth.

"Tell me, my good Korneliusen, what is the state of morals here in Bergstaden?"

"Oh, much as in the days of Noah, marrying and giving in marriage."

"What is the state of the different vices—let us take drunkenness for example?"

"Oh, about the same as before, d'you see; it might have been worse, it might have been better."

And they sat there silent for a while. Then it dawned on Sigismund that he was just as wise from the sacristan's answers. His words were as slippery as polished quartz. The pastor's annoyance at this smooth and meaningless answer changed nevertheless to amusement. This man from the mountains was certainly no fool. This calm, this assurance, and this tact and impudence at the same time were old Norse; Sigismund could have said old Norse culture.

"So we can say that on the whole the people in this parish are sober, Ole Korneliusen?"

"If we put it any other way, then people would have to be drunk the whole time. Then the Works would stop and the smeltery too, and the bigwigs would get nothing to eat."

Sigismund got up again. He couldn't exactly say that the sacristan gave him detailed information. And his time was a little too precious to throw away on this difficult man. Sigismund had still a good part of his inaugural sermon to write.

Ol-Kanelesa got up too. He was both hungry and thirsty and wanted to get back home to Elisabeth Cottage to get a little food inside him. Just then the church clock struck six; he should have been in his smithy long since.

They stood there side by side, pastor and sacristan, listening to the heavy strokes from the iron hammer in the tower.

"Our bell tolls, our time unfolds——"

"And eternity claims soon our souls," Ol-Kanelesa added hurriedly.

"Yes. And you're already an old man, sacristan."

Sigismund still felt that he wanted to penetrate the sacristan's armor a little. It would do him good to be reminded that all is vanity; his own too.

"I'm fifty-five. And the pastor?"

"I am thirty-three."

"The rest will go quickly," Ol-Kanelesa said. "After you're thirty, it goes like a flash."

He opened the door and stepped over the threshold. Sigismund remained standing in the door-opening holding the latch.

Ol-Kanelesa bent down and picked up a fiddle wrapped in a cloth, from the corner behind the door.

"You are a fiddler too?"

"Oh, nothing to speak of."

"But you have a violin."

"Oh, there's many here with a fiddle. And if all of them could play, there would be more than enough fiddling and dancing here in the world."

"So you were playing last night, sacristan?" Sigismund said sternly. "Is that not a frivolous occupation for a servant of the Church?"

Ol-Kanelesa put the fiddle under his arm.

"Is it worse playing at night than by day? I've never seen it forbidden."

It seemed to Sigismund that he was talking to a brick wall; this man was possessed of a cold, unbelievable calm, a calm which nothing and nobody could shake.

"Just one thing, sacristan, you must listen to the voice of conscience."

Ol-Kanelesa remained standing there thoughtfully for a long time, staring down at the floor. Sigismund became impatient, it seemed to him that their conversation would never end.

"So, does the pastor have to listen to that voice, then?"

"Yes, certainly I do."

"Then the pastor's conscience is too quiet. I think conscience has the loudest voice of all."

Now it was Sigismund's turn to stand there and reflect at length. He had a good mind to reprimand this low person for his speech and conduct. His speech was uncouth. He spoke as if he was speaking to an equal rather than his superior. Besides, he was not quite certain whether the man was sober.

"We will talk about that another time."

"Yes, we must have something to talk about another time, too.

And Ol-Kanelesa went down the steps.

"One thing more, sacristan." Sigismund leaned far out of the door. "Is there much dancing here?"

"Not so much as before."

"What can have caused dancing to decline?"

"I don't think they have the strength to dance quite so much as before; it's mainly dancing with their feet together."

Sigismund didn't understand. This was no doubt something poisonous, something quite impossible again. He thought, too, that he noticed a mocking smile on the sacristan's face.

He said severely: "What do you mean?"

"I mean people are too hungry now. Bad years and war all the whole time, that's nothing much to dance about."

"Is there famine here?"

"Yes, there's not much to eat up in the snowdrifts."

"Sad," Sigismund said. "Sad. Very sad."

His heart softened suddenly. It looked as if nature was now sowing with the wrong hand. War, pestilence, and famine! Jeremiah was right: "The bellows are burned; the founder melteth in vain: for the wicked are not plucked away." All the same. Finally the wicked *would* be plucked away. In the meanwhile one must not lose faith in the light.

"Farewell, sacristan."

"Yes, farewell."

Ol-Kanelesa left. As he reached the lowest step, a fiddle string vibrated. The sound touched his heart. He was both fiddler and blacksmith; steel, iron, the fiddle, and the stream up at the Works in the spring, they all sang the same song.

Sigismund sat down at his desk again. He sat and turned over the pages of the manuscript of his inaugural sermon; a new Sermon on the Mount! He had lost the thread of it. It was as if the sacristan, that infernal sacristan, had given him something bitter to swallow.

Sigismund read through page after page of his manuscript. His eyebrows contracted more and more threateningly. It was a worldly sermon. Just empty sword-play. No attack on wickedness, on the opponents of the Kingdom of God. What

he had written was a contribution to his own honor and glory
and not to the glory of Christ. "A new Sermon on the Mount!"
he exclaimed. "I who in no wise am worthy to unloose the
Master's shoe-latchet. I write a Sermon on the Mount? What
folly! Folly!" He was deeply moved. He threw himself down
on his knees by the chair and prayed: "Lord God of Hosts!
My crucified Saviour crowned with thorns! Because of Thy
bitter suffering and death, forgive me that I have sought my
own honor and not Thine. Forgive me that I forgot Thy
precious promise that that which we shall speak and say shall
be given us at that selfsame moment. Lord, think mercifully
of me in Thy Kingdom."

A Dream of a Golden Stone

The same day.

In Ol-Kanelesa's smithy up
in Mørstu Street it was more
than usually busy.

Spring quivered in the sun-warmed air. And the winter
tracks northwards toward Rugeldalen and southwards towards
Os would become impassable any day now because of the
thaw. So horses had to be shod for summer driving and
wheeled vehicles made ready.

The wagoners' horses stood around the smithy and snorted
without appetite at the mouldy hay. They were a collection
of nags, in bad condition after the spring shortages and pulling
heavy loads.

In Ol-Kanelesa's cottage, usually called Elisabeth Cottage,
up on the Mørstu hill, the wagoners sat playing cards to pass
the time. The cottage was small, beamed, and with a lead-
light window looking onto the outdoor smelting ovens. And
the small rough windowpanes were always covered by a grey,
sulfurous smoke—it was no good trying to look out of them.

The wagoners sat in there in half darkness, although it was the middle of the day.

Elisabeth Cottage had once stood out on the Røros estate and had been the doctor's wife, Mrs. Elisabet Jürgens's, sitting room. Here she sat through many long winters consumed by melancholy memories of her childhood at the court of Christian IV.* Her longing for more sun, milder climes, and more worldly magnficence eventually brought on both chest and liver complaints. In dark nights she knelt down by the little lead-light window and prayed with many tears and sighs all the prayers she had learned from her dear, departed mother. And during the worst nights, when madness sat with her like a phosphorescent ghost, she sang at each hour, with her face turned towards the ceiling, the songs of the Copenhagen night watchmen. She counted the days, the weeks, and the years until she would once again see the castles and the church towers; but then death came. And the fine lady was carried out in a costly oak coffin adorned with wrought iron. Then her brother, Director Arnisæus, an aristocratic gentleman with a self-torturing soul, moved into the cottage. Death came to him too. Then the cottage stood for many generations with shuttered windows and a rusty padlock on its door, until the blacksmith, fiddler, and sacristan Ol-Kanelesa bought it and transported it on a wagon up to Bergstaden, right up to Mørstu Street. Here, no other sun than the morning sun shines. But Ol-Kanelesa thought that it would be good to wake and get up in the morning sun. For it was brighter and more beautiful than any other sun. Close by hung the smeltery bell which summoned the smelters to and from their labors. The bell had its own melody—just like the iron and the fiddle. Everything had its own melody, but not everybody had the ears with which to hear.

The wagoners who sat in Elisabeth Cottage were all angry at the clerk in charge of supplies. "That Johannes," who was always trying to keep the price of supplies up and the cost of transport down. The youngest of them didn't mince their

* Christian IV, King of Denmark-Norway, reigned from 1588 to 1648.

words and said straight out that Johannes was a scoundrel.
Just like the charcoal tax-collector. The road inspector, too,
was as wicked as the devil. Soon it would be impossible to
move a wheel over the roads; but at this the older wagoners
protested. Roads! Roads! No, in their younger days there were
roads to complain about. Then everything which was transported in the summer had to go on the back of a horse. Iron,
copper, and salt! Was there anyone here who could pick up
a pack saddle weighing several hundred pounds and put it
up on a horse's back? "Eh? Hm!" And then all the gypsies and
tramps we had to contend with in those days. "Don't forget
that, my lads!"

Ol-Kanelesa had little to say today. He shod the one horse
after the other without saying a word. Being a blacksmith
was a pleasant enough job, but today he was angry. And
thirsty! The new parson had angered him. A malicious one.
Yes! If he'd thought of putting Ol-Kanelesa in his place, he'd
come to the wrong man. He had to laugh. Put Ol-Kanelesa in
his place? Use strong arm tactics with him! Ho! Ho! Sigismund wasn't the first high-up to try that. . . . First of all he
would teach Sigismund where the Aursund Lake lay. And
then he should be permitted to learn to understand what
people said, so that he didn't have to chew over every other
word that was said to him. "That's how it is up here in the
mountains! Ho! Ho!" The smith clenched his teeth and wielded
the sledgehammer so the sparks flew. "Bring the ladle here,
Embret!" he said. "We can't thirst to death." He emptied it at
one draught and threw it over into the charcoal bin.

Pastor Sigismund was also the subject of conversation
amongst neighbors these days. "What a tall, stalwart man the
pastor is," everybody said. "But he looks unpleasant and angry.
Lord preserve us!" And there was laughter from one doorstep
to the other all down the street. No one was so fearful that he
didn't dare to laugh. "He looks like our friend the Master of
the Royal Hunt, old nasty-face von Langen." And those on the
doorsteps laughed again. Then there was that story about him.
He had ordered Jens-Pettersa and Grelk-Per to come to his

office for being tipsy the other day. He'd put a foot wrong there! Grelk-Per had told him to mind his own business and not concern himself with what other people ate and drank. At this the pastor had thundered out, read them the riot act, and threatened to read out their names from the pulpit. To this Per had replied that if he did that the congregation wouldn't hear anything new: everybody knew that he had been "just a wee bit under the weather." This story, too, was repeated several times that day in Elisabeth Cottage. Some took sides with the pastor, others with Jens-Pettersa and Grelk-Per. And the matter was discussed many times with thumps on the table, as they played their game of cards. However, everybody was agreed on one thing: Sigismund should beware of mentioning that sort of thing from the pulpit. There was a limit to everything; also to what one could take from a parson.

The matter of the two smelters was also aired around the anvil in the smithy, so that they could hear what Ol-Kanelesa had to say. They wanted to hear his opinion; after all, he was the sacristan.

But Ol-Kanelesa would say nothing more than, "Everybody's got enough to do to keep his own nose tidy."

What he really meant by that, whether he was on the pastor's side or on Jens-Pettersa's and Grelk-Per's, no one really knew. And when they asked him how he liked the pastor, he said:

"How do you like somebody you don't even know?"

To this the wagoners could make no reply.

Many of the poorest wagoners couldn't afford to have Ol-Kanelesa shoe their horses; that cost extra money. They had to be content with getting him to make the shoes and supply the nails. And then they made a botched job of shoeing the horses themselves. It couldn't be helped if the horses got lame; every penny counted.

Tøllef, who had transported Pastor Sigismund in his charcoal wagon up to Bergstaden, stood there too with some worn-out horseshoes. He owed Ol-Kanelesa three shillings from before and trembled at the thought of asking him to make new ones. The tip the pastor had given him had gone with his other little bit of money to the sheriff at Tynset. The sheriff was after him the whole time. . . . The whole day he thought of little else other than the sheriff and his wretched debts. At night he dreamt of nothing but the sheriff and his debts. Now he owed money to all and sundry. His creditors were like birds of prey; one day, no doubt, they would pick his eyes out. . . . He sweated, froze, and his knees trembled. He didn't know where to turn, what to do with himself. Was there anyone on the face of the earth as badly placed as him? Scarcely.

Yet there was one night when he, too, had slept like a normal human being. And had dreamt like one, too. One single night! And that was the night he lay in the hay out in the travellers' stable and slept—it was as if he felt himself free as the air and secure, when he had the money on him he had got from Sigismund. And then he dreamt of the golden stone. God be praised and thanked for that dream! He dreamt that he had found a big shiny stone in the ground just outside the wall at home near Elgsjøen. He forced up the stone and carried it into the cottage. And it was so heavy that he only just managed it. And when he got in he almost died with joy; there was gold in the stone! Gold! Real gold! Now the sheriff at Tynset wouldn't be able to force an auction at Elgsjøen. And now people would have to stop calling out after him and roaring with laughter at him. And from now he would be able to live securely on his own land. What a joy! Just think, to be allowed to live in peace and quiet. And be allowed to die on his own land. Yes, no one could understand how good a dream that had been. For many days he had rejoiced over it. He persuaded himself many a time as he went for his load of charcoal that the dream was true. It made the way so smooth and agreeable.

"Well!" Ol-Kanelesa said suddenly. "Now perhaps you can pay me what you owe me, Tøllef?"

Ol-Kanelesa had little desire to stand here remaking old horseshoes for Tom, Dick, and Harry for nothing. If only he wasn't still so thirsty. And so sleepy. For four days and nights he had been up playing at the wedding of that Anders up at

Tanmæsa. What he got from the guests for his fiddling became less and less for every year that passed. Never had there been so many buttons in the collecting ladle as there were this time. But, honestly, he couldn't say much about it. Poverty was too great up here in the mountains now. It would soon be as bad as it was during the Swedish war.*

"You mustn't drive me too hard, Ol-Kanelesa," Tøllef whimpered. "You know the sheriff's after me the whole time, don't you Ol?" He stopped, the words wouldn't come out.

"Well, you must just let the sheriff take Elgsjøen and the rest of it. He won't give up until he does."

"Elgsjøen!" Tøllef shouted. "What d'you say, the sheriff take Elgsjøen from me?"

He shouted as if for his life. He had used the whole of it to save his croft at Elgsjøen. Was he to give up now? Had he then lived in vain? Lived and striven to no avail?

Ol-Kanelesa looked up; the others standing there looked up too. Tøllef's cry sounded like a cry for help. He stared at them, his mouth wide open, a cold sweat ran down over his grimy face leaving light stripes behind. He looked like somebody struggling with death.

"No, no," Ol-Kanelesa said. "Perhaps you can fix it there too?"

"I must fix it!" Tøllef said. "I can't leave my croft."

"Yes, sure you can fix it, Tøllef," someone in the crowd said, trying to comfort him. "You know you'll fix it." "Yes, if you can't manage to hang on to your farm, then no one else can," comforted a third. "And the way you've worked," a fourth added. "For that matter, you can be out of debt in a few years' time," a fifth person said. And they all began to comfort Tøllef. They all said, quite seriously, that he was still an able-bodied chap in his best years. And they abused the sheriff at Tynset, calling him the blackest names; the greedy louse! And all this comforting helped. Tøllef's voice became less gloomy. He hadn't the slightest doubt that he would manage to keep

---

* Røros was ravaged by the Swedes in 1678 and 1679.

Elgsjøen. Before he was an old man, he might for that matter
be rich; a squire! He began to laugh. A cold, mad laughter.
The wagoners looked at each other. His laughter was unpleasant; they shuddered. Poverty was depriving Tøllef
Elgsjøen of his wits.

"Bring your horseshoes here!" Ol-Kanelesa said. "Over here
with them, d'you hear!"

"May God bless you, Ol-Kanelesa," Tøllef said. "You'll get
back every penny I owe you. And if I ever get any power in
this world, you shan't have helped me for nothing."

The wagoners grinned; Tøllef was quite mad.

Ol-Kanelesa was serious. He went about his work and took
particular trouble with Tøllef's shoes. He even put the best
steel he had into the calks. And when he was finished, he said,
"Give me your hand, Tøllef."

Tøllef held out his hand slowly. He didn't understand what
the blacksmith really meant by it.

"Now we're quits, Tøllef."

"Are you daft?"

"Out with you!" Ol-Kanelesa said.

He took and pushed Tøllef out through the smithy door and
threw the horseshoes after him.

And the smith went on with his work. He forgot Tøllef, the
poor devil. He was thinking again about his own affairs. He
thought how well off he was, all the same, as long as he could
work in his smithy; the smithy was *his* world.

True enough he had his fiddle too. Indeed, if he hadn't had
that, he would surely have been lying under six foot of earth
a long time ago. And then he could sing. Yes, God be praised!
God hadn't forgotten him. But once he had possessed something that was much more than his fiddle, the smithy, and his
voice put together—but one should never speak of the snows
of yesteryear.

Gunhild Bonde

The traffic in the streets of Bergstaden had quieted down —there was only an occasional wagoner who, delayed by the melting snow, swung into Rau Alley with his skinny nag. The smeltery with its bellows groaned twice as heavily in the quiet, bright night. And the chimney stacks billowed forth their dark, thick, charcoal smoke over the rooftops.

The night was cold. Puddles in the street and in the courtyards froze over—closing up like tired, tear-stained eyes. And the enclosed gardens pushed their aged, frozen faces up out of the snow drifts.

It was quiet too in Ol-Kanelesa's smithy. The smithy door was half open; but inside near the forge and the anvil it was dark. The fire had gone out. And it was cold there too, colder than outside, for a cold draft blew through the sooty vent in the roof.

Ol-Kanelesa sat on the anvil, bare-headed and in red shirt sleeves. The handle of his sledge-hammer, worn smooth with wear, was rested against one of his knees. He had taken off his leather apron with the many burn holes in it and had hung it on the vise. The drinking ladle lay on the floor. After he finished work for the day, Ol-Kanelesa had to take a rest before he went up to Elisabeth Cottage. The day had been both hard and never-ending. It was as if lame nags swarmed up out of the very earth today. He had never seen so many ugly, scraggy nags as this spring.

And the people? The bones would soon be sticking through the clothes of half the wagoners.

"The winters. The winters," he mumbled. "The winters bide too long now."

His long hair fluttered in the through-draft from the vent.

"Is there a famine here?" the pastor had asked.

"Oh yes, thank you! We're just starving to death!" Ol-Kanelesa pursed his lips. Had anyone heard a more stupid question? He drank out of the ladle and threw it away; then rested his cheek on his hand and closed his eyes.

"Good night, your Reverence! Good night, the whole world!"
He dozed off.

Wasn't it Blacksmith Jens standing over there by the anvil,
playing? Ol-Kanelesa tried to sit up. Was he dreaming? No.
Blacksmith Jens was standing there, he saw him. He heard his
fiddle clearly. But Jens was dead. No. . . . Yes. Jens played
wonderfully. Yes, he knew how to handle the fiddle; what a
player!

Ellen! Was Ellen here too? Of course it was Ellen. She was
wearing her bridal wreath—but she too was dead. Ellen dead?
Not at all! Now she stood here between him and Blacksmith
Jens.

"Fancy meeting you again, Ellen!"

He tried to take hold of her but she glided away. She disappeared. And now Blacksmith Jens disappeared too. Ol-
Kanelesa awoke as someone came in and picked up the ladle.

"Were you just dropping off, Uncle?"

"Eh, was I asleep?"

The woman who came into the smithy was Gunhild Bonde.

She was just a little over medium height. Her face was sun-
burned. Her eyes dark blue. Her hair which was quite black
was arranged in two long plaits tied with red ribbons. When
she smiled, it was not her mouth that smiled but her eyes.
"Have you seen Gunhild's smile? Isn't it like a smile in one's
dreams?" Sigurd Olaus Dopp used to say when he felt con-
strained to be pompous. And the myopic secretary of the mines
could be pompous, at times.

She had a shining needle with a green silk thread in it in her
red woollen bodice. Today, too, she had sat making her bridal
gown—the one which never got finished—which never ought to
be finished, ever. She had sewn and pricked her fingers, sucked
the blood and gone on sewing again. If it were only her
shroud! She would have worked at that day and night, giving
thanks and singing praises; but a bridal gown? Oh! God alone
knew that she had shed more tears over it than she had sewn
stitches.

For three days and nights she had sat with the gown on her

lap and the needle in her hand. But tonight when the clock in the church tower struck twelve, and the shadows crept in through the windows onto her table, she had thrown aside her sewing–the bridal gown–her disgrace. And then she had run down to Elisabeth Cottage, and from there to the smithy. She had to get Ol-Kanelesa, her uncle, the only creature on this earth she dared go to in her distress, to plead her case with the new pastor. The pastor could, if he wanted, refuse to marry David and her, couldn't he? She had met the pastor in amongst the graves in the lower churchyard one morning– that was also one morning early before the sun rose. And since then she had so often thought about him. She didn't really understand why she had done so. She had–no–yes she had– she had thought more about him than David.

What's the matter, Gunhild?" Ol-Kanelesa asked.

She supported herself against the anvil. Her face turned as white as death in all this blackness.

"Uncle!" Her teeth chattered in her mouth. She shivered. "Oh, Uncle." She dug into the charcoal with fire tongs.

"My dear, what's wrong with you?"

He too was shivering. He clutched at his chest, tightly, as with claws.

"Uncle Ola!"

"Are you unhappy, Gunhild?"

"Yes, *now* I am unhappy, Uncle."

She thrust her face down in the heap of charcoal.

"You're making yourself dirty."

"I've dirtied myself already, I have."

"I've never heard the like; made yourself dirty?"

He walked over to the forge. He walked like a blind man– groping his way with his hands.

"I've never heard the like!" he repeated. "You, dirtied your-self?"

He took hold of her; lifted her up, carefully. He had not taken hold of anybody since Ellen. And that was now twenty years ago. Over twenty years it was.

"I'm not fit for you to take hold of, Uncle."

He stood there holding her. It seemed to him that his arms stiffened around her.

"It's me who's not fit to take hold of you."

Their words, their stammering words, sounded like a confession; to God! A painful and abject confession, in woe and anguish.

"You must talk to the pastor. And to her, the stepmother. It's she who's forced me into this misery."

"Is there someone else you're in love with, Gunhild?"

"I'm most in love with you, Uncle."

Ol-Kanelesa let go of her, horrified. He staggered backwards. He stared straight ahead, a fearful expression in his eyes. He had never heard anything so blasphemous.

"You don't know what you're saying, Gunhild."

She fell down on her knees by the forge.

"I've no one else who cares about me but you."

"Our Lord, Gunhild; He cares about you."

Ol-Kanelesa helped her up. They stood there a while, staring at each other. She was not shivering any more, and it became lighter—and the light came with peace and calm.

"I'll talk to Sigismund about this."

He took her and pushed her gently out through the door of the smithy.

"Tomorrow, I'll talk to Sigismund."

He closed the door.

The church clock struck one.

Pastor and Sacristan

The sun shone in through the east window of the room; it glowed like a fire in the middle of the wall. "God's light! The piercing light of God!" Sigismund sat up in bed, still tired, his hair tousled. He

straightened it out with his hand. He buttoned the gold button on his shirt. The button he had got from his beloved
mother, Margrethe Sigismund, née Brostrup, when he came
home from Copenhagen after his ordination.

Today, too, he prayed for his mother—his beautiful mother:
"Lord, God Almighty, encompass my precious mother in Thy
light, there where all weeping, all fear, is no more." He was
always very moved when he said that prayer. He could repeat
it over and over again. And now, too, he repeated it again and
again. He was so afraid that she might stand in the darkness
outside the gate, the Pearly Gate, and knock in vain.

A painful and tormenting feeling of loneliness came over
him. The world was again desolate and empty. He, Benjamin,
who should have sat at the right hand of the Father, was himself sitting without, in the darkness—damned and among the
damned.

He got up and put on some clothes. The day called him to
work, and to battle! Yesterday, his great dream of the future
had received a nasty blow. The post had brought him five
impudent, dunning letters. Five violent threats! The worst one
was from lawyer Wilgens. He threatened to make a scandal.
And now Sigismund would answer him. Half-dressed he sat
down at his desk and began. First of all, there was no question
of any immediate payment. He told the greedy usurers, short
and sharply, that he had been posted by royal decree to a
little parish consisting of poor, indeed famine-stricken, mountain peasants. And now, when war, pestilence, and crop failure
rode like a black-horned stallion over the kingdom, terrifying
the whole of humanity, simple Christian duty demanded
patience. To Mr. Wilgens he added: "Honored Sir. You should
in truth reflect that at your age you stand on the brink of the
grave. Soon, you ought to part from the goods and the gold of
this world; note well that the Bell of Your Life has already
begun to sound its last twelve strokes." Sigismund seized the
sand box and shook it energetically. He hoped that this powerful postscript would make the old miser tremble in his fragile
bones.

It was not completely without danger to write to his creditors in this way—but he would be a hypocrite and a coward
if he began to go on his knees and fawn on that corrupt sec-
tion of society which consisted of usurers and money-grubbers.
But supposing they took their petty revenge and set the civil
power at his throat? Well! He would then have to reconcile
himself to swallowing the bitter pill and take the two thousand
rix-dollars Kathryn had invested in an iron works in the south,
and throw them into their greedy maw. But then! Yes, then he
would see that they were shaken to the very bottom of their
souls. He would not hesitate to use the cat-o'-nine-tails on that
occasion. As he had sat there writing, Sigismund had worked
himself up into a rage. His anger warmed his blood. He became hot and flushed.

He started when he heard Kathryn cough in the small side-
room. The whole night she had lain there coughing. On reflection, perhaps the cold air here, mixed as it was with acrid
sulphur fumes, wasn't good for her weak chest. He consoled
himself, however, with the thought that the long journey, the
freezing sledges, and sleeping in cold bedclothes had caused
her health to deteriorate—and that with quiet and warmth and
the coming of summer it would improve. In any case there was
no immediate danger. Her expectoration did not sink in water.

Who was trying the door? In this old house there were many
strange sounds. During the night as he lay awake he thought
he clearly heard someone come in. He did not see anyone, but
there was no doubt that the door opened and closed. Was
there some unquiet spirit that couldn't find peace? Today he
would try and find out from Mr. Leich if anybody had committed suicide here; but a pastor in the 19th century could
hardly ask about that sort of thing either. He would make himself ridiculous. Of course it was ridiculous! Ha! Ha! Ha!
Superstition! Just superstition! Besides, he intended to fight
superstition. He would speak about it from the pulpit. He
would make people understand that it had its root in ignorance, in the terrible darkness of the Middle Ages.

Again there was someone at the latch.

Sigismund felt a cold shudder go down his spine. . . .
Spirits? He got up from his chair and called out, "Is anyone
there?"

His voice was uncertain. He didn't hear anything other than
Kathryn's coughing. What? He stopped in the middle of the
room and called out again.

"Come in!"

He was irritated by his own timidity. Witches and goblins?
With a bound he pushed the door open quickly.

"Is it you, sacristan?"

Sigismund felt relieved. He felt even more relieved than he
really wanted to admit. It would never occur to him to believe
in witches and goblins.

"Come in, Ole Korneliusen."

"You must excuse me that I'm afoot so early."

Ol-Kanelesa stood there in his working clothes, wearing a
leather apron and clogs. He held his cap under his arm.

"The early bird catches the worm," Sigismund said.

"Yes, so they used to say."

The sacristan stepped over the threshold and came in.

Now Sigismund remembered that he had a bone to pick
with the sacristan. Judging by what he had now heard, this
man's life and morals were not entirely irreproachable.

"Sit down."

He began to walk round the sacristan; silent, gloomy, and
ominous. Few things made people more submissive than to
walk up and down the room and look threatening. The late
Bishop von Arnfeldt had taught him that trick. It was very
effective. And Sigismund continued to walk; but he carried it
too far. Ol-Kanelesa saw through him and sat cold and indifferent on the edge of the chair. He sat with a face of stone,
he didn't flicker an eyelid. And Sigismund walked up and
down. Ol-Kanelesa sat there in the same way. Not even his
hands betrayed the slightest embarrassment.

Ol-Kanelesa's calm made Sigismund hesitate. He was looking at a face where every line spoke of a quick intelligence.

Then Sigismund went into the attack.

"You were once a schoolmaster, I hear."

"Yes. That's in the book, isn't it?"

Sigismund started. He groped for words.

"Why did you give it up then?"

"That's in the book too."

"Yes, it says that you resigned at your own request."

"Why d'you ask when you know it already?"

"Hm. Yes. But what was your real reason for resigning?"

"Aren't I permitted to plan my own life?"

The plan which Sigismund had made in advance to come to grips with the sacristan was going awry. He couldn't get in a blow at the man.

"Well," he continued. "Wasn't it so that you had to resign because of drink and gambling?"

"Where's the pastor got that from?"

"I have it from completely reliable people."

"Does the pastor know who's reliable and who's not in this place then?"

"I have every reason to believe that the person who told me this is completely reliable."

"Well, well." And after a while Ol-Kanelesa said, "Does the pastor think that people who immediately come rushing to spread evil about others are so reliable?"

Sigismund began to walk up and down again. Perhaps the sacristan was right? Gossip mongers were the least reliable. They were usually slanderers and backbiters.

He realized that his hastiness and his zeal had led him astray. He would have to investigate the matter further.

"There is, in any case, one thing I want to tell you, Ole Korneliusen. If I achieve full certainty that you had to resign from the school because of a dissolute life, then I shall have to speak to you seriously."

"Is that any business of the pastor's?"

"Are you not the sacristan?"

"I can finish today if that's how it is."

"Finish!" Sigismund said. "Do you want to finish?"

"Yes. At my own request."

That the sacristan wanted to finish, resign at his own request, as he said, put Sigismund in an awkward position;
dismissal was the very thing he had intended to threaten him
with. Had the sacristan seen through him and by cunning and
presence of mind struck his own weapon out of his hand? He
put his hands on his hips, drew himself up right in front of
Ol-Kanelesa, and looked him straight in the eye; but there
was nothing to be seen in his face which gave an answer to
anything. . . . Ice, stone, and iron were in it.

"We must remember that one day we shall have to answer
for all our actions, Ole."

Ol-Kanelesa got up quickly.

"Just so. You took the words out of my mouth. We mustn't
forget that, no."

Sigismund turned impatiently away from him.

Like the heathen Vikings this man tried to catch the enemy's
spear in the air. But now he *should* go; banished from the
temple. Finis!

"I must talk to you about something," Ol-Kanelesa said.
"About something important; I must talk to you about it."

"Is not what we were talking about just now also very
important?"

"Have I said that it wasn't?"

"No, no. Then speak out; but no duplicity."

"The third Sunday after Trinity, when you have preached
your inaugural sermon, there will be a wedding to officiate
at."

"Yes. What about it?"

Sigismund felt uncomfortable at being reminded of his
inaugural sermon. He had torn up the sermon he had written.
Well. He had Christ's promise that what he was to preach
and say on that occasion would be given to him at that same
time—but now, as the day drew near, it became more and
more difficult for him to hang on to that promise—to rely on
it entirely. Was he really one of the elect to whom the promise
applied? Yesterday he had gone up to the church again and
had knelt for a long time in front of the altar and prayed;

not for any answer to this question—but that this doubt-poisoned thought might leave him. And when he got up he felt that this had happened.

Today the doubt was there again. Today the old serpent from the Garden of Eden had appeared again, hissing. He heard its discordant sound. He was repelled by its cunning.

"You must prevent this wedding, pastor," Ol-Kanelesa said. "She, who is to stand there as bride, will say yes with her lips and no with her heart."

"What?" Sigismund said. "Am *I* to prevent it? Is there some legal hindrance?"

Ol-Kanelesa looked up. A strange smile came over his calm face. And it was a smile so twisted and ugly, so full of contempt, that Sigismund started back, horrified.

"Can I ask you something, pastor?"

Sigismund didn't answer. He just stood there and stared at Ol-Kanelesa.

"Are you a lawyer, or are you a curer of souls?"

"How dare you ask such a question?"

"Be not wrathful," Ol-Kanelesa said severely, switching over to a stiff literary style. "The feet of wrathful men lead to the abyss."

"To be sure I am your pastor. And the whole lot of you shall get to know it."

"Hasten in no wise too quickly along the path you are now taking," Ol-Kanelesa said. Whereupon he changed to his own dialect again, and said both loudly and authoritatively: "Have all those who have walked together to the altar been happy and lived a true Christian life just because the forms have been legal?"

"Take care," Sigismund said. "Guard your tongue."

He shook his forefinger warningly in Ol-Kanelesa's face.

"Yes or no, pastor?"

Sigismund sat down heavily in his chair. He had to try to calm down.

Ol-Kanelesa sat down too—slowly and carefully on the extreme edge of the chair

Neither of them said anything for a long time; and Sigismund battled with himself. Something of what the sacristan
had said was now written with letters of fire on the wall. He
had seen it before too. During the whole of his married life
with Kathryn, he had seen it; but in a slightly different form,
with slightly different words, but the content was exactly the
same. And then he was to hear it from this man of the people,
this depraved wretch! He forced himself to think slowly. And
to penetrate deeply into his own soul. "*Yes* with her lips and
no in her heart." Hadn't Kathryn and he, too, pitched their
tents on the same shaky foundation? Yes! Yes!

"Listen," he said. "Do not let us lose our tempers any more."

Ol-Kanelesa was silent.

"What are the names of this couple who are to be married
on the third Sunday after Trinity?"

"The bride's name is Gunhild—Gunhild Bonde. The bridegroom is David Finne."

"And you know the bride?"

"Yes, I'm her uncle."

"You are her uncle?"

"Yes. She's my brother's daughter."

Sigismund became more and more calm. He thumbed
through the yellowed pages of the church register without
his hands shaking. He read the couple's names a couple of
times. And he stood for a long time bent over the thick folio,
thinking.

"No," he said, and thumped the rough writing in the book
with the flat of his hand. "What my predecessor has done, I
have no power to change. And besides—" Benjamin Sigismund
bit his lip. "Nor have I received a request from either of
them."

"Gunhild doesn't want to have that David," Ol-Kanelesa
said.

"Has not she given her promise to David Finne?"

"Yes, with her lips, but not with her heart."

Ol-Kanelesa realized that the whole thing was hopeless. He
felt it useless to explain all the circumstances to the pastor.

All in all, perhaps the pastor was the last person who could prevent the marriage. No one on earth could save Gunhild now. She had gone too far.

He got up and bade Sigismund farewell.

"Farewell," Sigismund said, and closed the church register slowly. "Farewell, sacristan."

Benjamin Sigismund remained sitting there, thinking about Gunhild Bonde and her marriage to Finne, David Finne. He certainly couldn't get mixed up in this affair. It may be, too, that this Gunhild was a capricious female who wanted one thing one day and another the next. He had known many like that.

Then Sigismund began to think over his clash with the sacristan; it left a nasty taste in his mouth. From the sacristan his thoughts moved on to the two smelters. The people here in Bergstaden showed a lack of respect and an arrogance which he must come to grips with. His predecessor had not held the reins tightly enough.

And Sigismund got up and went over and opened the door wide. The blacksmith, the sacristan, had left behind a rank smell of soot and sweat.

When Ol-Kanelesa came out of the gateway Gunhild Bonde stood there waiting for him. She stared at him with frightened eyes. Her hands trembled. She tried to hide it by keeping them under her apron.

"Did you sleep last night?" Ol-Kanelesa said.

"Me, sleep?" she repeated. "There'll be no more sleep for me until I go to my rest for the last time."

"You must come to your senses, Gunhild."

He tried to remain calm and speak with authority now, too —but that calm and authority he'd had when speaking to Sigismund seemed to be taken from him as he stood down here in the gateway. He fumbled for words. He scarcely dared look up at Gunhild.

"What did the pastor say?" She had to support herself

against the wall so as not to collapse—it was as if she had asked whether she was soon to die. "Wouldn't he help me, Uncle?"

"I think he's one of them who won't help anyone except himself, is our Master Sigismund."

"Did he say no then?"

"Well, he didn't say yes, in any case."

She grasped a rusty iron ring on the back of the gate and held on to it with both hands. Her knees wouldn't support her.

"Then I shan't be true to him," she said. "This is happening against my will."

"Not true?" Ol-Kanelesa stammered. "If you're married you must be true."

"My marriage won't be valid. At least to Him who sees and knows all."

She let go the iron ring and ran up the street. People she met and knew, she pretended not to see.

The Third Sunday After Trinity

Today Benjamin Sigismund was to preach his inaugural sermon.

The streets lay grey and dry. Now nothing was left of the winter, the long winter, than a few big, white snowdrifts along the tree line in the mountains. Around the snowdrifts there were twisted birch trees, and here and there a birch tree rose up out of the snowdrifts themselves; they stood there with budding leaves. Lakes and tarns shone golden blue, reflecting the sun and the sky, the crags and the flowering grassland.

On all the roads leading to Bergstaden people from the country came driving in their two-wheeled buggies; sometimes with as many as twenty horses together. The menfolk sat perched on the shafts in their shirt sleeves and their waist-coats unbuttoned, letting one leg dangle down in front of the wheel, and holding onto the long reins with both hands. The womenfolk sat curled up close together in the buggies on hard-packed haysacks and between leather ropes smelling of tar. The iron-shod wheels bumped over the stones and ground into the gravel. And those who were sitting up there had to shout—the shaking and bumping of the vehicle cut their words in two. But that didn't affect these taciturn people—they hadn't so much to say to each other that it couldn't wait for another day.

Those who hadn't a horse or an ox to drive there with, went on foot, following the cattle tracks through the fields and forest—that, too, was a great treat, to be out walking in the warm weather in their Sunday best and without having the usual heavy load of provisions on their backs—now that the leaves, the heather and the moss were giving off their fragrance in the sunshine. And the mountain plover sang and the cock grouse shrieked, and the southern wind soughed in the grass and the flowers.

The fires in the smeltery's circular furnaces were extinguished, the outdoor smelting ovens burnt low, and the cloud of acrid smoke and sulphur which had lain over Bergstaden for a year now moved away northwards with the breeze. Now the town lay under the arc of the sun—it shone down into the dark backyards, into the holes and corners, and sparkled on the grey slate up on the rooftops. The air trembled, steely white, between the rust-colored walls of the houses.

Benjamin Sigismund had spent a sleepless night; a night of fear. And what was worse, it was fear of people, not of God. He felt queasy and ill at ease. For the first time in his life he was going into the pulpit without having prepared what he was going to say. His practice had been to weigh carefully in advance every single word he was to say. At times he had also shut himself up to practice his sermons. Everything was thought out and calculated, both what he said and the way he said it. And people had said that his sermons were

spiritual masterpieces; but were they all inspired by God?
Scarcely! No! He had been a conjurer. He had performed
instead of witnessing. He had arranged performances in the
temple, in "my Father's House." And that was why he now
felt the Master's scourge upon him. *His* wrath had fallen
upon him—the hawker of doves in the temple, the charlatan
Benjamin Sigismund. In the past his congregation had been
wanderers in the desert who, in vain, had hurried to the oasis
to slake their thirst—but who had had to wander back over
the hot desert sand with dry cups in their burning hands; the
springs of the oasis had been empty of the living water.

Yes, such had his preaching been. An abomination for God
and man. Today he would go into the pulpit with the bare
lesson of the day in his hand. He was to stand face to face
with a new congregation—with a people of cold and stolid
temperament.

It was only when the church clock struck eight that he got
up, tired and unrested. And contrary to his custom he dressed
himself slowly. He felt no joy at the morning sun. Nor did his
spirits lift at the sound of the church bells. Had his inner
life perished during the agonies of the night?

He continued to sit there looking at his hands. He was no
noble soul with clean hands; they were in nowise worthy to
touch the gleaming chalice, the paten, and the Holy Scriptures.
He had sunk into an abyss; the abyss of vanity.

Thy draught seems like honey,
But loathsome when drunk,
Vanity of vanities.

Tears forced the blood up into his moist cheeks. He put his
hands over his face and repeated,

. . . But loathsome when drunk,
Vanity of vanities.

He also thought of going in to Kathryn and waking her, to
ask her help in this bitter hour.

He was sitting in a boat with those of little faith out on the

Lake of Gennesaret. And the waves—the heavy waves were already so high that they could capsize his frail craft. If Kathryn and he threw themselves down on their knees and prayed to the Master to awake? It had always been so difficult for him to pray with anyone else; two people breathing, two hearts beating, broke the peace of the private chamber. Besides, Kathryn would find it hard to understand what was actually involved. He was on perilous seas. Kathryn and he were not as one soul. Had his mother been alive, she would have watched and prayed with him. They were one soul! His soul was fired by a spark from hers. On the morning of creation his heart had been formed under her heart. How often, when he thought of his mother, did he feel as if a part of his own heart now lay down there in her deep grave and perished.

He reached out for his Bible. And he opened it at random. His gaze fixed on Eliphaz' words, "Then shalt thou lay up gold as dust, and the gold of Ophir as the stones of the brooks. Yea, the Almighty shall be thy defence, and thou shalt have plenty of silver."

He closed the Bible slowly.

An invisible hand had placed a burning candle in his room. *In hoc signo vinces.* By casting his gold into the dust, by true humbleness of mind and spirit, and by the Sign of the Cross, he would conquer.

He remained sitting for a long time on a sand-scoured stool by the window, listening indifferently to the church bells. Now they had begun their final tolling.

No, their sound didn't move him; nothing moved him now. There were no memories, no emotions. He was tired.

"Benjamin," Kathryn called.

Sigismund didn't get up. Her arms round his neck every morning! What was the point of it? He sat talking loudly and excitedly to himself. Was he a cynic? Yes, he was a cynic! He ought to be ashamed of himself! He sat here working himself up and was in a bad humor. And then he let Kathryn get the benefit of it.

She was not completely without blame. If only she had been

a little different from the thousands of other wives with their routine and meaningless morning kisses—and their empty embraces; this self-deception expressed in empty caresses—this life of ten thousand others.

"Benjamin!"

"Yes, Yes. What is it?"

He pressed his hands against his bony knees to get up—to get up and go into his wife's bedroom. He certainly had nothing to reproach Kathryn with. They both belonged to the great grey mass. They were part of the ten thousand.

Kathryn was still in bed, with large, shining eyes after her sleep. He bent over her. And she threw her arms round her husband's neck. Not tightly! Not passionately! No, today as yesterday. He let it happen.

And then they began to talk about everyday things. About things they had talked about hundreds of times before: clothes, shoes, food, drink. He looked at hers and the boys' boots with parental concern. Yes, that was part of his role. He stroked her hair. That was part of it too.

"You have prepared your sermon, I suppose, Benjamin?" Kathryn said.

It gave him a shock. He woke up.

"Prepared?"

"Yes, I suppose you have learned your sermon off by heart?"

"No," he said. "Not at all, I have not learned it by heart."

"Benjamin!" She gave him a horrified look. "Today the church will be full of the best people in Bergstaden. Surely you have it prepared?"

"Kathryn, that is worldly talk. From now on it is not fitting for me to preach to people of rank and title, but only to the lost sheep of the house of Israel."

She was familiar with his rhetorical style. With him, excitement and flowery language usually went together.

Nonetheless Benjamin's inaugural sermons were among the great events of her life. Those Sundays with the bishop to dinner had been her red-letter days. On those days she, too, counted. But today it was in truth well that his Lordship

Bishop Peter Olivarius Bugge was unable to come. Yes, for Benjamin could fail, too. His ardor, power, and enthusiasm sometimes made him bend the bow too far. And his arrows flew wide of the mark.

The church bells began to toll for the second time. And the pastor hurriedly ate a piece of coarse rye bread. With it he drank a mug of cold well water. Then he put on his cassock hurriedly and stuck his prayer book into one of the folds; there was a hole in the pocket.

A painful, almost melancholy feeling of remorse seized him. He had in no way been as he should towards Kathryn today. Today, too, he had sinned against her, and at the same time against God. He almost went over and embraced her—but stopped himself, it seemed such a miserable gesture. If he had done wrong to Kathryn, it could not be atoned for by an embrace and a kind word. Atonement, that was no easy thing, it demanded daily contrition, its own deep suffering.

The Main Street and Rau Alley were packed with people as the pastor came out of the gateway of Leich's house. And at once it was as if a muffled shout arose, a whispering from mouth to mouth right up to the churchyard: "Here he comes, the new pastor." The venerable elders of Bergstaden had taken their places in good time along the walls of the houses and up on the steps leading to the doors, ready to touch the brim of their large top hats. Those who had only home-knitted caps removed them with great seriousness—people said that he "came bounding like a lion up the street." The women and the girls, who were not supposed to greet him, retired shy and frightened behind the backs of the men, and peered out with wide-open eyes.

Benjamin Sigismund walked quickly and with long firm strides. He held tightly on to his prayer book with his left hand. With his right he continually pinched the brim of his top hat. He did not look up, and took care the whole time to keep a severe, clerical expression on his face. He knew what the people were now saying and thinking. And this made it of such great importance that his first appearance should be a dignified one. The first impression was always the most lasting. His Lordship, Bishop von Arenfeldt, would on an occasion such as this have conducted himself like a general.

But Christ, the great Lord and Master, would He in this hour have walked here, conducting himself like a general? *He*, the King, who had come quietly riding on an ass and with the ass's foal. "In no wise! In no wise!" Benjamin Sigismund lowered his head. In remorse! In shame! His gait became less precise, almost shambling. And his expression, that stupid parsonical look on his face, disappeared. No one was greater than his Master. His face took on a dispirited, melancholy expression. Now he began to look up at some of the people who stood pressed up against the walls of the houses and greeted him. He nodded and smiled.

Two girls, two young seventeen-year-old girls from Flanderborg, stood arm in arm with pearl-studded bonnets and red chin-bands in the sunshine up by an old grass-grown grave. They nudged each other furtively with their elbows and their cheeks flushed as the pastor went past them. "My, what a handsome pastor he is!" one of them said. "Yes, but they say he's such a terrible bad temper," the other said. And with Kingo's hymnal in their hands they hurried laughingly up the steps to the church to get a place in the pews as near the front as possible. They had to have a closer look at the pastor. It was only when they walked up the nave, treading carefully in their low, copper-buckled shoes on the green juniper branches which had been laid on the floor, that the smile disappeared from their young faces. And they became like the others in there, pale and serious in the quiet and the cool air.

When Benjamin Sigismund opened the vestry door and saw the sacristan, Ol-Kanelesa, with the hymnal between his two black blacksmith's hands, he once again took on his severe clerical expression. He had now heard even worse things about this man. The Church could not be disgraced by having this morally depraved person in her service. And Sigismund banged the door demonstratively behind him. The penitents who were sitting along the damp walls, staring at the floor and ready to confess, jumped.

Sigismund gave Ol-Kanelesa a brief, cold nod. And he at once opened his prayer book and read the penitent's prayer quickly and nervously.

Ol-Kanelesa tried to clear his throat a couple of times to remind the pastor that a hymn should be sung first. The sacristan's mysterious coughings and strange gestures distracted the penitents, so they heard little or nothing of what was being read to them. Some of them even tried to catch Ol-Kanelesa's eye. Thus deep was their penitence.

As Sigismund stood ready to go in and kneel at the altar he felt that something was wrong—there was not the proper, heavy silence in the vestry. None of them who stood there looked sinful and guilt-ridden. Were they a lot of hypocrites who had come to confess? Or had his words and injunctions been without effect? If so, how would things go in the pulpit today? As he stood here he could scarcely remember the lesson for the day. Yes, today he had set the Word of God, the Master's promise, a hard test.

He was very pale, his cheeks as if whitened and with blue rings under his eyes, when a little later he appeared in the chancel door.

The drawing of hundreds of deep breaths could be heard. An involuntary turning of pages in heavy hymn books sounded like the rustling of dry leaves, from pew to pew, down through the church and up in the galleries. The gentry of Bergstaden, who sat in their expensive closed pews in the upper part of the church along by the windows, where they could impress the common people, forgot for the moment who they were. Like all the others they had to stare at the pastor.

Yes, there was nothing to say against his appearance. Whereupon they once again tried to outdo each other by putting on their accustomed stiff patrician faces.

One or another old miner, his sight weakened by gunpowder smoke and the heat of torches, shielded his eyes and stared for a long time up at the altar. "Fine parson," one of them mumbled. "He reminds me of old Pætter Abildgaard," another mumbled from down at the back of the pews.

Ol-Kanelesa came out into the nave and read the bidding prayer, and Benjamin Sigismund knelt at the altar. For a while he prayed warmly and earnestly to God for His wisdom in conducting divine service on this day. Not to his own honor and gain, but to His glory.

Then he stopped suddenly still on his knees, listening to the sacristan's beautiful voice. In this man's mouth the words took on a strangely beautiful sound. The sacristan's voice was like an instrument, tuned to the walls and the dome of the church. Sigismund felt his soul warmed at hearing God's Word enunciated in this way. He made a resolution: he would deliver his sermon just as simply and straightforwardly. He had something to learn from Ol-Kanelesa. And he understood it was a sign from God. Words and images must have the same limpidity and power to reflect thought as a clear stream had. Such were the words and images of Jesus. They were so clear and bright that the two thousand years which had passed since they were said had not been able to leave the slightest sign of rust on them.

Now Ol-Kanelesa was singing in a loud voice:

Illumine light of love the road,
To the heart's dark cavity,
And dwell there in this poor abode,
Now and to eternity . . .

Benjamin Sigismund now entered the narrow doorway leading to the pulpit for the first time, whither he had been called by the Lord God to preach the living Word. And for him this narrow doorway with its faded blue paint and its worn iron handle was in that moment changed to a pearly gate with a golden handle. And the sunshine from the many windows met him as he went in, like a wave of golden, blinding light.

Yet this door was no pearly gate for him and no entrance to the light, the true inextinguishable light. There would come a time when all the shining pearls he now saw in the spirit would grow dark and lose their splendour. And the light, the golden light, that too one day would lead out into the darkness, out into a long night.

He closed the book with the cross on it. Only the cross, the cross of Jesus Christ, was all he wanted to see at this moment. And he folded his white hands over this cross and began to sing with the others.

'Tis worldly honor you covet,
For this is all your aim,
My commandments you do forget,
For them no time does remain.
The world which shall ensnare you,
You hold so dearly to
Me have you quite forgotten.

The singing lifted his mind up from earthly light to an even stronger and brighter light. The Word of God which so often before had seemed contradictory and shadowed by the cold shadows of doubt and disbelief now emerged clear and pure. Was this the promise of Whitsun morning, the hour of the spirit and transfiguration? It was the same light which enveloped him now, as in that early morning hour when he first stood in this temple. His inner eye saw. And his inner ear heard. God was nigh!

He began to pray, calmly and quietly. His words grew in earnestness and in strength. In his mind his prayers became like the smoke of Abel's sacrifice; God could see it.

And when he read the lesson for the day, "And the Spirit and the bride say, Come. And let him that heareth say, Come. And let him that is athirst come. And whosoever will, let him take the water of life freely," it was as if breathing stopped down there in the church. Eyes shone. And faces grew pale.

He, who before had always been given to using powerful language about sin and death and the eternal and inextinguishable fire, spoke today quite quietly and subdued about the Son of God, the crucified one, crowned with thorns. He gave freely of the water of life to the thirsty and weary wanderer.

There was no sound of sobbing in the church. There was no fear in the rugged tanned faces.

What had they then to fear? "And whosoever will, let him take the water of life freely," was the message of the day to them. The day and the hour was full of sun and light and God's love and gentleness; Paradise lost had been regained—they all saw it so clearly now—it shone with unending magnificence and glory along streets of gold—there were babbling brooks and there were green pastures—and there was no hunger and no sickness and no death—and no poverty and no debt —and no sheriff with summonses, seizures, and forced auctions. There no one needed to spin and gather into the barn and worry himself about the morrow.

Yes, Paradise lost had been regained—almost regained. And whosoever would, could go therein and drink of the water of life freely.

A cloud passed over the sun which now stood right over Peder Hjort's white burial chapel. The light disappeared from the stained-glass windows of the church; Paradise regained was floating away. And the weather-beaten men and women sat there once more with their hymn books in their horny hands and stared into the old world, with its striving, its strife, and its everyday cares.

No, not everybody. The two young girls from Flanderborg sat there side by side with wet eyes and looked towards Paradise, towards the Garden of Eden. The garden with green birch trees around the snowdrifts and flowers and sun on the lake and on the tarns year in and year out.

Sigismund's sermon was not long; did the Lord God himself stand beside him and point his finger to where he should begin and end?

He could not expect the plaudits of the world for this sermon; in any case plaudits were to be despised. He had not spoken of the Lord of Hosts, of the God of the rich and mighty, but of the God of love. He who had not recognized difference between prince and beggar. He who led those who

stood poor and downtrodden in the gateway up to the east
end of the temple. He who brought the unworthy to sit beside
the worthy.

When the hymn "Each one of us his failing hath . . ." was
to be sung, it was Ol-Kanelesa and some old miners who sang
it. The others remained seated, staring down at their Kingo.
They were still filled with the wonder and warmth of the
sermon. They sat there without burden and without yoke. The
new pastor had scarcely said a word about sin, death, and
the kingdom of the Devil. No bad dreams of hell and eternal
damnation would haunt them tonight and bring a cold sweat
out on to their foreheads—as on so many a night before after
the fire and brimstone sermons of their pastors. The Good
Shepherd himself had led them by the hand up along the
way towards the lost Paradise. Up towards the land they had
so often glimpsed through their prayers and tears and long-
ings and dreams.

When the blessing had been pronounced, Ol-Kanelesa in-
toned the recessional hymn and the whole congregation, both
the gentry and the mining folk, joined in. And mine secretary
Dopp even tried to sing some of the verses in harmony. However, today no one seemed to bother himself very much to
appreciate his efforts. Not even his subordinates at the Works
showed any inclination to pay their proper respects to his
deep bass voice, by honoring it by keeping quiet themselves
and staring admiringly up at the pew where the small, vain
man sat.

Today there were no baptisms
after the service. And only one wedding. Yes, today Gunhild
Bonde, and corporal in the Ski-Corps and foreman at the
Works David Finne, were to be married.

And since it was two members of the middle class who
were getting married today, both the mining folk and the
gentry remained in their pews—partly out of curiosity and
partly to do honor to the bridal couple by staying.

The lofty, beautiful atmosphere of Paradise disappeared. Worldly thoughts crept into their minds once more. Even the two girls from Flanderborg quickly dried the tears from their shining eyes and began to gossip, whisper, and smile. Now they were to enjoy a wedding. And to go to the wedding reception dressed in their Sunday best, with pearl-embroidered bonnets and copper-buckled shoes, this was much the same as going to Paradise for these two seventeen-year-old girls.

But everyone was now talking about Gunhild and David. All down the rows of pews, both on the side occupied by the men and the side occupied by the women, and up in the galleries, everybody was talking in low voices about this marriage. And all were agreed that it was more than tragic; Gunhild was dead set against it. She was being more or less bullied into marrying him. Her uncle, Ol-Kanelesa, had one morning this week gone to the pastor and asked him to prevent the marriage; but the pastor had only become angry. But Parson Sigismund could watch out for himself. He and his missus quarreled continually. People said Mrs. Leich's maidservant Anne-Sofie had seen and heard a thing or two up at the pastor's lodging. Some were of the opinion that given time everything would come right between Gunhild and David; when wild ones like Gunhild got their first child everything usually went swimmingly.

Now the church was buzzing like a grinding mill. The gentry, too, leaned over to each other now and then and whispered a few words, very few—what they had to say was said mainly with their eyes, with brief nods and smiles. After which they sat back again with their stiff, stony faces silhouetted against the whitewashed walls.

The sacristan came and sat down quietly and solemnly on an old creaking chair under the plaque commemorating mineowner Lorentz Lossius, the distinguished-looking gentleman in a blue tail-coat and a sword of honor.

Today was the last day Ol-Kanelesa would officiate in church, if things went as he thought. He didn't intend to stay and be beholden to Benjamin Sigismund. Anybody who

thought that didn't rightly know Ol-Kanelesa. Besides, he had
lost bigger things than this miserable sacristan's job. Both life
and death had parted Ol-Kanelesa from that which was a
thousand times more precious to him than this beggarly little
job of doing service here on a Sunday. And now he would also
be parted from Gunhild. Now she was getting husband, house,
and home. Then there'd hardly be any question of old Uncle
Ola any more, would there? Of course he'd soon have lived
as much of life as it had been ordained he should. And then—
then the only thing left was to die. He crossed his legs and
yawned a couple of times behind Kingo's hymnal. He was
tired.

Those who sat in the pews right at the back—mainly young
people, and some servant girls and farmhands from the big
estates—turned round and stared wonderingly at the church
door.

Twice it had been opened slightly and then closed hard and
quickly again. What was going on out there?

Some thought they had heard a woman crying out, others
that people were fighting. But surely it had never happened
that people had begun to fight in church? It might have happened that some people or other had fallen to quarreling in
the churchyard, especially as there were several paths and
short cuts between and over the graves; but in the church
itself, never! No doubt there was many a hooligan nowadays
who cared neither about the church or the pastor, but that
they could take to quarreling inside the church porch. No, no
one was such a hooligan as that. No wonder then that a cold
shudder went down the backs of those who sat there in the
back pews.

At the same time, something both serious and unpleasant
was going on on the other side of the church door; for out
there someone was fighting for her life. It was Gunhild Bonde.

She and David Finne, together with the bridegroom's party,
the bridesmaids, and their closest relatives, had come up the
church steps. The bridal couple, as the custom was, went hand
in hand. Much as children go hand in hand. It really looked

as if everything was well between them. But when they got inside the porch of the church, Gunhild tore her hand away.

"No, I won't," she said. "I'd sooner die than do it, David."

David Finne stood there bewildered. He tried to seize her hand again but couldn't get hold of it.

Now the members of the bridal party began to get cross with Gunhild. A grown-up woman behaving that way! She ought to be ashamed of herself! And they forced their hands together again.

One of the bridesmaids said, "Just get her into the church, then things will be all right."

And another bridesmaid said, "Just stick together a little longer and it's soon done." And she added, "I dreaded it too."

At the inner door to the church Gunhild sank down on her knees in front of the threshold.

"Is there nobody here who will save me?"

She looked around desperately. No, there was no one who would now.

Then David Finne said, "If you don't want to, then you needn't."

He stood there helplessly, looking down at her. Things could never have been called good between them; but never so bad as today. It would be hard to lose Gunhild. But the shame, the talk and the laughter in the Ski Corps, in the miners' huts, at the charcoal dumps, and at the smeltery would surely be even worse.

Now it was David's turn to get a talking-to. Wasn't he a grown man? Surely he could show a woman who was the boss. He, a foreman.

And then Gunhild was lifted up; dust and dirt were brushed off her dress and her bridal crown was hurriedly rearranged and put straight on her head.

"Open the door!"

One of the bridegroom's party ran with short, stiff steps and threw the door wide open.

In the church it suddenly became quiet. The bridal couple moved up the aisle. Hand in hand. And as they went past the

church windows the sun threw a golden light on the bridal
wreath. It was woven of heather, leaves, and budding bird-
cherry blossom. The bridal gown which Gunhild had made
during the many light spring evenings, and with the shedding
of so many salt tears and bloody pricks on her fingers, suited
her. And her low shoes were not adorned with common copper. No, the buckles were of silver. Ol-Kanelesa had given
them to her the day before as a wedding present. For thirty
years he had had them locked up in his little green-painted
wall cupboard. He had only taken them out at long intervals
to polish them shining bright. And then Ol-Kanelesa had wept.
For once they had been destined for another pair of bridal
shoes, but of that nothing came.

David Finne looked good in his new uniform. If anyone
could be happy in this world, then it must be these two, both
finely set-up and handsome. And so well-off too.

Ol-Kanelesa got up in his sacristan's pew. He knit his hairy
eyebrows which met in the middle, and made a grimace with
one corner of his mouth.

So now the pastor was standing before the altar rail. . . .
The organist, who had stood bent over the railings of the
organ loft with his long hair hanging down in his eyes, jerked
back his head, rushed over to the organ, and began to play
a chorale.

Benjamin Sigismund looked more like a warrior clad in
chain and armor than a clergyman, as he stood there between
the enormous brass candlesticks with their yellow, home-made
altar candles. He only lacked a helmet and sword. For when,
after his sermon, he had spoken a few words to his good
sacristan, Ole Korneliusen, at the entrance to the chancel, his
despondency left him and he got back his old fighting spirit
again. And in full measure too. He was mightily angry.

What was it this common fellow was presuming? Yes, indeed, to remind his Reverence to stick to the ritual as laid
down by his Most Gracious Majesty! Surely, it could never
have happened before that a sacristan had dared to say that

sort of thing to his superior? Sigismund had told him straight
to his face and in a loud voice that just as certain as this was
the first Sunday they had conducted divine service together,
so just as certain was it their last. He wasn't going to tolerate
reprimand from his subordinates. Had he made a mistake, then
he would shoulder the blame himself.

"In short, sacristan, unasked-for advice is not wanted. And
that's final!"

And in that warlike frame of mind, Benjamin Sigismund had
gone up to the altar to officiate at the wedding.

He stood there for a long time, staring at the bride. And he
forgot the little skirmish with Ole Korneliusen at the chancel
door. He forgot his clerical dignity. His fighting spirit disappeared. His face again took on the gentle, melancholy expression it had had before the sermon, when he stood here looking
out over the congregation.

And not only that. His hands began to tremble. He had to
grip his old, worn prayer book tightly in order not to let it
drop on the floor.

Wasn't it she he had met on the first morning up in the
churchyard? Yes, of course.

Hadn't he also seen her once before, once long, long ago?
Yes. And when? He tried to remember something through a
thousand—ten thousands of years. . . .

What was her name? He groped for the piece of paper
on which her name was written. He read, "Gunhild Jonsdatter
Bonde."

When Benjamin Sigismund looked up from the piece of
paper their eyes met. Not in the flesh. No, only in wonder, in
great wonderment.

And it was as if Benjamin Sigismund suddenly stood on the
other side of a curtain between this life and another, a greater
and more beautiful life—where the streets were of gold and
where the light never disappeared into darkness and into
night, where one lived in dreams; in beautiful blessed dreams
—where one came so close to God and all the pure in heart.

At this meeting, this silent meeting, he stepped once more through the pearly gates of Paradise, where his mother and all the pure in heart and blessed were.

And a power stronger than his own power, stronger than his will, wanted to force him down on his knees and grip her hands and kiss them. Not in sinful, sensuous desire. No, as a father kisses his child's hands, so would he kiss hers. And it was as if he repeated and repeated: "Now we meet again. How long is it since we last met. Perhaps it was a thousand years ago? Have you forgotten me?" And his voice became full of a painful tenderness: "Have you forgotten my face and my voice? No! No! You know, too, that it is I."

He moved right over to the altar rail. He fumbled confused for words to begin his remarks to the bridal couple. His mind was a blank. He tried to reunite the threads but the threads were burnt.

The pastor's words were causing uneasiness in the church. Persons of rank and condition sitting in their closed pews once again exchanged brief glances with each other.

Yes, for right opposite them in the first row of pews sat his wife, Mrs. Kathryn Sigismund. She was now deathly pale, poor woman. She couldn't understand why her husband was having such difficulty with his remarks to the bride and groom.

The common people, too, were becoming restless and nudged each other.

No, this parson was worse than the poorest locksmith at speaking. Ol-Kanelesa would in truth have been a past master compared with this stammerer, a middle-aged Brækking man remarked, who stood there in yellow elkskin attire, supporting himself against the whitewashed wall up in the Baron's gallery. Had they once again got a tongue-tied parson? And how long would they be burdened with him? That sort of parson usually stayed for a long time in the same parish.

And the glow of Paradise in which they had all so recently sat now disappeared like dew before the sun.

The bride heard nothing of what the pastor said. She didn't even hear that he spoke so miserably badly.

Once she was inside the church she let herself be led wherever they wanted, without resistance. She had no will of her own any more. Had they led her to her grave she would have gone with them.

Now all her tears were shed. Now all her dreams were dreamt. Spring had passed. And she was not to know the summer with its sun and warmth. She had left the spring and gone straight into winter. Into a winter on the bare mountain with nothing but snow and ice as far as the eye could reach. And there she would be frozen to ice.

No, she didn't hear a word of what Benjamin Sigismund said.

Nonetheless, she felt at that moment that she was closer to him than to David.

But what if Sigismund had been David? She felt like tearing off her bridal wreath and throwing it on the floor, and then tramping on it, tramping on the leaves and on the flowers and on the white bird-cherry blossom. She had thought so many times that she would say *no* here in front of the altar. She thought also of it now—but her mouth was dried up.

Quite by chance, Benjamin Sigismund happened to remember that it was this wedding his depraved sacristan had asked him to prevent. He saw a way out of his difficulties.

Now his words came like sun after storm. Heads were lifted down the rows of pews. Up in the galleries people leaned over the rails so as to hear better. And the gentry also sat up and listened.

Kathryn's face lit up. Now everybody could hear what Benjamin Sigismund was capable of. She wasn't going to be wrong when she prophesied that after this people wouldn't fail to call on them. She longed for someone to talk to. And for someone to visit and someone to wait for. Her feeling of deprivation was worse than bad up here in these barren and desolate mountains. Her chest was giving her more trouble than ever before. And it was entirely due to this torturing and consuming dissatisfaction.

Yes, the days and the hours seemed many a time like eternity. Yet there were times when she thought that this Berg-staden, too, had its beauty—but alas! It was only her eye that saw this beauty. Her soul felt in no way elevated by it. Her heart flinched many a time, tortured at the bare thought of this eternally autumn landscape—and this desert—and this land of death. And what if she died here? She would also feel deprived in her grave. Benjamin Sigismund was, no doubt, a fine, a marvellous man. In truth, he shortened many a long and unending hour for her. And yet! A great man also cast big shadows. Everyone saw the sun and praised it; only *one* saw the shadows and sat and froze in them. And this one was the great man's wife. She sighed deeply.

She sighed so deeply that her children sitting beside her heard it. And they began shyly and sadly to pat her cold, white hands. And little Laurentius whispered, "You mustn't be sad, Mother. We'll be so nice to you, we and Father." She was too deeply plunged in melancholy ponderings to return their caresses. Moreover, her children's pats on her hand had become just one of many habitual things for her—it was only for the little ones that this was something new and rewarding each time.

Sigismund was now speaking to the text: "What God hath joined together, let not man put asunder." His interpretation was a solemn one: If we have no right to put two people asunder, then in the same way we have no right, forcibly, to join them together. And those who did so could one day expect to feel the full weight of the words, "Woe to that man by whom the offence cometh." Marriages were only instituted by God when two hearts, two souls—often through trial and tribulation—had found each other. In this connection parents and persons in authority had often, far too often, built up for themselves a capital of sin and criminal responsibility. And those marriages which were founded only on rank and this world's Mammon, without an inner strong and living desire, they were a crime against the All Highest.

At this thundering speech Gunhild looked up. She woke up as out of a faint. The pastor's words rang out like a song of revenge over all those who sat here and had done her wrong and caused her suffering. The one who had least blame in all this, when everything was considered, was David himself. Whatever happened, he mustn't be reprimanded now on his great day, though he had gone around like a living reproach and had nagged and begged her year in and year out to marry him. None of her relatives, with the exception of Ol-Kanelesa, had ever given her any peace or quiet until she had agreed to take David—and now at last they could enjoy the mess they had made. She could imagine them all sitting in the pews behind her, trying to swallow the unpleasant hash they had made. Much good might it do them! Yes, they were welcome to put a little on a spoon and to stick it in Step-mother's mouth too, while they were about it. She was hard of hearing and was getting out of it all too lightly.

Vengefulness and bitter scorn steadied Gunhild. They had been hard to her. Harder perhaps than they themselves realized. But perhaps a time would come when the wind would change and it would be her turn to be hard? If everything else had been bitter, revenge at all events would be sweet.

Benjamin Sigismund thundered on: "And let it be said to you two, who stand here in the sight of this congregation, that if your hearts be bound with the bonds of love, then ye shall now become one flesh to your days' end. But if it be not so, then ye shall in no wise become man and wife, even though I marry you a thousand times here before this altar. Beware lest ye be responsible for making this act, which should be pure and holy, an abomination. And not ye alone, but also your parents and kinsmen, who in this grave matter are equally responsible, I exhort to think seriously on it!"

Dopp in the mine secretary's pew and charcoal inspector Michael Brinchman in the smeltery secretary's pew both put their hands behind their ears at the same time. What on earth was this tremendous broadside about? And Ol-Kanelesa almost got up from his sacristan's pew. Now they were getting it, Gunhild's mother and all the others who had arranged this marriage. Serve them right! Serve them right!

The common folk sat as if paralyzed after this violent outburst. They all knew what the pastor was referring to.

Sigismund then opened his prayer book and read the marriage service with their names included. Both Gunhild and David said yes. She was scarcely audible. He spoke in a loud voice. After which the pastor quickly read the prescribed passages from the Bible. Then, without saying a word, he shook their hands over the altar rail and turned despondently towards the altar, and walked with a bowed head and long steps through the chancel and out into the vestry. Here he sat down on a chair, still holding his prayer book. And with his elbow on his knee and his hand under his cheek, he remained sitting there listening to Ol-Kanelesa's singing down in the church. He closed his eyes and listened. The singing was beautiful. Miraculously beautiful. He thought once again of his mother. This singing would have rejoiced her soul. "The singing of this ordinary man is as beautiful as your sermons, my son," she would have said. "You two can do great things together."

He sat there thinking of the corporal's young bride, Gunhild. She, who now went hand in hand with her husband down the nave. She was scarcely going to a bridal feast. Perhaps she was going to a life of sorrow and lies? Well, well. It was scarcely his affair if her life flowed out into a barren desert. The responsibility of his office ceased the moment they said the yes which bound them for ever.

Responsibility of his office! What was that? A phrase! He and his clerical brethren were slaves of the word and lazy dogs, the whole lot of them! He ought, when Ole Korneliusen came to him in his study that morning and spoke to him about this miserable business, to have investigated it thoroughly and acted on his own principles and judgment, and not relied blindly on his black-robed predecessor. Had he acted like a human being and not as a clerical tramp with a bag full of royal decrees, perhaps this beautiful young woman would have been spared entering a life full of conjugal misfortune.

When Ol-Kanelesa came into the vestry he found Benjamin Sigismund walking to and fro in an agitated state.

He gripped the sacristan's hands.

"We must be friends, Ole Korneliusen," he said. "We must try to understand each other."

Ol-Kanelesa ran his hand over his chin. And he remained standing there a while before he answered.

"Haven't we been friends, then?"

"Not entirely," Sigismund said. "And the blame is mine. I take all the blame on myself without reservation. I am an ungovernable fellow by nature. And one thing I must thank you for: the beautiful way you sang the psalms. Your throat commands an instrument more perfect than you yourself know."

The pastor spoke quickly and ardently. He was very excited.

"I want to thank you for something, too."

"What, do I deserve thanks?"

"Yes, for lambasting the Finne people and Gunhild's mother so thoroughly."

"I don't understand. What do you mean?"

"I mean that it was well done that you wiped the floor with the whole lot of them."

Ol-Kanelesa's eyes shone and he smiled maliciously.

"That I castigated those who have some of the blame that, today, a young girl, partly against her will and desire, stood before me to be married, is it that you mean?"

"Just that."

"Well, well. I repent somewhat that I did not listen to your advice on that morning."

"You're a stranger amongst us, you are, like all the other pastors have been."

"That I am, Ole Korneliusen."

Ol-Kanelesa remained standing there for a long time, reflecting on an important question.

Finally he came out with it; not in any ill-willed or disingenuous way, but quiet, almost meek.

"Yes, well, I suppose this is the last Sunday I shall stand in the nave and sing?"

"If God in his great mercy grant you a continued span of days, then you must just continue," the pastor said in a commanding tone. "Our church greatly needs your singing."

"But suppose we both stand by what we have said?" Ol-Kanelesa said. "In the long run perhaps we would get along better like that."

Benjamin Sigismund looked up, astonished. He felt respect for this unschooled man.

"But remember, it will reduce your income."

"Then I must work in the smithy and play the fiddle so as I make it up in that way."

"You intend to work in the smithy and play the violin?"

"Yes, I can't just sit here twiddling my fingers and kicking my heels, that I can't."

"So you intend to let your singing be silenced for good?"

"I can sing down in my smithy—alongside the fire and the forge."

"Your singer's voice has its place in the house of God."

"Hm. Yes. I thought it came to the same whether they were from Gerizim or from Jerusalem."

"Well. Nevertheless, we ought sincerely to strive to render to Caesar the things that are Caesar's and to God the things that are God's."

"Then perhaps we'd better meet each other halfway, your Reverence?"

"So be it."

Sigismund gave Ol-Kanelesa his hand again.

"Tell me, my dear sacristan, is the young bride, Gunhild Bonde, very upset?"

Benjamin Sigismund had the greatest difficulty in speaking in a reasonably calm and controlled manner. He was still in a deeply perturbed state of mind. Quite possibly it was the thought of his dear, departed mother that had brought on such a feeling.

Ol-Kanelesa didn't answer. He took his time and said:

"Can't a couple who sit rowing their boat each on their own course be permitted to draw in their oars again?"

"If they can be parted again?"

"Yes."

Sigismund made a deprecatory gesture. His lips trembled. "We two are not going to discuss that today."

"No, it may be a bit on the early side to talk about it today."

And then they went out through the vestry door.

The pastor stood there, looking out over the churchyard. The sun was baking the grey gravestones and the rotting, tar-daubed wooden crosses.

Once before he had seen a churchyard like this; it was in Spain, beautiful Spain! There, too, the graves lay naked of grass and flowers; the dry wind and the burning sun had killed the earth itself. It was as here, nothing but sand, stone, and sun.

"Where does the founder of Bergstaden, Hans Olsen Hitteraasen, lie buried?"

"No, there can't be anyone who knows that now." Ol-Kanelesa had pondered a great deal over that himself. "He must, I'd think, lie somewhere down in Litj Street, where the old church stood."

"Why has nobody looked after his grave?"

"It's been so toilsome just to keep alive here that no one's had time to think about them who's dead."

"Has the people's struggle for bread been so hard?"

"Yes," Ol-Kanelesa said. "Stones, bare stones, are a hard bread to live off in the long run; even if the stones are ever so shiny to look at."

"And where is your brother Jon, Gunhild's father, buried?"

"What, our Jo? He lies in the upper churchyard, he does. Down here, in the lower churchyard, only the gentry are buried."

"You shall show me his grave."

"Brother Jo's grave?" Ol-Kanelesa said surprised. "That's no different to look at than any of the other graves up there; but if your Reverence really wants to see it, then—"

They began to go up the stone steps of the terrace leading to the upper churchyard. Benjamin Sigismund lifted his cas-

sock up over his knees and ran up the first dozen or so—but
then he remembered his priestly dignity. A clergyman couldn't
run in his robes as if he were a small boy. And he walked
staidly and with long strides up the remaining steps.

"Yes, here he lies, our Jo-Kanelesa."

Ol-Kanelesa stopped by a neat grave up by the edge of the
terrace. A tall, ornamental iron cross bore the name of the deceased: "Foreman Jon Korneliusen Bonde." And underneath
was written:

Rest here wanderer thy foot so sore,
Here by Death's shadowy shore.

"Who, then, fashioned this remarkable cross, Ole?"

Ol-Kanelesa hesitated.

"I made it, such as it is."

"And this verse?"

Sigismund pointed at the words on the cross.

"I took them from a hymn."

"Which hymn? I can't remember it for the moment; is it by
Peder Palladius?"

"No, Palladius shan't be blamed for that, no. I must take it
on myself."

"Do you write hymns, too?"

"No, not at all. I'm just a nothing, I am."

Benjamin Sigismund stood with one foot on the grave and
glanced sideways at Ol-Kanelesa. He now saw that Gunhild
and he had the same clean, finely-chiselled features—the same
proud, erect head and the same strange, deep eyes. There must
be something out of the ordinary in this family.

"Mr. Korneliusen. Tell me something about your ancestry."

He had called Ol-Kanelesa "Mr. Korneliusen." And had done
so unreflectingly. The words came out by themselves, quite
naturally. He had never honored a sacristan or member of the
low orders in that way before; he had not even addressed his
curates in that way, even though they were supposed to be
educated men.

"We're supposed to be more German than anything. We're

supposed to be descendants of someone called Busch, Henrik Schlanbusch, if I remember his name aright."

"What was he by rank and profession?"

"He was a sort of secretary of state for the mines. Apart from that he was certainly a scoundrel; at all events Peder Hjort will have it so in his books, I see."

"Look here, sacristan. Will you have dinner with us in our quarters today?"

"Many thanks, your Reverence, but I'll have to eat down at the farm today where the wedding is."

"Gunhild's wedding reception?"

"Yes. We just call it a wedding."

Benjamin Sigismund became once again serious and thoughtful. He felt painfully moved at the mention of the wedding and this woman's name.

Why? He could give himself no answer.

On the way down the stone steps of the terrace, Benjamin Sigismund didn't run; he walked so slowly that Ol-Kanelesa got down to the lower churchyard a good while before him.

Ol-Kanelesa was wondering if he should show the pastor a grave down here with an even finer iron cross and on which, today, there lay a large wreath of juniper twigs—but he let it be.

Ellen von Westen Hammond's Birthday

Ol-Kanelesa didn't go down to the wedding reception. He hurried as quickly as he could down Rau Alley and slid like a shadow along the sides of the cow barns and towards home. He had buttoned his tail coat up over his chest and pressed his top hat down to his eyes. He would not like any-

one to recognize him just now. And like this he made his way
down to Elisabeth Cottage without being noticed. He pulled
the big outer-door key out quickly and locked the door from
the inside. He pushed his top hat back on his neck, and peeled
off his overtight church mittens and dried the sweat from his
forehead with them. It had been warm up there in the church
—but down here it was stifling. He thought of opening the
window but let it be; then he went over to the corner cupboard and took out a square green bottle and a little bronze-
gilt goblet and filled it to the brim, so that the golden schnapps
ran out over his thick, scorched blacksmith fingers. He stood
there for a while with the goblet in his hand, squinting furtively at the window with the small panes.

"Your bridal skoal, Gunhild!"

He emptied the bronze goblet at one draft; it measured a
quarter of a pint. Then he stood there again, listening with his
eyes. And once again he filled the goblet to the brim.

"And your bridal skoal, too, Ellen!"

Yes, for today was Ellen's birthday. She was born on the
third Sunday after Trinity, 1757.

And for the third time he filled the goblet full.

"And your bridal skoal, too, Ol-Kanelesa!"

He wouldn't have had anything against drinking a fourth
skoal but he had no one else to drink to. Out of humor, he put
down the square green bottle and the bronze-gilt goblet on
the unpainted folding-table. Then he threw his top hat on to
the peat box and lay down on the bed. He folded his hands
behind his neck—and let one foot dangle down over the edge
of the bed.

He lay there thinking of the way the sun had shone when
he and Ellen were engaged. Then the sun was brighter and
warmer, especially on Sundays—it shone in such a way that all
the mountains and all the streets and all the houses and paths
were like gold. The grass of the pastures and the leaves were
also greener then than now. In the evenings and at night the
Hitter Lake and the Gjet tarn were as if plated with silver.
And how the church bells rang! Now there must be cracks in

the big bell, the middle bell, and the little bell. They had all
got such a rough, unpleasant sound that it sent a cold shiver
through the body. He had even thought of going up into the
tower to see if this wasn't so.

His eyes became moist at the many memories. And his lips
began to quiver; it was painful to think of all that which once
was so beautiful, nothing would be like it again.

He jumped up from the bed. He knew of someone else he
should drink a skoal for; it was the pastor.

The goblet was filled. He lifted it high in the air. "Skoal,
pastor! You're the biggest fool of them all! Ho, ho!"

Ol-Kanelesa stood in the middle of the room and laughed
coldly and harshly while the tears ran down his newly shaven
cheeks.

Today, Ellen von Westen Hammond would have been fifty
had she lived. To him she was, today, as she had been thirty
years ago, a slight, twenty-year-old girl. But had she been
alive today, it was not at all certain that she would have been
his; it wasn't to be expected that a common, poverty-stricken
schoolmaster could have kept her for life. But now she was his
for all time; there, as she lay in her grave.

These were, at all events, the thoughts which Ol-Kanelesa
comforted himself with—today, as so often before during the
thirty long years which had passed since she died.

Was someone knocking at the door? He squatted down and
crept over to the wall. Plenty of room to hide here. Whether
they looked through the window or peeped through the key-
hole, they wouldn't see him here.

"Are you there, Ol-Kanelesa?" someone shouted.

He recognized the voice; it was Nils Tufte, the master of
ceremonies at the wedding. Ol-Kanelesa sat quite still and let
Nils bang and shout as much as he liked. After a bit it became
quiet. He heard Nils' steps as he went away.

Every summer as Ellen's birthday drew near, often several
days before it, Ol-Kanelesa went around as if in a daze. He
was filled with both restlessness and joy. The third Sunday
after Trinity was a red-letter day for him. It was Ellen's day.

And with the years the day had taken on a fixed and un-
changeable routine: first of all, to rise before dawn and before
other people were about and go to the grave with a big wreath
of fresh juniper twigs cut at Volen.

And, then, it was his custom to sing behind locked doors
down at Elisabeth Cottage the hymn:

Be comforted my heart,
From weeping refrain,
Reflect that for the best
God doth all ordain.

After this he officiated as usual at church for the morning
service.

And then—yes, then he took out the shoe buckles, the ring,
and the two letters he had had from Ellen that winter she was
at Brænæs. In the evening, at seven o'clock, he went for a walk
along the Hitter Lake, where he and Ellen had walked on so
many an evening the last spring she was alive.

He went solemnly over to the bureau and slowly unlocked
the lid, then drew out a secret drawer from under the other
compartments and carefully removed a thin gold ring and
two small, yellowing letters written in an elegant, fine, maid-
enly hand. Then he forced the gold ring with difficulty on to
the ring finger of his right hand and sat down heavily in an
armchair beside the bureau and began to read. He read every
word—these words which, already a generation ago, he had
learned by heart—now, as then, they were fresh and quite unbelievable, and went straight to his heart.

He remained sitting there for a long time with the letters in
his hand, staring. Now he looked back on his life. And what
he saw neither rejoiced nor enchanted him; it was, to be sure,
a wasted life. He, who once had dreamt of achieving so much,
had achieved absolutely nothing. As he sat here now, he was
not even worth a thank you. And now everything was too late.
Everything was against him now. The iron wouldn't obey his
hammer; nor would his fiddle sound as before. Everything he

had read he had gradually forgotten. Was the Almighty taking
everything He had given from him? If so, the Almighty had
every right to. Anyone who had misused God's gifts as he had
couldn't expect to keep them for all time. He had already kept
those he had a long time, long beyond all expectation.

Now somebody was knocking at the door again.

"Are you in there, Uncle Ola?"

It was Gunhild's voice. He jumped up from his chair,
twisted the gold ring off his finger, so that the skin came off
his knuckle and began to bleed. Then he put the ring and the
two small letters back into the secret drawer and turned the
key in the lid. Once again the three relics were to rest in peace
until the next third Sunday after Trinity.

"Gunhild, my dear," he cried, "is it you then, Gunhild."

"People are sitting at the table waiting for you, Uncle."

"Waiting for me?"

"Uncle," Gunhild said and caught hold of his hand. "I, in
any case, have no one to wait for but you."

"Wait for me?" he repeated. A childish joy came over his
worn mind. "God bless you, Gunhild!" He patted the back of
her hand. Her hand was so delicate, it reminded him of Ellen's
hand. This, too, affected him; today he associated everything
he heard and saw with Ellen; sun, light through the window,
a friendly word—in everything there was something which reminded him of her. Today, it was as if Ellen rose from her
grave and walked beside him.

"Did you talk to the pastor after the wedding service, Uncle
Ola?"

He looked sharply at Gunhild. Why in the world had she
asked about that?

"The pastor? I've nothing unsaid with him, have I?"

"Someone saw you and the pastor up in the upper churchyard."

"Hm! Yes. Of course. He's a stranger here."

"Wasn't there anything special he wanted with you, then?"

Ol-Kanelesa shook his head. He didn't want to talk to Gunhild about this, not today at all events.

"We must hurry," he said. "We mustn't keep people waiting any longer."

"Were you up at Father's grave?"

"Yes, we walked around there, too."

Ol-Kanelesa still couldn't understand why Gunhild was asking him all this. He took out his blue-bordered stocking cap and put it on; his top hat was only for going to church.

"Aren't you going to bring your fiddle?" Gunhild asked.

"No, the fiddle stays at home this time."

"Then I won't dance!"

"Won't dance, you, the bride?"

"Uncle!" she burst out, and flopped down in his armchair. "Just now I'd like to change places with Ellen, that fine Miss you should have had."

She wasn't crying. Her face was rigid and hard.

"I'm out of myself now, sure I am."

"Out of yourself, you say?"

He opened his eyes wide, horrified.

"Yes, I am. I gave our David a clout on the ear last night. And then when we got out of the church, I let him have it again."

"Take care, Gunhild."

"Don't start nagging at me on my bridal day," she begged. "Oh, merciful heaven! How's all this going to end?"

"You may well ask," Ol-Kanelesa said.

He went and wrapped his fiddle in a cloth. He'd take it all the same, if Gunhild really wanted it.

"You must play all the dances you know this evening, Uncle."

"That *would* be a lot, that would."

"Yes, for now I want to dance myself to death."

"Oh, don't blaspheme, standing there in your bridal gown," Ol-Kanelesa said solemnly. "Your words can one day bring you harm."

And they went out through the door. Both had been savaged by life, almost in the same way.

The wedding guests were breaking up and were ready to leave. Only a few young people, warm after the night, remained. The clock struck four; Gunhild was still dancing.

Ol-Kanelesa was sitting on a sunken grave in the lower churchyard where the clergy are buried.

The sun shone out between the large blue clouds over the mountains to the east; from the magpies and the thrushes it looked as if it would again be a warm day today, with nothing but sunshine.

It was still in the streets, as if the town was deserted; the houses stood in their rows, with locked doors. A watchman in a bare-worn reindeer skin coat sat on some steps far down the street, sleeping and shivering, with his back pressed up against a door. Now, when the smeltery was closed down and all the outdoor smelting ovens were out, and the townspeople up at their mountain farms, there was nothing to watch over; thieves and robbers didn't exist for miles around.

Ol-Kanelesa was quite sober now. Quite frankly, he had been terribly drunk during the night. And, drunk and depressed, he had taken his usual walk along the Hitter Lake with his fiddle under his arm. There he had sat for a long time on a stone, up amongst hillocks, and had waited for his hangover to pass. He wouldn't return to the resting place of the departed until he felt quite sober.

His fiddle lay hidden in the stiff grass by the side of the grave. Ol-Kanelesa himself sat with his face in his hands, thinking; not so much of her now, who lay here in the grave, but of Gunhild.

During the night Gunhild had danced the whole time. Danced as only someone who is unhappy can dance, here in this wicked world. At two o'clock in the morning Ol-Kanelesa had tuned all the strings on his fiddle so high that they broke; this dance had to end, too! But did it finish? No. Another with a broken-down fiddle was pushed into the fiddler's corner.

"Even if I have to sing and dance all by myself, the dance shall go on until sunrise!" the bride had shouted.

Gunhild had no self-respect any more. She had completely lost control of herself.

"It's hard to live, Ellen," Ol-Kanelesa said. "Though, surely, worse still to die?"

Now the light glittered on the tall iron cross behind him, the cross with the long inscription in copper letters driven into the iron: "Here rests the Honorable Miss Ellen von Westen Hammond."

At the base of the cross was written, "Blessed are the dead which die in the Lord."

Ol-Kanelesa had used full five years to make this cross.

And many from the east and the west and the south and the north had seen it, and had wondered who could have fashioned such a remarkable work of art.

And to that question only a very few had received an answer.

Benjamin Sigismund

Even if Benjamin Sigismund wasn't exactly the hero of the hour, he was at least the person who was most on people's lips up here in the mountains. Not only were his remarkable inaugural sermon and even more remarkable bridal address discussed, but also his own person. In the miners' huts when the tar lamps had been blown out in the evenings and the clay for the mine holes had been rolled, the miners talked about the pastor. And at the mountain farms, when the scythe and the rake had been set up against the walls of the shack, and dry juniper crackled on the fire, talk also turned to the pastor. The Lapps up on the moors and in the remote valleys also talked in their lilting tongue about the new pastor; they believed for certain that he possessed the Black Book* and had studied in Wittenberg itself,

* *Svarte bok:* a book of spells and incantations, widespread in Scandinavia in the 18th and 19th centuries.

far away in the land of the heathen. Then perhaps he could exorcise the ghost of Bjørk-Nils, who haunted and terrorized the Lapps, and get him back into his grave again?

At the birthday parties of the gentry in Bergstaden, there were heated discussions about the pastor, his lyrical sermon, and his frivolous bridal address. Was he a rationalist? His inaugural sermon said no! His bridal address said yes!

Mine secretary Dopp said curtly: "He's an adventurer!" In this he was flatly contradicted by the high-born matrons of the town; the young ladies, on the other hand, agreed with Dopp —oh yes, it seemed to them there was such an exhilarating aura about that word. And Miss Sara Mathisen said, loudly, and with her head thrown back, so that everybody could hear it: "I think the pastor is a great and wonderful person." A bold assertion, in respect of which the young lady was thoroughly teased by her cousin, Works' doctor Mathisen.

"Are you in love, Sara?" he asked aloud.

"And if I am, it's in no wise with you, Jens," Miss Sara said, hot and angry. "And you'd better look out! He's a learned man, both about healing herbs and about anatomy."

These words cut cousin Jens to the quick. If there was anything he prided himself on, it was his skill as barber-surgeon. On this he would tolerate no insults! Not the slightest hint! Otherwise he was a jolly man who liked a good joke, but there was a time and place for everything. For the common people the pastor was already and unreservedly a great preacher. The last part of his bridal address had left an irradicable impression on their simple, sincere minds; but the real question was, was he a man for the people? In these times when there was great poverty amongst the common people, it would soon be seen.

. . . In the pastor's quarters up in Leich's house little satisfaction prevailed.

Kathryn's chest trouble didn't seem to want to get noticeably better in the fresh air. It was not, perhaps, that it was completely without healing effect, but dissatisfaction and longing for other places and other people tore down what it had built

up. She felt continually tired and depressed. The many calls
she had hoped for didn't materialize. The only person who still
came up to see them was the sacristan, Ole Korneliusen. The
other day Benjamin Sigismund had invited him to dinner. And
to her great horror he addressed the man as if he were one of
them. Sigismund had also got him to sing some hymns with
him. Unfortunately, she was not able to rise to the same degree
of exaltation at his singing that Benjamin could. Well, she
could let that pass, but when Sigismund got him to play some
old folk tunes the torture really reached its climax; oh, horror!
She got cold shivers down her back at this caterwauling. How
people could be entertained by earsplitting wailing of that
sort was beyond her comprehension. Her husband on the
other hand was enchanted. He was now in the mood to accept
anything. However, it was only a matter of time before his
mood changed. Then he would mercilessly throw the man and
his ghastly instrument out through the door. Oh, Madam
Kathryn longed more than ever for cultivated companions.
But they didn't come.

Benjamin Sigismund was now in a deeply religious phase
again. That a cleric was completely absorbed in his ministry
and in his faith, no one could reproach him for that—but there
was nothing moderate about Benjamin. He always became
completely absorbed in just that one thing, with all his
thoughts and all his mind. Everything else became as nothing.
During such periods he could wear his cassock on week days
as well as Sundays. He could get down on his knees many
times a day with his hands folded over his Bible. He also had
his Bible lying on the table beside his bed. And he, a Protes-
tant pastor, got out his crucifix and kissed it tearfully. If he
heard anyone swear or use an indecent word, he thundered
out in violent anger. It had happened that he had caused the
townspeople to be called together for evensong in the middle
of the week. Then he was Peter; Peter, his great ideal in everything. Not the old, venerable Peter as bishop of Rome, but the
young, enthusiastic Peter who girt his fisher's coat about him

and cast himself into the sea and swam to the shore so that he could be the first to embrace the feet of Jesus.

And then Benjamin Sigismund could change. Abruptly, like a change in the weather. Then, too, he was Peter; the doubter, the denier. Faith had to give way to reason. He put on his robes only when he officiated in church. He dressed himself as a soldier, a knight; he got out his rusty rifles and pistols and polished them bright so they flashed like lightning. He bought some dogs and sallied forth as a hunter on long trips out into the wilderness. Then the world was everything to him; the hereafter lay away out in the blue. Politics and patriotism, the wars in Europe, the great and famous statesmen whose renown flew over the world; he discussed them all with everybody who came within range. Things divine must in no way violate the boundaries of probability. To be sure, he prepared his sermons with great care, then, too . . . And Kathryn sighed. The praises of the joys and delights of this world could then be sung in their house until the small hours. And less than modest poems were recited in French and in every other imaginable foreign tongue. His ambition and pride took on almost childish forms. He aimed at the highest offices. He labored from morning to night with scholarly and philosophical articles.

But, God be praised, these periods were relatively short. Afterwards his remorse was deep and sincere. He called together his fellow clerics and, tearful and tormented, did penance, and sought comfort and solace for his sins by constant recourse to the holy sacraments.

Kathryn prayed on her knees in her private chamber, with her children beside her, that God in his great mercy might summon home her husband at such a moment in his life, though it cause her all the woe, anguish, and earthly sorrow it might.

So that Benjamin Sigismund, too, might be saved.

Sun and Midsummer Day

The twenty-second of June, 1807.

Benjamin Sigismund had sent for Ol-Kanelesa. He came straight from the smithy in his clogs and his leather apron. When he got to Leich's house, he sent a message by the maid Anne-Sofie saying that he was waiting outside. He wouldn't go in in his work clothes.

The pastor came out onto the steps.

"Your Reverence must excuse me," Ol-Kanelesa said. "I'm not fitly dressed to come up to your study."

He looked down in embarrassment at his clogs and at his blackened apron.

"Have you come direct from your smithy?"

"Yes, that's just what I've done."

"Listen, my dear sacristan. Tomorrow is the feast of St. John the Baptist. According to the history of our ancient church this day was a holy day."

"It's been kept both as a holy and an unholy day, that day, for sure."

"We won't talk about the cruel persecution of the church, Ole, not today."

"No, no."

"How do you know that at one time this day was profaned?"

"Well, I've read a bit too—that's to say in days gone by, when I was younger."

"Yes, yes. Of course, you've been a teacher."

Ol-Kanelesa didn't answer. He stood there thinking of the time when he took large volumes with him into the smithy, and into the schoolroom. Leather-bound books with buckles on them, and with Thomas von Westen Hammond's name inside the cover. Now that was a long time ago. Anyone who battled with iron and charcoal year in and year out became forgetful, that's how it was with old blacksmiths. And he didn't any longer remember much of what was in the books. Just something here and there he could remember when he was reminded about it. He was an ignorant man.

Today Ol-Kanelesa was small and humble. In his own eyes

he felt worth nothing. Another thing was, he had been drunk at Gunhild's wedding, drunk and confused, and that was a great shame and a mockery. Had he anything to feel big about? Like Cain, his countenance fell, he shook his head, and held himself in the greatest scorn.

"Listen," the pastor said again. "We will ring the bells and call the people together for evensong tomorrow. What do you think of that?"

"There's no one here, the miners are at the mines. And up at the smeltery they're on holiday."

"But the directors and their families are still in Bergstaden, aren't they?"

"Your Reverence," Ol-Kanelesa said in a literary style. "Verily, they have ears to hear, but they are deaf at the same time."

"What do you mean by that?"

"I mean that you can just as well preach God's holy word to sticks and stones as to the upper classes."

"What!" the pastor shouted from the steps. "What are you saying, Ole Korneliusen?"

"I am a most unworthy and humble man, to whom it is in no wise given to try the hearts and reins of men; but—" At this point Ol-Kanelesa relapsed into his normal speech. "I'm afeared we're in Nineveh."

"Well," the pastor said. "We will return the lost sheep to their flock." He was brimming with zeal. "And the mine workers, Ole, are they also included amongst the unrighteous from Nineveh?"

"The miners, them? Oh, we had no doubt best reckon them as amongst the righteous."

"And they have all remained firm in the faith of their childhood?"

"In all the infirmity of the flesh, yes. We must believe that."

"God be praised, God be forever praised!" The pastor came down the steps and patted Ol-Kanelesa on the shoulder. "With the help of the Almighty's strength and support they, too, shall be preserved in the faith and in the communion of saints."

"We must believe that, too."

The sun shone right into the blacksmith's eyes; they smarted and were painful. He was more used to the light from the fire down in the smithy.

"Listen, Ole. Supposing we visit the miners tomorrow and celebrate evensong with them?"

Ol-Kanelesa reflected.

"The miners' hut is too small for a church, but we must do as the Master himself did—preach a Sermon on the Mount."

"You mean we should hold divine service out in the open?"

"Yes, if the weather is good enough, yes."

"The weather! The weather!" Benjamin Sigismund said excitedly. "We will go to Him who is lying in the boat asleep and bid Him awake and rebuke the storm. Which mine should we make our way to?"

"It would have to be at Aalberja."

"Arvedal, then?"

"Yes. Arvedal, yes. But we must perhaps find out from the managing director if we are allowed to?"

"What! From whom?"

"The director, Mr. Knoph."

"Well! Please fetch him to see me."

"The director?"

"Yes, of course."

Ol-Kanelesa walked slowly out of the entrance gate to Leich's house; Benjamin Sigismund stormed up the steps. Now the Lord's field here in the mountains should be plowed to the last inch and bring forth sixty-fold. Glorious!

When Ol-Kanelesa got out into the street, he remained standing there, confused, staring and peering up in the clear, glittering air. Fetch Director Knoph! No one had dared to do that; that sort of thing was just not possible. He'd have to go up to the pastor again and tell him how things were—but he was sure to think that he was trying to get out of it, and was being stubborn; the pastor was still such a stranger here, it looked as if it was going to be a time before he became familiar with how things were here.

"Now you're truly between the Devil and the deep blue sea, Ol-Kanelesa!" he said to himself.

And he began to walk up and down the main street with his hands behind his back. He kept close in to the walls of the houses, so as to be in the shadows. There was less light there than in the middle of the street. In this way people wouldn't notice him so much; people might think he was drunk again, loitering up and down like that. He didn't want anyone to think that now, when at last he had given up the brandy bottle.

No, he better go up to Elisabeth Cottage and think over this matter of old Knoph and the pastor.

He locked the door after him as he went in, and even pushed home the wooden bolt, to be quite sure that no one would come in.

He took down the board with tobacco from the mantel, and began to shred the tobacco into his pipe. He sat down at the gateleg table, put one arm up on the leaf, and smoked and pondered for a long time. It wasn't that he was afraid of old Knoph—but he might be so angry at being summoned by the pastor that he would throw him out. And then people would be sure to think that the sacristan had been thrown out for being drunk and disorderly. Whatever happened, it wasn't going to be that. He shredded some more tobacco—taking his time and thinking. And he rubbed it in the hollow of his hand for a long time, pondering. He picked up a fresh ember and lit up. The little room became thick with tobacco smoke, so that Ol-Kanelesa sat like a black shadow over by the table. He became thirsty, too, sitting there smoking and brooding.

Supposing he took a dram, a tiny one, a single sip? No, that couldn't help one way or the other. He got up and walked slowly, almost reluctantly, over to the cupboard and took out a wooden bottle containing some French brandy. He shook it with both hands. And it was as if the French brandy down in the bottle said, "You must beware of me, Ol-Kanelesa." He

shook the bottle once again; French brandy was supposed to
be shaken well before drinking. Now it said, "Drink up, Ola
lad! Then you'll be happy and you'll find a way out too!" He
unscrewed the lead cap. He wiped himself over the mouth
with the back of his hand. He lifted the bottle half way up his
chest—but now it was as if somebody stood beside him and
said, "But perhaps, all the same, you stand to gain most by
keeping your word, Ol-Kanelesa." He lowered his arm. Who
was it who said that, then? The voice seemed exactly like
Ellen's. If he could only be sure it was Ellen who stood here
warning him, then never a drop of brandy should pass his lips
again.

Besides, it wasn't the first time he'd thought Ellen was
standing beside him; begging him to give up drinking. He had
thought a great deal about it—thought and thought about it
and had always got just as near and just as far from an
answer—it was useless to think thoughts of that sort.

And then Ol-Kanelesa did something he had never done in
the whole of his life before. He went over to the fireplace and
poured the brandy into the ashes.

"You're still the big fool you always were, Ol-Kanelesa," a
voice said at once.

"Now you have kept your word of honor, Ol-Kanelesa," another voice said.

"Yes, yes. You're still the same old Ol-Kanelesa," he said to
himself. "A poor devil who continually drives off the road and
overturns in the ditch."

He screwed on the lead cap and put the empty bottle
quietly back in its old place in the cupboard.

What should he do now? He'd have to grit his teeth and go
down to old Knoph and do as the pastor had said. And, perhaps, he'd better put on his Sunday clothes; no, he wouldn't
bother about that—he was a fool and an idiot anyway. And a
fool, dressed up in his Sunday best . . .

Down at Director Knoph's office the matter took the course
he had thought it would.

"If there's anything the pastor wishes to speak to me about, he can see me here in my office," Knoph said.

And with that the interview between him and Ol-Kanelesa was at an end.

And now Ol-Kanelesa repented bitterly that he had poured all that good French brandy into the fire. Had he drunk it, perhaps he would have had enough courage to give that worldly and conceited gentleman a piece of his mind. But instead of leaving Knoph with a few well-chosen words from which he would have benefited for a long time to come, Ol-Kanelesa crept out of his office like some poor half-wit.

Knoph growled fiercely as Ol-Kanelesa was shutting the door. And this angered Ol-Kanelesa so much that he was on the point of turning and going in again. He would just have asked that mortal clay, Otto Knoph, what he was being so stuck up about. No, today there wasn't a bit of spunk in Ol-Kanelesa.

He was also annoyed that he'd had to run errands for the bigwigs in the middle of his work. He had promised to have four wagon wheels ready by this evening; they were for a couple of wagoners from Vingelen who had driven their wagons to pieces in the Haanæs hills. And what one had promised, one should try to keep. Even if one, otherwise, was ever so much of a miserable wretch.

In a trice Ol-Kanelesa was up at Leich's house again and got the maid Anne-Sofie to run for the pastor. And Benjamin Sigismund came out onto the steps once again.

"Well, Ole. Haven't you got Mr. Knoph with you?"

Ol-Kanelesa had to tell him what Knoph had said. And Benjamin Sigismund took this message very badly indeed.

"Well," he said. "We are not going to ask any director for permission to celebrate divine service up there on the Mount. The earth we walk on and the heaven over our heads are the property of God."

"And quite right too, in my humble opinion."

Nothing would please Ol-Kanelesa better than to see Knoph

taken down a peg. His arrogance had angered him more than once.

The next day at four o'clock Ol-Kanelesa stood outside Leich's country store with food in a knapsack on his back and waited. He was dressed as yesterday, but with his hands and face washed clean of soot and charcoal. Truly, his hands were clean but not white; Ol-Kanelesa had typical blacksmith hands, they looked like stone clubs. He always had to force them down into his pockets.

Benjamin Sigismund came walking with long strides out through the gate. He had his cassock, and a knapsack too; in it lay his Bible and a small piece of dry flatbread. Today Kathryn had neither butter nor cheese—but now in these hard war years with crop failure and long winters, there were many who had no bread. Kathryn had both cried and sighed deeply as she put the dry bread into her husband's leather knapsack. And it had touched Benjamin Sigismund's heart. He stroked her on one of her cheeks with the back of his fingers and reminded her of John the Baptist's food: locusts and wild honey. He reminded her, too, of the fowls of the air and the bees of the field, who neither sowed nor spun; but received their reward and sustenance from God.

Otherwise Benjamin Sigismund was in good form today. As far as Ol-Kanelesa could see, the anger which Knoph had aroused in the pastor yesterday had now passed completely; and so it was. True enough, the arrogant director's answer had kept him awake for a good part of the night, but towards morning he fell asleep and had slept soundly until Kathryn had called him and the clock in the church tower struck seven. The morning light of a new summer's day had illuminated anew the words of Jesus, "Whosoever shall smite thee on thy right cheek, turn to him the other also." He had even decided to go and see Mr. Knoph—that would be turning the other cheek; but wouldn't it, at the same time, be diminishing

ecclesiastical authority? Yes! Of course! He decided, therefore, to hold firm to his decision of yesterday; to celebrate
evensong on the Mount without obtaining the permission of
that high and mighty gentleman in advance.

"What," Ol-Kanelesa said, and stared in amazement. "Aren't
you going to drive to the mines, do you intend to walk?"

"Wander on foot, you mean?"

"Yes, go on foot, yes."

"You and I must always be wanderers on this earth."

"Yes, me perhaps, but you?"

"I too. Let us hasten."

"The way is long and we must take it easily—especially to
begin with

"The longer the way, the sooner we must set forth, Ole
Korneliusen.

"Yes, I know that's in the Scriptures but—we're not in
Palestine.

"Not yet, but a time shall come when both you and I shall,
by the grace of God the Almighty, cross the threshold of the
promised land.

"We must believe that, at least."

"Not only believe it but also be quite certain of it."

And so they set forth: Ol-Kanelesa leading; Benjamin Sigismund following a few steps behind him. His dubbined boots
were far too tight. Every step he took was painful—but it was
on bruised feet that one must go towards Canaan, on bruised
and bleeding feet. And one must arrive tired and weary, re-
penting, sorrowing, and thirsting. Knights with golden spurs
and those who drove in triumphal chariots could never enter
there. They had already received their reward; the Lord rewarded justly, no one was forgotten, no one got more than he
deserved.

And the sun shone down from a cloudless sky; Kvitsanden
lay glittering blue and warm—it looked like a dried-up lake;
as, indeed, it was.

In the peat banks along the River Glaama people were

working cutting the peats; steam rose from the frost in the many hundreds of piles of peats, and the sun glittered on the worn iron spades. And acrid smoke rose up between the piles; thus it wasn't to be wondered at that Benjamin Sigismund asked if there was a camp there.

Now and then a gust of wind coming down from the Hitter ridge blew through the streets of Bergstaden and whirled dust, sand, and dried horse dung up into the warm air. And before the pastor and the sacristan had managed to get as far as Mount Reimer they were grey and saturated with dust.

Up here on the hills something happened to Benjamin Sigismund. A small and insignificant thing seen from the outside. It was like a sun-kissed zephyr which dances on the smooth shining water during the long light days, but which can end in storm and great waves in the dark nights.

Beside the road there was a newly built, single-storied wooden cottage, with a window with small panes. There were no curtains at the window and no flowers on the unpainted window ledge. It was through this window he saw Gunhild Finne as he went past. She was standing there holding a rough clay beaker in her hand.

And this caused Benjamin Sigismund to forget that he was a scholar, a pastor and a parish priest. . . . His imagination was fired: now he was a knight in golden spurs, a young count with a great retinue, dashing across the spring fields on the big estate, over dykes and ditches. Hunting horns sounded from the woodlands, fire sprang from flint and firepan, shots rang out. He brought *her* his first hart. He lay the noble beast chivalrously at her feet.

"Get ye behind me, wicked thoughts, wicked and blasphemous thoughts. I am only a humble servant of the Lord."

He went on, shaken to the depth over himself. He was a reed shaken hither and thither by the wind.

"Won't you tell me something about the history of these parts, Ole Korneliusen?"

He had to try to absorb something into his soul, some fresh

impression of a place or an event which would cure his mind, just as the essence of a particular herb cures a sick body.

"History?" Ol-Kanelesa said. "I don't know much more than what's written in Hjort's book."

Ol-Kanelesa, too, was plagued by a multitude of things as he walked along in the heat of the sun. To begin with he had a burning thirst and a hangover, but he could still stand that— no doubt it would pass this time, as so many times before. It was worse to think that he was not a man who could ever keep his word. He walked along, sick with shame. That he should sink so low and get drunk again last evening, he could scarcely believe it. He was sacrificing both his temporal and his eternal peace by this degrading life. Had Ellen lived, everything would have been different. It was not unthinkable that he could have been pastor here instead of Sigismund. But it was futile to think of that now. He had become a drunkard. But in future he would be careful not to promise anything at all; he ought to spit in his own face. Yes, that he ought.

The trickling of a brook above the road caused his tongue to contract in his mouth. What if he took out the drinking ladle from his knapsack and tried to drink? But wouldn't the pastor realize he had a hangover? No, he'd have to wait for a while. He sneaked his tobacco tin out of his waistcoat pocket and bit off a long plug. Was it just one dram he'd had? One single one?

Sigismund tried to forget her whom he had seen through the window, by forcing himself to think about a learned dissertation he had worked at for a long time—but his thoughts wandered and made their way to a newly built timber cottage where a young woman stood with a rough clay beaker in her hands. She was beautiful.

"I say, Ole Korneliusen, how are the young corporal and his wife getting on?"

"You mean David and Gunhild?"

"Yes."

The pastor became hot and flushed. Yes, like somebody who during the first flush of passion hears his beloved's name mentioned by others. He hurriedly dried the sweat from his face

so that Ol-Kanelesa should not see how flushed he was. And
in order to confuse Ol-Kanelesa further, he said, "Yes, her
name was Gunhild, wasn't it?"

"Gunhild Finne, yes."

Was there a touch of irony in the sacristan's voice? Benjamin
Sigismund didn't dare ask again.

When they had walked for an hour, Ol-Kanelesa said, "Now
we're on the north side of Nyplads Bridge, your Reverence."

They stopped and leaned over the parapet of the bridge,
and stared down into the clear water which glided black and
soundless under the arch of the bridge. At the sight of the
water Ol-Kanelesa's thirst became unbearable.

"Supposing we rest here for a while?" he said. "We've still
a long way to go."

Now he *had* to have something to drink. He thirsted worse
than the rich man who saw Lazarus in the bosom of Abraham.

"Just as you wish, Ole Korneliusen."

Then they crept down and round the north end of the bridge
and put down their knapsacks in the heather; Ol-Kanelesa took
out his drinking ladle.

"Is the pastor thirsty?"

"Thank you," Benjamin Sigismund said, and seized the ladle
eagerly. "A good ladle of water in this terrible heat is not to
be despised."

He drank for a long while. Time and again he filled the
ladle and drank. Ol-Kanelesa thought he would never get his
ladle again. It seemed to him that Sigismund was drinking up
all the water in the world.

"Ah!" Benjamin Sigismund said, and filled the ladle once
again. "Wouldn't a bath in this clear water be refreshing, Ole?"

"Bath!" Ol-Kanelesa began. "Do you want to wash yourself?"

To bathe in the open on a weekday was hardly the thing for
adults. Had it been a Sunday, it would have been different.

Now Benjamin Sigismund began to ladle water over his long
thin hands. Ol-Kanelesa began to see stars before his eyes. He
couldn't stand it any longer. He threw himself down on his

knees like a thirsty old bull moose and drank from the stream.

"What is the time, do you think?"

Ol-Kanelesa raised himself up on all fours and peered towards the sun. "Five."

"So, five o'clock?"

"Yes, thereabouts."

Ol-Kanelesa was wondering whether his thirst would ever be slaked. He couldn't remember that he had ever been so thirsty before.

"Then we are in good time, Ole."

Ol-Kanelesa didn't hear. He just drank. Drank as he had never drunk before.

But Benjamin Sigismund ripped off his cassock and laid it with his leather knapsack under one of the piers of the bridge. Then he walked a little way up the river, undressed completely behind a willow thicket, and threw his clothes on to it. And to Ol-Kanelesa's great horror the pastor threw himself stark naked into the stream so that a mass of green foam welled up around him.

"Hey! You'll kill yourself!" Ol-Kanelesa shrieked. "D'you want to do away with yourself?"

He started running along the sandy bank of the river. He'd seen people wade out into still water up to their chest when they wanted to bathe—but he'd never seen nor heard talk of anyone diving headfirst into running water. No, that he hadn't!

Now, fortunately, it looked as if the pastor had really heeded what Ol-Kanelesa had said and he came wading ashore again. He shook the water off himself and stood there in the sunshine, enveloped in a shining silvery spray.

"Aren't you coming in, sacristan?"

"Me, out there?" Ol-Kanelesa said. "Not on your life; wild horses wouldn't get me out there."

"This water is our Bethesda."

"Hm. Yes. But we've only two arches, your Reverence." Ol-Kanelesa pointed at the arches of the bridge. "And the sheep's gate, where shall we have that?"

"We must do without that, Ole."

Benjamin Sigismund was in the best of spirits. He asked the sacristan to rub his back. Ol-Kanelesa was also in a good humor now. He laughed and rubbed the pastor's back up and down with leaves and birch twigs; that, too, was a quaint idea, to let someone stand there and rub the skin off your back. He'd get both the scab and scabies from it.

Wagoners who were moving in long convoys south towards Bergstaden walked beside their wagons and stared at the two people out in the bank of the river. "Gypsies," they all said. "Gypsies taking off some of their winter muck. It stinks of them for miles around."

And they laughed.

Ol-Kanelesa heard the laughter and felt ashamed.

They picked up their leather knapsacks again and opened them. And a large flat stone did service as our two cronies' dining table.

Sigismund put his dry, coarse, flatbread on the stone, folded his hands, and said half aloud: "Our table, Lord, is now prepared," but his thoughts dwelt on quite different things.

Ol-Kanelesa also took off his cap and solemnly folded his hands. His thick, worn, workaday fingers only embraced each other at their very tips. He said the words of the grace quietly to himself and found great comfort in them. And when Benjamin Sigismund said,

Grant us the reward of our sweat,
With the bread of life our souls sustain,
Which Jesus through the Cross did us gain,

Ol-Kanelesa bowed his head.

What he prayed for, deeply and earnestly, was the bread of life. This was the bread he hungered after; the bread which could give him the inner strength to resist sin and temptation —and the strength that was needed to tear his stumbling foot away from the cunning snares the great tempter laid.

Benjamin Sigismund and Ol-Kanelesa ate their rough, dry

bread in silence, taking turns to drink water from the ladle. Afterwards they sat there dozing in the sun. And then Ol-Kanelesa began to tell of that July day in the hard and wicked year 1678 when the Swedish general Sparre, with his two thousand soldiers half-dead with starvation, came riding down this road; and of the night when blasphemous cavalrymen used the old church as a stable for their horses, of the mockery of the service which the four Finnish chaplains held the morning after, and of the burning of the smeltery, the mines, and Bergstaden.

Benjamin Sigismund didn't listen very closely to what Ol-Kanelesa was telling him.

The Bell at Arvedal Again Sings the Praise of the Lord

Three hundred years older than the mine at Arvedal is its mine bell. This little bell, encrusted in verdigris, once had a higher rank and title than it has now, but that, too, was a long time ago. Those who heard it when it hung high in a church tower overlooking the sea on a little headland on the north coast of Zealand returned to the dust generations ago. Once upon a time it rang out not only over a populace of peasants and poor fishers but also over proud patricians and nobles in battle array, their trappings glittering—it chimed down over smiles and laughter and joy—and over sorrow and a thousand salt tears. And then one night the Lord let fire rain down from heaven over the church. Perhaps it had become an exhibition gallery for pride and human arrogance, a place of false doctrine and profane words and thoughts? Only the bell, which fell into the fire with the tower, was saved destruction; perhaps it was the thing which had been least abused?

When a new and mighty church was raised on the site of the old one, it also had to have a new and mighty bell. Then the old church bell came into the market. Until the rich, most noble Lady Cornelia Bickers bought it for a song and gave it to her husband, Jochum Jürgens, lord of the manor of Gjordslev and Westervig. He had it sent up to his mines in Norway; it ended up at Arvedal. Here it was hung up on the bare, weather-beaten mountain, between two rain-washed posts under a tarred canopy on the grassy turf-roof of the foreman's hut. Now it had to sing for grimy stokers, mine-hands, and other employees, every morning at cockcrow and every evening at sundown. It hung there tarnished and poverty stricken; in vain it tried to tell the grimy miners of its former greatness, of all the glory and splendor it had seen and been witness to—but its complaints and its dissatisfactions fell on deaf ears. During the storms and the dark nights, when the strong and invisible hand of the north wind grasped its clapper, its song competed with the howl of wolves and the cries of owls out on the moors, an eerie and terrible song. And when the shaking and confused hands of the foremen reached for its worn leather strap to give warning of danger from fire, flood, or war, the ancient bell clanged with a sobbing voice, out over the misery of this world. Would it never more sing the praise of the Lord? Yes, this evening, St. John's Eve! Now, once again, it would ring out to the glory of God. Not in the hearing of the rich and powerful, those dressed in silk and scarlet, who are to be compared with the grass "which is today, and tomorrow is thrown in the fiery furnace," but for the common laboring man over whose door it was writ: "In the sweat of thy face shalt thou eat bread." This evening, when the spring and the mountain were celebrating their nuptials, with green grass straws covering the grey bogs, newly budded leaf over the forest of crooked birch trees, yellow flowers along the trickling brooks, shining white moss on the hard rock, and the sun dancing over the snowdrifts.

This evening when God in his mercy had willed that all should be set free—when the unblessed and miserly spirits, brooding over their buried earthly treasures, would once again for a short while be able to clothe themselves in their earthly bodies and hold their treasures in their frozen hands—when the subterranean dwellers, the descendants of Adam's first wife, were allowed to reveal themselves to the eyes of Christian folk*—yes, this evening the bell of Arvedal would once again sing a hymn of praise to the All High.

All the miners at Arvedal were gathered together outside the mine. There sat the smith, old Jamt-Ola, with blond hair and beard, dark-complexioned, brown-eyed, and with hands seared by the fire and almost without fingernails. Beside him sat a man from Løbø, a powder man by trade, with a red scar over his right cheekbone from the cut of a Swedish sabre. These two had been messmates in the mining camp ever since they were boys. And now they went everywhere together. Now they were sitting on the runners of an upturned sledge outside the smithy with hands folded, and as immobile as if they were cast in clay. Per the wheelmaker also sat there, a giant in a leather apron reaching right down to his clogs. Yes, it was as big as a whole heifer hide and always freshly oiled with cod-liver oil. Per had never made anything in his life but wagon wheels. Thus he saw and thought of everything as round. This plagued him sorely and compelled him, even when he was sitting still, incessantly to draw circles on the floor or on the ground with a stick. It was his form of madness. He knew it himself, but could do nothing about it. He had sought advice and cures for it, but in vain. He had drunk the most remarkable brews.

---

* According to Norwegian popular belief both the dead and evil spirits were abroad on Midsummer Eve. The same belief also applied to December 13, which was associated with St. Lucia, or Lussi, or Løssi as she is called in Norwegian dialect. According to the legends of Adam in the Talmud, Adam's first wife before Eve was created was Lilith, who thus became the mother of demons.

And he had slept on the night of St. Halvard's Day, three times in succession, with thirteen sheepstails under his pillow; that did just as much good as all the other things! As he sat here on a piece of metallic rock, he had drawn four wagon wheels in the sand—and they were also wheels going at a tremendous speed, he had drawn, they ran into each other and around him; a grand drawing! But it was, as we have said, madness.

In the gateway to the mine, Iver, nicknamed the Sheriff-shy, was standing; he was a Selbu man who was quite convinced that he had caused another person's death. In his youth he had been thoughtless enough to fire a blank at a Lapp girl. What followed is not difficult to understand. She put a spell of fear on him. And ever since he had lived in perpetual fear that the sheriff would come and clap him in irons. And if he saw a man on horseback, it was the sheriff, and in a trice Iver was invisible!

Everywhere, on stones, sledges, and wagons, the miners sat, serious men with good, thoughtful faces—but with eyes too weak to stand the strong light. The long winter with its unending darkness, and the deep mine galleries with a flickering torchlight between the walls, had weakened their eyes. And the continual thundering of explosive charges, day in and day out, year after year, had damaged their eardrums. Like all people who are hard of hearing, they talked in loud voices.

It was a beautiful evening. The Aarv Lake to the north formed, together with Storklætten and the neighboring slopes, a multicolored, sunlit picture; and further north still two mountain lakes appeared as blue dots on the horizon. Mount Hummel loomed up to the south with its shining white snow drifts. From the mine tips over at the Christianus Sextus mine it gleamed as from millions of diamonds.

And then the bell began to ring. The miners took off their caps slowly and put them on one knee. And they bowed their heads. God was, in truth, abundantly good who had let them live to see a new St. John's Eve once again. There were no words on their lips; words were empty, they couldn't say enough at a moment like this. No, they gave thanks, silently, with their hearts. High over their heads the bell continued to ring; the old church bell from Zealand, from a sunlit coast along a gentle smiling blue sound.

Benjamin Sigismund sat out in front of the steps on a chair from the chief foreman's room—it was the same gilt, leather armchair which Henning Jürgens had sat in on so many an evening and gazed with his steel-grey eyes out towards the Aarv Lake and dreamt of his youthful love, Miss Tine Irgens of Westervig.

Benjamin Sigismund sat so that he had a view over all the mountains and moors. It was a hard, terrible landscape he saw; a landscape of snow and ice and rock. Only the song of the little church bell was beautiful. All the rest was ugly. He looked at the men who sat around him here—they were men in prison. And he, himself, was a poor priest in exile.

And then the bell stopped. Ol-Kanelesa and the choirmaster, Peder Nilsen Koch, mounted the steps holding each side of a big hymnal, the one with the key and the two crossed hammers imprinted over the cross on the cover. Their singing, their strong manly singing, broke like sunlight through the grey-cold mist which enveloped Benjamin Sigismund's mind. The mountains, the hard grey terrain, now emerged as a neighborhood, not exactly soft, but beautiful in its way. And the lifeless faces around him awoke and came alive—and they became men with a birthright as they heard the beautiful singing, in which they all now joined.

He was seeing both the landscape and them for the first time. Their faces had the same strong, chiselled features which Gunhild Bonde had. And then he himself began to sing with a loud voice—hadn't they all sat down here by the rivers of Babylon, by the Euphrates and the Tigris? He would now rise up and preach the glad tidings to this people in exile, that they today could, once again, take down their harps and set out on the way back to the valley of Lebanon and the land of Gilead.

The singing was abruptly interrupted by a loud noise from

the entrances to the mine. A young, lithe foreman came running up with a lighted torch. He was swinging it quickly in the air, so the flame went out. And a rain of sparks fell like stars around him. His face was white and his eyes wild.

He called out breathlessly:

"There's been a fall down at Cornelien!"

The foreman went on to say that two wheelminders, who were putting in the new water wheel, had ignited a charge with an old iron ramrod. And one of them, a man from Kvaksvolden, had had one of his eyes torn out. Now he lay prostrate over the axle of the wheel, groaning.

The pastor had jumped up out of his gilt chair, the chair from which the long-dead director Henning Jürgens had so often jumped in rage. Sigismund had understood little or nothing of what the young foreman had said in his dialect— but he had recognized the man immediately; he was, of course, the man he had married on the third Sunday after Trinity, David Finne, Gunhild Bonde's husband.

Benjamin Sigismund felt embarrassed at seeing this man. But why did he? He tried to understand. Finne had never done him any wrong or harm.

Now David Finne caught a glimpse of the pastor. It was understandable that a hateful expression passed over his face at the sight of this clerical gentleman. Sigismund's shaming bridal address had, without a doubt, given him many a sleepless night.

The most courageous of the miners hurried to make fire and light their torches. And then they hurried silently to the entrances to the mine. The corporal lit his torch again and disappeared with the others inside the mountain. He was shaken and far too impetuous. He shouted and gave orders. He went on ahead quickly swinging his torch all the way down the gallery.

Those who remained up above huddled together in groups and discussed the condition of the two injured men—probably they would both be blind for life; the surgeon, Jens Mathisen, couldn't manage much more than patch up broken shinbones.

No, he was no eye doctor, that was certain. But Hans Koldberger was supposed to have been a different sort of vet. He
had even, old and trembling as he was, taken people's eyes
out and washed them—no surgeon could do that now. In his
day there were very few blind miners. Now almost every
other man was blind. That is, amongst the pensioners.

"What. Has there been an accident?" the pastor asked Ol-
Kanelesa. He then explained how it had all happened, but the
pastor became no wiser. Stranger as he was to everything,
he couldn't get much idea of what had happened.

Now they brought up the two injured wheelminders. They
were carried carefully into the head foreman's hut and laid
on separate benches.

The pastor tore off his cassock at once and threw it over
the back of the leather chair. Then he rolled up his shirt
sleeves and ran in after them.

"Fetch some cold water," he shouted. "Quickly!"

Some water was brought in in a blackened pot; it was
David Finne himself who brought it.

"Have you got a clean cloth?" the pastor asked. What a
question to ask! A clean cloth in a mine?

The others who stood around also thought it was an idiotic
question. A clean cloth, the fool!

"Well!" Sigismund said. "We'll use what we have."

He caught hold of his shirt up by the collar, ripped it up
on the chest and right down. And then he began to wash the
faces of the injured. He washed the eye of the man from
Kvaksvolden; that gave them all a start. It looked as if he
was going to do even better than old Koldberger—anyway,
Sigismund was supposed to be a trained sawbones too; that
was what people said anyway. A mad fellow, to think of
tearing his shirt to pieces. A linen shirt too! Parsons, they
didn't have to wear hairshirts; nor the other bigwigs either.

"Shall I be blind?" the man asked.

He lay there biting his beard.

"Don't fear going through life with one eye," Sigismund
answered. "Worse things could have happened to you, lad."

When the two men had been washed and bandaged, and
Sigismund stood once again out on the steps, it was night.
He stood for a while looking out over the moor. And he
breathed deeply as if after a great exertion. Then he turned
to Ol-Kanelesa and said:

"We will continue from where we stopped, Ole."

He put on his cassock again. And then he spoke with great
fervor on the text:

"Surely there is a vein for the silver, and a place for gold
where they fine it. Iron is taken out of the earth, and brass is
molten out of the stone."

His eloquent interpretation fell on deaf ears. Those who sat
there on sledges, on stones, on steps and listened, did not
hear him. For them the night was no longer filled with midsummer sun and beauty—what had happened to the two
wheelminders could, at any time, happen to the others too.
And those who sat here now, fit and well, could, before the
sun went down again, be lying prostrate on a bench in there,
in the head foreman's hut. "Today me, tomorrow you!" If only
the pastor had talked of that. And of all the other things they
had to struggle and toil with.

Benjamin Sigismund didn't notice that he was talking to deaf
ears tonight. He saw visions. Glorious visions.

Yes, there was one who listened: Ol-Kanelesa. What the
pastor was saying he had once experienced in a dream. Well!
A dream was nothing to live off; but it could sometimes be
a comfort for the soul.

And then—then just before a new sunrise, the bell in Arvedal
rang out once more to the glory of the Lord.

An Old German Earthenware Beaker

The homespun — the black, shiny homespun, it would not turn on the loom. And the frame worked stiffly, just as if the reed of the loom was full of resin; the shuttle stopped continually halfway in the weave and the yarn kept on breaking. When one spun yarn on a birchbark spool, as she had done, one could hardly expect anything else. She kept on tying the yarn until her fingers became lacerated and bled. Suppose she took the scissors and cut down the weave? Cut it down to the last thread and threw it on the fire. Whatever she thought, it would be sinful and wicked somehow or other. If she cut down the weave, *he* wouldn't get any new clothes; no new waistcoat and no new jacket. Then he wouldn't go to church this winter. Yes, for he had taken the idea into his head that he would only go to church in clothes which she had spun and woven. Had anyone ever heard the like of such a notion?

And supposing she now said to herself, "I'll wear out the loom for the man I'm married to, and whom I care for more than anyone thinks. I'll sit up day and night and weave and think of him. He'll get his new clothes. And he won't freeze. I'll weave every single stitch in the name of God."

It would sound beautiful. And it would be a lie, too. In despair she gripped the frame with both her hands, put her feet on the treadle, and pedaled with all her might, so hard that the windows rattled. Half the loom fell to pieces; the reed hung there smashed on the frame, and the willow of the treadles flew clean off. She jumped up and looked for the scissors. Now her homespun should go! And into the fire with it, too! Every thread in it was spun with evil thoughts and ill will.

Where were the scissors? She looked for them in the table drawers and on the shelves, but she couldn't find them; her old, black iron scissors. There was nothing in its place any longer. Had there been silver or gold in them, perhaps the crows and the ravens might have stolen them—but not steel.

Yes, yes! Down it should come! She couldn't stand the sight

of it any longer. Wickedness and sin grew with it; for every stitch she wove, she wove a sinful thought into her life. If he wanted to stay at home because of his clothes, he would have to. If he wanted to be cold, he'd have to, too. She hadn't asked to weave homespun for him. Rather, she would set up her loom for someone she didn't know, a poor shivering beggar, than for—she wouldn't mention his name.

Yes, yes! Down it was going to come! She threw herself over it. She tugged and tore at the warp, but it held. Not a thread gave way; they were strong, as if spun of iron. What did it mean? Had He who governs and disposes everything taken the strength from her hands? She tried to lift a chair. That obeyed her. And again she dug her fingers into the black yarn, but it held as before. Was there perhaps someone she couldn't see who was making the threads strong, unbreakable? She became afraid. Ashamed and despondent, she sat down by the fireplace, her head in her hands. Now and then she glowered up at the homespun as at something horrid which was embittering her life. The loom took on a face; black as a stoker's it was. Long, gaping teeth hung in its mouth.

"You bitch!" the loom said to her. "D'you want to kill him, you bitch?"

She nearly cried out at it, its face was so horrible. She looked around for a knife, so as to have something in her hands to defend herself with.

She must be going out of her mind. For a whole month she hadn't slept, hadn't closed her eyes. If she went to bed, the bed burnt like a red-hot iron under her. She went to bed with shame and got up with even greater shame. When she got up in the morning she felt like striking herself in the face. "Fie, shame on you. Everything you do is lies and deceit!" Her heart was filled to the brim with hate and disgust. Her hands, which ought to have blessed, only cursed. She must be a lost soul, possessed by the Devil. And all of it came from her allowing herself to be tied to someone, who . . . Yes, what were the wicked faults she had to reproach him with?

None! She just wouldn't live under the same roof with him.
For nothing in the world! Who would she live under the same
roof with, then? And to that question she couldn't see that
she owed anyone an answer.

Yes, to one! God! Him she dared not answer. He wouldn't
support her; for it would be against His will.

But then the sun came out. First it shone on the window-
pane, and from there on to the loom. The ugly face of the
reed of the loom, its black coal-heaver face lighted up—now
it smiled. And the threads became golden.

The sun! Was it God who, in His great and everlasting
mercy, was sending her the sun to save her from this wickedness? Certainly it was God! He never sent darkness, but light.
Never curses, but blessings. Never hate, but love. In His name
she went back to the broken loom and began to tie thread to
thread. It was a test of patience. And hour after hour passed;
the clock on the church tower struck time and time again.
She was tired and nearly fell asleep over the loom; but if she
put her hand under her cheek, sleep fled.

Finally all the threads were tied together and a new reed
put into the frame. Then she could do no more. Weak at the
knees she crept away from the loom. And it was only then
that she remembered it was Midsummer Eve. It was strange—
why had she forgotten it? She, who every year had longed
and waited so much for Midsummer Eve and had counted
the days and the weeks to it, had this year forgotten it. But
how could Midsummer Eve make her happy. It would certainly never bring joy to her any more. . . . Oh, well, since
it was this very evening, she would follow the old custom all
the same and decorate the place a bit; not so much for this
evening, but so as to recall all the beautiful and happy Midsummer Eves of the past.

She went over to the green-painted wall cupboard, which
hung near the door, unlocked it, and carefully removed a
small earthenware beaker. It wasn't beautiful—but it was rare
and very old. And everyone who had owned it had been
afraid of it. Once upon a time it was supposed to have be-

longed to a German they called Old Bushy. His real name was Henrik Schlanbusch. It was only on Midsummer Eve they had the custom of getting it out and putting foliage of the birch tree in it. And then it was put in the window and remained there until the leaves faded. In days gone by people had watched the leaves in the earthware beaker. If they stayed green for a long time, it was a good sign. It prophesied luck and good fortune for the whole of the coming year. If the leaves withered quickly it prophesied misfortune and sorrow. Thus the tiny birch twigs in the old German earthenware beaker constantly received replacements of the fresh cold water. When they finally withered, be it early or late, the beaker was once again locked away in the green-painted wall cupboard.

Yes, that had been the custom, generation after generation. And the custom had been carefully followed.

And, as she stood there holding this rough earthenware beaker in her hand, two men passed by the window and took the road to the north.

The man who passed last turned round and looked in as he did so. She nearly dropped the earthenware beaker onto the floor. And she felt her heart beat. Her heart, which a long time ago had stopped beating—so she thought—beat again so she heard it.

And as in a dream she poured water into the little earthenware beaker. She went on pouring so that it ran over onto the floor—for she scarcely knew what she was doing. And then she ran out and broke a twig from a young birch tree. Poor young birch, which must lose its twigs and die of it! She put the twigs into the earthenware beaker.

Might it now be that these twigs never withered and their leaves never turned black!

The sun, the blessed sun, now shone in through both doors and windows. And it shone into her mind too.

She began to sweep the floor and scour the tables and benches with sand. Yes, it was Midsummer Eve. And shouldn't one then decorate, wash, and make everything beautiful this evening? The most beautiful evening of the whole year! She whitened round the fireplace with freshly ground chalk. And now the two who had just passed were completely out of her thoughts. She tied an apron round her and ran up to the hill to the juniper thicket and stripped green juniper; she strewed it on the floor and on the hearth and on the steps up to the door. She washed her face and combed her hair. And she hadn't a thought for those two now either. She fetched her Sunday clothes from the hallway and put them on—they had now become far too big and roomy for her. Then she stood there for a while, dressed in her Sunday best and in her pearl bonnet, looking about her. The loom stood there, complete and ready for use, with a new reed. Anybody could come and sit down at it and weave. The room was clean and tidy; the cobwebs had been swept out of all the corners. The fireplace stood there shining bright in its snow-white attire. And the floor was clean and white under the green juniper twigs. Anyone who came in now would, without doubt, think it pretty and cosy. Now she would go out. And she wouldn't lock the door. Anyone who came . . . Yes, there would be no need for them to lose their tempers and kick the door to pieces or take out the windows to get in. And if thieves came they were welcome to steal anything they needed. They might also take that old German earthenware beaker, but what would they do with it? Perhaps they would try to break open the cupboards and the writing desks and steal the silver spoons and the beakers—but they were not hers and never would be. No, they belonged to a stranger who lived here. It was no concern of hers to stand guard over someone else's property. Not even the cottage was hers. That, too, belonged to the stranger. So she might as well go.

From the new-timbered cottage she made her way down towards the upper churchyard. The stones on the way lay there so white and clean. And the light in the air was white and shining. There was no smoke

from the smeltery now. On both sides of the road the flowers
stood there still growing and becoming deeper and richer in
color for every day that passed—those which were pink yesterday were today red as blood—and those which were pale blue
this morning were already dark blue this evening. Everything
here had to hurry and grow in the short summer . . . Yes, for
otherwise they wouldn't be ready to die when the autumn
came, would they? A wren flew the whole time in front of
her, chattering and flicking its tail. What did it want? One
would rather not have a bird for company. Otherwise, she
didn't care who went along with her. Even if it was snakes,
it was the same to her.

And then she climbed over the stone fence into the churchyard, and walked slowly over the dry sand from grave to
grave, reading the names, both of those she had known and
those she hadn't known, which were inscribed on the sun-
baked flagstones—but she didn't think there was anything
sad in all these people being dead. Even though she well
knew that every grain of sand she trod on here had been
watered by salt tears, it was a matter of indifference to her
now. And those who had stood here and wept, they were
dead too. And she had read all the inscriptions so many times
that she knew them by heart.

At the edge of the terrace she stopped for a long time by a
grave with a big rusty iron cross over it.

Rest here wanderer thy foot so sore,
Here by Death's shadowy shore,

she read. She had read these lines many times before, too. And
as soon as she neared this grave she had always wept bitterly.
Now she stood there with dry eyes and stared at the iron
cross. It was terrible to stand here by this grave without being
able to weep. She had been in the habit, after she had wept,
of sitting on the grave and remembering everything that had
been good and beautiful. Today she could find neither rest
nor peace. She must leave. But where should she go? Did she

herself know? If it came to that, did anybody know where they were going?

She went now down the stone steps to the lower churchyard. She was carrying a heavy burden which was trying to force her down on to her knees. What sort of burden could it be? She carried nothing on her back and nothing in her hands.

Yes, the heavy burden was the tears she could not weep at the grave up there and which she had to carry down here with her again.

Down in the lower churchyard she stopped at only one grave, and read, "Blessed are the dead who die in the Lord."

She sighed heavily and walked along the wall of the church and out into the street. Supposing she now went down the street to Gunna Gate? No, she had nothing to do down there, either. The street was almost empty of people. She saw no one other than Mrs. Sigismund down by the German house. She recognized her by her cough. It sounded hollow and unpleasant between the walls in the quiet street, and in the hot air.

The sick lady certainly didn't flourish here in Bergstaden. And Pastor Sigismund had recently said to Ol-Kanelesa that his wife's days might soon be numbered.

Everyone had his or her cross to bear. She couldn't help feeling very sorry for the lady. And then Mrs. Sigismund went in through the gate of the German house. And Litj Street was quite empty of people.

She, who was standing up there, turned about and began to go up the street towards Mount Remmers. And it was so quiet that her steps echoed on the flagstones between the sun-baked and smoke-blackened walls. She saw herself the whole time in the black windows on both sides of the street—it was as if the two of them were accompanying her, footstep by footstep, one on each side. They moved like ghosts inside the windows—over the floors in there and through the walls and the locked doors. And they had her figure, her clothes, and her face, those two. For a while this ghostly company occupied her thoughts. Perhaps she, herself, was fey? She thought about it coldly and calmly. If she died now she, too, would no doubt get an iron cross. He who had fashioned the two iron crosses up there would no doubt fashion a third, too. She would ask him also to put on her cross, "Blessed are the dead who die in the Lord."

Then her thoughts moved from death to Mrs. Kathryn Sigismund. Every time she had seen the sick woman, with her pale suffering face and her large staring eyes, she had felt for a long while afterwards something she resented. Was it the woman's sick and unsympathetic appearance which did it? It could scarcely be anything else. She had never spoken to her. Nor had she ever had anything to do with her.

Up at Mount Remmers she met a mountain Lapp, who came leading a Lapp girl by a rose-patterned silk scarf which was tied round her neck. The girl, who was being led like a dog on a chain, smiled and laughed and was very pleased with herself.

Midsummer Eve was, of course, the day when the Lapps got married in Bergstaden. The mountain plover and the cuckoo sang and called, and now turned the mountain into a festive bridal hall. And when the bird cherry blossomed between the snowdrifts, bridal garlands were also blossoming.

"Have you seen our pastor?" the Lapp called out in broken Norwegian. We're going to get married on Sunday."

"He's living down at Leich's," she replied hurriedly.

"Is he handsome, the pastor?" the girl asked.

She, the other, turned bright red. What could she say to that?

"Certainly he's handsome."

The two Lapps turned round and laughed happily after her. And the man shouted out:

"Will you be our bridesmaid?"

She pretended she hadn't heard the Lapp's shout and walked quickly up the hill. To see those two so happy, that was also like seeing something evil—something which cut her to the quick.

Now she was once again back at the new-timbered cottage. It hadn't been her intention to come back here. Carefully, as if she was afraid of waking somebody who lay there
sleeping, she crept on her toes up the steps, pushed open the
door quietly, and peeped in. There was nobody there. Everything was as she had left it a little while ago. The loom stood
there as before. The earthenware beaker with the twigs in it
stood there looking so poverty-stricken and alone. Nobody
had been in and trod on the green juniper or sat in the chairs.
The fly which was buzzing in the window was still buzzing
at the same pane. As carefully as she had come in, she went
out again. She closed the door carefully after her—still as if
she was afraid of waking somebody who was asleep. Then she
jumped down the steps—as though she hadn't time to take
the steps one by one. And she started to run down the main
road. She made her way north. She was in a hurry. What was
it that was so pressing? Even she didn't know. Was she going
to meet anybody? She could find no answer. She simply had
to go on walking—walking! walking! walking! as far as the
road went, walking into all eternity! She must never again
think of going back to that cottage.

At Gubstenen she turned off onto the cattle tracks up
towards Voln. Now the sun was shining obliquely down over
the snowdrifts in the west. At Voln she found the remains of
a fire which had recently been left. The heather and the blades
of grass had not yet raised themselves up again after the
people who had been sitting there. She got down on her knees
and blew on the dying embers, put some dried leaves and
twigs on them, and got them to burn.

Now she was once again a little girl herding the cows,
warming her red, frozen fingers, drying her wet, ragged
clothes, and shaking embers in her worn-out shoes. Now the
ancient church bell at Arvedal was ringing in the new shift.
Now the moon was rising over the church roof in Bergstaden
and shone on the great clock face with its long hand. . . . It
was good to sit here for a soul which had gone astray and to
imagine that all dreams were real and all reality dreams. It

was good for an outcast to sit here and feel God's peace over her soul. Here could the sleepless sleep. Here could the tired and weary find rest.

. . . Blessed sleep! Blessed mountain plover who was singing her to sleep! She had heard it almost the whole time through her sleep; now close to her, now further away, and then close beside her again.

The sun had gone down a long time ago, but its rays were still in the air, in the clouds. The fire had gone out, there was just a slight smell of acrid smoke from burnt earth, moss, and heather.

What was that? Through the air came a heavy echoing sound; the church bell at Arvedal? Was it a fire or flood? Or mobilization? She climbed up onto a stone so as to be able to hear better and see further. It certainly wasn't a fire. She could see no flames. And it could hardly be a flood, now that the waters had subsided. Then it must be war, the enemy! The small church bell from Zealand must be warning the Mine Corps that they must turn out, every man of them. She knew them all in the Corps, both the men and the officers. She had danced with nearly all of them on her wedding night.

Yes, she had danced in a delirium that night. She thought quite calmly about all the miners who must now go out to fight and die. Coolly and calmly she thought of that which others thought of fearfully and tearfully. She, who now ought to have thrown herself down on her knees on the hard rock and prayed for one of them . . .

Yes, she would have paid with years and days of her life if she, too, could have stood here, her knees trembling with fear.

After a while she followed the cattle tracks further in towards Voln.

David Finne, foreman and corporal, came riding southwards along the road to Bergstaden. He was riding bareback on an old nag he had borrowed from a prospector of the 9th Company. At the Nyplads bridges he rode past the pastor and Ol-Kanelesa who were both on foot. He saluted the pastor, as was required by the regulations, but he wouldn't even look at Ol-Kanelesa, that gossip-monger! The corporal was not in a very happy state of mind as he sat there and was bumped along astride the sharp back of his horse on that bright summer night. The terror of what had happened to the wheelminders still pierced him like the cold point of a spear. And the blame for that misfortune would no doubt finally rest at his door, the fore-man's. And yet! David Finne was thinking of things which were worse to think of than that. He was thinking of Gun-hild. A witch and a calamity as a wife, she was. Now he wasn't going to put up any more with being treated as a stranger in his own home. If they shared the same table, then they'd sit on the same chair too! His patience had long since been ex-hausted. Before the sun came up he would have had it out with Gunhild. And then she could go to the pastor and com-plain as much as she liked. Anyway, he didn't want to hear talk of the pastor after today. . . . He was long since tired of hearing how fine and handsome a man Sigismund was. . . . He dug both hands into the mane of the horse and put it into a gallop with his long iron-pointed miner's stick. There was a slopping sound from the horse's belly and its shoes rattled, "Clunk! Clunk! Clunk! Clack! Clack! Clack! He rode at such a pace that gravel and pebbles hailed around his ears.

When he got home he threw himself off the back of the horse and ran up the steps of the door. It was ajar and he kicked it wide open.

"Gunhild!" he shouted. "Are you at home, Gunhild?"

He didn't get any answer. He remained standing there for a while in the middle of the room looking around. So Gunhild was out somewhere. No, she wouldn't sit at home on Midsum-mer Eve, the witch. Oh, what a bitch! He picked up his miner's stick and ran it through the weave so that the threads sprayed out. "Weave yourself!" He kicked wildly at the green juniper twigs with his knee boots. "Rubbish!" Then he caught

sight of the old German earthenware beaker standing on the
window sill. He hissed an oath at it, and took and threw it
into the fireplace. And then he sank down heavily onto the
seat of the damaged loom and rested his head in his hands.
His wrath and bitterness were spent. And now tears came.
They had to come out, too.

At dawn David Finne rode off again northwards on his
skinny, limping nag. He was a marked man.

And a quarter of an hour later Gunhild came into the cottage. Her clothes were wet and her shoes were full of sand
and gravel. The night dew glittered in her black, uncombed
hair.

She had stood up above the road and had seen David both
come and go. And she had also seen Benjamin Sigismund and
her uncle Ol-Kanelesa trudge past. She almost called out to
them—but her tongue had refused to speak.

She went over to the fireplace. There she found the earthenware beaker smashed. And the leafy twigs which lay on the
hearth beside it—they were black.

The Hittite's Wife

The short summer in the
mountains would soon be at
an end. Already the nights
were getting long, with mist around the tarns and the lakes
and up the river, and the bright leaves on the birch trees were
no more—everything was turning yellow, one leaf today, two
tomorrow, and the next day several millions. The north wind
was again finding its ancient ways from centuries past over
the bare mountain, the air no longer quivered in the midday
sun, and the sun itself made shorter and shorter journeys for
each day. The cuckoo, that happy bell ringer, had also stopped
ringing its brass bells for the bridal journeys of woodland

fairies. Now all the slopes were silent—silent as in great, deserted rooms.

To the young people who as yet had experienced so few summers and had not yet had their souls seared, this summer had been like a sun-kissed love letter, or a fleeting kiss, or an almost inaudible whispering in the ear. To the old people, the grey-heads in a hurry, both in thought and deed, with their long skinny fingers out after their neighbors' goods, this summer began yesterday and finished today.

. . . It was an evening well on in August. An evening with a full moon, with a golden bridge over the Gjet tarn, with faded hayracks, and long black shadows in the courtyards.

Benjamin Sigismund was walking to and fro along Langeggen. He wasn't in clerical attire but in a short jerkin and long riding boots, with a peaked cap on his head and a silver-mounted stick in his hand. There were many who saw him walking out there in the moonlight, but they all took him for the county governor Fredrick Trampe, that arrogant overlord. Nobody thought it could be the pastor.

Today he had spoken to her for the first time—to Gunhild Bonde, no, Finne now. He had run into her up in the upper churchyard. She was sitting on her father's grave. Her speech was that of the common people. Her clothes were also of the common people's, possibly more refined. That could mean that she had imagination, a sense of beauty; inherited taste, too.

What he had noticed in particular was her beauty—it wasn't dazzling, but it was individual. There was something intense about her whole being—something which had forced its way into him with violent strength.

Was she then that Bath-sheba whom the hideous wise-woman down at the Lakes had prophesied? No, a thousand times no! He felt no desire for her. He was no womanizer. Hadn't he bigger and more important things to do than to go around thinking about somebody else's wife? He had to laugh to himself. He, the Reverend Benjamin Sigismund, what concern had he with the daughters of Cappadocia? Now he could scarcely remember her face. Was she blond? When he met Gunhild Finne next time, it wasn't certain that he would even recognize her.

Stop, Benjamin Sigismund! You are lying! He beat the leg of his boot with his stick. You are a liar! You continually add one sin to the other. Your account has long been an abomination to Him whose servant you are. You are a wicked and faithless servant! And your sins are many and great. Mountains and high towers would be needed to measure them!

Yes, concerning that, and according to the words of the Scriptures, there could be only one opinion. He had been David on the roof of the King's house. His desire had been inflamed from the first morning they had met.

Through Him, who was capable of all, he could perhaps get strength to go away and sin no more?

And then Benjamin Sigismund went home to his house.

As he went up the stone staircase he heard Kathryn coughing in the sitting room. She went on coughing violently for a long time. And he felt a dread of going in, a dread of meeting those large, questioning eyes.

"Is it dangerous, Benjamin?" the eyes asked. "Shall I die soon?" The eyes could also cry out at him, "No, Benjamin, I don't want to die! I dare not die!"

He remained standing there for a while thinking of an answer he could have ready; a white lie on which Kathryn, again tonight, could sleep peacefully.

At this moment thoughts of Gunhild had vanished. But had they? No, oh no, they had not vanished—for they were thoughts of life, and of the joy and happiness of life. And thus they were the strongest.

The door opened. And Kathryn called out:

"Benjamin, are you there?"

"I'm coming now, Kathryn."

He went in resolutely—with closed eyes so as not to see the terror in her face.

"I thought I heard you out on the stairs, Husband. Oh, when you come I forget that I am sick and ill."

She put her arms around his neck, stretching herself up on tiptoe against his tall figure.

Benjamin Sigismund twisted his head aside and tried to smile.

"We are not on our honeymoon, my dear; we have to eat bark bread these days."*

"We don't, do we, Benjamin? No, don't move your dear head! Let me hold it a little longer between my hands. Oh, my dear one!"

He freed himself gently, but she continued:

"Tell me, Benjamin, don't you love me at all any more?"

"Yes, of course, you know I do."

"Lies, Benjamin Sigismund!" he heard someone cry out. "You love someone else now! Her name is Bath-sheba, the wife of Uriah, the Hittite."

The voice was so loud that he thought Kathryn, too, must have heard it. And the voice was the voice of God. And it seemed to him, in the half-light of the room, that he could see a fiery sword over his head; God's sword!

"I'm hungry. Can you give me anything to eat?" he asked. "I haven't eaten a bite all day."

That, too, was a lie. He had got himself into a web of lies with a thousand threads. The more he tried to free himself, the more entangled in it he became. There was only one movement he could make to free himself: throw himself down on his knees and tell her the truth. But wouldn't that be the truth that killed? Verily! Verily! He had no choice. He *had* to keep silent.

After supper Kathryn said almost elatedly:

"A note came for you today, can you guess from whom?"

"No."

"We have been invited to a party at the Knophs'."

"At Director Knoph's?"

"Yes."

---

* In time of famine bread was made from finely ground bark mixed with rye flour.

"We must think about it, Kathryn."

Sigismund was gloomy and silent. He still felt laden with guilt. A serious resolution began to take shape in his mind: to dismiss this woman he had met for ever from his thoughts. Wasn't an honest and sincere resolution infinitely better than an over-hasty confession? Verily! Verily! And, at once, the resolve brought him more peace. From this little stumble into the snares of Satan he would reap experience and acquire the wisdom to avoid a bigger fall.

"Yes, we must consider it, Kathryn."

Kathryn held out her thin hand over the table to him. She looked up at him, imploringly.

"Benjamin, it made me so happy that, at last, some of the gentry here in Bergstaden have invited us, that I accepted at once."

"I see. Then the matter is settled."

He took her hand and held it for a while—that thin, clammy, sick hand. He must never forget that this hand was given to him in trust and confidence when he asked for it. Should he then thrust it away from him now—now that it was tired, weak and near death?

"You must wear your canonicals at the party, Benjamin."

"Canonicals at a secular party?"

"The officers of the Mine Corps are to be in uniform and so are all the other officials."

"Well, that's another matter, my dear."

After a bit he asked:

"The officials, the minor ones, are they also bringing their wives?"

"I didn't ask about that. Why do you ask, Benjamin?"

She began to clear the table. There wasn't much. Just a few pewter plates worn thin with use, two or three knives, and a couple of empty milk jugs, that was all.

"No particular reason. In other words, it's going to be a largish party. Did you hear if there was any special reason for its being held?"

"No." She looked somewhat roguishly at her husband. "Are you afraid you will have to speak?"

"In that case we must hope that I shall survive it. What do you think, Kathryn?"

She laughed. She stroked his hair.

"Actually, I am terribly anxious about you. You ought to see about getting an Aaron in your place, dear Moses."

"In that case Aaron would have to be Ole Korneliusen."

"Ole Korneliusen!" Kathryn cried. "That terrible drunkard!"

"Don't speak so loud, gracious lady. We all drink, according to how thirsty we are."

"He is assuredly very thirsty, Benjamin."

"Yes, assuredly," Benjamin Sigismund said very seriously. "Both hungry and thirsty! Anyway we shan't discuss that matter, and even less pass judgment on it, my little lady."

And the conversation continued in a tone midway between jest and gravity. They had achieved a short armistice in the battle between them, those two. Kathryn then told him what she had recently heard from her maid Anne-Sofie: Ole Korneliusen was a dreamer and an adventurer. In his youth he was supposed to have been secretly engaged to a pastor's daughter, Miss Ellen von Westen Hammond. At that time he had big ideas of becoming a pastor, and studied Latin in the schoolroom—it was at the time when Ole Korneliusen had taught school for a few weeks during the winter.

"But wasn't that a highly laudable ambition, then?"

"Yes, yes, of course. But you must admit, Benjamin, that the engagement was something of a—of a *mésalliance,* not to say a scandal."

"No, I don't admit that at all, Kathryn," Sigismund said heatedly. "Didn't life give them the right to it?"

"What do you mean, Husband?" Kathryn asked, horrified. "A young lady with 'von' in her name and a blacksmith, that doesn't sound very promising, does it?"

"It sounds excellent," Sigismund said. He was still irritated. "What happened to them?"

"Miss von Westen Hammond died before her parents found out about it. And then, of course, Ole Korneliusen gave up his Latin. His house of cards collapsed. The idea of a blacksmith becoming a pastor is, to say the least, absurd, isn't it?"

"Not at all, my dear. Not at all. He is a very talented man. Don't you know that he is supposed to be descended from a certain mining chief up here?"

"He, Ole Korneliusen? Well, well, that is nice to hear."

"And then what happened, Kathryn?"

"After the lady's death, Ole Korneliusen began to drink heavily. In any case, he has never been very temperate. And, as you know, he had to leave his post at the school because of that."

"Yes, I know about that."

"And you know the story about the cross on the grave, as well, I suppose?"

"The cross on the grave? No."

"I think it's beautiful, all the same. No one could believe a drunkard capable of fashioning such a work of art, let alone to be inspired by such a lofty idea."

"Tell me about it."

"Just after Miss von Westen Hammond was buried, Ole Korneliusen came up to her father and implored him with tears in his eyes to give him permission to execute a cross to be put on her grave. After some consideration von Westen Hammond gave him his permission. He had no doubt a suspicion that there had been some sort of relationship between the two of them—some innocent relationship we must hope it was. Ole Korneliusen worked for five years on this cross."

"Five years!" Sigismund repeated. "Five long years?"

He began to walk to and fro across the floor. "Yes, truly, love can bring mountains together, Kathryn. Tomorrow I shall go and carefully inspect this cross. He is in truth a remarkable man, this Ole."

It was long past bedtime for the pastor and his wife; the children were already sleeping the sleep of the just and Kathryn prepared her husband's bed. She smoothed the patched white sheet carefully with her hand. And she furtively kissed the little pillow, which was filled with eiderdown and covered with a blue silk pillowcase.

Kathryn herself used a linen pillowcase stuffed with straw. She undid the bed tassel from a peg in the beam and put a clean handkerchief into the handgrip. And then she quietly opened the door into the living room and whispered:

"The bed is made, Benjamin."

"Thanks! Many thanks! I'll sit here for a while and work on my dissertation."

"Are you still writing it?"

"Yes."

She tiptoed in. Her knees were trembling. Her hair, which she had combed with a coarse comb, hung down over her narrow, bony, square shoulders. Her arms had become so thin and wasted.

Now she wondered anxiously whether Benjamin would get up from his work and kiss her when she said good night. He didn't do it very often—but now, at this late hour, with a night mood enveloping everything, perhaps he would? Oh God! Everything about Benjamin Sigismund was so uncertain. Violent and uncertain! He had always been like April weather: suddenly sunshine, suddenly cloud. He walked on divided paths: one foot on the narrow path, the other on the broad—but there would come a day when Benjamin, too, would have to choose; might God, then, because of his goodness, lead him gently over on to the path which led to eternal life. She bent down towards him and whispered:

"Good night, Benjamin."

"Good night."

He didn't look up. His hand continued to write.

The Cherubim's Flaming Sword

Dating from the time of the late, lamented director Henning Jürgens, the Works' directors had been in the habit of holding a big party in the autumn for persons of rank and condition and lesser employees of the copper works. There were very few of the present generation of Bergstaden dwellers who knew the original reason for this festivity: it was the birthday of the Lady Tine Irgens of Westervig. Now it was almost two hundred years since that noble lady had been wrapped in her winding-sheet and laid in her coffin. And Henning Jürgens, who in the small hours had sat up at the tavern with his friend and confident Jens Tausan, Master of Arts, emptying one pot of ale after the other with many powerful drams in between, and had dreamt of her, he, too, was now gathered to the bosom of his forefathers. His dreams had returned to that unknown and beautiful kingdom from which they had come. And the toasts for the beautiful, the proud one! All the winged words, all the tears which for her sake had run down the strong, weatherbeaten face of the old miner; yes, now it was all written down on tables of clay and preserved. The salutes fired in her honor, the ringing of bells at the mines and the smeltery, were forgotten. A black stallion which on a summer day had carried her on its back over Mount Storvarts had been given a pagan burial, fully saddled, under some great stone blocks out at Pinsti. Its grave, too, had been forgotten. Only the annual party remained—but, like all poor ghosts, a faded version of its former self.

The present managing director, Knoph, who was a loyal servant of the crown, had turned the occasion into a festivity in honor of his Majesty Christian VII and his Royal Highness, Prince Fredrik. Therefore, into uniform all of you worthy to bear it! And ladies of quality in the town had not a little work during the preceding week, polishing buttons, pressing tunics, and patching riding breeches. And there was much cleaning and polishing at Knoph's official residence for the occasion. Washerwomen armed with tubs, buckets, troughs of sand and other scouring materials climbed up steps and ladders. Knoph himself kept a close watch on everything to make sure that it was as it should be. His gloved hand was in action everywhere.

Scolding and abuse all round! It was instant dismissal and consignment to hell on the spot, if the slightest speck of dust should attach itself to the tips of white gloves. The slaughterers in the town busily sharpened their long knives in the darkness of the early morning hours. The cooks sat, half-asleep from tiredness, over their brown sausage fillers. But if the severe Mrs. Knoph found them dozing, they at once began to stuff sausages like madmen. Long tables were being laid in all the rooms. Wooden ale bowls moved over a fixed route between the cellar and the wash house.

The most important guests came on horseback. Mine secretary Dopp hadn't any further to go than across the street, but he came, nevertheless, on horseback.

In the passages hung the side arms of those in uniform—swords that had never tasted blood, but which now and then received a few drops of salt brine to give them the red, honorable rust which decency demands a man's sword shall have.

The guests were seated according to their rank and station. Benjamin Sigismund who, obviously, was the man to propose the royal toast and the toast of the United Kingdom of Denmark and Norway, was placed near the head of the table—but solely for that reason. He was still new in the town. He was not yet admitted to the inner circle. And not a mother's soul here in Bergstaden thought of calling him by his first name. Everything took time. And besides that his family background could scarcely be said to be the most distinguished. True enough, his father had been a worthy civil servant in the western part of the country. Heavens above! Nobody could say anything against that. All the same, there were quite a few degrees of rank above the Sigismund family, even if some of its members took the opportunity of showing off somewhat. That Mrs. Kathryn Sigismund hopped up on a perch alongside the most distinguished ladies, on account of her husband's office, was to be expected. Her gowns were not new, and testified mainly to lack of means. Otherwise she was both sweet and well-behaved, the poor sick lady. Her cough bothered her a good deal. Especially amongst so many strangers. She had to sit continually holding a handkerchief to her mouth.

It at once aroused the embarrassed attention of the guests that Sigismund had not come in clerical attire—in his ruff and cassock. He had not even bothered to put on the ordinary long frock coat with lace sleeves; instead he had come in a short jerkin and a low jabot. It was a quite fantastic attire, better suited to an itinerant juggler than to a cleric. Nevertheless, there were many honest matrons and graceful maidens who looked admiringly after Sigismund as he walked with long steps up to his chair at the head of the table.

The host's face blanched and stiffened at the pastor's arrival, but by a great effort he preserved his composure. Mine secretary Dopp was enjoying himself. He had prophesied to himself that it would be a remarkable evening. In short, he scented scandal! And, to control his merriment, he began busily polishing his spectacles. Those thick spectacles were always a safe and convenient camouflage. If things got really tricky, he polished the sidepieces as well.

By an error David Finne and his wife, Gunhild, had been shown to seats at the host's table. True enough, they sat down near the bottom—nevertheless, it was quite preposterous! David's place was not even amongst the apprentice engineers and the chief foremen. He was only an ordinary foreman. Nor had he anything else to his credit which gave him the right to sit where he now sat. Unfortunately, the error was discovered too late for it to be put right.

His wife, the young Gunhild, was dressed in her bridal gown. There was nothing wrong about that. And together she and her husband made a pair. And who, then, should be happy on this earth if it wasn't those two? Ol-Kanelesa, the sacristan and blacksmith, had also, strangely enough, been given a seat at the same table. Here, too, Dopp had a finger in the pie. It had to be remembered, he insisted during a conversation with the hostess a day or two previously, that he (Ole Korneliusen) was a man of mature years, well read and well informed on many subjects. Even in Latin he was by no means uninformed. There was no doubt about it, he ought on this occasion to be honored. It was of great importance for Dopp, personally, to have him sitting as far up the table as possible, but he was wise enough not to mention that. But Ol-Kanelesa didn't allow himself to be taken off his guard. He was already sitting unperturbed in the center room between the ore sorters and the Sunday watchmen; the latter having been graciously invited this time, in order that they, too, could have a bright and beautiful memory to take with them into their old age. And when Ol-Kanelesa could not be induced to change his seat, Michael Brinchmann, the smeltery manager, was quietly assigned the place which had been intended for the sacristan. And now, as far as could be seen, everything appeared to be in apple-pie order.

True enough, to begin with the atmosphere was very stiff. Most of the guests were not used to grand occasions. The long time which had passed since they had participated in society life in the more spacious South made them uncertain. And the young people who had been born and bred in Bergstaden had no training whatsoever. What had been impressed on them in the nursery by their anxious mothers concerning the manners and tone of good society, in truth, didn't take them very far—maternal exhortation had been mainly concerned with sitting still, curtsying, bowing nicely, and saying thank you—but there was a great gulf fixed between that, and being able to conduct oneself with decency, and in a completely free and natural way, so that it appeared that this was quite an ordinary everyday; and it was a gulf which made a young maiden tremble. And once one began to tremble seriously, one was hopelessly lost.

And even the host himself, who had taken part in so many magnificent and wild parties both in Copenhagen and Amsterdam, and at the famous dinners at the Falun mines in

Sweden, sat there taking a good grip on himself. The pastor's
somewhat unusual attire and the completely wrong placing
of guests down at the bottom of his table left him distrait.
His fingers itched, too, to give that idiot of a butler a good
dressing down. And so it was that the hand of that former,
so urbane man-about-town, and present lord of a not-incon-
siderable manor, shook as he stammered out a welcome to his
guests and drank their health. And when, during the main
course, he proposed the customary toast to the Røros Copperworks and its high associates, he even spilled some drops of
wine on the tablecloth. He asked those present to drink this
toast with him to the last drop. They all got up and emptied
their glasses in silence. Only Kathryn and the two sisters, the
Misses Bjørnstrup, played false and only sipped. The gentlemen, on the other hand, responded to the request as one man.
No, not really everybody. Ol-Kanelesa only lifted his glass
to his mouth. Not in order to give expression to any dissenting
opinion. He was far too indifferent to the Røros Copperworks
and that overfed pack which went under the name of the high
associates for that—his reasons were quite different. He was
no rebel. He was simply Ol-Kanelesa, a common blacksmith
by trade. And he was discussing his profession in detail with
the man sitting beside him, the Sunday watchman, Rasmus
the wheelwright. He was close to ninety and was not lacking
in experience in repairing worn-out horseshoes and whetting
mattocks. He had for a whole month one summer been a smith
at the Christianus Sextus mine. And that time, that one month,
he remembered as one of the happiest times of his whole life.
The whole of that month the sun shone. He couldn't remember that there had been such unbroken sunshine either before
or since. In any case, there had been more sunshine both summer and winter when he was younger than there had been
in recent years.

Then Ol-Kanelesa said:

"Yes, the sun gets smaller and warms less as time goes,
Rasmus."

"Wasn't it that I've doubted!" the old man said excitedly—

for this agreed to a *t* with what he himself had thought and
believed, but he had never brought himself to say it to anybody before. Ol-Kanelesa was the friendliest man he had met
for many a year. The old man had to laugh. He threw back
his head, closed his small grey eyes, and laughed with his
mouth wide open.

Pastor Sigismund's speech proposing the royal toast was
awaited with great expectations. Wasn't that a speech of the
utmost importance? Yes, without doubt it was! Benjamin Sigismund had long since confirmed his reputation as an orator.
Every Sunday the Bergstaden church had been tightly packed.
All the pews and galleries were full. And the people stood in
two rows in the nave right up to the altar. People came from
afar to hear the new pastor. Although his sermons were long,
often up to two hours, they sat and stood, listening patiently.
What he said and how he said it did not exactly belong to
the realm of the real and the possible—no, on the contrary, but
it was something they themselves had dreamt and longed for:
a new heaven and a new earth. When he stood before the
altar and officiated, it was as if the arched roof of the church
was lifted from the walls. The high heavens with the sun and
its clear light became the real vault of the church. In his
interpretations of the Scriptures, Sigismund was certainly the
equal of Pastor Jens. He was supposed to have been unique.

Now Sigismund was tapping his glass, and got up, pushing
his chair far behind him with one foot.

Knoph straightened himself in his chair and sat stiffly with
a stony expression on his face. Dopp pushed his glasses deftly
over his ears and hurriedly hid his green polishing cloth in
one of the pockets of his tail coat. Brinchmann tried to catch
the eye of the youngest Miss Bjørnstrup—but that shy young
lady had scarcely dared raise her eyes during the whole of
the meal. For this, Brinchmann himself was mainly to blame.
Kathryn flushed a bright pink. Would Benjamin's speech be
well received? Oh! Her heart beat more quickly now than was
good for it. She loved him as he stood there. He, that erect
and handsome man, was her husband before God and the

whole world. David Finne and Gunhild, who hadn't exchanged a word at table, now looked up—first quickly at each other, and then at the pastor. And, at the same time, Gunhild looked into the pastor's eyes. And she, too, felt her heart beat. David, in a great show of arrogance, tried to ape Knoph by sitting stiffly erect. He was so preoccupied with this foolish impulse that he didn't notice what was going on around him. He didn't even see Dopp's mocking wink with one eye at him. But what he failed to see, Ol-Kanelesa saw, although he was sitting so far down the table. Not that he was surprised at what he saw. Hadn't the children of man been more or less the same since the time of Adam? He folded his big black hands under the table and listened to the pastor's speech proposing the royal toast. And from the expression on his face, it looked as if he was all ears.

Sigismund's speech was a disappointment. His Majesty was only mentioned in a few passing words. Head foreman Aas, in particular, was incensed at the lack of admiration for the King and his person which the pastor, it was obvious, had deliberately shown. So much so that Aas had almost interrupted him—but at that moment he met the warning eye of Mr. Knoph. And Knoph was, of course, Aas's superior. Nor did the latter part of Sigismund's speech have a soothing effect on the angry head foreman. Sigismund was now talking of the great and the powerful in this wicked and beastly world, and the responsibility they had in these times to the poor and hard pressed. This, in the view of Mr. Aas, was seditious talk. Didn't his Reverence realize where he was? Besides, Sigismund himself already had a bad name for his, speaking frankly, quite unparalleled miserliness. He really ought to express himself a little more carefully. If necessary, they could call Bernt from Tuften as a witness. As everybody knew, the pastor had cheated him out of two rix-dollars. And was there a poorer wretch here in Bergstaden than Bernt? The chief foreman couldn't restrain himself any longer. He got half up and shouted:

"Is it the board of directors you're referring to?"

Dopp rubbed his hands with the speed of lightning. Now! Now there would be a scandal! As has been remarked, he had scented it the whole time.

Had the roof fallen in, consternation could not have been greater. Had Mr. Aas drunk too much? No. No, he was an extremely moderate and careful man. No, of course, it was only his touching loyalty to his superiors that had led him to this somewhat violent and improper outburst.

Mr. Knoph raised his forefinger with the big signet ring. And that was more than enough to make chief foreman Aas sit down. He gripped the arms of his chair with both hands and let himself down into it again.

Sigismund took it calmly. In his Copenhagen days he had learned to take such disturbers of the peace for what they were. He nourished no ill-will towards Aas. One must respect a man with opinions. And, as if nothing had happened, he passed smoothly over to a poetic and high-flown disquisition on the distinctive natural beauty of the area. A natural beauty which had a face that was stern and almost unapproachable— but an eye and a soul with an enchanting smile; it could not only delight but also intoxicate. Had anyone seen anything more beautiful than the Hitter Lake on a spring evening when the high mountains with snow, flowers, and budding leaf were reflected in its shining mirror? Had anyone, however far travelled, seen a valley like Arvedal? And just as the natural beauty was stern and unapproachable at first sight, but beautiful and deeply enchanting in its nature, so were the daughters of the mining community.

At that, Dopp, sly, scandal-loving Dopp, nudged his neighbor with his elbow.

"Wasn't that what I said?" Dopp whispered. "I knew that he would end up on the distaff side."

Now chief foreman Aas also began to find the speech more congenial. True enough, it was still a speech which had little to do with the toast Sigismund was supposed to be proposing, but the chief foreman was born and bred in Bergstaden and any praise of the town and its inhabitants made his heart glow.

And to make amends for his rashness, he called out, "Here! Here!"

The part of Benjamin Sigismund's speech which now followed was for all intents and purposes addressed to Gunhild. But it was so poetic and lyrical that not many noticed. Yes, two did: Dopp and Ol-Kanelesa. The worthy matrons and the young ladies had tears in their eyes, and the men became animated.

And when Sigismund proposed a toast to the snowy, flower-bedecked mountains and their beautiful mountain women, everybody got up, smiling and pleased, and drank to them. David Finne and Gunhild, who had never drunk a toast before, stood there quite lost with their filled glasses. For them both the whole thing was like a dream. David felt himself tremendously honored to be reckoned amongst persons of rank and condition. Gunhild felt happy and confused that Benjamin Sigismund had looked at her and smiled. Fancy, Benjamin! . . . She blushed and became hot all over.

"He did us out of drinking his Majesty's health, chief foreman," Dopp said ironically to Aas as they had got up from the table.

But chief foreman Aas was once again the serious man. In any case, he didn't want to discuss that particular matter now.

"Mr. Dopp. I assume that later this evening you will find an opportunity to drink his Majesty's health."

"Me!" Dopp said. "Such a thing would never occur to me."

And he went off to look for Ol-Kanelesa.

He wanted to hear what that old scamp thought of the pastor's speech.

"Ole Korneliusen!" he shouted.

Ol-Kanelesa appeared.

"In whose honor do you suppose the pastor was really speaking?"

"Hm, yes. Wasn't it in your wife's then?"

"Yes, maybe it was," Dopp mumbled, and edged away.

His smile became a grimace. "Anyway, I could see that you knew that, Ole."

Mrs. Georgina Dopp was in every respect an honest and good person. But she wasn't beautiful. Thus, it was scarcely in her honor that Sigismund had spoken.

Nobody paid very much attention to Sigismund during the course of the evening. In the first place he was a stranger amongst them. And, besides, no one was certain where he really stood. Another thing was that no one could know how their host, Mr. Knoph, felt about the pastor after what had happened at table. It was best to be a little careful. Mr. Knoph was known to be a capricious man. Once he had been put in a bad humor, it wasn't so easy to get him out of it again. But, by way of compensation, everybody devoted a great deal of attention to Mrs. Sigismund. They flocked around her. And time and time again she had to tell them how they had fared in their previous parish—neither the pastor nor she had been very keen on leaving there—but when her husband had received the posting to Bergstaden from the very highest authority, there was no way out of it. A pastor in the state church had, unfortunately, no choice but to obey.

And how could his Reverence keep himself informed about all the things that were going on in the world outside nowadays? Kathryn smiled proudly. Yes, how should she explain it? In the first place the pastor subscribed to the newspapers and journals which were printed and published in Christiania; there was a great deal in them, though not everything. And, in addition, he often got long letters from his clerical colleagues both in Denmark and in Germany. They were in much closer touch with great events than we were in this country. Besides, Benjamin was unique in his capacity for acquiring knowledge on everything under the sun. Many a time she couldn't understand how he could absorb it all—for example, this so-called surgery and the art of the barber-surgeons. Every single thing he knew about. If people only knew what he had said the other evening. Yes, he had said that in a short time we would be afflicted by a severe outbreak of enteric fever.

"How terrible!" they all said. "What could cause that?"

Yes, during his many walks in the summer the pastor had

come across a number of small animals. "What were they called, now?"

"Benjamin!" she called out. "What are those small animals called you discovered in the mountains?"

"Myodes lemnus."

"Yes, that's it, myodes lemnus." She was badly bothered by her cough. "These animals will foul our drinking water, my husband says."

Everybody thought that sounded terrible. One must hope that it would only be a mild visitation. And in order not to hear more of this unpleasant prophecy on this festive occasion they took Kathryn over to the refreshment table. The Misses Bjørnstrup even put their arms round her—for these Bjørnstrups were really lovable people. It was characteristic of the whole family. Old Mrs. Bjørnstrup sat year after year by the window and knocked on the pane with her chiselled ring to the poor people she saw out in the street, and invited them into the kitchen to drink a bowl of milk. This ancient lady had certainly earned herself a passport to paradise in this way.

"I say, chief foreman," Dopp said to Didrich Aas. "Now I have something really nice to tell you."

"Well," Aas said, sucking at his long clay pipe. "What may that be?"

"According to a rumor, his Reverence has prophesied something of a plague."

"What!" the chief foreman said, horrified. "What are you saying?"

"He has promised us a violent dose of lemming fever."

"Lemming fever? Ha! Ha! Ha!"

And the two gentlemen slapped each other merrily on the shoulders and roared with laughter.

Sigismund sat out in the hallway. This had for the occasion been turned into a little room, with check-patterned rugs on the walls and yellow homemade wax-candles in large brass candelabras on the shelves, in place of the dusty pieces of ore-bearing rock which the director had brought home from his journeys in the mountains and which otherwise lay there

the whole year round. In the corners there were iron-pointed
miners' sticks, which mining experts from afar were lent when
they came up to Bergstaden on a visit. Some old flintlock rifles
hung there just for decoration; Knoph was no huntsman. On
one of the end walls hung the battle-axe of Lorentz Lossius,
inscribed *Anno 1637;* it was a wicked, rusty weapon with a
curved handle four feet or more long.

Benjamin Sigismund sat on a stuffed horsehair stool in the
inmost corner, smoking his iron pipe. And to sit there puffing
away at his own pipe instead of sticking politely to his host's
new clay pipes was also tactless. He sat with his legs stretched
out. Over his head there was a candelabra with seven wax
candles, but the light from it didn't fall on his face, unless
someone went through the door and the candles fluttered. He
was pale. Perhaps he sat there feeling rueful?

No, Benjamin Sigismund was not feeling rueful. He was
entirely satisfied both with himself and with everybody else.
Hadn't he got these loyal monarchists to raise their glasses for
quite different things than Christian VII? He had driven
them on a tight rein round and round and round, so that they
resembled small circus horses with tassels dangling on their
foreheads and their tails tied up. Even the hot-blooded chief
foreman had had to appear in this circus ring. When night
came, and they were lying in their beds twisting with overfull
stomachs, they would, as their intoxication left them, realize
what they had done. And the thought of this amused him for
a long time. He almost burst into laughter.

It was only later in the evening when the lights began to
burn low out there in the hallway, and the strong Dutch
tobacco began to taste bitter and didn't please him any longer,
that he began to think that he was strangely alone amongst
all these people. What, were they avoiding him? Only the
host had come up to him a couple of times and inquired how
he was.

Of course, they were avoiding him. He could quite clearly
see how they all hurriedly turned their backs as soon as they
got near the doors. This amused him for a while. Yes, what

had he in common with these so-called persons of rank and condition? They had been too long up here in ice and snow; their thoughts and opinions had become distorted. He had not come to these parts to be a socialite but as a— Besides, he had so many scholarly interests to pursue. He looked forward to plunging into new tasks.

He sipped carefully at his beaker. He lifted it up to the light. There were strangely many beakers here. This silver one looked old with its small dents and its half-worn embellishments. And it was a good and refreshing wine the director had given him.

This hallway was strangely like the hallway at home, in his mother's house. The walls, ceiling, and the worn floorboards with their round, vertical wooden nails were the same here as there. In his mind's eye he once again saw his beloved childhood home: up there on the shelf lay *Sabati sanctificatio—* printed on wooden blocks and bound in tanned deerskin and with inch-wide brass clasps. Near the exit door hung his father's sword of honor. And there stood his gold-knobbed cane with his monogram and witnessed to former greatness. Hm! That cane also bore witness to the decline of the family; now it had also become an unpleasant measuring rod of it. . . . And these memories made him feel now, as always, weak and melancholy. He passed his hand over his forehead. He wouldn't think that sort of thought now.

From one of the innermost rooms he heard the sound of dancing. He heard a violin too; it sounded like Ole Korneliusen's. Could it be possible that it was the sacristan who sat there playing for dancing when his pastor was present? Well, if so, Ole Korneliusen ought not to have done it. When they were alone he would speak a serious word to him about it. True enough, Ole had also played for him. And he had to confess that Ole with his blissful instrument had driven many a dark cloud from his mind.

At that moment Ol-Kanelesa came in quietly through the door. "No, are you here?" Benjamin Sigismund called out happily. "And I thought it was you playing in there."

"I'm no fiddler for the bigwigs, I'm not."

And Ol-Kanelesa made as if to walk on. He didn't consider it proper that he, one of the common people, should hang around the pastor now. There were enough silk-clad apes here to do the talking to the pastor. And he, for his part, had no desire to be the wee bird who tagged along after the cuckoo.

"Won't you sit down, Ole?"

"Thank you very much," Ol-Kanelesa said. "But I can talk to your Reverence later, I can."

Benjamin Sigismund jumped up.

"There is no one I would rather talk to than you."

He took Ol-Kanelesa by the arm and sat him down beside him. And to his great astonishment he saw that the sacristan was quite sober.

"Haven't you drunk anything, my dear Ole?"

Ol-Kanelesa sat there embarrassed.

"Thank you for asking. I'm well satisfied."

Benjamin Sigismund seized his hand.

"Will you forgive a personal question, Ole Korneliusen? Is it correct that you were engaged to Miss von Westen Hammond?"

Now Ol-Kanelesa became even more embarrassed. He sat for a long time looking down.

"We liked each other."

"So you were in love with each other?"

"Yes."

"And then she died?"

"Yes. She was too good for this world."

"And that beautiful cross over her grave, you have fashioned?"

Again, it was a long time before Ol-Kanelesa answered. He sat as if he was looking for something far away.

"She deserved a cross that was even prettier. I wasn't a good enough smith. And so the cross became what it is."

Benjamin Sigismund's eyes became moist and wide. His strong face contracted and he lay his hand on Ol-Kanelesa's head.

"May God bless you, Ole Korneliusen. You are a sterling fellow."

"Thank you, your Reverence, for your blessing."

And after a while he added:

"We mustn't talk too loudly about a sterling fellow."

"Yes, yes, we must, you are one."

And the pastor and the sacristan sat there silently side by side. Both of them felt that they understood each other best in that way, without words, and without any further explanation. Were they both thinking the same thoughts? Their faces were serious. They breathed heavily and deeply. And there was a great silence around the two men, although the violin sounded louder from the inner room and more people danced and laughed and sang to the dance.

Then the pastor took out some tobacco leaf, filled his pipe afresh, and then passed the tobacco to Ol-Kanelesa.

"Thank you. I have a little myself, too."

"Fill up with this, Ole!"

Ol-Kanelesa took out his pipe from his waistcoat pocket and tore a couple of leaves off the tobacco and filled his pipe. After the meal he had also smoked one of Knoph's long clay pipes for a while—but, by chance, he happened to see himself in the large mirror in the gilded frame out in the hallway. Then he saw that the clay pipe didn't suit him at all. He had, therefore, quietly put the pipe aside and crept out almost shamefaced. Yes, that's what happens when a wretched, bent-up blacksmith tries to play the bigwig. He looked like a fish out of water!

He made a paper spill, lit it from one of the candles, and passed it to the pastor. And then they sat there again, smoking and saying nothing. The pastor again leaned back comfortably with his long legs stretched out over the floor while Ol-Kanelesa sat bent forward over his knees with his brown, scorched pipe-bowl buried in his great fist.

After they had been sitting there like that for a while, Ol-Kanelesa suddenly sat up.

"Uncle Ola, can I talk to you for a bit?"

It was Gunhild. She stood there flushed and warm after the dance. And as she stood there now she was even more beautiful than usual.

"There will be an opportunity for that later," Ol-Kanelesa said.

"No, in truth, you shall sit here with us two," Sigismund said. "Your uncle and I have had a long conversation on some remarkable things."

He got up and let her sit down in his seat.

Then he got himself out an ancient three-legged stool which stood hidden away under another; this stool was peasant work and far too crude to be used for the present festivities. Director Knoph was in the habit of sitting on it in front of the fire on evenings when he wished to fortify the more primitive impulses of his nature, something which this highly placed miner used to joke about when he was in a good humor. He was not always good humored.

The pastor sat down astride the stool. Who would believe that he was Bergstaden's parish priest as he sat here now? Rather, Benjamin Sigismund resembled one of those people from the Black Forest who once passed through Bergstaden—true enough, it was now almost a generation ago, but old people still remembered them and talked of them; gypsies and low-down scum they were, but nevertheless they called themselves counts and mine experts.

"I hope I'm not disturbing you?" Gunhild said. She looked around shyly

"Well, we're disturbed as it is," Ol-Kanelesa said.

Gunhild answered smartly:

"Then you're like me."

"So you were the first bride I married here in Bergstaden!"

She sat there rubbing the backs of her hands. And Sigismund noticed that she was not wearing a ring.

"Yes. I suppose I was."

"And certainly the most beautiful bride I shall ever have to marry."

She looked up. Her eyes shone.

"Oi! Now you're going too far!" she said. "Me, a miner's wife?"

Ol-Kanelesa and Gunhild laughed, but Benjamin Sigismund only smiled faintly—he still found it difficult to understand the dialect of the people of the region. There had been a fusion of German and Swedish in the language which had long ago been reshaped by popular speech; it was a resonant and musical dialect. In Gunhild's mouth it sounded like an echoing song from the mountains themselves. Perhaps he would do some research into this dialect at some time. An account of that particular aspect of it would offer much of interest.

So that Ol-Kanelesa and Gunhild should not find it boring to sit here, he began to tell them of his journeys abroad. Mainly about a journey to Spain. He told them of bull fighting, that dangerous game. He had once seen a bullfight himself.

"The Spaniards make very clever blacksmiths, don't they?" Ol-Kanelesa asked.

"Clever smiths?"

"Yes. I once read about it in a geography book."

"Quite possible, Ole. I really hadn't thought about it!"

"I could certainly have done with learning something from them."

"Ugh, Uncle," Gunhild said. "How would you like being a Spaniard? Don't they wear heel plates in their ears?"

She laughed. Her laughter was icy cold.

"Heel plates?" Ol-Kanelesa said. "What a horror."

He got up, chuckling. And then he went through into the drawing room, holding his pipe in the palm of his hand.

Benjamin Sigismund grasped Gunhild's hands quickly.

"Tell me, Gunhild, are you unhappy?"

She looked down—but made no attempt to withdraw her hands.

"Supposing I am, what can I do about it now?"

Sigismund was perplexed and confused. And he sat there listening with his eyes. A loud chanting and banging of feet began to reach them from the inner room. They could feel the beat of the dance on the floor as they sat there. It was a wild dance, that was not difficult to hear.

It was the junior employees of the Works, young foremen and overseers, who were dancing now—it was more or less a set performance for the gentry, who stood watching in groups in the doorways. And among them was Kathryn, with the elder Miss Bjørnstrup's wizened arm still encircling her.

David Finne was among the dancers too, eagerly encouraged by Mr. Knoph himself. He had the reputation of being a brilliant dancer. And this evening he danced so that the sweat dripped off him. His yellow bandolier shone out brightly amid the other uniforms. And his feet moved like drumsticks. He was the women's favorite.

"Gunhild," Benjamin Sigismund said, "Are you in love with someone else?"

"I daren't answer that. Perhaps some other time, perhaps never."

Then he let her go. Perhaps he had touched something which was on the point of breaking? Not only in her mind but also in his own. His face became very pale. They were both standing on the edge of a precipice, a dizzy abyss had opened at their feet, it was the earth itself which had opened. And it was a sweet and enchanting fear he felt in looking down into it—it enticed him, it called to him.

Once again he remembered the ugly witch down at the Lakes. Her wicked prophecy must never be fulfilled—no, never.

At that moment Ol-Kanelesa came through the door carrying an ale bowl filled to the brim. He moved slowly between the table and the chairs, looking carefully where he went. And he held his tongue rigidly between his teeth in his efforts not to spill any.

"A wee drop for your thirst!"

He handed the bowl to the pastor.

"Gunhild first!"

Sigismund made a slow gesture with his hand in her direction. His hand was white too.

"No, you first," Gunhild said.

Then Sigismund took the bowl and handed it to her. She took it hesitatingly and drank. She was not thirsty. Then she passed it to the pastor.

"Thank you for the drink, Uncle," she said to Ol-Kanelesa. "God bless you!"

Sigismund drank hardly anything either, although he was thirsty and his throat was dry. Either the beer was sour or something was wrong with his palate.

And then Ol-Kanelesa drank. And he drank for a long time, thirsty man as he was.

Gunhild and Sigismund stood on either side of him, not daring to look up—yes, now fire was let loose in the sky, and the stars were ablaze! Could they escape? They could do nothing.

Seconds became hours, days. And the worthy sacristan drank his draft for a thousand years. And when his thirst was finally slaked, and he turned his back and went out again, they still stood there in the same position.

"Gunhild."

She didn't answer. She saw him standing like a shadow against the candles which burned low on their long black wicks. Her feet which wanted to flee were bound. Her hand which wanted to defend herself refused to move.

"Gunhild."

The candles burned as if in fear. Now they were to die. Those two standing there barely glimpsed each other's faces. She wanted to sink down but had to stand. She wanted to cry out, but had to be silent.

"Gunhild."

He still got no answer.

Then somebody came, whom she didn't see, and took the chain from her foot and the shackle from her hand—the chain which no one had heard rattle and the shackle which fell silently down onto the hard stone floor. He drew her in to him. And he whispered down on to her pale face:

"Today our fate is sealed."

Her beautiful head lay heavily on his arm. Her lips were still silent.

"Do you remember the first time we met, Gunhild?"

Candle after candle burned low in the candelabras. And now the one who had loosened the chain from her foot and the shackle from her wrist, the one whose very steps are silent, came and blew out the lights one by one. And there remained only a few red wicks, which lay there smoking and glowing, on the tiny, shining sconces. And a black curtain was lowered over Lorentz Lossius's battle-axe and the ancient shotguns with their rusty nipples. There were to be no witnesses.

"Do you now remember the first morning?"

"Yes, Benjamin."

Now Kathryn's laughter sounded from amongst the dancers. She who had not laughed for twenty years was laughing. And it was as if a heavy sword had fallen between them. The cherubim's flaming sword! Had God, from whom nothing shall be hid, struck down this doomed woman with laughter? Terrified, Gunhild rushed out of the door. And Benjamin groped around him with both hands and sank down on the horsehair stool. Through the thick timber walls he heard her steps on the wooden gangway out in the entrance. And the iron-bound door creaked on its hinges with a cold, jarring sound as it was slammed to.

The First Winter Night

The winter was at hand. Spring with its white nights, its clear light of day in the north — the light one could read one's prayer book and book of homilies by when the clock in the church tower struck twelve midnight—this had now become a dream, a beautiful memory. And Midsummer

Eve, with its flowering bird cherry—the tree which in our mountains blossoms snow and shining stars of ice—had become a memory of paradise. And the summer with its flowers, gold and red and blue over all the fields and round the tarns and lakes, that, too, was buried with the memories of the sun.

To none had it been vouchsafed by right that they would live to see a new spring and a new summer. The winters were so long, so cold and hard. The cold, in which one could mint thin two-shilling pieces of quicksilver, that was the breath of Death itself. And so the gravedigger had dug a big grave in the upper churchyard, a common sleeping chamber for the dead of the common people. Here they would sleep with hands folded, side by side, free of all fear of the sheriff and starvation.

Their bread! May the Lord bless it, such as it was! Now it was baked of bark and moss, watered with salt tears and baked on the embers in the grey dawn. It filled no one any longer. Bark was short, too. Even the God-fearing man was now driven into his neighbor's forests on dark nights, and flayed his twisted dwarf birch with long knives. A few rotten bones in a bag was a gift. And God's blessing was called down over a handful of corn. The ore in the mines, that golden rock which for two centuries had provided the miners with food, sank in value—there was war, too, in all the lands, it was the sword and not the busy and peaceful hoe which humanity had in its hands.

In the mountains and in the narrow valleys people prepared for winter. They were like the bear who dug his way in under the giant roots of the pine tree, or sought refuge in mountain caves which had served as winter lairs from time immemorial —in short, people now prepared for hibernation. Houses were made tight with moss. Enormous birch trunks with branches on were raised up against the north wall of the dwelling house, cowbarn, and stable, so that they could act as a snow-guard and be a protection against the many winter storms. Peat and hay were carted in and placed under a roof. And then the winter could come! Women and children now had to sleep much and eat little. On the other hand, both horse and man had to be prepared to be more active and hardworking, and be chilled to the marrow transporting charcoal and ore over the long distances. And for many a man and many a horse this winter would probably be their last. Those who had frozen much usually suffered different fates when the spring came. Pneumonia came treacherously with the sudden change in the weather. And then one light night, when the ptarmigan was cackling outside the window and the grouse was calling up on the hillside, Death came stealthily—relatives might catch a glimpse of him moving over the floor. Then the prayer book was brought out and a prayer said for the sick and the dying. And a hymn was sung with tearful voice. God himself, who had placed this hardworking and conscientious man in his humble and poverty-stricken station in life so that he had had little or no time to think about the next world, now brought him an assurance of eternal blessedness through the death of Our Lord Jesus Christ.

And the horse, the man's faithful comrade during snow-storms and the hard cold, couldn't stand the abrupt change to good weather either. It stood in the stable, getting thinner on its short spring rations. Its shoulder blades were broken down from the hard wooden collar, its hooves cracked from the rough nails; and then the strangles came with pain in the breast. And then one evening a neighbor came with a loaded flintlock rifle. He was silent and serious. He hid the rifle quietly behind the cow-barn door. And very patiently he managed to entice the sick animal out of its stable and behind a wall. Yes, things moved slowly through the stable door and the gateway. There wasn't exactly any hurry. He said "gee-up" and pulled the reins gently, cajoled him and made encouraging noises.

Meanwhile the children looked with tearful faces from behind the green window panes—now Brownie was to be shot. And Mother sat on a stool near the fire, holding her hands over both her ears, so as not to hear the rifle shot. Finally, Brownie had reached the back of the cow-barn wall. The

neighbor went back and fetched his gun. He crept up on tiptoe round the corner. Then he took aim on the corner and
shot. Brownie, who had drawn many a heavy load of charcoal
and ore, had to be spared the terror of death—that was simple
Christian duty. But the fatherless little ones behind the lattice
windows had got another memory to take out into life with
them. A memory which later tortured them many a time in
their dreams, and brought tears to their eyes long after they
had grown up and had wrinkled cheeks.

Well! Things didn't need to be as bad as that. The winter
was long. But spring could come too, with nothing but joy
and delight for old and young, for horse and cow, and small
lambs too—they, who would come into the world around
Candlemas. There could be no doubt, God nevertheless arranged everything for the best, one could be sure of that.

The winter brought great dangers. Many rotting crosses
with rusty nails in their decaying nameboards bore witness
to that, as they stood there, lopsided in their moss-grown heaps
of stone. Here, people had frozen to death. Nevertheless, these
lopsided crosses in the mountains had none of the eeriness of
graveyard crosses. On the contrary. Here were hawks and fal-
cons. Here the south wind and the north wind played their
melodies in turn on the little grey sliver of wood; it sounded
like the stroke of a bow on a single string. And the hawk and
the falcon sat hour after hour in the mist and the rain on
this decaying piece of wood, listening to its music—for it was
the most glorious music in the world, it went straight to their
hearts. And they, too, had a heart, a serious heart, these far-
seeing birds of prey.

The miner, who penetrated deeper and deeper into the
mountain searching for the golden rock, feared the long winter least of all, although there were few who faced so many
dangers as he did. A block of stone could become loose in the
vault above him, crush his torch and his smoky train-oil lamp,
and end his life. And, unbelievable though it may sound, even
worse things could happen to him: a premature explosion
could tear out his eyes and cast him through the gateway into

eternal and never changing darkness. Gunpowder was of the
Devil. Full as it was of wrath, it caused nothing but misfortune, whether it was in the barrel of a shotgun or in a bore
hole. It was better in the days of the crossbow and when the
rock was split by fire. But that was now so long ago, that
there were only legends left of that day and age; legends
which were told at intervals of years in front of the fire in
the miners' huts when the driving snow and the north wind
raged.

Also at the manse in Bergstaden preparations were being
made for winter. For several days Ol-Kanelesa had been
stuffing moss between the window frames and the timber
walls, and he had re-covered large areas of the roof with turf
and flat stones. And he had planed the living room floor,
which had become uneven through wear, dancing, and sand
scouring, and had put new wooden nails into the decayed
beams.

Benjamin Sigismund, who had never had a tool in his
hand, understood little about house repairs. He sat for half
a day at a time in a chair and watched, thoughtful but not
particularly interested; but he imagined, nevertheless, that he
was in charge of the work and made sure that everything was
done as it should be. If he passed any remarks, and as the
master builder he was obliged to do so, they were usually quite
nonsensical. And it often delayed Ol-Kanelesa for a long time
to dissuade him from his senseless ideas.

Otherwise, Ol-Kanelesa didn't say very much when he was
working. He had been trained to hold his tongue when he was
working with an axe, a saw, or a hammer. People who talked
a lot about everything under the sun during their working
hours got nothing done. They were drivelling idiots. Thus he
would often be very short with the pastor. But at the end of
the day over his plate of porridge and bowl of milk he was all
the more animated. And then the two of them discussed difficult matters and subjects with great knowledge and insight.
And Kathryn, who now and then came in to listen, was more
astonished than ever that an uneducated man possessed so

much learning. But she still couldn't understand it that Benjamin sat there and addressed the sacristan with such respect —she must say, it was too much of a good thing. Yes, even if Ole Korneliusen was the worthiest of men. Her father would never have done it.

"Listen to me, Ole Korneliusen," the pastor said one evening. "This winter you must take up your schoolteaching again."

But Ol-Kanelesa shook his head sorrowfully. He didn't want to hear with that ear. No, he wouldn't, not for anything in the world would he be a schoolmaster. He was a blacksmith. Really, he was nothing at all. But in any case he felt happiest in his smithy.

"I have heard that you were very capable."

"You shouldn't listen to what people say. Our friends praise us, our enemies blame us. That's the way things are."

"Did you not like your work in the school?"

"I would have said so, then—but that was before I got the poison in me, your Reverence."

"Poison?" Benjamin Sigismund exclaimed, astonished. "Have you ever drunk poison?"

"We all drink poison. And then we begin to die of it, internally, bit by bit."

"What sort of poison do you mean?"

"That poison the world brews for the lot of us. Some stand less, some more of it."

"Wickedness, you mean?"

"We can well call that poison. That grinds us down at the finish, too."

"Perhaps you mean lies, backbiting, and cruel words?"

"They're the worst killers. A proper devil's brew. There is nothing that kills quicker than that. It's just a pity that we carry on giving it to each other, as hard as we can."

"You are right, Ole! You are right! So it is no good talking about your schoolwork?"

"Hm. No. In any case, I've a sort of school down in the smithy, I have.

"You run a school in your smithy?"

"No, I'm the pupil. I learn from them I shoe horses for—the charcoal carrier and the wagoner. They've thought about a lot of things, them that go for loads year in and year out—a lot of things I haven't thought about before, and which you won't find in books and in the Scriptures."

"I understand. That's what is called the school of life, Ole Korneliusen. Tell me, what is it you most learn down there?"

"Mostly what I learn is, at the bottom, what the Master taught us: Judge not!"

"You are a great disciple, Ole. Let me shake your hand."

Kathryn had sat listening to this conversation and the next day she decided that she must address Ol-Kanelesa as an equal. It seemed to her that she must do so, since he was both a righteous and a well-read man, and since Benjamin had done so for a long time now, although it was scarcely quite proper.

After the party at Director Knoph's she had felt much better, and had been brighter and more light-hearted than before. And now members of the gentry began to visit her. The two Misses Bjørnstrup came every day. They were very interested in her embroidery work and praised it. Her designs were among the most beautiful they had seen. They took some of the patterns home to try for themselves. When they didn't turn out as they had hoped, they sought advice and guidance from Kathryn. The French patterns were especially difficult, but then they were so graceful. And when Kathryn could get somebody to look after the children, she visited the Bjørnstrups too. They sat round an old, sand-scoured table in the center parlor, where a lot of maps of mines and their underground passages, and sketches of German smelting works were hung up on the walls. They drank tea from large blue cups. The Bjørnstrups were well known for their tea—regularly, every spring and autumn, they received a small consignment direct from Amsterdam. They had a brother-in-law down there who was both a rope-maker and a big business man; he too was called Bjørnstrup, Georg Abraham Bjørnstrup. Eyebrows were raised in the family when it turned out that the pastor's wife had not heard his name before; but they were, of course, tactful enough not to let her see it. Mrs. Sigismund had, it was true, been married so young and, otherwise, had not had much chance to become acquainted with such things, so by and large it was both understandable and excusable. Yes, they were delightful people. Mr. Bjørnstrup could also, every now and again, sit down at the sand-scoured tea table and smoke a pipe and be particularly entertaining and gallant. And that was almost more than one could reasonably expect of a man in his position and with his great responsibility. The number of his subordinates grew continually. Nevertheless, he contemplated the future of the Works with great misgivings. Especially the future of the forests which the Works owned. They declined continually.

Kathryn could at times be in great spirits. Her chest trouble improved the whole time. She didn't cough anything like as much now as formerly. Also at home she was more settled and could be friendly and jocular.

"Benjamin!" she could exclaim. "Before the year is out I shall certainly be quite well. There's little chance of your getting rid of me during the next two hundred years. Aren't you delighted?"

"Yes, yes. Of course."

"Perhaps I shall also live to see you a bishop, Benjamin?"

"Yes, let us indeed hope so, Kathryn."

"Bishop Benjamin Sigismund!" she said, and beamed with happiness at the thought. "And then we'll move from here, Benjamin. Oh, what a glorious day, when we pack our trunks. If it would only happen in the autumn. An autumn day like today. Next autumn? A year today?"

"Why especially an autumn day?"

"Yes, then we will be able to follow the sun and the summer and the migratory birds on their way south. A part of the way, at all events. Oh, we're living in exile up here, I feel it so acutely when my malaise at living here is at its worst. Then it sometimes feels as if my soul is tearing itself away from my body and is fleeing . . . Have you ever felt that, Benjamin?"

"No. Well, maybe to begin with, but not now any longer. Time, which never pauses, cures excessive feelings of that sort."

"What! You are surely not thinking that we shall remain here in this wilderness?"

Her heart quivered with fear. She stared horrified at her husband.

"Well, there's no bishop's palace up here."

He looked up at her gaily, it was a somewhat affected gaiety.

"You must be clever, Benjamin, and hurry and become a bishop. Yes, you will, won't you?"

"As quickly as possible, my dear."

Benjamin Sigismund was grateful to her, in spite of everything, for believing in him. She had not always done so. No, on the contrary, hardly ever. Also, he had often been disappointed at her indifference to his career. He felt that he had the ability to become a bishop.

She could read in his face that he, too, meant it seriously. Benjamin was a very ambitious man, she knew that. And her fear disappeared as quickly as it had come. There were many things she had to talk to him about now. She began with the children.

"Laurentius is making great progress with his German, Benjamin. He takes after you."

Yes, that was something Benjamin Sigismund liked very much to hear. He sat up in his chair and nodded approvingly.

"And you're teaching him French and Latin, Benjamin?"

"Yes, of course."

"But to change the subject: don't you think you could come in with me and the children? We can quite well sleep in the same room, now that I am so well. And then we could use this room exclusively as your study and sitting room."

He sat there, fanning himself under the nose with his large

quill pen. He sat and thought—that is, he didn't think. He just felt a need to be alone. Alone with himself and his work and his thoughts. And with—no, he put that thought out of his head. He hadn't seen Gunhild since the party at Knoph's. Yes, he had seen her once. It was up at the churchyard, where he had met her for the first time; but when she caught sight of him, she turned and disappeared down an alley. Besides, she was another's. And he was another's too. And it was incompatible with the Word of God. What had happened in the late night hour at Knoph's must not happen again. *Ein Mal ist Kein Mal.** For both of them the command was, Go and sin no more. He would never offer it a single thought again. And far less her, this woman of the people. He continued to fan himself under the nose with his quill pen.

Kathryn cleared her throat. She was waiting for an answer. And again she looked up almost anxiously at her husband.

"Well, what do you think about it, Benjamin?"

"We must give the matter further consideration. My new book demands peace. And first and foremost an undisturbed night's sleep."

"Well, then we won't say any more about it for the present."

Benjamin Sigismund was now fully occupied with his new book. But he couldn't make any real headway with it. And he found it difficult and tiresome to become absorbed in his material. In the first place, the small library he had at his disposal gave him little or no help, and secondly, he lacked a clear inner vision. He lacked, too, Christian zeal. The light of his spirit which before had burned so clearly had now, somehow or other, been put under a bushel. Well! He would strive seriously to put it up on a candlestick, so that it gave light to all that were in the house. He would call for fire from above, from Sinai itself! His prayers, too, had lost their power, their aspiring strength. He must, in full seriousness, knock on the gates of prayer, which now were closed and locked to him. Had he lost his good companion, the Master? In this, too, he resembled Simon Peter; and yet Simon was the greatest of the

* Once is not always.

twelve. Wasn't it precisely Peter's mistakes and errors which revealed the most powerful traits of his character? Simon Peter's earthly progress was now wavering, from one side of the road to the other, now measured and certain of its direction, and now again prostrate with his face pressed down in the cold, wet gravel of the way. And then, once again, quickly forward on sore and bloody feet, sure in the knowledge that the Lord went ahead. He was the great example of the *only* way humanity could attain to the everlasting life.

And he, Benjamin Sigismund, was no exception. He always felt himself clad in the worn coat of Peter. He was also girded about with the great disciple's spiritual sword; the Lord God had ordered him to put the sword of iron and steel into its sheath for all eternity.

He fell on his knees beside his desk and prayed, fervently. Like Jacob of old he had to wrestle with God. And like Jacob he rose up blessed. Now all was transfigured. The gates, the gates of prayer, were once again open. He still saw himself as Peter, but even more wavering, even more tired and weary.

Already tomorrow he would carry out his plan of visiting the sick and the suffering, the cast down and the poor, and bring them the glad tidings. He would resolutely continue to do so from day to day, until it pleased his Lord to call him from the fields, in from the great vineyard, down from the walls of Solomon's temple to give an account of his day's work. And then might his Lord say: "Well done, thou good and faithful servant." He must be zealous. Far too many hours had been wasted of the precious days of his life. Supposing he had already entered upon the eleventh hour? A feeling of dread possessed him at the thought of that and of everything he had neglected. All the great things, even if they were small in the eyes of God, he had dreamt of doing, were still undone.

The whole of that night he sat working at his new book. He covered a great number of pages. Words stormed down on him. Images welled forth. . . . He felt it as one of the really great moments, with the furnace full of fire and flames. He must strike while all the irons were in a glow of light,

while they glowed white-hot and had the sun's, God's own,
shining light in them. Oh, never before had his spirit streamed
so powerfully from him—that which alone could mold a beautiful and perfect form.

That night the winter came. It came from the north; first
with snow which shone like flying hoar-frost in the clear silver
light of the full moon. And then the snow began to cover all
the black earth-roofs of the houses; it covered the brown,
tarred roof of the church, too, right up to and above the windows in the tower. The cherub on the spire had a white garment thrown over its thin shoulders and over its trumpet; a
garment adorned with snow stars and ice diamonds. Over the
graves, white sheets with pale silken fringes were spread—
the crosses, both the rotten ones, with only a few awkward
initials on them, and those with an elaborate and expensive
inscription on them, received garlands of large white roses.
The two churchyards, which neither spring nor summer could
embellish with a wild flower or a blade of green grass, were
changed by the snow into fairy paradise gardens. Down the
streets white, soft carpets were unrolled. A white cloth was
laid on the high stone steps leading up to the doorways. They
looked like white-clad altars, these old, rough granite steps.
And the footprints in the new snow of both people and horses
were wiped out at once—the first winter night would have
none of that; nothing living and sinful must set foot on this
shrine. And the town lay there white, beautiful and shining.

Benjamin Sigismund looked out through the little lattice
window. And the sight which met him: it was a new town,
conjured forth as if by magic, supernatural in its brilliance.

He tiptoed into the bedroom. Kathryn, too, must see this
new town. But Kathryn slept deep and soundly. Her breathing
had once again become slow and regular. Neither had she
any longer the red, flushed roses on her cheeks. Had an angel
laid his hand on her? Angels could do that at the command
of the Lord, couldn't they? She, who had been marked out
for death, lay there hale and hearty.

He went quietly out again without waking her. And he

didn't reproach her any more for sleeping too much. He saw it differently now. Sleep, peaceful, dreamless sleep, stood guard over one's health—although Mother Sleep was the half-sister of Death, and blind and white as she.

He stood once again at the window. And he felt painfully alone. Alone, as Adam was in the Garden of Eden on the first night. Here, no one stood beside him with a pounding heart. No hot breath touched his cheek. No arm rested heavily on his. No soul beside his soul was mirrored in this glass.

He thought only of one; of Gunhild! If she with her spontaneous spirit had stood here, would she not have absorbed this fairy vision with all her acute senses? She would have delighted in it, as a child delights in pretty decorations. For in this white enchantment there was something matching her own beauty.

His thoughts of Gunhild blended with thoughts of his own beautiful mother. And at the memory of her Benjamin Sigismund felt, as always, a light being lit in himself. Her memory was the light which shone on everything beautiful, everything wondrous, he saw. She was herself the most beautiful of all the earthly lights.

What was that? He leaned over his desk and pressed his face up against the window pane. He heard trumpets in the air. He heard drums and kettle drums. He heard the whistle of the flute. All the white on the roofs, on the steps, on the streets, and on the graves was torn away. Hands, feverish hands, grey, shadowy hands tore it off and threw it against the walls, the doors and windows.

It was the north wind which had come, the north wind and the long eight months of winter. Would it be granted to him to see the light nights and the long sunny days again?

A cold terror, a grey serpent, came and crept into his heart. And the serpent and the terror said:

"God, the All Highest, disposes in that."

Sigismund lit a fresh tallow candle and continued writing his new book.

How Can the Blind Lead the Blind?

In the narrow streets the snow lay a good two feet deep. Walls, window frames and doorways were clogged with driven snow. And cold rose from everything. White is always cold, be it snow or linen—one's vestment on Judgment Day. Yes, even the flower of the bird cherry, the daisy, and the chickweed wintergreen, as it stands there in the sun and the warm air, is cold—it is the soul of whiteness that is cold.

The old grey men who had said farewell to the mines and the smeltery now got down their thick, patched, winter attire from the clothes loft and put it on. There was no prospect that the snow would disappear again this year. The fields were long since deep frozen and one could drive across the marshes, the lakes, and the tarns. To go and long for more sun, spring, and mild weather—no, that was futile, to that longing there would be no end. It was better to give up at once and let oneself be snowed up and frozen in. If only man and beast had enough food! Starvation was the worst thing of all to contemplate. One could perhaps reconcile oneself to grown-up people being hungry, going to bed hungry and getting up hungry; but to have to look on while the children became paler and thinner every day, that was a tragedy. And to have to lie awake during the long dark nights and hear the beasts in the cow barn and the stable bellowing because of empty bellies, that was not much better either.

No, nobody could know what trials and tribulations the winter would bring. The war continued, too, both at home and abroad.

Mine secretary Dopp was now well informed on what was going on in the world outside. He too now subscribed to the newspapers which were printed in Christiania. Ol-Kanelesa, too, was informed. He borrowed Dopp's newspapers and read everything. Yes, Ol-Kanelesa was a reader. The Scriptures never stumped him. He was more of a bookworm than any parson.

Benjamin Sigismund had once again put away his outdoor

attire. He spent the day visiting the sick and the dying. He read from the Holy Scriptures in a clear, soft voice, adapting the text for the poor in spirit so that its truth became as clear to them as the light of day. In the Scriptures and in the sacraments he had received the keys of heaven. Should he then withhold entry to any? He prayed on his knees with those who prayed. He prayed as if for the salvation of his own soul.

Day after day he went out to the suffering. And he concerned himself not only with their spiritual sufferings but also with their physical ones. He tended and bandaged wounds and brought healing herbs for aches and pains—for such were the things a good samaritan ought to do. The whole of humanity, himself included, had fallen amongst thieves: the multiplicity of our sins! Everyone needed oil poured into their wounds.

. . . The twenty-first of November.

That day was remembered for generations to come because of the frost. Pine stems cracked in the forests, and blackened magpies lay in the streets of Bergstaden—they had fallen down stone-dead from the edge of the chimney stacks where they had tried to warm themselves in the smoke from the peat. In the cow barns and in the stables, cows and horses stood, hanging their heads and shivering. And in the low-timbered cottages people sat huddled together in front of the fireplace. The old people, who had the thinnest blood in their veins, put on old skin coats, dried up and shrunken. They could with quavering voice tell of the cold in days gone by, too; they were gloomy and ghastly tales.

Benjamin Sigismund woke feeling frozen. Was it the cold of the plague? Quickly he felt his pulse, but there was nothing quick or violent about it. Then he understood that it was the cold in the air. Presently, he heard Kathryn call from her room.

"Benjamin, I'm so cold—"

And presently the children called out:

"Papa! Mummy! Are you awake? We're so cold, we are too.

"Get into the same bed," Benjamin Sigismund called out. And it was done. The boys got into their mother's bed.

Sigismund jumped up. The cold pierced the soles of his feet like sharp knives. A feeling of wild terror gripped him. Had the earth been changed to ice and enveloped in eternal darkness? After much groping along the wall, he finally got hold of the outdoor clothes out in the hall and spread them over Kathryn and the boys.

"Where is our tinder box, Kathryn?"

"It's up on the mantlepiece."

She could hear that her husband was not in a good humor. He was always so jumpy when his sleep was disturbed. Nevertheless, since the party at Director Knoph's Benjamin had been kind and amenable. That, too, had contributed much to the improvement of her chest and making her feel more lighthearted. Goodness was life-giving nourishment for her. It was balsam, manna in the desert.

Benjamin Sigismund could not find the tinder box. He knocked a brass candlestick on the floor. Angrily he shouted:

"There's no tinderbox here!"

"I'll get up and look myself, Benjamin."

"Lie still," he ordered. "I'll find it, I dare say."

He felt around the mantlepiece. Now a copper jug fell on the floor. Angrily he kicked at it, but hit the leg of a chair— it was laughably painful, and made him grasp his toes and jump around on one leg, grimacing.

"Why don't you put things in their proper place! Are you still cold in there?"

No, it was better now. Laurentius's back was a little cold, that was all.

"Good!"

He jumped back into bed again but that, too, had become icy cold.

"Ow!" He was up again. Now he *had* to find the tinderbox. He knocked down more things from the mantlepiece and clattered over chairs, but the tinderbox, no! It had disappeared. And so he was forced back into bed for a second time. He pulled the sheepskin blanket over his head and tried to breathe underneath it. In that way he got some warmth into his body again. Now he became tired, dozy. His eyes closed slowly.

A bad dream, a sort of nightmare, began to torment him. It seemed to him that he had been put into one of the deeper mine galleries at the Works. Round about him a cold darkness brooded, a slippery, thick blackness. It penetrated his clothes, his body, and took possession of his soul. Now, it was slowly and painfully prizing his soul out of him. It couldn't be stopped. Yes, one thing could stop it: light; a strong, blinding light! But there was no light here, there had never been any. Never had a beam of the sun shone on these barren rocks. They lay here full of cold and darkness. And thus they would continue to lie until the Day of Judgment, when heaven and the earth would be ignited and come ablaze. If only he had a lamp. If nothing more than a smoky wick. He was completely in the power of this terrible darkness. In his terror he began to call for light: "Lord! Lord! Send in thy mercy a ray of thy sun." His fearful cries were echoed back from the rocks. No one was at hand. No one heard. God had hidden His face. And in this fear he awoke, clammy and sweating over the whole of his body. And to his joy he noticed that there was now a light somewhere. Where it came from he couldn't decide. Was it a magical light which could shine through sticks and stones? He sat up in bed and looked around with confused eyes.

Yes, there it was. The sun was shining down through the chimney. It was shining on the rime-covered stones of the hearth. But the rays of the sun were so cold that the frost didn't melt.

God be praised, it was again day. The Lord's bright day! He jumped out of bed and dressed quickly. It was still icy cold but it didn't feel so terrible any longer. He found the tinderbox lying on a chair in front of the bed. He had put it there so as to have it to hand. How could he have forgotten it? That sort of thing mustn't happen again. And with great strength and determination he lifted the steel and struck. The hard flint promptly produced some blue sparks, but he couldn't catch these in the tinder. He struck again. Hard and with determination—but no.

Then the door opened. And a man came in, with silent footsteps and miserably undersized. He was clad in furs, grey deerskin. On his head he had a pointed cap with blue and red beads. He dragged a stick, longer than he was tall, through the doorway and put it down carefully on the floor.

" 'Morning!" the man said, and bared his teeth.

Sigismund couldn't decide whether it was a smile or pain he saw in the man's twisted face.

"Be you our pastor?"

"Yes. What do you want?"

Sigismund remained sitting on the hearth with the tinder-box in his hand. Where had he seen this deformed creature before? Yes! Now he remembered him, he was the man he had met on his first morning in Bergstaden; the first morning when he met Gunhild.

He saw again a picture of Bergstaden and her, just as he had seen it on that spring morning.

Yes, that spring morning! It seemed to him to be so eternally long ago, although there was only a summer and an autumn between then and now.

Years could become days, and days could become years; time could not always be measured in hours and dates and years, but with heavenly joy and gladness, longing and woe. At this moment Benjamin Sigismund measured time in the last of these ways. To measure it in that way was to change hours and days to years. It seemed to him that he had known this Lapp from the beginning of time. He forgot that this man had stood and laughed and called after him, indeed, had made a fool of him in public. He felt on the contrary an inexplicable goodwill towards this stone-like creature. He could lift him up and put him on his knee, and pat his bushy black hair; it was as stiff and wiry as a horse's tail. He had once seen hair

of that sort on an idol. Then, he had felt the deepest repug-
nance at it; but now it was quite the opposite. Oh, no one was
always the same. Yes, one was: the All Highest! But man was
inconstant and always fickle from cradle to grave. He gave
the flint a new blow with the steel.

"Me make fire for you," the mannikin said. "Me do it!"

Benjamin Sigismund gave him the tinderbox and the Lapp
struck the flint and ignited the tinder at one go. In a short
while the fire was burning on the hearth. The Lapp even got
the frozen wet wood to burn. The whole time he stood with
his face in the smoke and mumbled. Was it some heathen
incantation? He was also making some very mysterious signs
and gestures with his arms over the fire.

"What are you doing, my man?" Benjamin Sigismund called
out, "Are you calling up the fire?"

The Lapp stared uncomprehendingly at the pastor. He
didn't understand.

"Eh?" he shrieked in his singsong voice. "Eh! Eh!"

Was the man standing there laughing? It was the sound
of laughter, but his face expressed sorrow, suffering. What was
he trying to say?

"Is there anything you want?"

The Lapp didn't understand that either. He looked quite
helplessly at the pastor.

"No understand what pastor say."

Then, like lightning he bent down, groped for his long
stick, dragged it with him out of the door and disappeared.

Benjamin Sigismund sat and stared after him. What did the
dwarf want? Was he a being of this world? Superstition! He
made a peremptory gesture with his hand. Nothing but superstition! He put more wood on the fire. And then he warmed
himself on all sides until he was warm all through.

There was sun in the fire. Sun, gathered up and preserved.
Especially in the pitch of the pinewood—there was much sun
there. He would buy more cords of pinewood. Then they
could have a fire in the hearth the whole night and protect

themselves against the dark and the cold. Not only their
bodies, but also they could keep their souls pure of darkness
in that way; for darkness was impure. It was the enemy of
God, the soul and sphere of the Devil.

The ice patterns on the window now began to melt. The
sun itself breathed with its red mouth on them from the other
side of the window panes. And it dripped springlike from the
lead-lights down on to the rotten window frame.

What sort of life was Gunhild living now? He never dared
ask anybody about it. Not even to Ole Korneliusen did he
dare put such a question. Every time that greying wise man
came up to his study, or when they met in the choir of the
church, he felt a violent urge to greet him with, "Have you
seen anything of Gunhild Finne recently?" But every time it
was as if his tongue was nailed to the roof of his mouth. Was
then this question so great a sin, since the Lord every time
struck him with dumbness? How often had he not laid this
matter on the scalepan of his conscience. And sometimes the
scale dipped one way and sometimes another. He had also
prayed to God for a sign to guide him but he had received
no sign. Was it that his Lord would give him no sign other
than that which was written in the Holy Scriptures? Did he
in no wise desire Gunhild? No, it was a lie! He desired her!

He jumped up from the hearth.

No, in no wise did he desire her. Another lie! His whole
soul was ablaze with desire for this woman. All his longing
was for her.

No! No! He didn't feel it in that way. His desire was not
coarse and earthly. . . . He had seen nothing of her at church
since the party at Knoph's. For what reason did she stay
away? Every pew in the church was taken, the common people stood tightly packed all up the nave and up in the galleries—nonetheless, to him the great church was quite empty
when Gunhild was not sitting down there.

But she was right to stay away. Yes, but she must come
once more. Just once more. Then he would speak so that the

very walls would weep. He would storm the gates of heaven. The golden gates of heaven.

The door opened. The dwarf stood there again with his long stick. Ol-Kanelesa came with him.

"Good morning, sacristan," Benjamin Sigismund called out. "It is a long time since you were last here. How is Gunhild Bonde?"

Now it was done. The word which was spoken couldn't be taken back.

Ol-Kanelesa started. And he took his time before he answered. Finally, he caught hold of his chin and looked up at Benjamin Sigismund.

"Gunhild? She's sitting there moping the one day like the next."

"What, is Gunhild still unhappy?"

"She's having a bad time," Ol-Kanelesa said straight out. "She should have said no up at the church, that she should."

"Yes, yes. Naturally that would have been the only right thing, Ole Korneliusen."

The pastor sank down on the curb of the fireplace. So, she was having a bad time. He felt quite dizzy with sorrow and grief over it—no, dizzy with joy, of a quite inexplicable joy. She was having a bad time. Perhaps she was thinking about him?

"Must hurry, our Klætta wait for pastor," the Lapp mumbled.

"Your Reverence," Ol-Kanelesa began.

Benjamin Sigismund didn't hear. He asked:

"And have you talked to her recently?"

"Yes, last night."

"Last night?"

"Yes. But you must go on a sick visit, pastor. There's a Lapp girl who's dying up in the mountains."

"What do you say, Ole? Is somebody dying?"

Now Ol-Kanelesa explained briefly that the wife of the Lapp, Nils from Bu, lay dying up at Flensmarken.

"Is your wife so ill?" Sigismund said to the Lapp; but he only looked questioningly up at Ol-Kanelesa. "What pastor say?"

"Your wife, Nils. Very sick?" Ol-Kanelesa said.

"She die."

Benjamin Sigismund couldn't see any particular anxiety in the Lapp's face.

"How old is she?"

Ol-Kanelesa had to translate that, too.

"Two and twenty. Two and twenty, one week from Michaelmas."

"What! Twenty-two?"

Ol-Kanelesa nodded. She was no older than that.

"And you, Lapp?"

"Four and seventy."

"And now she shall die and you live?" Benjamin Sigismund said. And added in a conciliatory tone: "Yes, yes. We mustn't call Him to account about that. His ways are not our ways. . . . You will come as interpreter, Ole Korneliusen, will you not?"

"If I can help to open up the gates for a despairing soul, then I must try."

When Benjamin Sigismund, dressed in a fur coat and Lapp shoes which Leich had lent him, was going out of the gateway, Gunhild stood there.

She didn't greet him. The cold and the gold of the morning sun made her unusually beautiful, although she was tired and hadn't slept.

"Gunhild," Benjamin Sigismund said, and went up to her and took her hand. "Why don't you come to church any more, Gunhild."

"Do you want to see me *there*, then?"

"Yes! Yes! He held her hand tightly. "It's just there I want to see you."

A sledge swung up to the door at a trot. Sigismund climbed hurriedly on to it. Ol-Kanelesa followed, carrying a small

wooden box. They went at a trot along the whole of the main
street. Everything happened so quickly that Benjamin Sigismund didn't even manage to say goodbye to Gunhild, who
stood there, thinly clad and cold. She stood alone for a while,
looking at the disappearing sledge. And then she began to
walk—to walk with long steps along the track of the sledge
right up to the smeltery. There she turned and walked quickly
down again. She had nowhere to go.

                                 Up at the Hitter Lake, Ol-
Kanelesa said:
   "It's cold today, your Reverence."
   Benjamin Sigismund made no answer to that. He said:
   "I asked her to come to church, Ole."
   "Who?"
   "She."
   "Gunhild?"
   The pastor nodded. For him Gunhild Finne had become
she, the only one.
   And then they were both silent for a long time. Ol-Kanelesa
sat covering his face with his woollen mittens. There was a
searing cold wind. He couldn't remember that he had ever
known it colder. The peasant, whose sledge it was, sat behind
on the back seat and drew his head down in the collar of his
fur coat—but Benjamin Sigismund sat with his head upright.
His great eyebrows became white with hoarfrost, and the hair
which stuck out by his ears curled up grey and frozen over
his temples.
   Ol-Kanelesa couldn't understand that the pastor didn't get
frostbite. He watched closely to see whether any white patches
appeared on Sigismund's face, the sign of frostbite. Then he
would have to rub snow on it.
   No, Sigismund felt neither the cold nor the biting wind. He
drove recklessly with tight reins. And the world, that old
wicked world, was at this moment beautiful and wondrous to

live in. Look at the birch trees along the edge of the lake.
Every twig burned with a white light. Light which radiated
from the living flame in the interior of the stem. The stone
markers they drove past on the ice also had their light. And
the snow! Tinted scarlet red by the sun, it was a carpet rolled
out over forest, rocks, and frozen water.

He cracked the whip in the air. The horse threw up ice and
snow from its shining iron shoes around the ears of the three
people on the sledge.

Then the large hands of the peasant gripped the reins and
held them back:

"You're not driving my horse to death, pastor!"

Benjamin Sigismund looked up amazed. The peasant on the
back seat had brought him back from fairyland. Now he, too,
began to feel the cold. It cut his ears, and made his hands so
stiff that he could scarcely move a finger. And only now did
he see the snow: cold and unending; Death's great winding
sheet.

"What is the man saying, Ole Korneliusen?"

"He thinks your Reverence is driving mighty fast."

"No doubt we are driving quickly, but do you not think
that Death drives even quicker?"

"Yes, well yes," Ol-Kanelesa said thoughtfully. "He drives at
his own pace. Whether he drives quick or slow there's not
much use our trying to compete with him, is there?"

The pastor tore the reins out of the peasant's hands. And the
whip cracked once again. He permitted no interference whatsoever. Wasn't the redemption of a soul more important than
anything?

Now Nils the Lapp was catching up with them. He was
driving a reindeer sleigh. He hollered and gesticulated with
his arms and whizzed past like an arrow.

"Go, go, pastor!" he shouted. "Klætta wait."

The peasant on the back seat, a wiry-haired, red-bearded
man from Malmagen, made new protestations. It wasn't going
to help him to have his horse lamed. "Whoa there, whoa!" He

had driven with road surveyor von Krogh between Malmagen and Bergstaden plenty of times, and he was a swine to drive, too, but even he didn't drive that crazily. Perhaps the pastor would pay for the horse?

"How much do you want for your miserable nag, my man?"

"How much? I must have seven rix-dollars for it."

"Well, we are soon agreed on that price."

Sigismund was excited. Now the whip really began to crack in the air. And it was easy to see that it wasn't the first time he had a pair of reins between his hands. The horse reared, threw itself against the shafts, and off along the lakes they went.

Ol-Kanelesa and the peasant from Malmagen exchanged furtive glances; but neither of them had any great desire to speak to the pastor. It was really Ol-Kanelesa who approved such conduct least of all. There was no certainty that our Lord would overlook the wrongs we had done to animals. We had to remember that He hadn't given them tongues to speak with. The peasant, on the other hand, was content with the thought of the seven rix-dollars. He could get a reasonably serviceable gelding for five; and it would be good to have two dollars in his purse when the land tax was due. Every time he thought of it, he came out in a sweat.

"If she is released from her chains, will her lucky star then rise, Ole Korneliusen?"

"Whose?"

"Gunhild's."

"Her. I thought you meant the Lapp girl."

Ol-Kanelesa sat there again for a long time and thought.

"I don't know what would be the heaviest to bear, the shame or the chains, do you?"

"The shame? You mean what people would say?"

"Yes. One must be strong to bear that burden, too."

"God's judgment is heavier, Ole."

Ol-Kanelesa was silent.

After a while Benjamin Sigismund said, "Well, is your view different?"

"I don't know. He who is the righteous judge judges mercifully, doesn't He?"

Then Sigismund was silent for a long time.

"You are right, you are certainly right. God judges in love, people in malice."

The sun, the short day's sun, which had burned like a great blazing fire over the tops of the pines, now began to glide down between the trunks. The blaze condensed into one big, glowing bonfire which threw a red flicker of fire onto their faces.

"Oh, what magnificence and glory," Benjamin Sigismund said. "The merciful God is shining his great light on our countenance."

Here in the desolation there were no tracks from horses or people, but away over on the flat moors was a broad track made by thousands of reindeer in the mild weather, and now frozen to ice.

To Benjamin Sigismund the whole journey was something unreal; it could well have been a dream. Before, he had always dreamt his beautiful dreams in the sunny morning hours when he was sitting in a chair, his cheek on his hand. The most beautiful came at the point when sleeping and waking met— they were the intoxicating ones. He leaned back in his seat and closed his eyes. Now his good friends, his blissful dreams, could come. Now they could come and lead his soul into their world, where friendly elves, the small servants of the angels, danced with flowered garlands in their hair and with gold harps in their white hands.

Idle fancies, adorned with the red roses of irresponsibility! How constant in its weakness was not the flesh we had inherited from Adam, right from that late evening hour when the two had wandered hand in hand out through the gate of Paradise, past the cherubim and with the dusk of the night on their faces!

He let the horse go at a walk. He folded his hands over the reins and prayed: "Lord, Thou who created us from the cold clay, perfect and in Thy image, that which we daily destroy

and cast asunder, do not in Thy mercy call us too hardly to
account, for we are yet, in spite of all our faults and defects,
Thy children, which through Christ's suffering and death must
be our certain hope and firm belief."

They stopped at a Lapp hut on an open place in the pinewood. It was here Nils lived.

Nils opened the door, an untanned reindeer skin stretched
over strips of wood from which the bark had been removed,
and crept in.

Sigismund and Ol-Kanelesa shook the snow off themselves
and crept in after him. On a mat made of woven pine branches
a young Lapp girl lay, her large eyes wide open. Beside her
squatted an old woman. There was something demonic, shadowy, about this old woman which made Benjamin Sigismund
start. Was she a being from the world of shadows? She let out
some short howls. Did they express sorrow or malediction?

"What is your name?" he asked the sick girl, and put his
hand over her heart. It had almost stopped beating.

"Klætta."

"Klætta," the old woman repeated.

"Klætta," Ol-Kanelesa said too. He saw that the pastor had
not yet grasped the name.

"What does that mean, sacristan?"

"I suppose she was called after the mountain where she was
born."

Benjamin Sigismund turned to Ol-Kanelesa and said in a low
voice:

"Death has already done his work here. This young woman's
soul is on the threshold, ready to leave its earthly habitat. It is
our duty to accompany her through the blackness of death
with the glowing light of the Word and the Promise."

And after a while he said:

"How like Gunhild Finne she is."

Ol-Kanelesa made a grimace. Was Sigismund thinking about
Gunhild now, too? Yes, yes. It was no business of his. Everybody had eternally enough to do with scrutinizing himself. He
merely said:

"We're all children of Adam."

He, also, thought that she resembled someone: Ellen!

The pastor stood for a while holding the thin hand of the dying girl in his. What beauty cruel Death brought to the young! The pale light from Death's lamp, the lamp he carries under his trailing cloak, and which he takes out now and again and shines on human faces—that weak and pale light which makes all living things start in mad terror, made at the same time all that was earthly disappear so that God's image could come forth.

"Do you believe in God and in our Lord and Saviour Jesus Christ?"

Yes, but her sins were great, they were like the tall, dark mountains. All the days of her life had been full of misdeeds and mistakes.

To Benjamin Sigismund's surprise she spoke Norwegian well, but her voice failed.

Would she then confess her transgressions?

Yes.

And did she wish to receive holy sacrament?

Yes.

Ol-Kanelesa and the others went out. They sat down silently beside each other on a log outside the wall of the hut.

And on his knees beside Klætta's bed the pastor heard her confession. She had married the old widower for his hut and animals. Her mother had for many years begged her way from valley to valley. Klætta didn't want to inherit that. And she and Nils had had a child, a little boy. Fearful that the child should come to resemble its father, she had wished it dead while she was carrying it. God had not failed to punish her, the child was stillborn. Now the Devil was standing outside the wall of the hut, waiting for her. She had seen him several times today putting his head through the door opening to see whether she was dying. Last night and the whole of today she had tried to pray—but it was as if God was so far away.

Was that all? Were there not other sins? Yes, ten thousand

others too, but they were the sins we commit as often as we
draw breath and take a step.

"Little friend," Benjamin Sigismund said, and stroked her
forehead. "In the name of Jesus Christ I promise you merciful
forgiveness for all your sins." And he continued: "Our Saviour,
Thou who in Thy woe and suffering on the cross wast ready
to take a robber, a murderer, a wretch who had transgressed
all God's laws, by the hand and lead him in to Thy glory, come
Thou to us and lead this erring soul over the dark waters of
death and up to the new Jerusalem, the city whose squares
resound to the blessed music of the harp. Let Thy holy angels
hurry to meet her with palms, the sign of everlasting blessedness, the blessedness Thou grantest to all Thy redeemed.
When Thou now stretchest out Thy sickle and cut down this
mountain flower in the early morning hour of its life, then we
know with full assurance that Thou in Thy inscrutable love
hast destined it to be an even worthier and more beautiful
adornment in Thy mansions."

Sigismund got up and took the chalice and the communion
plate out of the wooden box. His hands shook.

Then the dying girl whispered joyfully to herself, "Now I
hear they are singing so beautifully in the mountains—they
are singing around Langkjønna, round Klætten and over
towards Viggela."

He put down the chalice and the plate on the hearth and
gripped her hand again, which was almost lifeless and cold
now.

"Who is singing?"

"The angels are singing. Can you also hear them singing?"

"Yes."

He could hear nothing but he had nevertheless to say yes.
Yes, for the singing was there, he felt convinced of that. A song
from the other side, from Paradise. It was just that he hadn't
the ears to hear it with.

Klætta tried to sit up. Her gaze was fixed in the far distance.
And a smile in which the peace of God was reflected shone in

her large, staring eyes. She lay there with her head on her arm. She lay as if she were lying out on the moors asleep.

Now Sigismund opened the door and beckoned with his hand to those who sat outside. They came in, Ol-Kanelesa, the Lapps, and the peasant, and took off their caps and stood round the fireplace, bending down under the low beams of the roof.

"Bend your knees. Verily, the Lord is here!"

Nobody did so. Silent and with their caps in their hands they stood there, like sharp shadows in the cold clear light which streamed in through the open door. As if to shun the light which came in, the old Lapp woman crept into a dark corner where some reindeer skins were hung up to dry and began to recite something—it sounded like an incantation, and only Nils understood it. He tried to silence her.

"Klætta dead? She dead, Ol-Kanelesa?"

"She has left us now, Nils."

The Lapp fell down on his knees by the hearth. It was as if an old dwarf birch was blown over and collapsed, joints and limbs creaked inside the hairy furskins. He thrust his head down in the ashes. And his fingers dug into the blackened stones like claws. And he began to howl. It sounded like a cry for help.

"Get up," the pastor said severely. "The Lord has been good to your wife."

Nils got up obediently. He sat down on a stone which jutted out from the hearth. His eyes were red and without tears. Perhaps he was weeping inside?

Ol-Kanelesa laid out the dead girl on the twig mat and carefully closed her eyes. They heard the horse shaking itself in the shafts outside.

Then Benjamin Sigismund let the peasant help him on with his fur coat. And he offered Nils his hand.

"She has gone on ahead, into God's glory. Try earnestly to find the same way. You, too, have not many steps to go before you stand at your own grave."

He felt no sympathy for the old man. A marriage founded

on the earthly lusts of a decrepit old man's body was an
abomination. And the pastor turned his back on Nils in disgust.

"What pastor say?" the Lapp asked, and grasped Ol-Kanelesa
by the arm of his coat.

"He says you must behave yourself so you can find the way
Klætta has gone. You know that way is steep and hard to
follow, Nils."

"Klætta in heaven?" Nils asked.

"Yes," Ol-Kanelesa said. "She heard the angels singing."

"Oh, Klætta in heaven." Nils held his head. "Oh, Klætta in
heaven."

And when they had got up onto the sledge, the three of
them, and drove away, they still heard the Lapp repeating:

"Oh, Klætta in heaven."

The cold got gradually less as they approached Bergstaden.
The sky was blue over the church and from the roof of the
smeltery it was dripping; the dripping had its own spring-like
sound—the full moon came up and white quartz and shining
ore glittered and glowed out over the whole of the smelting
area.

At the entrance to the courtyard of Leich's house, the pastor
took out his pocket book and gave the peasant seven rix-
dollars.

"Eh?" the peasant said. "I don't want to sell my horse, I'm
blessed if I do!"

"It is my horse," Sigismund said.

He took the horse out of the shafts, removed the harness,
and threw it onto the empty sledge. And then without further
ado he took the animal and led it by a tuft of hair on its head
through the gate.

The peasant stood and stared after him. What a parson, had
anyone seen the like?

Hour after hour Nils remained
sitting on the hearth with his face hidden behind his crooked

fingers. He looked more like a dog than a human being just now, did old Nils.

The Plough, which Nils had looked up at on so many a winter night, now rolled with its glowing wheels over his turf-covered hut. He didn't look up at it any more. He pondered only one thing: was it true that Klætta was dead?

His mind grew more and more dark with the night. In a delirium he began to sing an old Lapp song that he had learned from his grandfather; his name was Nils, too.

Colonel von Bang's Brigade

Once again a long winter had passed. The inhabitants of Bergstaden had frozen more than in any previous winter. The cold had been a heavy scourge, but hunger was harder. Bread made from ground bark and rye flour had been daily bread for months on the miners' sand-scoured tables. The Lord be praised for that bread, too! In many countries they hadn't a bite to put in their mouths; travellers from afar could tell of that. Now starvation and pestilence, enveloped in the gunsmoke of the cannons, crossed all the frontiers. In the south of the country Norwegian soldiers were fighting for more than their honor; they had covered themselves with glory in the engagement at Trangen. The name of Captain Dreyer was on everybody's lips. Yes, so it was said by those who came driving in coaches from the south.

Early in the morning, long before the sun was up, the first of the vanguard of Colonel von Bang's brigade came marching into Bergstaden.* They were not completely unexpected. Mr.

* Colonel von Bang's brigade was in Røros in 1808. Because of the alliance of Denmark-Norway with France, Norway was at war with Sweden, which was allied with England.

Dopp, who was well informed about everything that had happened and would happen, had, at a tea party at the Misses Bjørnstrup, not been able to keep his knowledge of this to himself. "We can, any morning now, be awakened by trumpets," he said.

"Swedish trumpets?" the elder Miss Bjørnstrup asked, and paled considerably.

"We must not believe anything so dreadful, beautiful lady."

This apparently simple piece of information helped the lady to regain color in both her cheeks; Dopp knew what he was talking about. In his youth he was supposed to have been one of the irresistible young men, but now his eyes were dimmed and his hair grey; time consumes us all. And from the Bjørnstrups' the news didn't take long to reach Kathryn, and after that it ran briskly from house to house.

Oh, the soldiers, they could be as ragged and bearded as they liked, they were nevertheless soldiers, and from time immemorial welcome guests in Bergstaden. Even Swedish soldiers, out-and-out enemies, had been received with far-too-open arms. What hadn't happened that Christmas when the Swedes under General de la Barre marched in?

The evening before Colonel von Bang's brigade arrived, two lieutenants appeared with their orderlies. They rode up to Director Knoph's office and tied up their horses outside the office window. Mr. Knoph came out in person, went hurriedly down the high stone steps and shook both the lieutenants by the hand while they were still in the saddle. Mine secretary Dopp, who saw this from his office window, polished his spectacles and remarked that Mr. Knoph, considering the high office he held, demeaned himself a little too much. A managing director of the Works didn't fall over himself to press the hand of two lieutenants, two dressed-up young whippersnappers. Later he heard from Brinchmann that the two lieutenants had handles to their names. At this, Dopp somewhat changed his opinion of Mr. Knoph's courtesies.

David Finne, who had already been promoted from lance-corporal to corporal, found a place in the director's stables for the lieutenants' horses. The orderlies' horses were let out to graze out by the Gjet tarn.

Posthaste the Works' chiefs were called together in Knoph's private office. The pastor was also called. During the winter he had had to give much assistance to the Works' surgeon, Jens Mathisen, to fight a rather severe epidemic of bilious fever, which had ravaged Bergstaden. The pestilence, which they had also experienced in the black year of 1786, had already early in the winter filled the communal grave in the upper churchyard. Sigismund had also another assignment at the Works. He assisted the keeper of stores, Johannes Aas, at the stores depot. Benjamin Sigismund's star was rising. He was also well versed in the law. Mr. Knoph had consulted him on legal matters quite a few times. Sigismund knew how to keep himself in the limelight.

A list was drawn up of the most well-to-do members of the bourgeoisie who, without particular inconvenience, could have the colonel's officers billeted on them. Mine secretary Dopp, for whom the pastor's penetration into the inner circle was a constant source of irritation, permitted himself quite often to make more or less reasonable remarks about the proposals which his Grace put forward. Whereupon Benjamin Sigismund answered curtly: "Mr. Secretary. You have no right whatsoever to delay the proceedings with your insubordination."

Before Dopp in his excitement had managed to polish his spectacles and open his mouth, the matter had usually been settled as Sigismund wanted. An important contributory factor was that Dopp was not exclusively amongst friends in this gathering. He was not the man to spare an adversary when an occasion arose which gave him the opportunity to hit out. He always hit out with full strength—but, excited as he always was, he was not particularly accurate in his aim. In big and important questions he could show a fearless honesty. In small matters he was a great rogue. His exaggerated ideas about his forebears and, in general, his feeling of belonging to the upper ten often led him astray. This was something he shared with the rest of Bergstaden's gentry. The whole of their lives they had been the bosses, and they had played Providence for so many thousands of people cowed by hard toil and poverty, that they thought they alone dominated existence. All this humble "yes Sir" and "no Sir," all these poor men's caps in thin, embarrassed hands, had nourished their inherited conceit until it became comic. They were blown-up, one-eyed trolls in the land of Lilliput. Was there, then, no one who dared murmer? No! Never! And yet they had a kindness of heart that was worth its weight in gold—but it always had a strange outcome. What didn't Dopp do the other day? A peasant came into his office with his cap on. This angered Dopp to breaking point. He shouted and made angry gestures with his quill pen: "Out! Out! Out in the passage and take your cap off!" Well, the peasant went out and came in again with his cap under his arm. He greeted Dopp, and Dopp greeted him. Just as if they hadn't seen each other for twenty years. Indeed, Dopp even patted him on the shoulder and asked him how many unconfirmed children he had now. "Nine," the peasant said. "Nine?" Dopp said. "Have you really still nine unconfirmed?" And then the peasant, on Dopp's express orders, was led out into the servants' quarters by a confused bookkeeper so that he could eat porridge and milk.

Colonel von Bang's soldiers filled all the streets and the alleys in Bergstaden. Their uniforms and their general appearance did little to distinguish them from the laborers at the Works. They were not far from being barefooted, and their tunics were covered with mud and with ash from campfires.

Their training was to take place at Faste Johannesen's meadow out at Stormoen. The Works' Corps also had a daily parade there now. Corporal Finne had been given the task of training some elderly miners, as so many of the young men had fled to Sweden. They were a collection of slow-moving and stubborn fellows who preferred to sit along by the fences, chewing tobacco and telling each other stories about elves and goblins—stories which were laced with juicy, down-to-earth folk humor from the mines, rather than stand here taking orders from that Finne boy.

None of the troops had any firing practice. Powder and bullets were as precious as gold. Their camp was set up at the Hitter Lake. It was here, too, that General Sparre had camped on the occasion when he burned Bergstaden. Here, on these blue August evenings, campfires were reflected, now as then, in the shining mountain lake. And, by a strange coincidence, three long Swedish swords lay in the earth just where Colonel Bang had his campfire. These were found later by two people who were collecting turf for an outbuilding roof down at Flanderborg.

Fiddlers and girls from the town went up to the camp. And here the hungry and ragged soldiers danced with the miners' daughters until reveille sounded in the early hours of the morning. Here, on the grey matgrass and the rust-brown heather, they forgot their hunger and many of their sorrows. Dancing also took the edge off their terror at what might happen in a few days time when they came into contact with Swedish lead and the hard, sharp edges of Swedish swords.

Down in Bergstaden, too, there was dancing. And much entertaining. And that was no less wrong—now, when hunger and shortage of corn were so widespread in the country.

Colonel von Bang and his two lieutenants, with their glittering uniforms, their swords, and their merry jests, came like rays of the sun into the houses of the gentry. French and German, those very elegant languages, which the good citizens only spoke haltingly, now had to be given an airing. Reading those languages! Heavens above, that was nothing! But when one had been out of practice for so long, it was much more difficult to express oneself in them. The few French books they possessed were now quickly dusted, corners of pages turned down, and casually arranged on sewing tables—and a well-thumbed French novel immediately gave the place a better appearance—after all, even up here in the mountains one knew something.

And then the Colonel held a big reception. He was a soldier. And, perforce, it had to be arranged in a soldierly way. Up by the Hitter Lake a large dance floor was laid out, true enough only of rough planks. With Dopp's permission the planks were quietly borrowed from the Works' depot. Well in advance the brigade's band had been detailed off to practice some lively dance music, but no low-class stuff—remember that! Tunics were washed, rinsed, and hung up on the trees to dry in the sun; and don't forget your rifles and sabres, and get a good shine on them buttons! They had plenty of ash, just the thing for putting a polish on buttons and side arms.

When the gentry arrived everything was in tip-top order. The soldiers were lined up on both sides of the road. The Colonel himself was on horseback. Looking at him, one could easily think of a certain emperor called Napoleon. He made a speech from the saddle to his guests. Whereupon he called on all ranks to give three cheers for King and country.

"What? Bless my soul, he's forgetting the noble board of directors!"

It was Dopp who angrily mumbled this to apprentice engineer Ole-Jensen.

"Oh, they won't die of that, Dopp," Ole-Jensen answered.

Dopp started back, horrified. What sort of rebellious talk was this an apprentice engineer was permitting himself to utter? He had to polish his spectacles.

The reception was a unique occasion. Magnificent! The bigwigs shook each other by the hand. The whole thing was unforgettable. The ladies had tears in their eyes. And the noble board of directors felt themselves remarkably enlivened.

Up on the slag heap, and on the other side of the lake, the sentries walked to and fro with slow, measured steps, to and fro—their dark figures, with long gunbarrels over their shoulders, stood silhouetted against the clear sky and the mowed fields.

David Finne was on guard there as duty corporal.

Benjamin Sigismund came in his extraordinary riding garb with knee-high jackboots. He looked more like an adventurer than a minister of the gospel. He very seldom wore clerical attire now. He had even officiated at a wedding without it. Illegal, of course! Dopp had even remarked that this deliberate and blatant misdemeanor ought to be reported to his Lordship the Bishop—but when consideration was taken of the fact that the pastor had come direct from putting splints on a broken leg up at the smeltery, which one must confess was an act of human kindness, this somewhat delicate business was hushed up. If nothing worse than that could be laid at the door of the Reverend Benjamin Sigismund, one would have to wink at this little irregularity—that was the considered judgement of persons of rank and condition.

Sigismund was in his element today. He talked French to the officers. He made jokes. He laughed.

"But where is Ole Korneliusen?" he said, and looked around in the crowd. "He is a man, Colonel, you would have pleasure in meeting."

"Who is this man? What sort of position does he have, your Reverence?

"He is a blacksmith."

"Blacksmith," the Colonel repeated, and wrinkled his nose so that his long moustaches stood straight down like two wings. "Well! What interest should I have in meeting a black-smith?"

"Tubal-cain was also a blacksmith, Colonel, and now as then no small luster attaches to this blacksmith's name."

Colonel von Bang had never heard of a blacksmith of that name. His knowledge of blacksmiths was on the whole not very comprehensive.

"Good!" he said, and tried to hide his ignorance. "Bring the man here. Ha! Ha! Ha!"

Some zealous souls, who had heard this, began to call for Ol-Kanelesa, but the reply came that he was not here. He had just been seen down in Mørstu Street. He was then wearing a leather apron and clogs.

And a piercing voice called out from the back of the crowd: "He was drunk, too!"

Benjamin Sigismund pretended not to have heard. He said
to Gunhild Finne, who was standing there:

"Is your uncle not here, Gunhild?"

"Uncle hasn't time. He had to work at the smithy, he said."

"Will you not try and get him to come?"

She shook her head. She didn't think it was any good.

That his Reverence, without further ceremony, addressed a
woman of the people caused a certain consternation. The
officers stood there for a while looking her up and down. She
was a good-looker, too. A mountain rose!

Yet, none of them could remember having seen her at any
of the dinner parties. They would have remembered a face
like that.

"Very well," Benjamin Sigismund said. "I will come with
you, Gunhild."

She stood there for a while, uncertain. She felt many eyes
on her.

The Colonel, with a bellowing roar, now summoned a non-
commissioned officer to give him some pressing order.

"Yes, yes." Gunhild tied the black silk ribbons of her bonnet
with white, quivering hands. "We can try. If Uncle listens to
anybody, he'll listen to you."

And without looking either to the right or to the left, they
ran rather than walked down the shortcut over the sandy
ground to the smeltery. They talked and laughed and jumped
over stones and mounds. Benjamin Sigismund was not the man
to be left behind.

Even now nobody dared look up or notice anything. Mrs.
Sigismund was standing there, of course. She stood arm in arm
with the Misses Bjørnstrup. And they were just talking to her
about a new way of embroidering.

But now Mrs. Sigismund was seized with an unpleasant fit
of coughing. Her cough had again been rather trying of late—
up until now it had come and gone. She coughed so much now
that tears came into her eyes. And she had to sit down on a
stone by the lake shore and rest a little. It usually got better
when she sat down. And then there was her heart! Benjamin

thought that it was quite good—but it made her feel afraid. Especially at night.

The elder Miss Bjørnstrup knew something about it too. Mrs. Bjørnstrup—that is, the wife of the Bjørnstrup in Amsterdam—had been plagued with heart trouble for many years, also brought on by coughing. She also used to get it when she cried. And for her, too, the night was the worst time. She was much better now.

The Misses Bjørnstrup exchanged half-concealed glances. And then with pursed lips and black expression they shook their heads behind Kathryn's back. They felt really sorry for her. She had been delivered into hard and ruthless hands.

The elder Miss Bjørnstrup was very good at finding words of comfort: Mrs. Sigismund must not think that there was any danger in the pain around her heart. Once she had become accustomed to the climate, she would see that she would master the condition—but it took time. The same thing happened to their sister, Mrs. pastor Wilden, when she moved from Løiten to Arendal. Then, for many years she was affected by the change of air—but now she too was better.

But Kathryn was difficult to console. She had always been optimistic about her illness—but today everything was so black and hopeless.

"Here comes Sigismund with old Ola!"

Two carpenters in leather aprons and with hammers, who had just completed laying the dance floor, stood nibbling at a plug of tobacco with their front teeth and stared with a wicked glint in the corners of their eyes down towards the slope along the Hitter Lake, which the pastor and Ol-Kanelesa were now crossing.

"Looks like parson has lost his Gunhild, don't it mate?"

"Then we'll have to send out a search-party; if we find her, Sigismund will pay the reward for return of lost property. He'll be real glad to get her back."

The carpenters' jests were both coarse and daring. And many of the bystanders heard them. They turned away so that no one should see them laughing. They were madcaps, these carpenters. Supposing Mrs. Sigismund heard what they were saying?

Kathryn dried her tears quickly. Benjamin mustn't for anything in the world see that she had been crying.

"Nobody can see anything from my eyes, can they?" she whispered to the Misses Bjørnstrup. "No, well, no, no one can see anything now."

"Benjamin!" she called out. "Just think, Benjamin, you have got the sacristan to come."

"Yes, of course. Our wise man allowed himself finally to be persuaded. Heh! Heh!"

And he patted her on the shoulder. And that made Kathryn smile and look up gratefully at her husband.

"This evening we, too, must dance, Kathryn."

"We? Can we dance?"

"Why not? Dancing in the open air is good for the health." He straightened himself up and looked out over the gathering. "We who mourn with the afflicted, shall we not also rejoice with them that rejoice?"

"Yes, but—your parishioners, Benjamin?"

"What, my parishioners? I will tell you what, my dear, I shall teach them to distinguish between the sheep and the goats."

"Perhaps so," she sighed. "If that is what you want."

She was so very grateful. No one was like Benjamin. . . . The dejection he had caused her from time to time was nothing compared with the joy he had so often given her. Now, for the first time, she fully realized how much she owed her husband. Yes, with the years, everything became clearer. A strangely vivid light now illuminated everything. The range of one's vision became extended, one saw more and more. . . . She saw now, as never before, that Benjamin was the one man, the one will.

The Misses Bjørnstrup once again exchanged expressive glances; but they were glances of a considerably milder kind.

Pastor Sigismund was, in spite of all his faults, a charmer. The good ladies couldn't resist it. . . . He had a marvelously winning smile, that man.

"Ole Korneliusen!" Benjamin Sigismund called out. "Will you not sit down and talk a while with Mrs. Sigismund?"

Kathryn shifted her position on the stone—as if moving away from something; it was not always so amusing to have this Ole Korneliusen about continually. And least of all here. Well—it wasn't his fault. All the same she would prefer to be let off now. And then she had the dear Misses Bjørnstrup.

Ol-Kanelesa took his time. He lit his pipe with an ember. He also got the opportunity to whisper to an old smelter, "Give me a shout after a bit, Øven." Yes, Øven would give him a shout.

And then he came up. He greeted Kathryn modestly in the manner of the common people. He inquired as to her health.

"Yes, thank you. Better than expected."

"Aren't you thinking of getting married soon now, Ole Korneliusen?" the elder Miss Bjørnstrup asked.

"I think of it day and night; without a doubt it's the thought of matrimony that gives me my queer look, I might say."

Miss Bjørnstrup blushed; Ol-Kanelesa aimed well, he scored a bullseye this time too. The point was that Miss Bjørnstrup had been hopelessly in love for the past twenty years—it was a heavy burden which she was reluctant to lay down; the gentleman in question was a mining engineer called Olsen, who was now at Kongsberg—but her prospects of getting him had not increased with the years.

Benjamin Sigismund's happy and animated voice was now heard from over by the bonfire, where the officers stood. And then Øven called out, "Ol-Kanelesa!"

Ol-Kanelesa got up; but then strangely enough Mrs. Sigismund gripped him by the arm. He mustn't go. Not yet.

"Yes," Ol-Kanelesa said. "I must see what's doing. He's surely never burning up?"

The Miss Bjørnstrup, the one Ol-Kanelesa had scored off,

couldn't contain herself. She felt a great need to get her own back. And so she asked:

"Have you seen anybody burn up then, Ole?"

"He can burn up, internally. He, like so many others."

Miss Bjørnstrup felt a blast of cold air from that arrow too. She blushed again. She wouldn't answer him.

The band struck up for the dance. The gentry led off. And to the great amusement of the lower orders.

It was not exactly seductive ballroom melodies they were dancing to—it was more like dancing to a thunderstorm.

Sigismund danced with his wife. It was the first time the people had seen a pastor dance. It was rather a painful spectacle. . . . The Colonel danced with Mrs. Dopp; they danced as if for dear life. His riding boots, his spurs and long sabre; no, it was no joke.

Kathryn couldn't dance for long. She also had an unpleasant feeling that it was not quite proper. Yes, wouldn't people think it scandalous? She asked to be allowed to rest. She curtsied and made her thanks. He bowed.

And Kathryn was handed over to the Misses Bjørnstrup. Benjamin Sigismund went over to Ol-Kanelesa and old Øven and sat down there.

"You are enjoying yourselves," he said. "What are you both laughing so heartily about?"

"Our Ol here has been telling the story of when Maasaa-Jørn sold seven billy goats to old nasty von Krogh. Ugh! I could kill myself with laughing."

When they saw that the pastor didn't seem to want to hear about Maasaa-Jørn and his goat deal with von Krogh, they began to talk about other things. Benjamin Sigismund, deep in thought, was making himself a spill out of some birch bark, to light his pipe. He sat for a while sucking at it—and then made himself another spill and generally speaking looked very abstracted.

"Has Gunhild Finne not come back, Ole?"

Øven started. He could scarcely believe his own ears. Was

there, all the same, something in what people had been saying?

"No. She went off home, I think."

"Yes, I see."

Benjamin Sigismund sat there smoking for a long time, without saying a word. The others, too, smoked and said nothing. Ol-Kanelesa sat thinking of how it looked here in his youth, when Ellen was alive. The Hitter Lake was bluer then than now. And everywhere was covered with flowers, red, yellow, and blue ones. And just here, there was a big rowan tree. And under it was a red-painted bench; the illustrious Peder Hjort was supposed to have had it put there as a resting place for the tired of foot—himself included. According to what old people had told him, he used often to walk here with his long, silver-mounted walking stick after the end of the day's work, this noble director with his white wig. Now the rowan tree had been cut down and the bench burnt; nowadays, everything had to be destroyed, that was how the new age was.

"Why did she not come back?"

Benjamin Sigismund stared along the road to the south. She had given him her word that she would come. She had also promised to dance with him—a single dance. And then—she daren't do either. And solely because he was a pastor. Pastor! Pastor! The mirror of the Hitter Lake grew dark when she was not here, and the sounds of the horn and the clarinet became a tortured whining, ear-splittingly out of tune. The stars of the heavens didn't shine. The whole of nature was depressed. He got up quickly. He would go down to the town and look for her. She must know that he waited here, tortured with longing—disturbed in his innermost soul.

Oh, he felt like shouting out so that everybody could hear: "She's mine, stone us! Strike us to death! Tread our names underfoot. Tread them down in shame and disgrace. Well done! We will not submit ourselves to your judgment, because you are the unjust. You self-righteous hypocrites, you yourselves shall wet the steps of heaven with tears and climb them on bloody knees!"

A lieutenant stood in front of him stiffly to attention and at the salute.

"Our Colonel wishes to drink a toast with your Reverence."

"Your servant, Lieutenant. Please convey to Colonel von Bang my most obliged thanks for this honor."

The Colonel handed Benjamin Sigismund with his own hands a beaker filled to the brim, an ancient, dented stoup, embellished with inscriptions which, in resounding phrases, praised the heroic deeds of its many owners; its last and present owner, Colonel von Bang, not least.

Other persons of rank and condition already stood with glass in hand. Some of them had to make do with an earthenware beaker. One of the lieutenants made a sign to the band to stop playing. And then the Colonel bellowed forth a speech in honor of his guests. He thanked them on behalf of the brigade for the hospitable reception they had received here in Bergstaden. Now, at this very moment, the brigade had got its marching orders. They had to proceed without delay into enemy country. For many of the soldiers of the brigade this attack against the enemy would mean that, in a few hours, the sand in their hour-glass would have run out. He asked his Reverence to pray for their souls. And for the Fatherland. And for Norwegian arms, that they might be granted an honorable victory. I give you the toast of His Majesty, the toast of the Fatherland! Three cheers and a royal salvo for them both! But only one shot from the smallest field gun thundered out. Before the sun rose they would perhaps find a better use for their powder than using it to shoot salvos into the air.

After this Benjamin Sigismund spoke. He lifted the ancient, dented silver stoup high in the air.

"Soldiers! Noble sons of Norway! Brave men from the mountains, from the valleys! You shall never die a forgotten death. Your memory shall be wreathed and adorned with the unfading roses of honor and love unto the most far-flung generations. And when you exchange sword blows with the enemy, then know, that across your shoulders you are wearing a chain armor whose every link has been forged with our most fervent wishes for your victory. Let him be dubbed knight who fights with a true and upright mind for this kingdom, for this ancient, Christian kingdom!" And then he said something which aroused consternation: "The day may be near, it has already given warning of its approach in the clear, shining glimpse of day in the east, when you will be called to battle, no longer under the banner which has descended from heaven, but under the ancient banner of the Norwegians, the banner of the raven. Then, even more than at this late night-hour, you must show that you are Norwegians."*

The clinking of beakers after this speech was in no wise overwhelming—many of them were not at all sure if they dared drink to it. What had he meant by it? Was he being disloyal to the king? Of course, Colonel von Bang drank with the pastor; but before they clinked their beakers he mumbled something about soldiering in general. He hoped that in this way the toast got a somewhat more indefinite character.

The reveille sounded.

David and Notler

On the east side of the Hitter Lake, David Finne walked to and fro between the sentries, his bayonet on his shoulder. He saw the bonfires being lit on the other side. The fire, the light, forced the dark and the shadows even deeper into his soul. He saw men and women coming in big groups up over the sandy banks. Some of them, those who came in pairs, used the cattle tracks along by the stone fences. He recognized one or another of them by their

---

* According to legend, the Dannebrog, the national flag of Denmark, fell down from heaven at the battle of Reval in 1219. "The banner of the raven" was the banner of Odin, used by the Vikings.

clothes and the way they walked. He recognized the pastor. Yes, thank you very much! He ought to have sent him a welcome greeting from the mouth of his rifle. That's what he richly deserved. He recognized Gunhild too. What did that bitch want there? David was evil now.

Had he done rightly, he should have tied her hands and feet together and locked her in the house—but as like as not someone would have found her there, wouldn't they? And the sweat came out in great shiny pearls on David Finne's thin, careworn face.

He was being tortured now; he was tortured night and day.

He gripped his rifle with both hands to cock it—for there were the pastor and Gunhild running up over the sandbanks.

"Stop!" he shrieked. "Or it'll go off."

He was too low-spirited and too full of misery to put his resolve into effect—too tortured, both in body and soul. No doubt it would end one fine day with his turning the muzzle of the gun on himself. He was frightened of that, too. He shivered when he thought of it. The grave was dark and deep. Would she weep a tear at his grave? She, the only one. Was he the one who should go to the grave, wasn't it the robber? He, who came and took the poor man's only lamb. He, David, shouldn't have lost his nerve that night last spring, when he lay out in Gjøsviken and had the pastor in his sights and his finger on the trigger—but his finger became numb. He also felt a cold hand, a hand he couldn't see, grip him round the wrist. He shouldn't have bothered about that, but fired—shot down the robber on the spot. No doubt he would have ended on the gallows for it, and with a blue ring round his neck. But rather that than— And David began to rage and curse himself for his cowardice. Oh, you're a poor devil, David. You don't dare anything. You just go around threatening the worst, promising all sorts of things, but nothing ever happens. You're a miserable wretch, you are. If you acted aright, you'd give both the parson and that woman a good hiding. No, he hardly deserved anything better than he'd got.

His rage turned into tears. Perhaps he couldn't hate any-

body. Not even Sigismund; but Sigismund could let Gunhild
be. He sat down on a stone out by the lake, choked with sobs:
"Gunhild! Gunhild! Were you born without a heart?"

Then two trumpets sounded on the other side of the lake.
Was it reveille? Dizzy and confused he jumped up, dried his
face on the arm of his jacket, and listened. Dancing! He just
couldn't understand there was anyone happy enough to be
able to dance—dance—dance.

One of the sentinels shouted out:

"Relief, corporal!"

"Number nine on guard!" David shouted.

Number nine came running and stood to attention.

Number nine was not completely sober.

He started babbling:

"Yes, I'm ready for my watch; but you, David, you'd better
watch your Missus a bit better than you're doing—she's a cow,
she is."

"Pay attention to your guard duty, you Torber."

Had he any guts now, he would have given Torber a clout
on the ear, and not stood here taking lip from him. No, he
was nothing but a weak-kneed twerp. . . . And then he had
to run over to sentry number ten who was also shouting to
be relieved. Here, Notler was reporting for duty. Notler, the
drunkard, still a junior engineer. He was a volunteer. Now
Notler was sixty and, as might be expected, was no soldier
to speak of; but as a sentry Notler could give just as good
service as a man in his prime. He had good eyesight had
Notler, and he heard even better.

Notler was supposed to have been one of the brightest and
most intelligent engineer apprentices. He could see where the
ore went and hear the water coursing far inside the mountain.
He could, long ago, have been the managing director of the
Works if his need for the brandy bottle hadn't been so great.
He was born thirsty. He drank himself tight in the tavern
before he was confirmed. If all the ale and spirits Notler had
poured down his throat had been collected in a pond, one
could easily have drowned the whole Works' militia in it. This

thoroughly pickled gentleman with the quick head was still on the staff of the Works and received a small yearly salary. But all authority had been taken from him. It was only when the managing director, the superintendent, and the foremen were standing down in a shaft, drumming their fingers and not knowing whether there was ore there or not, that Notler was sent for and asked. He was seldom wrong.

Now Notler, by and large, was a decrepit old man. Both his body and his soul had been subjected to long and hard wear and tear. When the high-ups at the Works asked his advice on something or other, he was in the habit of saying, "Let me have a dram first." And then he would point with his miner's staff at his head and add, "The lamp up here is burning rather badly, it needs oil." He got his dram and many refills besides. "Now its getting brighter," he said. "Now I can see the ore. Now I can hear the water."

However bibulous Notler was, his heart was still in the right place. Every fourth Friday, when he had collected his small salary from Dopp, he always popped into some cottage or the other where he knew the family hadn't enough to eat and pushed his money into the housewife's hand.

"Buy some barley," he said. "No beer, no schnapps, that leads to the Devil."

"But what about yourself then, Mr. Notler?" the poor housewife might object. Everybody addressed Notler with respect; he belonged, in spite of everything, to the gentry.

"I don't need any bread," Notler said and laughed. "I'm never hungry, only thirsty. And I'll get enough to drink in the tavern, the lads from the Works will see to that."

Yes, Notler was now a soldier. He carried his sporting rifle with a straight back. He listened. He peered. He knew his duty.

"David," he said. "You need a stiffener tonight." He unbuttoned his tunic and pulled out a bottle. "Take a swig, David. Don't think so much about your wife and less still about that parson."

"Keep quiet, will you, Notler," David said with a catch in

his throat. "Don't say any more or I'll give you one over the head with the bottle. I feel I'm going berserk, that I do, Notler."

"Pull yourself together, David. Drink! Women are treacherous. Yes, that parson— It would be no trouble to knock his brains out and hide him in the sand, just as a certain Moses did with the Egyptian. You, too, could always find your way to the land of Midian afterwards. And there you could choose yourself a new Zipporah. But whatever you do, don't stay here and whine."

"Notler, now you've said enough."

"Drink up, David. Your soul's on fire; swallow this."

Then David seized the bottle, and drank it dry. It seemed to take a weight off his chest.

"Thanks for the drink, Notler."

"Idiot!" Notler said. "You should give up going around eating your heart out over a bit of skirt, something out of the gutter no one else dared marry; you were a brave lad, Finne!"

He patted David on the shoulder. And then Notler went off to his watch. He knew his duty as a soldier.

David Finne walked unsteadily down the path to the shore, put his rifle down beside him and sat again on a stone. Here he regained his calm. He heard the music on the other side, and saw the campfires burning with red flames in the dusk and their reflection in the Hitter Lake. Here, he had sat fishing on so many a fine spring night and dreamt of her. Then everything was light, now everything was dark; he could weep both over the light and the dark. He heard the colonel speaking and caught one or two throaty words. He also heard the pastor speaking—but that was no speech, it was like the howl of a beast of prey.

Reveille? Sure it was reveille! And the people began to go down to Bergstaden again. Up by the elk pits he thought he saw a couple walking arm in arm; it was Gunhild and the pastor. David got hold of his rifle, rested it on a stone, took good aim, and fired.

Merciful God? What had he done? He hurried to reload

his rifle. Now there would be a general alarm and weapon inspection. It was best to have his rifle loaded. With trembling hands he poured powder down the barrel, rolled a bullet in after, and rammed it home with his ramrod.

Two weeks later.

An ore-wagoner was coming over the mountain towards Bergstaden. He was Trond Henningsa, Old Henningsen as he was popularly called, driving his rattletrap; its woodwork was grey and rotten from standing out in all weathers the whole year round, nails were dancing up and down in their holes, and the iron plating which was covered with red-brown rust was nearly falling off. The horse, too, was grey, but the greyest of all was Old Henningsen himself.

Yes, how old was the old crow really? Nobody knew. And certainly not himself. He was supposed to have been born on the day of the Seven Sleepers, but in which year? It was in the church register of course, but that was a book which wasn't very much read. He said himself that he could remember the dragoons, and that they burned the wood used for smelting at the Works, but that was almost a hundred years ago. Anyone who had lived so eternally long had much to remember; but recent years had shrouded much in oblivion. He remembered worst of all what had happened yesterday and today. Now, all he was fit for was to drag himself along beside his old nag and hold the reins. All his days he had been a wagoner at the mines. He believed that he still was, and an able-bodied one at that; but he spent most of his time sitting in the wagoners' room warming his back. His back was always cold. His horse was old, too, toothless and stubborn; it was as much as it could do to drag the old rattletrap after him.

The autumn moon hung over Mount Hommel, red and enormous. And all the mountains were bright and shining. It was no bother finding one's way along the rough track in such splendid moonlight. No one had put a spade or pick into the track they were now going over. It had been made by the

tramping of people and horses. On the smooth rock where
the foot of man had not been able to leave an imprint, horseshoes and wagon wheels had left their mark. This is the way!
the scratches said. Otherwise the packsaddle was still mainly
in use. It was easier, it was more comfortable too, it didn't
rattle as the wagons did. Old people were of the opinion that
it wouldn't be long before the wagon fell into disuse and the
packsaddle returned to its former honor and glory. Old Henningsen was also of that opinion. Wagons were only for transporting rock up from the mines; they were no good for driving
over the mountains and through the valleys.

Two soldiers came trudging after his cart in full equipment
and with sporting rifles on their shoulders. One of them was
Anders Lien, and the other Peder Klausen Haugen.

"What's the name of the man who's lying in the back?" Old
Henningsen asked.

"Notler," Lien answered.

"No, good lord, is it Notler then? Has he been shot by the
enemy?"

The soldiers went on walking for a long time before they
answered. They had told the old man this time and time
again, but after a while he had forgotten it again.

But it seemed to Lien that he had to tell Old Henningsen
once again.

They had been on patrol up in the Ruten mountains, he
said. They hadn't seen any Swedes. Peder Klausen, or Per
Klasa as they called him, had also been on a trip over the
border and had even been to a dance in a village there.

"Did you dance with the enemy too?" Old Henningsen
laughed.

"Of course I danced," Per Klasa replied. "I danced the soles
off my boots, too, but then I bumped into a fellow there and
grabbed his boots, so I managed."

"Yes, you're the boy, you are, Per Klasa," the old man said,
and shook his head. "You're a proper wolf, you are."

Lien continued: As there was no danger from the enemy,
they thought, one night when it was so raw and cold, that it

would be good to make a fire. They kindled a fire in a cleft in the rocks, and then they gave Notler a shout. He didn't answer. They shouted again, then both shouted, but no. Then they went up into the mountains to look. And there they found Notler. He lay there stretched straight out—dead, stone dead.

"Ugh!" the old man exclaimed. "Ugh! Ugh!"

And it made just as deep an impression on him now as when he heard the story for the first time.

And as the horse tugged and pulled for all it was worth to get the boneshaker up the slope from the Hitter Lake, the church bells began to toll. A corporal had ridden on ahead to report Notler's death to Sigismund. He had at once, with Ol-Kanelesa's help, got hold of two smelters to ring Notler home to Bergstaden.

Solemnly and mournfully the three bells rang out in the morning sun. And in the sun-drenched mist, which lay over the rooftops, the bells sounded like strongly vibrating chords.

A couple of magpies that sat sunning themselves in the window on the eastern side of the tower flew out—but they weren't afraid, they merely made a circular trip over the churchyard and then returned and sat down in the same place, flipping their tails. It didn't arouse any surprise that the church bells were ringing so early in the morning. In these troubled times everybody was quite used to them being rung both in and out of season.

On the fourteenth Sunday after Trinity, Hans Christian Notler was buried in the lower churchyard. As a mark of respect he was given the burial place which his birth and rank entitled him to.

At his graveside Ol-Kanelesa sang:

With sorrow and weeping keep bounds . . .

And it is told that people who stood out on Langeggen heard every word clearly and distinctly.

Benjamin Sigismund used as his text, "Stolen waters are sweet, and bread eaten in secret is pleasant." If the deceased had neglected his earthly career by allowing himself to be misled by stolen waters, he had at the same time not neglected to put hidden bread into the thin hand of the hungry. What then had we to praise ourselves for above this man?

"Oh you rich and powerful ones! You with piles of silver and gold in your coffers, rend your garments beside this grave, and confess that you are immeasurably poorer than he who now has been lowered into the womb of the earth. You who harden your hearts and close your hands over the precious corn in this time of war and famine, take good care that this corn be not changed to blood and pestilence between your grasping fingers."

This oration, too, greatly scandalized the gentry. Had they not been standing at the graveside, they would have shouted to him to hold his peace. It went too far! Did he himself know what he was saying?

Gunhild stood right opposite Benjamin Sigismund. She stood amongst the miners' families, though now she could well have stood with the others. She was, after all, Mrs. David Finne now. She was proud of Benjamin Sigismund for his bold words. Now there were many who were hungry. Now small children cried at bedtime for food.

The honorable burial place and Sigismund's flattering funeral oration were not the greatest honors Notler was shown. No, there was an even greater one. For many years to come, when the bird cherry blossomed, the miners' children came with blossom and leaves and laid them on his grave. And then they would stand around it and tell each other about Notler. About the Notler who gave away all his few shillings—but the Notler who sat in the tavern and who staggered home drunk in the small hours to sleep it off, supporting himself on his thin cane which trembled in competition with his thin, quivering legs, that Notler no one remembered any more. He was forgotten.

And in the large childish eyes, there were no tears and no sorrow, only joy

. . . As he was getting ready to go to Notler's funeral, mine secretary Dopp stood and stared for a long time from behind his thick spectacles at his Sunday hat. What? A hole in the top of the crown? He remembered that it had fallen off his head, just as if a hand had knocked it off, as he was going home on the night the brigade left. At the same time he had heard a shot. Was it a hole from a rifle bullet?

The Tower Window

Up in the church tower, with the window from which two magpies flew out every time the church bells rang, was an old bench. It had at one time been in the old church. It had scarcely been a bench for the common man; for that purpose it must, originally, have been far too good. Quite a remarkable picture was carved on its back: some reindeer, a dog, and a mountain Lapp with a pointed cap, on skis; but the name of the woodcarver had been forgotten. Some ecclesiastic or other had no doubt thought that the bench didn't suit the new big stone church. And so the bench had been carried up into the tower, so that the bell ringer could sit and rest on it.

It was here that Gunhild and Benjamin Sigismund met. Four years had passed now; it was the year 1812. A love which had only stolen embraces to keep it alive could hardly last very long; Sigismund knew it, Gunhild suspected it.

To begin with they only met up there in the light of day. It was far too unpleasant, especially for Gunhild, to cross the churchyard after dark. And it made the unpleasantness so much worse, that she went there on an errand which was both sinful and unlawful. When she went up the dry, creaking wooden staircase with beating heart and quivering knees, it seemed to her that someone came creeping after her—got hold of her from behind and tried to pull her down again. "Turn

back, Gunhild!" a voice called to her from between the rafters.
"The road you are treading leads to perdition." Benjamin
Sigismund could also have something of the same feeling. He
was always the first to arrive. Once he fell down on his knees
on the worn staircase, folded his hands and exclaimed: "Lord,
I a poor wretch of the seed of Adam can, like him, no longer
distinguish between right and wrong; I alone am the guilty
one!"

Here by the narrow window they sat well hidden, and at
the same time they could keep a good watch on everybody
who crossed the churchyard. If anybody approached whom
they thought might come up to the bells and into the tower,
they fled into the loft above the nave. In dread, in sweet and
mortal dread, they held on tightly to each other. They sat
silently and listened to each other's pounding heartbeats. For
him, pastor as he was, it must be said that it was an exciting
game—no, it was serious beyond words. He knew well enough
that the citizens of Bergstaden were now talking about their
relationship, but as yet nobody had caught them red-handed.
Kathryn, too, had her suspicions. No one had said anything
to her, but it hung in the air. And in this, Benjamin Sigismund
came face to face with one of his greatest sins: the lies of their
daily life together, in words, in caresses, and in concealment.
This sin was the smoldering flame which consumed the ties
which once had bound him so fast to his Lord and Master;
this sin was the bed strewn with thorns and thistles on which
he lay, and which kept him awake during the long nights. He
had lain on thorns and thistles before: the thorns and thistles
of economic difficulties and worries. No, they were not thorns
and thistles, they were flowers and roses. His living and his
appointment as quartermaster and surgeon at the Works had
turned out to be more profitable sources of income than he
had ever thought possible. Those hideous old usurers and
money-grubbers had long since been paid what he owed them
—together with a stiff letter, calling on them to reflect that this
life had in no wise been given them to heap up piles of gold
and silver, but treasures of more lasting value.

Sigismund and his wife had now moved from the cramped dark room in Leich's house into a large and spacious house just opposite. Now they had what they needed. And Kathryn's health had all the time got better and better. His reputation as a preacher travelled far. His church was packed with worshippers. The esteem with which his fellow clerics held him rose continually. He had already been appointed dean of the southern valleys. The next step up, when would that happen? Yes, the Lord had rewarded him, his bad and unfaithful servant, with a great reward: the accomplishment of his dreams of youth. But had he made just use of this rich reward? No, oh no! And was he today that which one understands by a happy man? No, no! There, where sorrow and anxiety had disappeared at God's command, he himself had brought a new sorrow, a new anxiety into its place. This was to ignore the words of the Scriptures: "But godliness with contentment is great gain" He showed the way to true happiness. He pointed it out to others. He himself walked to the side of it. Therefore his limbs were so weary and his feet so sore.

. . . As time went on their assignations became more and more confined to the late night hours. They both became bolder, as they got used to the churchyard, the graves, and the crosses with their black shadows on the moonlight nights— the dark staircase, the dismal whining of the wind in the crossbeams and through the banisters, the creaking of the stone walls which settled under their own weight, didn't make them start any more. And they had been here so many times that there were memories attached to almost every step in the long and many staircases—memories which through the days and the years lost their dark side, their cold grey clamminess, and increased in beauty and joy.

It was the third Thursday in September. Benjamin Sigismund sat in his big, bright study and impatiently turned the pages of his dissertation.

He took it out today. There was plenty of dust on it now. In recent years he hadn't had time for scholarly work. The dissertation was not good; it seemed a stranger to him—yes,

and to such an extent that he could well imagine it written by
somebody else. His views and his judgements had changed.
Besides, he felt no urge to continue with the work. Nothing
but superficial ideas! The subject he had chosen was also far
too thin and incapable of being shaped into anything of value.
It was mainly to kill time that he took it out now and looked
at it while he waited for the clock to strike seven up in the
tower. Then he would meet Gunhild. He didn't look forward
to this meeting. Every time could be the last. The hour for
parting was moving towards their frail bower of love, bathed
in shadows and sun—soon it would knock on the door with its
iron finger—soon its black cloak would darken the entrance.
And once it had entered it would go to work inexorably: with
brutal hands it would tear their twin soul apart. It would kill
life, the inner growing life. And then one would enter into
an empty and featureless world. Into a world where no one
answers when one asks, where no one comes when one calls
—for there are no others.

In the world he now lived in, two people at any rate had
loved him: his splendid mother and Gunhild. True enough,
Kathryn loved him—but with a different love. Her soul had
never eaten its way into his; they had always been two, never
one.

The clock in the church tower struck six. The heavy strokes
made his heart beat quicker. Yes, what then would the next
hour bring? Today as he came out of the storehouse and went
down the steps, a man was standing there. His face was distorted. He stood there intoxicated and furious, and hissed an
oath up into his face. He lifted his stick to give the man a
blow—but let it fall.

There was a knock at his study door. He didn't start. He
could tell that it was Kathryn. Had she come to wring a new
lie out of him? Every day, without realizing it, she added new
stones to his heavy burden. But even if she had known, would
she then, out of sheer human kindness, have stopped? Hardly!
She would have let out a shriek of terror. And her quiescent

tuberculosis would have again come to life after that shriek. Had the Lord closed all the gates around him and shut him up with his sin?

"There's a man, Benjamin, who asks whether he can see the pastor."

"Show him in, my dear."

He felt almost happy that it was only a visitor. Soon he would not be able to stand upright if more stones were added to his burden. His knees might give way at any moment, and then—

A dirty-looking fellow came in. His eyes gleamed as if he was deranged. He could perhaps be nearing sixty.

Yes, Sigismund had seen many a half-dead wretch during these years, but none like this one. His shoes had no soles, his clothes hung in rags on his emaciated body. It seemed to him, too, that he recognized the man—wasn't he the man who had transported them up here when they came?

"Does the pastor recognize me?"

"Yes, is it not Tøllef?"

"Yes, Tøllef Elgsjøen."

He sat down slowly on a chair. And he remained sitting there a good while staring at the walls, at the weapons hanging there, pistols, rifles, and ancient halberds.

"Oh, that gold nugget, that gold nugget."

"The gold nugget?"

"I mean the gold nugget I dreamt about."

"Have you dreamt about a gold nugget, then?"

Yes, many years ago he had dreamt of a great gold nugget which lay deep in the earth outside the walls of the cottage at home at Elgsjøen. It must have been the best dream anyone on earth had dreamt—but the worst of it was he had believed the dream was true. And then he had begun with this accursed digging to find the gold nugget. This spring, too, he had hit on something shining far down in the earth. Then he had felt so happy that he began to cry with joy. He cried and dug and laughed—it was a joy no one could understand.

"Did you find it, then?"

Had he found any gold nugget? No, things hadn't been arranged that well that he found anything. And in a month, a month today, his little property at Elgsjøen would come under the hammer. And now he had burnt down the cottage and everything in it.

"What! Have you burnt down your cottage?"

Yes, that he had. He had gone there looking at the cottage, there where his father and mother and grandparents had lived and striven. And the more he looked at the cottage and its old furnishings, there was the bed, the table and the cupboard, the worse it seemed to him that strangers should move in and take possession of it. Then there was a voice which said— He even thought it was his mother talking to him from far off in a mist: "Set light to the whole lot, Tøllef! Burn it up! Make a clean sweep of it! Then you won't have to see strange faces behind the window of your cottage." That voice had given him no peace either day or night. And then one night he did it—but when the flames blazed up round the gables, he realized it was wrong and tried to put it out. But the fire couldn't be put out. It was a rather strange fire, too. It had long glowing arms with wicked claws which seized hold of the timbers and tore them off the walls, down into a glowing mass of embers. What did the pastor think, was what he had done a great sin?

Benjamin Sigismund was taken aback. He didn't know what he should answer.

"What do you think yourself?"

"I was crazed when I did it, pastor."

"We must try to believe that it was not a great sin. At the most, a sin of infirmity."

Tøllef continued:

"Now the land will be sold. And then I'll have to leave home. Leaving the place where you've been born is like going to the grave. One's grown together with everything at home— every stone and every tree, one's grown a part of it."

The clock in the tower struck seven.

Sigismund jumped up. He had to go. A weight passed from his mind. He slid into a gentle, melancholy, almost anxious mood.

"Tøllef," he said. "How much do you need?"

"Eh! What do I need?"

Would the pastor help him? No, he must never imagine that. That was a dream, too; a dream! dream!

"Yes, what do you need?"

"A hundred rix-dollars."

"You shall get a loan of a hundred dollars from me."

Benjamin Sigismund was now in an agitated state of mind. He *had* to go. Go to his fate.

Tøllef remained sitting there. He must have heard wrong. That sort of thing was a dream. And he was afraid of all dreams. Especially dreams which one could call more or less good.

"Do you not want to borrow the money, Tøllef?"

"Borrow! Can I really borrow it?"

"Yes, that is just what I am standing here telling you."

"May God bless you!"

Sigismund took out a new shining key from his waistcoat pocket and unlocked his new cupboard. He had got a carpenter to design this cupboard. And Ol-Kanelesa had forged the metal fittings. Yes, it would be a hard nut for robbers and thieves to crack, if they felt like trying. There were quite a few suspicious characters in Bergstaden nowadays. He had recently noticed several down-at-heel, depraved-looking vagrants wandering around in the streets of the town. They had all looked wicked and repulsive.

And then Benjamin Sigismund wrote out an IOU which he asked Tøllef to sign. He owed this man a helping hand.

Tøllef staggered over to the table and made his mark on the paper; it looked like a worn-out heel plate. Otherwise he had no idea what he was signing. He was not even quite sure whether he was alive or not. It might well be that all this was happening in another world. He picked up the money and shook the pastor by the hand. His mouth stayed closed—there were no words to express what he felt.

And then Tøllef the charcoal wagoner went out of the door, down the steps, and up the main street. He carried his cap under his arm and held the hundred rix-dollars in his hand. His lodgings were down at Tuften. There his horse was and thither he should go. But then he went in the opposite direction.

. . . It was a September evening in Bergstaden. The sun flamed in the yellow-gold of the birch groves, two or three trees in a clump, which stood close to the stone walls. The grass pastures lay almost black; the scythe had cut close this year, the grass was so short that it had to be swept up with a broom. The small birch barns, turned grey by wind and weather, stood there with enormous turf roofs hanging out over them; they were almost empty. What was there to keep cows, horses, and draft oxen alive with? Of all the famine years people had heard tell of, this was the worst. The mountains were already white with snow. The mountain lakes were already covered with ice—yes, the mountain Lapps who came down to Bergstaden could tell of that. Nor had the ptarmigan hatched this year, and the reindeer were so thin that they were only skin and bone; but the wolf and wolverine and the lemming multiplied. In the miners' cottages hunger was a daily guest, their minds were in a ferment; were they going to starve to death?

But this September evening was just as beautiful, as if there was no hunger, no destitution, and no pestilence. The sky was blue, the ridges and the mountains threw sharply defined shadows just as in times of plenty, the air glittered, as if it was shining onto great mirrors somewhere, from which the light was thrown down onto the roof tops, down onto the great chimney breasts and onto the sandy grey streets. The north side of the church was white and light; the south side almost black. The boundary between day and night lay in a sharp line across the tarred wooden roof of the west transept.

People and animals moved slowly. Hunger had set its mark on all living things. When people met in the streets and along the way they asked each other the same despairing question: "What are we going to live on this winter, friend? We've no hay and we've no corn. And the war never ends." And they parted without saying goodbye and without looking back.

. . . Benjamin Sigismund was walking up towards the church. Up by the churchyard he overtook Per-Hansa, who was carrying an iron-shod wooden spade on his shoulder. He was leading a horse by the bridle. Per-Hansa greeted him, tugged at the bridle, and intended to pass.

"Where are you going with your horse?" Sigismund asked.

"I'll need to go out onto the marshes with her now."

"What are you going to do there?"

Per-Hansa stood there for a bit. It was as if he couldn't bring himself to talk.

"I must slaughter her and bury her."

"Why must you do that?"

"I haven't got any hay to give her."

And then Per-Hansa tugged at the bridle again, made a sucking sound with his lips, and bashfully swiveled the spade round on his shoulder. This evening was the last evening he and Brownie had together. They had been together a great deal, those two. They had lived through much hard work together, but they had also had many a pleasant hour. Time and time again Per-Hansa stopped. It seemed to him that he couldn't bring himself to put one foot in front of the other any more. When he had come north along the ridge he turned suddenly and walked south towards Bergstaden again. He walked quickly, too. The horse had to trot after him. And the thin, loose horseshoes said, "Click, clack, click, clack."

"We must try, Brownie," he said. "We must go on trying as long as we can." He realized this evening when he was sharpening his knife that he wouldn't bring himself to stick it into Brownie—that it was impossible for him to do it. It seemed to him that he could just as easily stick it into himself. How he was to keep the horse alive during the winter—no, it was no good thinking about that. He wouldn't think about it this evening either. Just now he was only so heartily glad that he had turned back.

Benjamin Sigismund tried to force himself to be calm. He had to try and let reason govern his house—while feeling, the deceiver of reason, would have to put up with waiting outside. He forced himself to make a detour round Miss von Westen Hammond's grave. He supported himself heavily on his stick and stared absentmindedly at the ornate iron cross. Yes, where was his relationship with Gunhild going to end? He tried seriously to weigh things up—but then he discovered that feeling and reason had exchanged abodes.

What was the use of brooding over it—he had brooded over it for a hundred sleepless nights—this thing which became more inexplicable the more one was preoccupied with it. Yes, it was like searching the heart and the reins. Who could do that except one, the Almighty? Had anyone completely explored the realm of love? No one! No one! For thousands of years its territory had been crossed in all directions. Every grove, every tree, every flower had been looked at with large, wondering eyes. Every path, every grain of sand, every stone in it had been watered by the salt tears of the wanderer and colored red with the blood of his bruised feet. And everybody came back with the same report: a country, both real and unreal, a country where joy and sorrow could not be plumbed to the depths—everything there is limitless, everything is nothing. Had anyone read the law of love? The law whose paragraphs are legion. No one! No one! Though it was written down in every language and proclaimed in every tongue, no one could interpret it.

He walked towards the church door. He walked—he, like the rest of miserable mankind, when it concerned the future, with his eyes blindfolded.

Gunhild was already there. She sat fingering something in her pocket.

In her face there was something frozen, hard; her mouth was not as full as before. Her eyes had lost much of their brightness. She had also got thinner. But her head was as erect as ever. There was something defiant, now as always, in the way she could lift it up—especially when she spoke.

This evening she had waited a long time. Contrary to her custom, she had come early. She was cold. There was such a draft through the window in the tower.

Wouldn't Benjamin be here soon? She held her breath and listened. Yes, now he was coming. He ran up the stairs. And something of joy illuminated her mind. Benjamin Sigismund still desired her—but what help was that now? Now there was only one road for her to take: away from Benjamin! Now she must go out into the black night. She recalled one of their meetings two years ago: it was out on Langeggen; Benjamin remained behind. And when she had gone some distance from him, she began to walk backwards, so that she could see him the whole way. And now, when she had to leave him for good, she would walk in the same way. It would be like holding a light in her hand—holding it up to her face.

She jumped up and met him over by the banister. There she remained, holding on tightly. The church tower swayed to and fro—the walls were no longer straight.

"Gunhild," he said. "Why are you so pale?"

"Benjamin! Now I must leave you. Now the time has to come!"

He didn't answer. He took and carried her over to the bench. He grasped her hands and threw himself down on his knees. And he pressed his face against her knees. Words froze on his lips. He wanted to sob but couldn't. The well of tears in him had dried up a long time ago. They would not be filled again. Not in this life. Perhaps in another? In a life where the sun not only scorched, but also brought dew to flowers and to leaves. He had lived another life before this—it was when he was a boy and knelt at his dear mother's feet and held her hands and wept over them. Those beautiful hands—those all-loving hands he would never hold in his again. In Gunhild's hands he had regained hers. These, too, were to be torn from him. Oh Fate, inexorable Fate!

In great anguish he gripped Gunhild's hands tighter.

"No, no, Gunhild, we must not part!"

"Benjamin! I don't belong to your class."

"Has our love ever bothered with class?"

She reflected and then spoke calmly.

"Not before—no—but there may come a time when it will ask for that too."

"Never! Never!"

Was there any other reason? He dreaded asking. Again he had to think of that face he saw today when he came down the steps from the storehouse. The features of the face were distorted, full of hate and wild rage. He had heard an oath—no, it was a shriek full of torment.

"And now you want to leave me, Gunhild?"

"I must. I dare not have his life on my conscience."

"But what if he takes yours?"

"Mine," she said in a hard voice. "My life! Do I live any life now that's worth talking about? Me, a married man's mistress."

Benjamin Sigismund had encountered some of this proud defiance once before; it was from Gunhild's uncle, Ole Korneliusen. It was her ancestor, the proud *Oberberghauptmann*, who was raising his head. What could he offer her? Nothing beyond what it was today. And was that anything for her to exist for?

"Does my love repel and disgust you?" he asked, but did not let go of her hands. "Have you ever regretted it, Gunhild?"

"Have I ever said so?"

"No, no, I never heard you say it, it is just a question—but it is not right of me to ask you about that. No, it is not, my dearest."

"He's already at the edge of the grave."

"Who?"

"David."

"Your husband?"

"Yes, David. The one you married me to. Why didn't you listen to Uncle? *You* could have prevented me from——"

"You must not reproach me for that," he interrupted her. "At that time you were still a stranger to me, weren't you?"

"Stranger or not, what does that matter? A human being in distress, isn't he to be saved just because he's a stranger? I was in distress then, Benjamin."

"Why did you not resist the pressure from your family, Gunhild?"

"Why!" she said bitterly. "The strong usually win over the weak."

"Gunhild, my beautiful dream, let us not quarrel. Tell me! Is David threatening to commit suicide?"

She thrust her hand into her pocket and drew out a leather strap.

He started back; a halter!

"Oh, horrible!" he said, and sat down on the bench beside her. "Is there anything more cruel than love?"

She sat there calmly holding the halter in her hand. Her face looked sallow in the blue of the twilight.

"You dear, sweet girl of the mountains, you will never have hateful thoughts about me, will you?"

"I dare not promise, perhaps I will hate you too."

She turned suddenly towards him and threw her arms around his neck. And she whispered close to his face:

"Yes, because I love you so much that I can hate you. There's no one on earth you can hate so much as someone you've given your soul to."

"Don't you remember what I've said to you once before: your soul belongs to God, Gunhild."

Her arms relaxed and fell down slowly over his chest. She lowered her head—resigned—tired.

"You've woven a thread you didn't spin, Benjamin."

They sat for a long time, silently; Benjamin Sigismund held her close to him. Just as if he was afraid she would tear herself away and flee from him.

Then he asked:

"Do you want me to resign my office here?"

"Even if you do, we still have to go over two corpses and two graves; can we do that?"

"No, no! We, too, have to die!"

"Isn't it better that those two should go over our graves, then?"

"Yes, perhaps. I have no means of knowing what has been ordained from all eternity. He by whose mercy we draw breath does not write in sand; it is in no wise granted to us to be able to wipe out or change that which has been ordained—verily, we are in the hands of fate."

"Preacher!"

She tore herself free, and moved to the far end of the bench.

"What do you mean?"

"It seems to me that you and the preacher speak in turns. Why don't you, right now, at this moment, try to be just an ordinary human being?"

"Gunhild," he said hotly. "I will rend my clothes asunder, my vestments too, would you then be satisfied?"

"Clothes!" she said in a hard voice. "Clothes! Have clothes anything to do with it?" She turned her head away. "Words," she mumbled.

Then the bell ringer came up the stairs to ring the ninth hour; that sweet, gentle reminder the inhabitants of Bergstaden got every evening to betake themselves in the name of God to bed, and receive from His good hands the blessed hours of quiet slumber and rest. Now all lights were to be extinguished, now all shutters were to be closed, the embers raked together on the hearth, and the evening prayer said: "Bless the sweat of our brow and our work, our bread and our food, our hands and the work of the hands. God preserve us from the blood-stained sword and sudden death, from famine, from disaster by fire and water, and all evil."

The little bell was used to ring in slumber and rest for tired and weary limbs. It sings like the children sing when they gather the first yellow flowers along the brook in spring. It never proclaims evil tidings, fire, pestilence, famine, and war, that's the job of the two larger bells. Otherwise, its voice is heard when the bells call to worship on Sundays, and when the great festivals are rung in. When small children are lowered into the earth, the little bell also sings, alone—but then, too, it is more a song of joy than of sorrow. Then it sings in joy over a new small angel of God who is once again on the way to heaven.

The bell ringer was an old man. And he walked with slow, quiet, somewhat irregular steps. He also stopped at each turn of the stairs to draw breath and gather strength for the next flight.

Gunhild and Benjamin Sigismund didn't hear the bell ringer until he was on the landing just below the last flight of steps.

In great haste they fled into the loft above the nave. Here, he enveloped her in his arms. She made no resistance. And the dark, the quiet, and the eeriness in there in the musty, foul air, and her dread, forced her close to him.

Here they stood as usual without saying anything—for no one can know in the dark how close a listening ear or a peering eye is.

When the bell ringer's white-haired head came up to the next level, he stopped and listened. Was it a ghost? Or was there, in spite of everything, something in what people had been talking about, that the pastor and Gunhild Finne had been meeting up here and that they hid in the loft when anyone came? Yes, there were many people now who could tell that they had been standing down in the street late at night and had seen both Sigismund and Gunhild go past the window in the tower when the moon was up. He, the bell ringer, had also seen both this and that which could indicate that there had been people up here at night. Last autumn he had found a whole rix-dollar up here and no one had ever claimed it. That was more than strange. Once he had found a shilling in the upper churchyard. Eight people had come to claim that. Who could afford to lose a dollar in these times? Besides, he noticed that there was never any dust on the old bench here by the wall. Why didn't the dust gather on that, as on everything else? Well, it was no business of his.

He continued up the stairs and over the loose planks to the window. He was always in the habit of standing here a short while, looking out over Bergstaden, before he rang the bell.

This evening he remained standing there longer than usual. He wondered: How many children are there now lying down there in the cottages, crying in their sleep because they have had nothing to eat? He had gone hungry himself; it was a hard bed to lie on. He had lived through the famine year of 1773; the whole of that year they hadn't had any food other than a few black oats from the soldiers, they rolled them out with a stone on the hearth. And that spring the birches on the mountainsides were white, all their bark had been flayed off. It was a wicked sight. An old man called Vil-Iver walked through his wood up by the Hitter Lake one night that spring, weeping bitterly. He hadn't found a single green tree.

"Hunger is a sharp sword," the old bell ringer said solemnly. "Who can save his neck from it?"

And then he went over and pressed the pedal to ring the bell. He rang it longer than usual. The old man had much to remember and much to ponder over. And his foot went on pressing and pressing. And the little bell went on singing out its monotone evening song.

For the couple standing in the darkness of the loft, time became long. It was as if they were in prison, fearful of judgement and of the executioner's bloody axe. Through a little window in the roof of the west transept a grey strip of light flickered across the dust-grey floor. A light without hope and comfort, it spoke only of death and the last light—the last glimmer the eye would see. At any moment they could expect the bell ringer to tear open the door and find them in there. Then—

At long last the bell ringer left. The clapper of the clock clicked twice in preparation for striking.

Benjamin Sigismund then opened the door noiselessly and put his head out and listened. He heard no other sound than the old man's careful footsteps far down on the stairs.

"We must go, too," Gunhild said. "We must, Benjamin."

"For the last time?"

"I am afraid so, Benjamin."

They began to go down the stairs. She first, with her hand firmly on the banister. He a couple of steps behind.

"Gunhild!" he said down by the door of the church. "Don't harden your heart."

Now Gunhild could bear it no longer. She sank down by the door. Ah, once before, she had felt these hard, bumpy floorboards under the knees.

Sigismund wanted to take and lift her up, but she begged him to let her be. She got up on her knees. Her long plaits had come undone and her hair hung loose over her back and shoulders.

"Benjamin, you're a surgeon for the military, can't you give me some poison so I can die?"

She threw herself down again with her face on the floor.

"You're hysterical, Gunhild."

She lay there, sobbing, crying, and praying:

"Help me to weep, walls, steps, doors."

Then he took and lifted her up onto her feet. And he brushed her dress haphazardly with his hand.

"Pull yourself together, now."

"Yes, I'll pull myself together now. Just wait a little and I'll do it, Benjamin."

Her right hand fumbled for the key. And then she leaned her head towards him and whispered:

"You mustn't forget me. If you never see me again, you mustn't forget me."

And then she tore open the door and rushed out into the street. A group of Swedish wagoners in long, white tweed coats went past at that moment. She disappeared amongst them.

Benjamin Sigismund staggered out after her onto the church steps.

"Gunhild!"

His voice failed. He then drew his cloak tightly around him and crept, half-bent, up towards the vestry. Here a black figure detached itself from the whitewashed walls, lifted a

hand and gave him a blow over the neck, so he fell and remained lying there.

"Lecher!"

"Who are you?"

"Uriah!"

The pastor tried to get up, but he got a fresh blow and a
kick from a heel.

About midnight Ol-Kanelesa found him. He lay stretched
out over the grave of Hans Christian Notler.

Night in Bergstaden's Church

It was the Saturday before
All Souls' Sunday.

The clock in the church
tower had struck eight in the
evening.

In David Finne's cottage a tallow candle was burning with
a long, black wick—but the brass scissors which lay on the foot
of the candlestick remained untouched. The idle hands in there
would do nothing about it. No, nothing. David, who sat with
one elbow hanging loosely over the corner of the red-painted
table top with its bright-worn iron rivets, didn't notice that
there was anything wrong with the candle. And his wife, Gunhild, who sat by the window, staring fixedly out into the darkness, made no attempt to get up and attend to it.

David Finne had now been accepted as an engineer apprentice at the Works. His capability and grasp of the work had
accelerated his promotion. But, in spite of that, happiness was
further away from him than ever—resentment, grief and a
thousand miserable hours were his silent, cheerless companions. What good did his white coat and his leather apron
do him? His cap, with the Works' coat of arms on it stamped

in brass, which for the other engineer apprentices was an honor and an adornment, was for him nothing but trumpery; his horns stuck up through the crown.

It was gloomy and cold in here. The spiders' webs under the roof had been allowed to hang there for years undisturbed, the dust on the cupboards and walls was turning yellow with age, the hearth was never whitened now—ever since Gunhild found the old German earthenware beaker broken on the flagstone, she hadn't bothered to make it look nice. The floor received a wash every Saturday evening around the hearth as elsewhere; but the hand that washed was sluggish.

The bed stood there broad and unmade, with sedge grass sticking out at the ends. In it a little girl was sleeping. The grandfather clock with its two heavy iron weights had stopped.

"Well, have you seen anything of your parson this evening, Gunhild?" David asked. And when he got no answer, he continued: "He passed by twice yesterday evening." And when David still didn't get an answer, his tone became coarser: "You'd best take a trip up into the church tower to see if he's sitting there. He can freeze to death waiting for you."

And then David Finne went on sitting there for a long time waiting for the effect of what he had said; but Gunhild was silent. She sat as before with her face turned towards the window, and with one hand on the frame.

"Why won't you have your kid baptized, Gunhild?"

Now she answered, but without turning her head. She half shouted:

"Ellen is baptized!"

"Yes, baptized by yon Ol-Kanelesa. And called after that fine female he used to go with. What about the pastor then, isn't he going to baptize Ellen?"

"Is there so much hurry, then?"

"Hurry! Ha! Ha! Ha! No doubt you're both nervous, both you and the pastor. I'm sorry for you."

"What concern of the pastor's is Ellen?"

Gunhild half got up. She dug her fingers into the palms of her hands, hunched her shoulders and shrieked out:

"David! Your smile is horrible. I can swear Ellen's your child. D'you want me to?"

"That's not necessary. I don't want you to perjure yourself."

She sank down in despair in her chair again, her whole body contracted. It was hopeless. The same thing over and over again, evening after evening. His bitter words, his derision and mad laughter—oh, it was as if a saw with long sharp teeth was cutting small pieces off her body. When he was sober, he was the worst of all. If he was drunk, he driveled, cried, and promised to better his ways. Then she too promised to better her ways. She promised to sweep away the cobwebs and the dust, whiten the hearth, and make the bed. . . . But when the morning came with a hangover, all the poison and bitterness came out of him again. And that paralyzed her hand and put paid to all her resolves. And so the grey spiders' webs under the beams remained hanging there in peace, and the dust lay there undisturbed. Then all her longing and all her thoughts fled out through these doors and in through others. It was into Sigismund they then fled. She hadn't met him for nearly two years. He hadn't forgotten her, had he?

The child awoke and began to whimper. She let it lie there. This evening she hadn't any heart even for her wee child.

"Pick the kid up," David ordered.

She got up, picked it up, and began to feed it; but it continued to cry and Gunhild tried to sing to it—but it was no bright and happy cradle song.

"My, my, you're singing!" David wouldn't give her any peace this evening. He had no peace himself any longer.

"I've sung for you too.

"You've sung for me?"

"In the spring when you lay ill, I sang for you then. I sang a hymn.

"Yes, you sang for me, but your thoughts were elsewhere. It was an unpleasant song, Gunhild. . . . You sang like the Devil himself, you did."

Then her temper got the better of her. She jumped up with the child at her breast. And her voice nearly failed her.

"Is that the thanks I get for sitting up with you night after night.

"Sat up with me? You sat there waiting for me to die."

"Now you've said enough, David!"

"Yes, now I'll soon have said enough."

David took the candle out of the candlestick—then he sat there for a while with it in his hand, staring at the wick which smoked and glowed, his eyes fixed and protruding. And he began again as if he was talking to himself. "Yes, now I've said enough." And after a bit: "Yes, I should have been silent a long time ago, I should."

And then he got up and put the candle in an old rusty iron lantern.

"Goodnight, Gunhild. We're through with each other now." He held out his hand.

She didn't take it. She had heard these words before, too—many times. The first time she heard them she was afraid. In her terror she had lied, and had sworn that she had completely forgotten Benjamin Sigismund.

Now there was no longer any terror in what David said. No icy cold blast. No threat. If he went, he would come back again all right, also this time. There was no end to it. She had been put into a grinding mill which ground and ground with hard stones. And the stones—they were her hate for David and her love for Benjamin Sigismund. There was no joy in her love for Benjamin anymore. No, it was torture! A cry of woe and lamentation! If she happened to see him pass outside in the street, she felt as if she stood naked to the waist in hot embers. Perhaps she could bind her eyes and keep them bound for days and years so as not to see him again. Lies! Lies! Lies, all lies! Oh, she would have to resign herself to standing patiently hour after hour, shivering, her teeth chattering in the cold wind, peering, just to see him cross the street to the tax inspector's office. Every time she heard someone come running in jackboots up the stone steps, she turned hot and cold. If she had been out on the peat bogs or on the grazing grounds, she began to peer down the road as soon as she approached the cottage—were there footprints in the gravel? Last spring when the birch trees began to leaf and the bird cherry to flower, she filled her window with cuttings. If he came past, perhaps he would understand that it was for him she had done it. One evening, when she knew he would come riding from Brækken, she had also strewn some juniper twigs on the street outside the doorstep. The whole of that night she had sat up and watched, so that she could see him high up on horseback as he rode past. And when, towards morning, tired and sleepless, she heard the sound of hooves up the street, she jumped up and locked the door. Later she heard that it was Michael Brinchmann who had come from the Fæmund smeltery. Benjamin Sigismund didn't come until late the next day.

David held out his hand to her once more. He repeated: "Goodnight, Gunhild. You must take my hand now. Even though it's hot as fire. You must—it's the last time."

"Keep quiet with that talk, David."

"Goodnight then, Ellen." He wanted to take the child in to his breast, but she wouldn't let him have her, either. Then he gripped her arm so tightly that he made it feel numb. It was the grip of a man, and it made her start. And she let go the child and let him have her. He held her up to his face and whispered over and over again, "Good night, good night, little angel. It's not your fault that you have come into this wicked world." And with great emotion, he mumbled, "May God protect and keep you all the days of your life." Then he put the child carefully back in its mother's arms. At the same time he inclined his head towards her. As usual she moved away—now too, in disgust. And then he remained standing in the middle of the room as if pondering something. His eye fell on the clock, and he went over to it and drew up the weights, set the pendulum going and moved the hands to nine.

"You must watch the clock," he said. "It will stop when it's done."

"Done, what do you mean by that, David?"

He didn't answer. He only buttoned up his overalls and went out of the door, without looking back.

Gunhild sat there and heard him rummaging around with something out by the outer door. Now it struck her that there was something unusual in the way David had left. He had never before, when he went out, taken hold of Ellen and had been kind to her. And fear gripped her—fear that something would happen tonight.

"David!" she called out. "What are you going to do?"

And with the child in her arms she ran after him, shouting out once again, "David!" Then she turned and went in again. She dared not create a disturbance. Now fear gripped her more and more. It gnawed with greedy teeth at her breast. It tore and tugged and bit its way further and further in. . . . She had never felt such a terrible fear. Would David really do what he so often had said he would: make away with himself? She wrapped little Ellen in a sheepskin blanket, put an apron on, threw a scarf over her head, and rushed out again.

In the streets everything was dark. Only a gleam of yellow light flickered on a window pane here and there from dying embers on the hearths.

She ran down the main street and stared hastily at everybody she met and passed. She stopped and stared for a moment up at the windows where Benjamin Sigismund lived. There were still lights in all the windows. What was it she heard? Benjamin Sigismund was singing. He was singing a hymn. She crept in to the wall and listened:

Alack, 'tis cold in the world,
All its light is but a shadow . . .

"Benjamin! Benjamin!"

What concern was he to her now? At this moment all her thoughts were for David. It was he she was out looking for. Why was she looking for him? Did she know herself?

She crept along the wall of the house and made her way through a side street.

She didn't find David. And so she had to go back. She went to bed fully clothed beside little Ellen. She folded her hands and tried to pray for David. . . . It was like praying for a stranger. And what should she pray for? That he might come home again so that they could continue their life of discord? And heap sin upon sin? Could she pray for that? No! She lay there, apathetic and helpless, staring at the grey glimmer of light on the panes.

In the quietness, and with the ticking of the clock, calm finally descended on her. And far away she heard a voice singing:

Alack, 'tis cold in the world,
All its light is but a shadow . . .

Hounded, persecuted, driven to madness and terror, terror of life, David Finne ran up across the churchyard, a leather halter in his hand. Now darkness enveloped him. It rolled forth from under the sky and swept in waves up from the earth.

The cherub revolved with a hoarse shriek up on the tower; its golden trumpet glinted like lightning in the light from the stars. A mountain owl dived down from a window on the east side and landed with a screech on the lopsided cross of a grave. There it began to hoot. To David's ears its hollow, eery voice sounded like the words, "Beware of an unhallowed death, David! The grave is deep and dark, remember that, David!"

He groped down between the graves for a stone to throw at the owl.

Then the owl began to laugh: "You're a fool, David. Everybody laughs at you. Gunhild laughs when you cry, Sigismund laughs when you're tortured, Ol-Kanelesa laughs too!"

He found a stone and threw it into the darkness.

"Quiet, you mountain wolf!"

Was it flying right over his head? He felt the cold air from the tips of its wings. A bad omen. Its shriek meant death, he knew that. But he couldn't turn back. He had no power over himself any more—it was as if he had to do what he had not willed. It was as if someone was running after him, whipping him—Don't stop now! Keep going! Keep going! Now everything was one thick blackness. He could just glimpse the white church wall.

Everything creaked and groaned around him. Dead leaves rustled over by the graves of the bigwigs. Earth and dust whirled up. The entrance to a nearby house blew to and fro. To and fro. Just as if someone was going in and out, in and out. The noise as of a whole platoon, riding, driving, and marching.

He felt up and down the church door with his hand, found the key and turned it. That shrieked, too. Tonight everything had got tongue and voice, both the dead and the living. But was there a key in the inner door of the church? Beret-Lusia Bentz, who cleaned the church every Saturday, was in the habit of leaving it there. Yes, it was there. He turned that, too. Out of habit he took off his cap and put it under his arm. A gleam of light from the iron lantern fell on the pews and the rows of chairs.

What was it he saw? All the seats were full of people.

He retreated backwards to the door again and stood there, staring into the vast, dark church.

No, the seats were empty

He mustered up fresh courage. And he went quickly up through the nave. His big, heavy hunting boots clattered on the hard floor. Was he really afraid of dying? He who for many years had wished for death—death which would be his friend and embrace him and kiss him.

Death's kiss was cold. No, the kiss of death was peaceful. He longed for that peace now. And then for a good grave.

Now he would make his rope fast up on the pulpit. Sigismund could have the pleasure of finding him here. Tomorrow, when he came from the vestry—when he came on his way up to the altar, then a sight would meet him and Ol-Kanelesa, the last thing they had imagined. Benjamin Sigismund would, at last, stand face to face with his crime. Then his days as pastor and dean would be numbered. Disgrace and shame would be

branded on that pious man's brow. Judas! The soldiers in the
Works' militia, the miners, and every man of honor wouldn't
hesitate a moment to chase him out of the church with their
sticks.

And Gunhild, the whore! She, too, would at last eat her
bread with salt tears on it.

He softened a little at the thought of her and the child,
little Ellen. In truth he didn't wish Gunhild any harm. She, too,
had been a victim. If that trash of a parson hadn't been after
her continually, things wouldn't have turned out so badly with
her as they had done. And little Ellen. At the thought of her
David Finne burst into tears.

He lifted up his hands with the halter and called out:

"I'll bring so much shame on you, Sigismund, that you'll become the stone everybody spits on."

Sobbing, he put down the lantern on the altar ring. Now he
was again standing on the same spot he had stood on when
Gunhild was with him. He would kneel here once again. Once
again he would bend his knee in front of the altar and try to
imagine that Gunhild was beside him.

He closed his eyes. He saw himself in uniform. He saw Gunhild with her bouquet in her hand—but then that horrible figure of a pastor came forward with his prayer book in his hand.

David jumped up and brandished his clenched fist over the
altar rail.

"Go!" he shrieked. "Go! Go! Seducer! Go to hell!"

Not even now, when he was on the brink of the grave, was
he to be spared seeing that beastly parsonical face.

What was that? He jumped up. He turned around and
stared about him.

From the galleries, from the pews there was also a shriek:
"Go! Go!" Was it he who was being called? Who was it who
was calling?

Up in the tower the little bell began to ring. Who was ringing so late at night? Perhaps he was listening to his own
funeral bell. No, bells weren't rung for suicides.

"Ding, dong, ding! Ding, dong, ding!"

No, it was not the little bell; it was up in heaven they were
ringing now—

He got up, ready to jump over the altar rail. Now he had
only to tie a knot in the leather halter. And then—the light
flared up. Who was standing there? Lorenz Lossius! And there
stood Hans Aasen. And there came Jocum Jürgens and his wife
Elisabeth walking round the altar. They who had died over
200 years ago, they stood here as in life and stared at him.
More came, people in strange attire, people he had never seen.
There stood a clergyman in all his vestments; was it Jens
Tausan?

He took a couple of steps backwards down the church; they
came striding up after him with noiseless steps, serious and
silent. And then the rusty iron lantern clattered down on the
floor. And the darkness closed around him. He continued to
walk backwards down through the church.

Wanderers in the Desert

Sunday afternoon. The night
frost, the silver-grey night
frost, had almost melted up on
the pastures which lay on the
sunny side. On the slopes which lay away from the sun, and in
the shadowy marshland between the high ridges, the rime lay
day and night; there was too little sun. The roads, too, were
frozen hard. The noise of wagon wheels, the sound of hooves,
could be heard from far off now.

Up on one of the pastures above the Hitter Lake a man in
yellow, tawed elkskin trousers and a blue jacket with tails was
ambling around. In his left hand he had a long miner's stick
with an iron spike.

Here he found a stone and threw it outside the fence—there

he found a rotten twig which he picked up and placed quietly on the fence.

His face was bright. His hair, which had been golden yellow, was now as grey as the night frost. It hung down over his shoulders and back.

He was Jon Haraldsen Bentz and was a furnace minder at the smeltery. The days of his years hadn't made any impression on this man, although he was now in his seventies. If one disregarded his grey hair, he looked like a young man.

This piece of pasture here was Jon's pride; it was the great work of his life. And it had been created out of the surplus strength of his body and the exuberance of his mind.

Some thirty years ago it was only a stony matgrass moor here. Then he bought it from the Old German, as they called him, for five rix-dollars. Now it produced winter fodder in plenty for four cows.

It was in the long, light spring and summer nights that this pasture had been cleared. When work for the day at the smeltery was finished, Jon got out his crowbar and rake and came up here to break stones and clear the land. People said he was a fool and an idiot to work on such a stony wilderness —but Jon had only laughed at them. Every spring there was a new little turnip patch and a few more yards of fence around it. Every foot of land here had received a good dose of sweat from him; but that was nothing to talk about—at the furnace down at the smeltery he also had had to leave a good dose of sweat behind every day, and was there anybody who said anything about that? No, that was how things were. In the winter he had scraped together dung from the wagoners' horses out on the ice, and had transported it on a sledge up to the clearing. Then, too, people said he was a fool and an idiot—there was no sense in ruining his health on all that horse muck.

Now there was no one who said he was an idiot and a fool— no, now everybody said that he had done a real man's job. The pasture had been called after him Jo-Harald's Piece. And Jon Haraldsen Bentz strutted, like a lord, stick in hand, down to his hay barn. To his eyes this birch-built barn down there looked like a castle in the September sun. He scented the smell of new hay from it long before he got there. Today, too, he had to peep in through the barn door and look at the hay. Oh, how golden green and full of yarrow and flowers it was! He also had to take a wisp and smell it; what incense, what myrrh! What? Had somebody been sleeping in the barn during the night? There was a deep groove. Yes, some poor homeless creature had, no doubt, been obliged to take refuge here, so as not to freeze to death. There was nothing wrong about that. Other haybarns were locked now, but he had never locked his. It had never happened that anyone had stolen his hay. Here in this world there were not so many thieves as people made out. If the worst happened and someone took an armful of hay and gave it to a starving animal, there was nothing much wrong with that either. In this time of famine one should only rejoice over every starving mouth that God fed, be they humankind or dumb creatures.

Outside the barn door there was a big stone, a big, grey flagstone; that had been Jon Haraldsen's dining table and resting place many a time. Now he would sit down there and have a smoke. The sun shone so beautifully. He shredded his tobacco into his pipe and lit up. Life was wonderful! He felt filled with a great and deep gratitude to God, who had given him such good health that he had been able to clear this land. He took off his cap, put it down beside him on the stone, folded his hands and thanked God with a sincere heart for every stone he had moved, for every blade of grass which had grown, and for every time he had sat here eating his food and resting.

And then his pipe was smoked. And then the sun went down. Then that happy and satisfied man got up and ambled down the path to Bergstaden. He little suspected what he today would be witness to of this world's sorrow and misery.

Jon Haraldsen walked along looking at all the stones along the side of the road—they were so white and clean, he knew them all, that he did. And to each one of them a little happy memory was attached. Yes, it was as if they all had an inscription on them with the year. "Today was a pleasant day, then the sun shone," was written on a stone. On another was written, "Today it rained wondrous well. And the grass grew so one could almost see it, what a day!" And on a third stone was written, "This evening little Harald went with you past here." He knew every small birch tree. He remembered every single spring, when the tiny branches budded and leaved; that was a miracle too. Yes, a new miracle it was every time it happened. A new, great miracle of God. God hadn't forgotten any of them. Some shepherd lads had stripped the bark off that birch tree there some three years ago. Then he had taken and bandaged it with a rag and stuck some earth around it; now it almost looked as if it would survive. And in the spring he would get some manure and spread it around the roots, that he would; it would be granted a long life yet, that birch, too. A wee birch like that was surely just as fond of life as we humans were.

"But it's not your birch, Jo! It's Lang-Per's birch!"

"Isn't that one and the same thing, then?"

And the man with sunlight in his soul walked on. He saw the new snow on Mount Hommel and knew that it was winter which was on its way. The winter with dark and cold and snowdrifts. The winter which laid a covering of ice many feet thick on all the lakes and froze the earth a couple of feet deep. He didn't dread it. After the winter the spring would come. Then, with God's help, he would clear another quarter of an acre of virgin soil up at his pasture; he'd make a champion turnip patch out of it! Besides, winter wasn't all bad either. Even the worst weather could liven one up; there was nothing like a good north wind to make the body feel lithe and gay. And then he had his ptarmigan snares to look after up at Volen; that was real nice work in the evening when the moon was up. When they got past Candlemas, the days were already so long that there was light when he went home from the smeltery. Then they moved on gradually to near the end of February when they could try some fishing out on the ice.

Then the rooks came back, the first birds of spring; then the magpie began to build its nest in the church tower. And then the first bare patches emerged from the snow up on the fields at Aas, so the young people could play their games again on Sunday evenings. He himself had done so several Sunday evenings last spring. Yes, he thought of doing the same thing next spring too. Was there, then, anything to dread about the winter? It made him laugh. And if one whined and carried on, and however much one dreaded it, what did it help? One was inclined to think that the winter wouldn't go any quicker that way either. And now he laughed aloud.

Down by the smeltery Jon Haraldsen turned off to take a short cut behind the cow barn belonging to the Ophus people.

Just where he turned, a whole lot of wagoners and miners were standing in a group talking loudly and excitedly.

"Well, are you going home to bed and starve to death, Jo?" one of them called out to him.

"Me, starve to death?" Jo repeated. "Why should I starve to death now, more than before?"

"You'll see when you go to the storehouse and buy grain with the new money," the answer came. "You won't get any more for a dollar now than you can carry home in your cap."

"Ain't the new money as good as the old, then?"

No, it was just that, it wasn't. The new money was something the big shots had thought up, just to cheat the people who did the transportation and the work up at the Works. People were getting nothing for it; it was no more worth anything than— The man who said it blew mockingly on the palm of his hand. There were even some of them who remembered the Works' banknotes; that was nothing but barefaced forgery. And it was the same now, they had proof enough of that; so don't tell us, Jo!

He realized it was no good arguing the toss with them about it. And so he left them. He went at an angle out from the wall of Ophus's cow barn and turned round the corner. Here he stopped suddenly and staggered backwards over the edge of the slope. It was just as if somebody had stood there waiting and had given him a blow on the chest. He dropped his stick. He flailed the air with his arms. And then he turned right about and ran back the way he had come.

"You must come here!" he shouted, and waved his arms at the peasants who still stood down there discussing the miserable new money. "There's someone here its all up with!"

"Eh? what are you saying? It's all up with somebody?"

"Get a move on!" Jo shouted. His face was as white as a sheet.

"Is there somebody who's done himself in, then?"

"Yes, Lord preserve us!"

They raced up, slipping on the stones, stumbling and gripping the ground with their hands.

"It's David!" a youngster shouted.

"Who?"

"David Finne, the apprentice engineer!"

David Finne was hanging there on a ladder; his feet almost reached the ground.

Jon Haraldsen took out his sheath knife.

"What are you doing?" someone began. "Don't you know it's an offence to cut down someone who's hung himself?"

"Yes, I'll take that punishment," Jon Haraldsen answered. "Just hold him," he ordered.

And then he cut the leather halter. And they took and laid him carefully on the ground. He was cold; it must have happened early in the day.

They stood around the dead man for a long time; they said nothing, just stood there and stared. And Jon Haraldsen forgot to put his knife in its sheath. He was the first to pull himself together.

"Wait here for a bit, I must let Gunhild know about this."

After a little while he came back and said that neither Gunhild nor little Ellen were at home, but the door was open. He still had his knife in his hand.

Now they picked David up and carried him home between them. But when they got to the cottage and stood there man to man and shoulder to shoulder and saw how neglected it was in there, anger began to awake in them all.

"All this is Sigismund's fault," one of the wagoners said angrily. "Now we'll go down to the manse and break his windows. We'll let him know we know who's driven David to his death.

"Yes! Yes!"

They intended to go round by the ore dump and get some stones, there wouldn't be a whole pane of glass left in the manse

"Afterwards we'll drag the scum out and knock the daylight out of him," someone suggested.

And they were ready to rush off.

Then Jon Haraldsen called out:

"Take care now, lads! The pastor's wife is lying at death's door too. And I'll tell you something else: let him who's without sin cast the first stone."

They were taken aback. He went on:

"And remember another thing, our David won't be brought back to life, even though you break all the windows in the world."

Yes, Jon Haraldsen was a man they had respect for, in spite of everything. Perhaps he was right in what he said. Tempers subsided. And they left, one by one. In any case it was so cheerless here that they were glad to get out. And finally Jon Haraldsen was alone in the cottage. He hadn't thought of leaving, not yet. He began to straighten out David's feet and tried to fold his hands together over his chest. He got some water in a wooden ladle, washed his face, closed his eyes, and tidied his hair. What a fine fellow he was, real handsome! It was just strange that Gunhild hadn't cared for him any more than she did—but now that was a thing Jon Haraldsen didn't understand much about. He found a dusty hymnal up on the shelf and then he sat down on a chair beside the corpse. He wetted his finger tips and laboriously turned the pages. Time and again he lifted the book up towards the light from the window—but the letters ran into each other; it was quite impossible to distinguish a single word. He rubbed his eyes and tried again—but no.

Then he closed the hymnal slowly and sat there with it in his hands, and tried to think coolly and calmly about this tragic happening. Yes, what had now become of a poor misguided soul like David's? Had he now found the peace and rest he had sighed so earnestly for in all these years? Would God have mercy on one who had not found enough peace and quiet here on earth that he could wait for his appointed hour and time? Jon Haraldsen turned over and over in his mind what he remembered from his Sunday school teaching, and what Pontoppidan's catechism said about ending one's life? by one's own hand: "Have we the right to take our own life? No, God alone who has given us life has the right to take it back." But there was also another question from Pontoppidan which came into his mind now: "Can we come to destroy our neighbor's soul?" "Yes, when by bad example we seduce him and cause him to sin and thus contribute to his soul's damnation. Woe to that man by whom the offence cometh." When he thought of this it seemed to him as if there was some hope for David too. . . . No, it was no use an ignorant man speculating on that. Besides, the Lord himself had said: "Judge not that ye be not judged." In the midst of his deep ponderings he went and picked a piece of straw from David's clothes. Had David slept out in some haybarn or other last night? Surely it was not David who had slept in the barn up at his pasture by the Hitter Lake? He saw now that David's clothes were full of straws. Jon Haraldsen got up and picked them off one by one—quietly, as if he was afraid of waking David. No agony, nothing unblessed could be seen in David's face—but the stamp of death was there. And then Jon Haraldsen took the hymnal and placed it under his chin.

Once again Jo sat down to wait for Gunhild. He had to be here when she came home—if possible to try and soften the blow a little when she saw her husband. Gunhild was hardly wicked. He had known her since she was a little girl. She lost her father early; may God protect all the small orphans.

In these days of war, pestilence, and famine, many a child would be without a father.

And the hours passed. And the dusk came. It got so cold that Jon Haraldsen shivered and froze as he sat there. He straightened his back and buttoned up all the buttons in his blue tail-jacket. Gunhild must come soon, mustn't she? Yes, now she would have to carry a wee, fatherless creature on her arm through the door. It was good that the sight little Ellen would meet this evening would be forgotten after her first sleep.

Hm! how cold it was! He who otherwise never felt cold was so cold now that his teeth chattered. In truth he must light a little fire on the hearth—but there was not so much as a sliver of wood in the house. He searched high and low. All he could find was a bundle of sulphur matches up on a shelf over the door. It seemed to him that he could hardly burn them. Otherwise, it looked as if they were well off. The house was full of shoes and outdoor clothes; only food and fuel were lacking.

That was Gunhild, wasn't it? He heard footsteps out on the steps. What on earth was he to say to her? He tried to find the right word of comfort—out of the many he had sat there and thought up to have ready; but it was as if all his words had fled.

He couldn't think of one.

Now her hand was on the latch—now she was coming in, now—Jo wished himself many miles away.

He drew a sigh of relief: it was Ol-Kanelesa who came.

Ol-Kanelesa was bare-headed, without a coat and without a stick in his hand.

"I heard you were sitting here waiting for Gunhild. She's down at Elisabeth Cottage."

"How's she taking it?"

"We can't get a word out of her."

Jo didn't ask any more questions. They stood there for a long time, side by side, looking at David.

"Yes, our David was a wanderer in the desert, who went

round all the oases he saw; but he never went into one. He heard the whispering of the palm trees and the trickling of the water. Like Moses he had to be satisfied with just looking out over Canaan."

To that Jon Haraldsen only answered:

"Perhaps there's something in what you say, Ol-Kanelesa."

And then there was a question Jon Haraldsen wanted to have an answer to. Could anyone say that anybody was to blame for David Finne's having done away with himself?

Ol-Kanelesa, that well-nigh learned blacksmith, that night owl! didn't dare answer that any more than Jon Haraldsen, that naive and ignorant miner.

Then they went quietly on tiptoe after each other out through the door; Ol-Kanelesa locked it and put the key in his waistcoat pocket.

The one went with slow steps and bent head up the street, the other with even slower steps and an even more bent head down towards the churchyard. Neither of them bid farewell.

"Mountains, Hide Me, Envelop Me"

Was winter drawing near? The days were no longer warm with quivering sunshine; no, they were all overcast and grey—they became one with the long nights. He did not long for the next dawn when he stretched his limbs out in the evenings to rest after the bell ringer had rung nine hours. He did not jump up at the first rays of sun through the windows, elated, strong, and bursting with zest for work. He did not sit in the late evening hours listening for footsteps outside the house. His heart did not flare like a flame in his breast when a hand quietly touched the door latch. He did not rush eagerly and happily to meet Ol-Kanelesa when he

caught sight of him up on the street, in the hope that he had
a greeting from her. . . . Oh no, when all the days had become
grey and all the hours empty and all the nights sleepless,
nothing at all happened which could bring him a new and
fresh joy any more.

He knew that gossip was now carrying his name soiled and
besmirched in and out of every door. He knew that in the
minds of all the people he went around as David Finne's murderer. He knew that all the eyes that stared at him hated and
detested him. But it wasn't at all that which made his days
grey and his hours empty. He would have stood proud and
upright in spite of all this—had it not been that the axe of fate
with a terrible blow had cut his life off at its roots, and in
so doing had deprived him of access to the sources of renewal.
Thus the tree which bore the name of Benjamin Sigismund
withered slowly and surely. The blow had not descended on
the day David Finne had committed suicide, but in the late
night hour when Gunhild ran from him at the church door.

No, Benjamin Sigismund was no longer the fine, ardent man
with a summer breeze in his mind. He was an unshaven and
untidy man with heavy dragging gait and threadbare clothes.
Now, when he had gold and silver to buy things with, he
bought nothing. When he had nothing to spend, then he
bought. What was the good of purple and scarlet? He was
threadbare in more than his clothes. . . . As before he performed his everyday work with great industry. Nevertheless,
his big ledgers and folios were full of mistakes of spelling and
arithmetic. And he thundered out his long and carefully prepared sermons to almost empty pews. Only that part of his
congregation who came to church out of habit, and whose
worship had thus become a slothful routine, came and sat
there and listened to him with deaf ears—but those who hungered and thirsted for the Word, the water of life, they stayed
away. Also in the pews of the gentry, on which heavy dues
had been paid, there were now many empty places to be seen
on Sundays.

Who was there now for them to show off their finery to,

their power and their riches? To each other? Since the new
managing director of the mine, Daldorp, came and had put
new life into the social life of Bergstaden, they had more
than enough opportunity to show off in their own circle. Another thing was, no doubt, that they were no longer so certain of their uninhibited and choleric pastor; Sigismund had
taken to mentioning names from the pulpit. And worse than
that, he didn't hesitate to condemn both high and low in the
same breath. Many of them, too, had the suspicion that it
was Ol-Kanelesa, the sacristan blacksmith, that malicious outcast, who had stuck his loose mouth a little too often and a
little too close to the pastor's ravenous ear. Now he was about
the only person Sigismund associated with.

. . . The 13th of January 1816. Benjamin Sigismund was
standing at his writing desk, cutting some quill pens.

Now and then he raised his head and stared out into the
street; but today he was not looking for anything definite. He
didn't see the people who walked, rode, and drove past his
windows.

Yes, today he had received a letter from a Swedish cleric,
Gustaf Tornhjælm. That highly-regarded prelate and court-
preacher had written that his Royal Highness, Crown Prince
Carl Johan,* intended, according to the most reliable sources,
most graciously to bestow on him, Benjamin Sigismund, the
great distinction and honor of making him a Knight of the
Order of the North Star—in recognition of the warmhearted
and excellent speech with which he had welcomed his Royal
Highness to Bergstaden and its mines. The Reverend Mr.
Tornhjælm added his own congratulations. Yes, it rejoiced him
beyond measure that a Norwegian brother of the cloth would,
in a very short time, be reckoned amongst the knights of the
Order; Tornhjælm was himself a Knight of the Order of the
North Star.

* Carl Johan, formerly the French Marshal Jean Baptiste Bernadotte,
became Crown Prince of Sweden in August 1810. After the union between Norway and Sweden (November 4, 1814) he also became Crown
Prince of Norway.

Benjamin Sigismund had put down the letter on his writing
desk as something which didn't concern him. The news had
come too late to rejoice or strengthen him. It ought to have
come before—before the evil years came, before the grey days
and the frost came. The bright radiation which emanated so
naturally from all joys could no longer penetrate through the
shadows and reach him.

No, he no longer yearned for the light which radiates from
honor and joy, but for the light which transfigures. He yearned
for one thing only: to see his life transfigured in the clear
light of God. The word of the Holy Scriptures which once had
been a lantern at his feet, yea, more than that, a glorious sun
on the road, had become more and more obscured. Had his
misdeeds laid scales on his eyes? Had his sin darkened his
understanding? In his worst moments darkness came rushing
in over him from all the four corners of the world; cold and
penetrating it was, penetrating to the marrow of his bones.
And with the darkness came questions in a numberless host:
Why? Why? Why? "The mountains, the rivers, the forests,
not even the stars of the heavens can answer you that, Benjamin Sigismund," a voice said. "You, who have locked yourself out from the light and into the darkness, are not worthy
of any answer."

His knife stopped at the outmost tip of the quill pen. His
gaze became fixed. Had his soul already been put in chains,
to be kept there until Judgment Day? He must tear it free.
He would and must settle his account with God before the
fiery clouds descended on the shining scales—the scales which
the stern and righteous judge held in his hand. Perhaps there
was still time left? The deep blackness of the grave had not
yet set a boundary between time and eternity. No, not yet.

The door opened quietly and the elder Miss Bjørnstrup
stuck her head in.

"Your wife wishes to speak to you, Mr. Sigismund."

He nodded.

And Miss Bjørnstrup closed the door silently.

Benjamin Sigismund took his head in both his hands. Once

again he must away to the loom, to continue weaving the winding-sheet in which Kathryn was to be swathed and buried. Every thread of this sheet was woven with lies; a winding-sheet, black in color! Supposing today he cut the whole tissue down, tore it to shreds, and burnt it up before her very eyes?

In the light of that flame she would read the truth; that he, her husband, had loved another. She would fall back dead at the sight of this fiery writing on the wall. She would close her eyes in an eternal and unblessed sleep.

"Lord, show me now the way. In many nights of vigil I have listened for Thy voice, but my ear has heard it not."

"Thou fool! Why didst thou not ask in the first watch of the night? Know thou that ye both are come to the fourth. She to the eleventh hour."

"Lord and Master, we perish."

No answer. Nothing beyond the words of the Scriptures.

What could it help that the words of the Scriptures were opened to him now? He, a blind man. The Word was now changed to stone and the drinking vessel was broken against it. He was condemned to cry into the hollow of his hands and slake his thirst with his own salt tears.

He went into her. The distance from his study to Kathryn's room was seven steps; for him today it had become seven leagues. He staggered like an old man through the door. His hand groped powerless and quivering for the back of the chair. And then he made a sign to Miss Bjørnstrup that he wished to be alone with Kathryn. He sat down and grasped his sick wife's thin hand.

"Thank you, Benjamin. You'll sit here for a long time now, won't you?"

"Yes."

"You know, it was wonderful."

"What was it that was wonderful?"

"When you stood in your vestments at the altar. . . . No, I must have imagined it all. I thought you had become a bishop. I heard the organ. It was in a big church I had never seen, perhaps it was a cathedral? And then I thought that I was quite well again, well as during the first years of our marriage. Don't you think it was a premonition?"

"Of what?"

"That before long you will be appointed bishop? And that it will be vouchsafed me to live and be restored to health? What is it, Husband, you are so pale?"

"Am I?"

"Then you don't think it was a good omen? Well, well, things will be as they will. All the same, I'm so happy.

"Are you?"

"Yes, when I am only assured of one thing: that you have always loved me—you, the greatest and grandest of all. In that assurance I shall, nevertheless, die happy. When you see that I am ready to depart this earthly realm, will you then say to me, the last thing you say to me, that it is me you have loved—the whole time."

He stared at the floor. He, the executioner with the axe in his hand! He felt his hands digging into its long handle. He felt his arms rise mechanically in the air. His heart stood still. And the blood in his veins stood still. He only glimpsed the shining blade of the axe quivering over his head. He was no longer master of it, no more than over a flash of lightning which streaked down.

"And supposing it was not so. . . . Supposing I have loved someone else—more than you."

"What! What!" She got up on her elbow. She stared in wild madness at him.

"Who was this other one, Gunhild Finne?"

"Yes."

He dared not look at her, dared not meet her gaze now.

"So, it was true after all—true."

She didn't cry out. She only sank down quietly onto the quilt—struck down by a terrible blow. Her eyes closed slowly; her face filled with agony. And some tears forced their way out from under her long black eyelashes.

Benjamin Sigismund jumped up from his chair. He threw his arms around her, called out and kissed her: "Kathryn! Kathryn! No, it was you I loved—you—you—oh my God!"

His shout had not reached her. Death had already closed the gates between them.

Then he put her down. And he stood there, his head sunk on his chest and mumbled:

"Mountains, hide me, envelop me."

And then—then came the silence.

The Spinner

The spinning wheel rumbled like a salt quern from early dawn to far into the night, and the grey wool yarn which ran through her thin hands was seven leagues long; no, seven times seventy leagues long it was! Oh no, it was never ending! For four years Gunhild Finne had been spinning it. Yes, time and the wool yarn were never ending.

Even more endless was the thread of her thoughts; was she responsible for David taking his life?

The spinning wheel, the shining spindle, and the grey wool yarn were allowed to rest in the dark; but in the quiet night hours, the wheel and the spindle of her thoughts went on spinning—spinning, spinning. Its wheel whined on its axle and carried the same cold whining into her soul, day and night:

"Didn't you kill David?"

"What do you think, Uncle Ola, did I kill our David?"

Ol-Kanelesa left without answering. And he sat for a whole day and a whole night down at Elisabeth Cottage, his hand on his forehead, thinking.

The next day he came back.

"Every living thing on this earth does nothing but plague the life out of some other living thing. And most everything is living, so it seems to me."

"But not sticks and stones, Uncle?"

"There's a sort of life in them too. Hadn't the log which fell on the head of Big Rasmus up at the smeltery life in it? And the block of stone which fell on Grelk-Hans down at Aalberja? That was alive enough, I should think."

And then she asked Jon Haraldsen.

"Was it my fault that our David went and hanged himself?"

He answered:

"Was it your fault that David married you?"

She shook her head with an anguished smile.

"And you knew full well that your life with him would go awry?"

"Awry? I knew that the whole thing would lead to disaster."

"And you told David that?"

"Yes, many a time—but his ears were deaf, were our David's."

"And you said the same to your mother and to his family too?"

"Did I! I wept and begged them let me be in peace—but they were even harder of hearing than David."

"Then it's my opinion that they are more to blame for David doing away with himself than you are, Gunhild."

After that conversation with the happy and simple Jon Haraldsen, the wheel of her thoughts stood still and rested awhile—but then one day it was as if a finger crept in between the spokes and set it going again; she treadled away, too, with her tired foot. Now it turned with even wilder speed than before. And now it shrieked and whined to high heaven: "You have killed our David! It's your fault he now lies in his grave and that Ellen has no father!"

And the dust lay in peace on the tables and benches and beams in Gunhild's cottage, the cobwebs hung in peace under the rafters, and in the soot on the hearth one could write with a slate pencil; the window panes which once had been so clear, and twinkled and shone in the sun, they had long

been yellow and crusted with sulphur smoke. The whole day
she sat in there in the half-light and spun. And she didn't go
on spinning and spinning to keep need and poverty from
her door. In the big chest in her bedroom dollar bills lay
yellowing, antique silver lay corroding; on the walls clothes
hung piled on top of each other, on the beams under the
roof sheepskin blankets and coverlets hung for the moths to
eat, and along the walls stood rows of shoes and boots which
had never been used. The two generations before David and
her had spent all the days of their lives, and had shunned
neither water nor fire, to scrape together all this. They, who
had possessed so many new and fine clothes, had always worn
their patched ones. And they, who had possessed new foot-
gear in abundance, had walked from cradle to grave in
cracked and rotting shoes the whole of that long way.

Now, the young, well-to-do widow lived here, sharing the
lot of the poor women of Bergstaden, spinning wool for Hjort's
orphanage. An occupation which demanded all the skill of the
hand but nothing of the mind. Her mind was filled with one
thought: was it her fault that David had put a rope around
his neck? She sat there, Sundays as weekdays, like a beggar
woman, ragged and unkempt with her flowing hair combed
only by her fingers. She often became confused as to what
day it was, so that many a Sunday she went on sitting there
behind the wheel believing it was either Monday or Saturday. She span in a delirium. Who cared whether she, a fallen
woman, dressed well or badly? It was more fitting that her
body which contained such a wicked and vile soul was clad
in rags; in the worst and ugliest clothes she could find.

Yes, there was one occasion since David was buried that
she had dressed herself in new clothes and had worn them
for a whole week.

She sat one Tuesday evening spinning as usual. Then she
heard someone coming quickly up the steps to the door—
someone in big heavy riding boots. She jumped up and hooked
the iron hook onto the door frame. And then she threw herself flat on the floor, stopping her ears with her forefingers.

She lay in this way until late at night when the frost came and forced her up and into bed.

The next morning she combed her hair and went to her bedroom and put on her Sunday clothes. The whole week she sat behind the spinning wheel in her finery with a silver brooch on her breast—listening over the wheel for footsteps on the doorstep outside; but no, they didn't come again—would they ever come again? On Saturday evening she stripped off her new clothes in great anger. She pulled out her brooch and threw it on the floor. She tore off her bodice and skirt so the hooks broke. She kicked off her shoes. For a whole week she had sat there making a fool of herself.

"Into rags, into patches with you, you bitch! Who's going to visit you? Everybody who passes your cottage, runs past your doorstep in disgust."

The whole of that night she spun in an angry rage. Who was she so angry with? With somebody who went under the name of Gunhild Finne. Ha! Ha! Ha!

Her bitterness grew continually. And why shouldn't it? She who year after year sat here, an outcast, imprisoned between these cold walls.

If she ever went out, it had to be after the sun had gone down and it was gloomy and dark in the back-streets and alleys. How could she strew flowers on the paths of others when they only threw thorns onto hers?

"Love thine enemies," Ol-Kanelesa said.

"Isn't that asking too much of such a one as me—someone who has only enemies? One enemy, two enemies, I might forgive, even love—but someone who sees an enemy in every single face, can he do that?"

"If you are such an important person that you have so many enemies, then perhaps you are big enough to forgive many of them? You know, there was one who could do that, too."

"Hm, yes; but me? Me, a lost creature?"

"You must begin, Gunhild; one today, two tomorrow. Begin with the one you think has done you most harm. Then you are over the worst."

"Yes, Uncle Ola, I've already done that; he who has done me the most harm, I've forgiven him."

"Is he alive or dead?"

"Those who lie in the grave need to forgive us, not we them."

Ol-Kanelesa said no more.

And so the days passed, the one after the other, in there behind the sulphur-stained windows and behind the humming spinning wheel. The grey woollen thread which ran through her thin hands would never come to an end. And the raging wheel of her thoughts whined and shrieked:

"You've killed our David! You! You! You!"

Ol-Kanelesa and the New Ellen

In Ol-Kanelesa's cottage the windows were clean and shining, the dust carefully wiped from beams and rafters, the hearth was whitened every Saturday and stood out snow-white between the brown walls, and when the Works' bell rang in the new shift the hearth curb and the sand-scoured floor were strewn with juniper twigs.

Now no wagoners were allowed to sit in Ol-Kanelesa's home with their brandy bottles and cards. He made quite sure that the bolt was closed on the outer door. If they wanted him for anything, he was available all day down in the smithy.

Ellen was in the cottage now, a new little Ellen. And swearing and drinking and cards were things a little angel like Ellen should have no contact with.

In his old age Ol-Kanelesa had set up house. His household was in no wise big; besides Ellen and himself there was old Løsi. She was well on in years and no longer capable of washing floors and staircases for the gentry. Here at Elisabeth Cottage she was as good as any.

One afternoon in the summer Ol-Kanelesa met her down at the pump. She stood there scouring a bucket when he came by with his sledgehammer and pincers. He stopped and began to talk about this and that; Pastor Thomas von Westen Hammond was also mentioned. Løsi had been in service in his house for many years; now it was almost a generation ago— yes, time went. She had rocked Miss Ellen to sleep many an evening.

"And now we have got a new little Ellen, Løsi."

"Eh?" Løsi held her hand behind her ear. "Good Lord, where's she come from then?"

"She's the daughter David left."

"And now she's living up with you, Ola?"

Yes, that she was. And it looked as if she was getting along real fine there, and she only really cried when they said she'd have to go home again. That being so, it was best she remained up at Elisabeth Cottage, wasn't it? Hm, yes, maybe it was, Løsi said too. She thought slowly and she spoke slowly, the old woman.

"You, who were a mother to the one our Ellen here is called after, you'd better be a mother to this one too, hadn't you, Løsi?"

"Hm, no, I'm too old to take on such a big responsibility."

Ol-Kanelesa laughed, just as if what Løsi said was only a joke. And he continued on his way with his sledgehammer and his pincers and with a smile in the corners of his eyes.

The next day Løsi came. Yes, only to look in and say hello to Ellen. She played for a while with her, tidied up some cups, and darned a pair of the child's stockings. And the next day Løsi came again, just to look in. And in that way she came to stay.

Ol-Kanelesa said that now she should have four rix-dollars a year in wages; but at that Løsi collapsed into a chair.

"Had you said four shillings, Ola, there would have been some sense in it."

"Both Ellen and me have agreed that it should be as I have said."

Ellen and him! He thought of her, the first Ellen. He turned towards the wall and closed his eyes; it was a great miracle that he should live to say "Ellen and me." It seemed to him that it was a beautiful dream he had dreamt a long time ago which had now come true. "Ellen and me! Ellen and me!" And, moved to tears, he thanked God that it should be granted to him to say anything so wonderful as "Ellen and me! Ellen and me!" He had to say it over and over again many times to himself.

Every evening now Løsi sat beside Ellen's bed, and sang the hymns and read the evening prayers she had once sung and read to Miss Ellen. On the first evenings her voice was trembling and her memories groping and hard to recall; but it went better later.

And the busy hands of time which both bind and loosen, they bound the three of them closer and closer together for every hour that passed. Now it was Ol-Kanelesa and Ellen who really ran things and made the decisions, and Løsi was the serving maid who, without objection, quietly accepted everything, just as she had learnt to do down there at Mr. Thomas von Westen Hammond's.

Sometimes the old wise woman would say to Ol-Kanelesa, "You and Ellen, yes, you and Ellen!" But she took good care not to say it too often.

Ellen and Ol-Kanelesa! In the evening, when he came from the smithy tired and dirty, she met him at the door. The sound of her small shoes inside and her happy cries of laughter! Oh, for him it was the song of the angels. Her two arms around his knees in the doorway made him stand upright under the burden of his years. And when she sat beside him on the bench at the little red-painted table in Elisabeth Cottage, he felt rich and powerful, and wise! He knew things now he had never known before. Then History threw open its rusty iron portals; the Future set its sundrenched doors ajar. And so they sat there with shining eyes betwixt these two worlds and stared; but their faces were turned in different directions. His towards the world as it once was. Hers towards the world of the future. One with tears in his eyes, the other with a smile.

One Sunday after church service, and after Ol-Kanelesa had taken his usual siesta, he and Ellen went hand in hand up to the churchyard to the grave of Miss von Westen Hammond. Here they sat down on a bench and chatted. He told little Ellen about she who lay in this grave.

"She was called Ellen, she too. And it's from her you've got your name, Ellen."

And then Ol-Kanelesa told her that the evening she died a whole host of angels came down to earth to fetch her. They clad her in white clothes, put flowers in her hair, and on her back she got large white wings, and a big palm branch in her hand. And then she flew off with them up to the stars, up to heaven, up to God. It was there she now was.

"Up there?" the child asked wonderingly, and pointed up to the clouds. "Right up in heaven?"

"Yes.

"Did you stand there and see it, Uncle Ola?"

What was Ol-Kanelesa to say to that? If he said yes, it wouldn't be true. And to lie to a child, that was more than anyone dared do.

"No, I didn't, Ellen."

"How do you know it, then?"

"God told me."

"When did he tell you, then?"

"He told me in a dream."

"Did he?" Ellen said excitedly. "Then I shall also ask him to tell me something in a dream; do you think he would?"

"Yes, that he will."

"Then I shall ask him to tell me if Father is up in heaven."

Ol-Kanelesa writhed as he sat there. As long as Ellen didn't ask him how her father died, then he would have to take the great sin on himself and lie—lie to an innocent little child.

"Why have I got Ellen's name?"

God bless the little creature. He took her close to him and stroked her hair.

"You got her name so you shall be as good and kind as she was."

"But then I would have to die and become an angel, wouldn't I?"

"Yes, when you are old—much older than Løsi, then you'll die and become an angel."

"Shall we all become angels, both Father and Mother, you and Løsi?"

"Yes, all of us."

"Oh, I look forward to that, Uncle."

She clapped her small hands.

Then Ol-Kanelesa got up suddenly, took the child by the hand and went down out of the churchyard. He didn't come up here with her any more. And after that day Miss Ellen von Westen Hammond's name was seldom mentioned at Elisabeth Cottage. For many reasons. And the shadow of death always rested over the names of the dead.

Good Friday

The church clock had just struck seven; it was the morning of Good Friday in the year 1825.

Benjamin Sigismund, now a Knight of the Order of the North Star, sat fully robed in his study, bent over his Bible.

This big room where everything had once been in order and in its proper place, from the quill pen and the sand-box on his desk to the chair and the straw mat down by the door, was now in complete disorder. Ancient leather tomes with buckles lay together with rusty pistols and broken swords. A wolfskin coat, which hung by the window, shed a few grey hairs every day down onto a heap of yellowing documents which lay on the floor. And a table with three legs, with fantastic carvings on it, was turned over on its side. Here, as in Gunhild Finne's cottage, indifference had taken over the running of the house.

He had again begun to get up early in the morning. Not out of zeal to get on with his work; no! but because his nights had become evil as never before. Coughing, sleeplessness, and a myriad of torturing thoughts crept into bed with him. So, why not try to shorten these nights of torture by getting up early?

His days were numbered; the Lord had already prepared his scythe. He, too, had contracted consumption. Was then Kathryn's end, in that way, also to be his? Every day now the Lord's scythe cut through another of the many and powerful bonds which had bound him to life and to this earth; in a few months, at the most a year, it would cut through the last one.

His steps were being directed towards the grave. Every day he entered new and unknown regions. The world with its honor, gold, and precious vessels could at times lie so far behind. Time was also put out of joint. When he lay at nights with his eyes closed, recalling the life he had lived, it seemed to him that it must have been a thousand years ago, ten thousand years! Time had lost its years, there was nothing to measure it with any more. Only very rarely did the living life come close to him now. If it did, it was only in fits and starts. Yes, one night during the winter he awoke suddenly and had a strong feeling that Gunhild was standing in there beside him. He could see nothing. He knew, too, that it wasn't so. Nevertheless, he got up. He walked to and fro, groping in the darkness for her. Even if she wasn't there, standing there, she was all the same near. Yes, so near that he could feel her breath. It seemed to him that a great happiness, an unearthly great and pure joy had come in through his door.

. . . Now Benjamin Sigismund sat preparing his sermon.

The lamp of his spirit burned with too low a flame now, its light did not fall so strongly and illuminatingly on the Word as when he was in his prime.

He began to read the lesson of the day aloud:

"And he came out, and went, as he was wont, to the mount of Olives; and his disciples also followed him. And when he was at the place, he said unto them, Pray that ye enter not into temptation. And he was withdrawn from them about a stone's cast, and kneeled down, and prayed, Saying, Father, if thou be willing, remove this cup from me: nevertheless not my will, but thine, be done. And there appeared an angel unto him from heaven, strengthening him. And being in an agony he prayed more earnestly: and his sweat was as it were great drops of blood falling down to the ground. And when he rose up from prayer, and was come to his disciples, he found them sleeping for sorrow, And said unto them, Why sleep ye? rise and pray, lest ye enter into temptation!"

Sigismund became deeply moved. He saw the Master in agony on his knees in Gethsemane. He saw His sweat, which became drops of blood, gathering up on his perfect, beautiful face. He saw Peter, James and John sitting there in the darkness weighed down by sleep. Not even Peter, the disciple with the passionate and jealous soul, Peter with sword in hand, was able to keep watch through the fourth watch of the night. He, Peter, the rock! Already the Tempter stood bent over him with shadowy face and cloven tongue. But He whose soul in this hour was pierced by the cold agony of death also saw the great danger which hung over the three disciples; and He had deep concern for them.

He too, Benjamin Sigismund, had like Peter neglected to heed the Master's counsel, and arise betimes and pray that he might not fall into temptation. But had he avoided that fall? He sat up in his chair. Yes, had he avoided that fall? Had then his, Sigismund's, path led to Gethsemane?

Coughing shook his emaciated body. He tasted blood in his mouth. And, as always, terror came with it; but this terror was colder and more icily penetrating than all other terrors.

It was as if he sat in cross currents from many eternities—some with a grey cold light over them, others completely in darkness. Was it the agony of Gethsemane? The disintegration of his body was in full swing.

He remained sitting there, remembering something he had experienced one night last winter. It seemed to him that the great silence, which only comes when a human being has drawn his last breath, enveloped him. And suddenly Kathryn was standing beside his bed. She took his hand in hers and smiled sadly. "Do you wish, Husband, that I shall pray for you, that you may still live?" she asked. "Here, from where I now am, it is not such a long way to God as from the place where you are." Her voice was without reproach, and all fear and suffering had left her face.

"Oh, my dear," he had said. "Do not intervene in the wise counsels of God. Don't you hate me, Kathryn?" She smiled again. "There is no hate here. No, Husband, I love you more dearly now than when I lived—but it is with another love, a love purified of all self-love."

But he couldn't quite decide whether this was a dream or a vision. Now, when his earthly happiness was in ruins, his spirit became more and more liberated. The eyes of his soul had the land of Canaan in sight. He had come closer now. He noticed it in so many things.

He got up and put on his hat with both hands, like an old man. He heard the maid struggling with the boys downstairs —but it was all happening so endlessly far away. In reality it was nothing to do with him. Yesterday, his concern for the boys was as great as ever. Yesterday, he and his sons still stood at the parting of the ways. He came from life; they were on their way to it. Today they were already far on the way. And far, far from each other they had already come.

Down on the steps an elderly man dressed for church and with a bright happy face was standing.

" 'Morning!" he said, and took off his cap. "I must thank you once again."

He took the pastor's hand and let it go quickly as if he had got hold of something cold and dead.

"Who are you?" Sigismund said.

"Don't you recognize me now, either?"

Benjamin Sigismund shook his head.

"I'm from Elgsjøen I am; it's Tøllef."

"Is that so."

"But pastor, don't you know me then?"

"No."

"It was me you saved so I didn't have to leave Elgsjøen."

"Is that so."

"I was going to church today. And then it was as if I couldn't bear to go past. I had to come up and thank you."

"Thank God, my good man."

"Yes, I've done that—as well as I could, that's to say."

When Benjamin Sigismund got up to the churchyard and saw the church and the tower he suddenly remembered who Tøllef was. He remembered now that it was on the last evening he met Gunhild up there that this poor peasant had come up to the manse. He remembered everything now, clearly and plainly: the light which fell on the whitewashed walls of the church, the golden sound of the clock chiming in the air, and all the people he had met in the street.

The feelings which had filled him that evening, the mood and the atmosphere he had experienced, streamed down on him again; they were paler—yet they were infinitely more beautiful and more pure, just as if they had been away for a long time and had been cleansed in the sun.

How long ago was it now?

Oh, it might be a generation ago. Or it might have been yesterday; so far and so near that evening was, as all else had now become.

Would these memories be amongst those which would be remembered in another life, on the other side of the grave? Everything from that evening was inscribed in words and images on his soul.

After he had gone up Litj Street and stood, dead tired, in his vestments in front of the altar of the Bergstaden church, while the Good Friday sun and the clear spring light streamed in through the windows, he was once again projected into a non-earthly existence. All this light, didn't that, too, belong to another world? No! Now he stood in the same place he had stood when he took divine service in this church for the first time. Here he stood when Gunhild had been led in as bride. Yes, then he stood, without knowing it, at the parting of the ways. One road was the road of arrogance, pharisaism, and self-righteousness, the other the road of error, humility, and knowledge. Was there not also a third road, the road to perfection? Yes! On that road there was only one set of footprints to be seen, those of the Master! Thousands thought they were walking it. And then they trod the path of the Pharisee and the self-righteous. He had come onto the road of error; Peter's road! Had the Lord taken him by the arm and led him onto it? For from this road there was a little path which led over to Gethsemane, the one Peter followed. From there to paradise the way was short.

And Benjamin Sigismund began to read the service as if talking aloud to himself. His voice was broken. Coughing and hoarseness prevented him from singing now. He forgot that down there in the pews hundreds of worshippers were sitting —it was not for them he was reading. No, the words were not for them but for himself. God and him! He now stood before his God, stood with his hands before his face and confessed.

And neither did he, when he stood up in the pulpit pale and emaciated and with blue shadows under his eyes, see those who sat down there.

But they saw him. And for the first time since David Finne ended his days by his own hand did they fail to point the accusing finger at Sigismund. His wasted figure told them that he, too, had lifted with trembling hands the cup of suffering to his bloodless, tortured lips. And they could also see that he had been lashed and chastized with a scourge of iron. Everything that they, through all the years, had wished he should suffer, he had now suffered. . . . It seemed to them that justice had now been done in full.

He himself had no idea that his parishioners had now changed to the path of gentle reconciliation. In general, what people thought of him had gradually become of less and less importance to him. Whether they condemned him or acquitted him was a matter of indifference. Soon he would be standing before a higher judgement stool—and before a higher and more just judge.

Today, no fulminations were heard from the pulpit of the Bergstaden church. Those who sat down in the nave and up in the galleries, their hands sweating for fear of being chastized by name, went free.

Today Sigismund was completely engrossed in the lesson for the day; by the tragedy of Gethsemane. Today his words did not go in one ear of his listeners and out the other. No, today they made their way to the doors of their hearts. And today these doors were opened. Yes, even the hard and stubborn of heart opened up. And their inner eyes became strangely clear-seeing. They saw Him and the eleven as they passed at that late night hour over Kidron, they saw the quiet black water glide silently past in the reflection from the stars —they saw the three sleeping disciples. And they heard Him, God's son, praying out there in the darkness. They heard his agony and his distress. And they saw the light from the angel, the strong, all-penetrating light. They witnessed the journey on the road up to Calvary. The cross, the heavy bitter tree of death, which weighed down His innocent shoulders, also weighed down theirs. The women, the young weeping women, who went with Him, their faces veiled, also passed by. . . . And when Sigismund folded his hands and prayed, "Help us to love Thee alone," many folded their hands and prayed with him, "Help us to love Thee alone." He, the pastor, and his congregation, they had all transgressed against the law of God; they were all equally responsible for His son's suffering and death.

Those who had heard Sigismund's inaugural sermon and still remembered it forgot the intervening years from then until today, they forgot all his hard words; they also forgot his many mistakes; now their thoughts were only concentrated on the crucified one. . . . And the angel's light, yes, an even stronger light, fell on the tree of the cross and on the head bowed in death; the head crowned with thorns. In that light everything of this world vanished, all worldly thoughts were extinguished.

None of them had ever heard such a Good Friday sermon before. Hadn't it gone beyond the preaching of mortal man? The Lord Jesus himself must have been amongst them. *He* had risen up vivid and lifelike before them.

When the service was over and the people began to make their way slowly and quietly down the nave, Sigismund called out from the choir to Ol-Kanelesa.

"Yes, your Reverence."

Benjamin Sigismund stood with his face turned towards the window.

And the light, the pale light from the spring snow outside, fell on his face. Ol-Kanelesa started. The doomed man stood there looking young and vigorous.

"At three o'clock our Lord Jesus's body will be taken down from the cross."

Ol-Kanelesa nodded.

"And then this day, this Good Friday, is over."

Again Ol-Kanelesa nodded.

"And then we can once again look forward to Easter Morning, to His great and glorious resurrection."

"Yes."

"Ole Korneliusen." Sigismund turned towards him. "Through His cross we are all equal. None is learned and none is ignorant. There are no commoners and no nobility. From now on, won't you call me by my name, Benjamin Sigismund?"

Ol-Kanelesa looked down. He who always had a ready answer now groped for words.

"Hm! A pastor's a pastor and a sacristan a sacristan."

"But many that are first shall be last," Sigismund said. "Not a word more about this, Ole. It shall be as I have said."

"No, your Reverence," Ol-Kanelesa answered. "We'll address each other as we have always done. I can't climb up to where you are and you can't climb down to where I am. Even if you dressed yourself in sackcloth and ashes, you would still be a Knight of the Order of the North Star. And though I decked myself in gold and crimson, I should still only be a blacksmith."

"I see. I understand that you feel it would not be natural for you."

"I think it would be lowering for us both."

"Then let us continue as before. Until we one day take each other by the hand on the other side."

To this Benjamin Sigismund received no answer.

"Listen, Ole. Would you be kind enough, that is to say after three o'clock, to accompany me on a little walk. I see now that the spring is coming, and—" Sigismund breathed deeply. "I want so much to go out and meet it once more—" He stopped once again. He was very moved. His white, thin hand gripped tightly round his old prayer book.

"Yes," Ol-Kanelesa said. "When the church clock has struck three, I'll come down to the manse."

. . . The evening was light and bright. In the streets of Bergstaden it was muddy and impassable. Today, Good Friday, the snow had begun to melt. The change in the weather had come suddenly. And although it was a holy day and everybody was in his Sunday best, they all had to rush and get out their iron-shod wooden spades and start shovelling the snow from the rooftops. A joy and a delight it was; for now the spring was coming! the spring! and it was coming early. Their minds and spirits, frozen hard by the winter, were now filled with gratitude to Him who had checked the cold and the driving snow, and had sent mild winds and sunshine.

When Benjamin Sigismund, leaning on the sacristan's arm, came up the street, the air was full of cheerful voices and happy laughter from every rooftop. As the two passed, caps were raised.

Sigismund walked slowly. It was terrible to see how consumption had ravaged that once so upright and vigorous man. No one had suspected that things would turn out like that for him. Oh yes! Some had suspected it right enough—for whatsoever a man soweth, that shall he also reap. But he had been a remarkable man in spite of everything. And it would perhaps be a long time before Bergstaden got such an outstanding pastor again. His good sides were now being appreciated. Now, when death had already marked him.

And lumps of snow from the rooftops splashed down into the street. Down there boys and girls were making snowballs, and with shouts and much noise they threw them back at those who stood up there shovelling.

At the churchyard both the pastor and Ol-Kanelesa stopped.

"Ought we not today to take a look at the graves of our dead ones, Ole? Here, both you and I shall one day be laid to rest."

"Yes, we must do as your Reverence says."

First they went over to Kathryn's grave. Here Sigismund stood for a long time, supporting himself heavily on his stick, staring down at the grave. He said nothing. His face was rigid and immovable. And then they went on in silence past engineer apprentice Notler's grave and over to Ellen von Westen Hammond's. Here Benjamin Sigismund read half aloud, and in his thoughts: "Blessed are the dead who die in the Lord."

"Is she still dear to you, Ole Korneliusen?"

"I think that she was the best—now as then."

He said it quietly. There was no sorrow in his voice. No complaint. Now the wound had healed. Now there was only joy over the good and the beautiful in the memory of her that remained. Even the shadow of death over her name was gone. In a way she had almost come back to life again. Especially after little Ellen had come. She took so much after the one whose name she had. Ol-Kanelesa could not believe other than that God had arranged it so—to bring joy to him. Certainly, he was not worthy of so great a joy. How could he, miserable and wicked creature that he was, do something that would rejoice God? He had thought much about it, but it was as if his thoughts stopped halfway.

"Oh, you happy man," Sigismund said, and patted Ol-Kanelesa on the shoulder. "It has been granted to you to carry a living light in your hand down through life—down to the evening shadows of old age. Do you know what that means? Do you also know what it means to have the light in one's life lit late and extinguished early. That man, too, must live his life."

"Yes, I do. I think that I have a sort of idea of what you mean—," Ol-Kanelesa stammered.

They went on up the many steps to the upper churchyard where the big communal graves were, where the miners and the miners' women and children were buried.

Now Benjamin Sigismund no longer ran up the steps as he did the first time he mounted them. Now it was Ol-Kanelesa who had to wait. And he waited willingly. For now the snow water trickled and ran down from step to step like a waterfall. It was a trickling he liked to listen to; it was the spring which, once again, was singing its first song of the year. In that song there were melodies which were always fresh. It didn't matter that he had heard them before, they were all the same new to him. A waterfall here right in the middle of two churchyards; a waterfall that came and disappeared and came again, it was impossible that its melodies could be the same as another waterfall. Every spring it came and sang to the dead. Just as if it only had one message: to tell them that it was now spring on earth. Spring! Spring! Spring!

Who could know if this was not the last spring he would hear these sounds. Nobody knew the day and the hour of the Lord. Tomorrow he would bring Ellen up here so that she could hear the same melodies. It had become so important to him to pass on to her young pure child's mind everything that was good and beautiful. So that when the evil days came, when the world began to cast shadows, then the good and the beautiful would keep guard.

They stood longer by the grave of Ol-Kanelesa's brother than by any of the other graves. Neither of them said anything about this grave. He who was buried here was, of course, Gunhild Finne's father. Since Kathryn's passing her name had not been mentioned. Not in so many words.

"Whose grave is that over there by the stone wall, the one with a new iron cross on it?" Sigismund asked, and pointed with his stick.

Ol-Kanelesa turned half away. He knew well who it was who lay there—but this was not the time or the place to speak of it now. That grave was not one of those graves people talked about; it was a grave which was to be forgotten, tramped on! Therefore it had been dug as close to the wall as possible, where there was much shadow, where not a blade of green grass grew, and where the snow lay until far into the summer.

Was that right? No!

And in anger at it Ol-Kanelesa had forged an iron cross— it was rough and not well finished, but it was a cross all the same and raised over a grave. He who lay there was well worth this memorial. He had been lonely in life; a human being surplus to the requirements of this world. There had been no place for him here. No one had opened their doors to him—no, they had been closed when he approached. He died alone, as he had lived. Alone and by himself he now lay and slept the long sleep until the morning of resurrection. His coffin had been dragged one evening in the driving snow and the north wind over the stone walls and laid in earth without priest and without the sound of the bell. The churchyard, too, had closed its doors on him.

"Who lies there?" Ol-Kanelesa repeated.

"Yes, who is it? I have not seen that cross before."

"Oh, it's a poor wretch that rests there, he, too."

Then something happened which caused Ol-Kanelesa to move aside: Benjamin Sigismund began to walk over to the grave. He walked with long steps and bowed head between the graves—as if driven there by a power he couldn't resist. Had he a suspicion as to whose grave it was? And then he stopped some distance away and read the name on the board: "Engineer Apprentice David Finne." He turned and walked back unsteadily in his own tracks down towards the steps.

Ol-Kanelesa followed him at a distance. He heard the pastor groaning as he went.

The Fourth Night Watch

Easter Sunday. The good weather had ended suddenly. Now there was frost, north wind, and driving snow again; but nevertheless it wasn't winter now, even if they were getting winter weather all the same. Spring had entered into their minds; and that was the important thing. What did it matter if it snowed and blew cold? That was nothing to talk about. Every night that came was shorter and shorter, the sun came up earlier and earlier. . . . Spring, the wonderful, the inexplicable! Was it strange then that the old people, the custodians of memory, they who carried the past and what had happened in it with them, spoke mainly of springs past and gone? The winters, the long, dark winters, were forgotten. The winter, the snow and the dark, had been nothing remarkable; their minds had liberated themselves from the winters as time had passed. No, it was in the blue spring days, in the pale nights that the saga lived on. In the brooks which were released on the mountain sides, in the rivers which rose out of the ice, on the bare mountain, in the ice which moved in great shining floes on the tarns and lakes, in the young leaves, in the white bird-cherry blossom; there, the saga had its roots. And the fairy tales too! No one had seen a woodland fairy on a winter night, no one had heard the hill folk's delicate brass bells ringing to the north in the hills in the driving snow and darkness, nobody had seen stately knights on black horses with gold bridles and silver shoes on All Saints' Day—no, St. Hallvard's Day and Midsummer, that was the time.

Today, Easter Sunday, the church bells were ringing in snow and wind, but with a springlike sound. And people were on their way to church, in groups, by themselves, bright in thought and buoyant in will. They had come from afar, from the mountains and the out-of-the-way valleys, they came on skis, driving, and on foot.

When the final peal had been rung and the church was full to overflowing and they sat with their hymn books open, the sacristan, Ol-Kanelesa, came out into the nave and read the bidding prayer. He had a large volume of sermons under his arm. He was pale. And when he opened the book and began to read from it, everybody knew that the pastor was absent.

Was he ill? Yes, he was. Someone who sat up in the front pews whispered to the people next to him that Benjamin Sigismund had had to take to his bed on Good Friday after the service. It was said he was very ill. Would he get over it? Hm! Well! The regimental surgeon had been up to see him, but what he thought no one knew. Doctor Wellerop never let anything out.

This news now passed from mouth to mouth down through the whole of the church—and all this whispering disturbed Ol-Kanelesa in his reading, and he stopped for a moment and glared severely and commandingly over his spectacles down at the congregation. It had its effect; Ol-Kanelesa was not to be trifled with, even if he was only a blacksmith and an unfrocked schoolmaster. Then he continued his reading. Of those who were at church today, there were some who had neither heard Sigismund's inaugural sermon or his Good Friday sermon two days ago, and who had only been witness to his fulminations; it seemed to them that it was almost more edifying to listen to Ol-Kanelesa. Yes, for once in a while at all events—and then there was Ol-Kanelesa's singing. He sang so the organ almost stopped playing.

Nevertheless, there was an air of depression over the people in Bergstaden's great church today. . . . The thought that perhaps they would never again hear Sigismund made them understand, for the first time, how fond they were of him. He had, in spite of everything that could be said against him, been close to them. Yes, closer than any other pastor had been in living memory. That he had thundered at them and had chastized them was perhaps nothing so very much to object to when they really reflected on it. He did, after all, clear the air. He raised up their hearts and minds. If a new pastor came it was not at all certain that he would be able to help them in their spiritual and physical need as Benjamin Sigismund had done. When had anybody known him to say no when they came to him? Never! Night or day, it was the same to him. He had fleeced them, that he had, made them pay down to their last shilling—but he had never turned them away when they were in need. But where was there a parson who didn't demand his dues? And all that talk about him— no, that couldn't have been as bad as the gossips had made out, either.

Especially, there were many of them who had been confirmed by him who today quite openly grieved at the thought that he would soon be gone forever. All of them had some bright memory or other from the weeks they had spent up at the vestry preparing for their confirmation. . . . One he had patted on the shoulder, another he had praised although he had hardly learnt anything. And the things they had been reprimanded for were now forgotten. Even those who had failed, however bitter it was, and however much they had wept over it then, they too had forgotten. . . . And wasn't it a joy and delight when they sat around him in the spring sunshine up there? If they could have that time over again, they wouldn't hesitate. And those who had lost some of their loved ones, and there were many of them—they could tell that Sigismund wasn't a man who made their burden heavier. "Rest assured, my dear friend, that the dear departed has entered into the joy of his Lord; there where there is no more weeping and no more fear, but where God himself has dried every tear from their face. In a short time we shall, through the merits of our Lord Jesus, be joined with them again, never more to part." They were words they knew by heart. When sorrow laid them low and the days became long and their poor hearts suffered woe and distress, then they remembered Sigismund's words. Then things brightened, then life was worth living again—even during the long days of sorrow and longing, life was worth living.

The spring passed. And it became summer—it was the time when the bird cherry flowered and the sun shone all day.

Benjamin Sigismund continued to keep to the house. He was not more ill than before; but his strength was broken. Death was quietly working away at him. In Bergstaden's church the Reverend Holger Hannig, the parish priest of Aalen and Holtaalen, officiated every fourth Sunday now. He was a quiet and pious man—but, no, he was not Benjamin Sigismund. They were all agreed on that. He always visited his sick colleague when he visited Bergstaden. Sigismund received him coolly and formally, as he sat silent and withdrawn in his chair. And the confession which Holger Hannig expected from Sigismund failed to materialize. Sigismund treated the other persons of rank and condition in Bergstaden in the same way when they came to see how his Reverence was. He had nothing to say to them. Nothing! In general he was not very friendly. And however much worse his illness became, he did not drop this, frankly speaking, stupid air of superiority. Thus Mr. Dopp one day got such a reception that it took away all his desire to continue with his short visits to the manse. "Mr. Dopp," Sigismund said, "have you nothing better to do than to wear out my doorstep?" At which Mr. Dopp had

taken his hat, bowed, and left—but he remained standing out
on the steps for a long time polishing his spectacles—he even
polished the sidepieces. That man-eating prelate could just
be permitted to sit there.

And then the exasperated mine secretary walked with small
quick steps over the street and into his office. There he tore
off his spectacles and threw them over onto an open ledger
and rubbed his eyes.

His bookkeepers saw that he was annoyed—but they took
good care not to inquire why. He would tell them right
enough as soon as he had collected himself. Provided they
took care not to contradict him, but agree with him, he was
usually in such a good humor that they were given the rest
of the day off. And to be let off now on a summer's day, that
was just what they wanted—for they all had houses and gardens to look after.

But there was one person to whom Sigismund never showed
the door: that was Ol-Kanelesa. He was always welcome.

But Sigismund didn't say very much to him now, either.
He had become a silent and withdrawn man. The two of them
could sit for hours at a time without speaking. Ol-Kanelesa
got used to sitting there and not speaking. He kept up the
fire on the hearth, passed one or another book to the pastor,
and moved the candle near to his chair.

But all these books were a gold mine for Ol-Kanelesa. He
spent more than one evening, sitting on the curb of the hearth
and with his glasses on the very tip of his nose, holding an
old chronicle up in the light from the fire. Here, with all this
learning, he spent many a good hour. And there was much
in it which reminded him of the departed von Westen Hammond's days. In a way he relived part of his youth again. On
the evenings he was not down at Sigismund's, he sat at home
in Elisabeth Cottage and told little Ellen about what he had
read—about what he had read now and what he had read
before, when the other Ellen was alive. And the child sat
there beside him, listening with large, shining eyes. She, too,
in that way, entered into a new and unknown world; a world

far, far away beyond this world. Her mind will be the richer for it, Ol-Kanelesa thought. . . . It was a treasure which gold and silver and precious stones could not equal.

Nor was Benjamin Sigismund idle now—now on the brink of the deep grave. He taught his sons languages and was busily engaged in equipping them for life. No doubt he was moving farther away from them for every day that passed. He didn't grieve so much over that now.

But no. One day when Laurentius, the elder boy, came in with his Latin grammar, pain at the thought of parting from him overwhelmed him. He drew the boy to him, embraced him, and sobbed.

"Laurentius," he said. "Will you promise your father one thing, one thing you *must* keep?"

"Yes, Father," the boy said. "That I will."

"Will you promise me that you will never pass judgment on your father?"

"What do you mean by that?"

"You are still far too young to understand—but will you remember what I have said?"

"Yes, Father."

"Good. Now let me hear how much you know."

He felt reassured. He had settled an important matter.*

* A different passage appears in the 1925 edition: "Benjamin Sigismund, too, was at times more preoccupied with the past than the present. . . . It seemed to him sometimes that he was moving backwards down towards his grave, with his gaze fixed rigidly on the life which had been lived. Then his thoughts revolved constantly around his children. It was difficult for him to realize that they were now no longer children, but grown men—and that they had already reached the stage he had reached some years before. Time marched quickly on—both for those moving away from life and for those moving towards it. He suffered, too, from continual self-reproach at not having watched more over their intellectual development when they were small.

"And yet, had he formed them in his own image, it would scarcely have been entirely to their advantage, would it? Now their characters would receive the stamp and mould their inner qualities entitled them to. And his correspondence with Laurentius took on more and more the character of a correspondence between two scholars, between two people who were more or less strangers, than between father and son. Their

Otherwise, Sigismund was glad when his parishioners visited him. Now, when he was ill and couldn't come to them, they came to him with all their small and big troubles and sought advice, guidance, and help.

"It is only now that I have become the pastor of this mountain people, Ole," he said animatedly to Ol-Kanelesa. "Now that I stand, staff in hand, ready to depart, my ministry is beginning. Can you understand it?"

Ol-Kanelesa moved his spectacles with two fingers up onto his forehead and put the book he was holding quietly down on the hearth.

"Yes, I think I can understand that too."

"Do you really?"

"*He* wants you to have your reward, you too."

"Reward, I?"

"He said, you remember, that those who came at the eleventh hour should get just the same reward as those who had worked in his vineyard all day."

"I, reward? No, Ole, I have in no wise earned any reward."

Ol-Kanelesa picked up his book and continued reading. He, with his poor learning, couldn't discuss the words of the Scripture with a scholar.

But when Ol-Kanelesa had left and Benjamin Sigismund was left sitting in his cushioned chair—and the night with its long hours came, and the quiet and the loneliness came, then Fear came, too, tiptoeing up to him. It stared at him with its face close to his.

"Sigismund," it said. "Your hour is approaching. Do you know me? I am the ashen cheek, the dimmed eyes, and the folded hands.

He said:

---

personalities, too, were quite different: Laurentius was the son of his mother. Now, when the years and the days had cast a redeeming light over everything, Sigismund was satisfied that it was so. At all events he attempted to be—attempts which nevertheless required no little effort and self-control.

"Get behind me, Fear. Why are you always waiting on me?"

"Oh, thou foolish and blind man. I have waited on every-body. Everybody, I tell you, Benjamin Sigismund. I have entered into all hearts, into all minds. Yes, I tell you. On this earth there are not hearts created that I have not entered into. Have you thought of eternity, Sigismund?"

Now Fear began to shout at him:

"Don't you merit eternal life then, my dear sir? Haven't you worked zealously and in the sweat of your brow in the vine-yard from the early morning hour? After all, you're already a Knight of the North Star."

Benjamin Sigismund trembled and his teeth chattered. He froze. He burned, sweated, and froze. Eternal damnation and eternal death were already here, ready to seize both his hands and take him into the darkness——

Then he heard Ol-Kanelesa's voice:

"*He* said, you remember, that he who came at the eleventh hour should get just as great a reward as he who had worked in the vineyard all day."

Out of the mouths of babes and sucklings the law of God shall be proclaimed.

Now Fear departed. He heard its flat-trodden slippers clat-tering on the threshold.

And the summer passed; and the autumn came. Autumn, the hardest of all the seasons, harder than winter itself. In the cold, dark autumn much is to wither and die; it is the autumn and the darkness which kill.

One evening, at the end of November, Benjamin Sigismund had Ol-Kanelesa sent for.

"Today, when the door was open, a white bird came in, Ole. It came right over to my bed. Do you think it was an omen?"

"Was it a ptarmigan?"

"Yes, perhaps it was a ptarmigan."

"It might have been frightened by a hawk, then?"

"It is possible that it was, Ole. But why should it seek refuge just here in my room? Had such a white bird come into me when I was well, it would have rejoiced me, but now —now when I am in bed, weak and exhausted, everything that happens which is a little out of the ordinary becomes a messenger of death. I see death in everything now. I believe for certain that that white bird was an omen."

"Heed not the cries of birds," Ol-Kanelesa said.

He thought, bad though it was, that the pastor was right this time. Without a doubt it was an omen—but he was not the man to confirm it. Hadn't Sigismund suffered enough now anyway? He could clearly see from day to day how suffering ploughed deeper and deeper furrows in his face. He was a strong man, Benjamin Sigismund; it took time. Suffering had still many furrows to plough.

Sigismund lay there with closed eyes, thinking of what Ole had said about bird cries; they were words from the Scriptures.

"Do you know, Ole Korneliusen, what I have decided to do today."

"No, your Reverence."

"I will burn my boats—my miserable, insignificant boats. They have all been carrying the garish sail of vanity. You see, there is a whole lot of my scholarly work lying here, a couple of theses, the whole lot products of the arrogance of my manhood. Will you light a fire on the hearth."

And while Ol-Kanelesa took down the flint and striker from the mantlepiece, Sigismund got out of bed. He was afflicted by a pain in his side and had great difficulty in getting on his clothes. But gradually it was easier. . . . The fire and the light stimulated him. And then he began to empty all his drawers and cupboards and chests.

"Here, Ole. Let everything be consigned to the flames. Quickly, so that I am not tempted to take it back. Here is a dissertation which cost me my sleep for six months. Into the flames with it!"

And Ol-Kanelesa put the dissertation in the fire. He didn't say anything, but he thought: Is the pastor going off his head? He, Ol-Kanelesa, was standing here now, making himself a guilty party to something which was certainly quite wrong.

Sigismund was on his knees beside a big chest of drawers holding some letters which were tied with linen thread; old, yellowing letters addressed with an old-fashioned hand, they were. He half-closed his eyes and passed the letters to Ol-Kanelesa—without looking in his direction.

"Quickly, Ole. Quickly!"

As Ol-Kanelesa was on the point of putting the bundle into the fiery glow, Sigismund called out: "Stop, Ole! Not those; they are my dear mother's letters. No, I cannot burn these. Will you promise me that you will put them in my coffin—they shall follow me to the grave." His voice was almost stifled by sobs. "Never has a mother penned such a sum of love as these letters contain. Remember, they must lie on my left side, right up against my heart. Do you promise that, Ole Korneliusen?"

"Yes, if I survive your Reverence, it shall be done."

Sigismund got up with great effort. He face was wet with tears.

"Thank you, Ole. Thank you, thank you." And he added, now in a brighter tone, as he went over to the cupboard where documents and securities were kept. "The fire shall receive, by way of recompense, a little compensation for what we have just deprived it of."

He took out his Order of the North Star.

Now, Ol-Kanelesa was horrified.

"Your Reverence is surely not thinking of burning that up?"

"Yes, just that. No one shall be permitted on my behalf to make a show with this tinsel at my grave."

And he took and threw the order into the blaze. It burnt
well—

Thy draught seems like honey,
But loathsome when drunk,
Vanity of vanities,

he said.

Now he sank down exhausted on the curb of the hearth
and continued to sit there staring into the lapping flames.

Was he now ready for his journey? Yes, soon. . . . There
was only one thing left.

. . . When Ol-Kanelesa that evening, stiff at the knees,
groped his way slowly and carefully down the dark back steps of
the manse, there was someone who suddenly gripped his arm.

"Is it you, Uncle Ola?"

"Gunhild!" he said. "You standing here?"

"Is yon Benjamin very bad now?" she whispered, without
letting go her grasp. "Is he dying?"

"Sigismund, you mean?"

"Yes, Uncle," she said firmly. "I mean him, yes. Him and
no one else!"

"No—he's out of bed, now and again that is."

"Is he up this evening too, then?"

She didn't whisper any more. Her words sounded more like
a cry.

"He's getting ready for bed now."

Ol-Kanelesa wanted to pass but Gunhild held him back.

"Has he asked you about me any time?"

"Not so far as I can remember, Gunhild."

"So he hasn't asked you then?"

"No," Ol-Kanelesa said. "He hasn't. He has more important
things to think about now, has our Sigismund, than that
there——"

"Uncle," she interrupted. "I don't know you any more."

Ol-Kanelesa relented. He put his hand on her shoulder as
she stood on the steps below him, and said—now with a kind
voice:

"Are you still thinking about Sigismund?"

"I should think I do."

"Hm. That's been a dangerous fire to put out."

"Evening after evening I've stood down here on the steps, listening and waiting for you. . . . I've heard the church clock strike one hour after the other. Three evenings you passed me here without seeing me. All three times I reached out for your arm but missed it. And when I tried to speak I couldn't open my mouth. Uncle, will you come with me up to Benjamin?"

"Now, tonight? No, it can't be done, Gunhild."

"No. No. Perhaps it can't." She stepped aside so that he could pass. "I must surely never come up here again."

And stiff in her joints and limbs after standing still for so long on the narrow, cold stairs, she began to go down them.

Ol-Kanelesa came silently after her.

Down in the entrance gate he said:

"Things aren't good for you now, are they?"

"Not good," she laughed. "Was it not good you said, Uncle?"

Her words had an inner hard, mocking sound; they cut the old blacksmith to the quick—for only someone who was destined to be damned both in this world and the next, and saw no chance of salvation any more, could find it in them to talk in that way.

"So I won't get to see Benjamin any more now. Not before we——"

Ol-Kanelesa guessed what she was going to say. And he interjected:

"Keep quiet, Gunhild. Not another word." He spoke so loud that people who were passing in the autumn gloom out on the street stopped. "Pray to God to keep you from wilful sin, Gunhild."

She staggered backwards towards the wall as if avoiding a blow. She had never heard him speak so loud and harshly before. Had he, too, become someone else? If so, then it was only she who had to go here on this earth and be always the same.

"You can see Sigismund again. I promise you that, Gunhild. Whether you'll feel worse instead of better after it—well, that must be your own affair. Just reflect on it. If you want to see him, then you shall. But you need time to think it over. Don't hurry. He won't die yet."

And then he went. And without saying farewell. And without turning to see whether Gunhild followed him. He had to hurry up to Elisabeth Cottage to say goodnight to someone there—someone who had lain there struggling with sleep, waiting for him, little Ellen; God bless her! May God give her a brighter and happier lot in life than that granted to her poor misguided mother.

Candles were burning up at Gunhild Finne's. And candle after candle burned low. Finally, she had no candles left. Now it was only the light from the hearth which illuminated the dark, uncared-for cottage—for the cobwebs still hung in peace under the beams, as did the dust which was now many years old; the window panes were always yellow.

The spinning wheel stood with yarn in the spool in the middle of the room—it didn't occur to her to move it over to the wall when she had finished with it, as others did. Here, the wheel could just stand where it stood, in the middle of the floor. It didn't stand in anybody's way—it was ages now since a visitor had set foot inside the door.

The house was more revolting to look at than ever before. Not even the floor was washed once a week now, it was scarcely swept with a broom. Nor was the ash on the hearth carried out at intervals—no, Gunhild had simply piled it up against the side of one of the walls. And when a storm blew from the north and gusts of wind came down the chimney, it blew dry ash from the heap over the floor and up onto chairs, table, and benches and down into the food dishes. It was worse here than in the worst miners' barracks, where there were only men.

There tonight, in this terrible hole, in this horror, was Gunhild Finne, dressed in her best, dressed for church! She had put on her silver-buckled shoes, the ones she had danced in at her wedding. Down over her breast hung her bonnet strings embroidered with pearls, over her shoulders she wore a rose-embroidered, fringed kerchief from Jönköping in Sweden. Her dress, in the dark, severe style worn by young married women, suited her. Sorrow and pain had tried in vain to mark her face with their sharp plowshares.

For a whole week she had gone in her church attire. For a whole week she had waited and watched. However tired she was, sleep helped but little. If she lay on her bed or sat down in a chair, sleep fled—it was as if it grinned at her from the door and had only made a fool of her.

"Will you sleep while he watches?" Sleep called out from the door. "Will you slumber and rest while he struggles with death?"

And then she began to walk to and fro across the floor, from one window to the other. She tried to peer out through some round patches on the windowpanes, where the sulphur smoke from the outdoor smelting ovens had not gathered. It was as if she stood there looking for somebody. Sometimes she would stand there in the middle of the room holding her breath and listening. But she didn't hear the wagoners' bells, chiming through the night outside, nor the sound of the horses' hooves. . . . She only heard the quiet. Not the quiet on earth; no, the quiet of eternity. Of the eternity into which we shall all one day enter. Was Benjamin Sigismund entering it now? When she stood there and closed her eyes, it seemed to her that she already saw him in there. He stood there erect. And with a long, black, ankle-length cape round his shoulders.

Then she began to call out:

"Benjamin, wait for me! I will come with you, Benjamin!"

Had she called out? No, not with her lips and voice. Not with words. Nevertheless! She had certainly never called so loudly before.

The wood out in the woodshed had been burned up. She

hadn't, like the others, supplied herself with wood and peat for the winter. Nor with food either. What did *she* want with fuel and food? Would the wood warm her? Would the food fill her?

Now only a few red embers flickered on the hearth. She sat for a while on a stool, bent over, staring into them. And then they went out too. . . . Then she jumped up. She dared not be in here any longer. She was afraid of the dark.

On the sulphur-yellow windows she saw that the moon was shining. Was it a full moon? It was better to be out under the open sky than sit here. Why was the air so suffocating? Dust. Dust, which had eaten its way into tables, benches, walls, roof.

Then she went out. She went without putting on her coat. She had the feeling, too, that she was no longer alone in here. Was David here? Or Benjamin Sigismund?

Just as she got out onto the steps, the clock in the church tower struck two.

Wasn't it more than two o'clock? She thought it was at least five. Would this night never end?

The night was cold and clear. She saw there was snow in the air. And the light from the moon cast a blue, silvery sheen over everything. . . . She now began to feel really cold.

Would this night never end? What should she do with herself? Go down to Ol-Kanelesa and little Ellen? No. Besides, she had no thoughts for Ellen now. Although she was Ellen's mother. But could a mother forget her child? Yes—No. All the same, tonight there was someone—someone, who was nearer to her.

A terrifying thought! What if God decided to take little Ellen from her?

"Lord! Lord! Be merciful and do not punish me so hard," she prayed. "Truly my sins are great, but thy mercy is greater."

She ran on, the lash on her back. She had no more tears to weep. If only she had.

Here, on her right hand, she had the churchyard. The grave crosses stood there, casting black shadows. By each cross a

figure stood enveloped in a black cloak—silent and immovable
they stood there. No, they were only the shadows from the
crosses she saw.

And over there by the stone wall an isolated cross stood:
David's cross! Wasn't there someone standing there by the
cross calling to her?

"Gunhild!" it called. "Gunhild! Gunhild!"

Was it David's voice? She turned her face away—and ran,
ran. She ran for a long time—mile after mile, hour after hour
along a naked, stony strand. The churchyard, the crosses, the
shadows, sailed along silently out there.

She only came to herself when she stood outside the wall
down where Benjamin Sigismund lived and stared up at the
windows.

Was a light burning up in his room? No, of course, it was
only the moon shining on the window.

"Benjamin! Benjamin!"

Here calm descended on her again. Now she began to walk
up the street again. The clock still hadn't struck three. She
walked as if delirious. Where should she go? Home? No! She
daren't go there any more; up there somebody sat waiting for
her. She couldn't rid herself of the thought that David was
there tonight.

At Ol-Kanelesa's smithy she stopped. And almost without
thinking she turned the key. A grating sound came from the
big rusty lock. She started in a cold sweat. Tonight everything
had got a voice. Everything she touched shrieked. To high
heaven! And with her hand on the worn key she stood for a
long time and listened.

No, now everything was quiet. Now everybody and everything slept. Even at the big hostels for the wagoners both
men and animals were asleep. No gates were opened and
shut. No horses' bells rang at the entrances to the big courtyards.

She crept into the smithy. She groped her way forward to
the forge and sat down on a chopping block beside it.

In the quiet and the dark in there a heavy drowsiness came

over her. She felt more secure now. She could again think
calmly and composedly about things. And strange though it
was, she thought more of David now than of Sigismund. She
wondered whether David had lived through the same terrors
the last night he lived as she had tonight. Had fear pierced him
to the marrow as it had pierced her during these long hours?
Yes, for Retribution never let its stinging scourge rest—it was
vigilant and watched carefully that no one sneaked away. For
whatsoever a man soweth, that shall he also reap. So many
times, as she sat behind the spinning wheel and spun and
spun, she had tried to imagine how David had really felt on
that night. And just as she had imagined it—so had she experienced it herself tonight.

"Oh, David! David! Did I cause you so much pain? Now
everything is too late. . . . Nothing can be put right again. And
to sit here and repent, that is little help to you, David."

The clock in the church tower then struck three. Not more
than three strokes did it strike!

Again the rusty lock creaked. The door opened slowly.
Ol-Kanelesa stood in the opening with an oil lamp.

"I knew it was you, Gunhild. Are you cold?"

His voice was cold and severe. He came in and seized her by
the arm.

"Are you cold?" he repeated. "Come now! You can't sit here
destroying yourself."

"Uncle," she began. "You must let me be in peace."

"Come!" he said severely. "Now you must do as I want,
Gunhild."

"Can't I please myself then?"

"No. Nobody can do as he pleases. Come! I've said."

His grip was firm and hard; there was a rugged will in that
grip. She dared not resist. And she went with him. She staggered in front of him up to Elisabeth Cottage. He blew out
the lamp and trotted after her, close on her heels.

At the doorstep outside the cottage she stopped.

"Come!" he said again. "We've further to go, we have."

"Why can't we go in here?" Gunhild asked.

She stood there supporting her back against the railings.

"The door's locked," he said. "Little Ellen's not going to see her mother—not as she is tonight."

Then, finally, tears came.

"Oh, let me go in to Ellen, Uncle. She's my child."

"Not tonight. Come now!"

"Uncle Ola! Are you so heartless?"

"One thing at a time, Gunhild. Come, do you hear?"

"No, I can't bear to go past this door tonight."

"Tonight you must choose between two things: either to go in to Ellen and never see Sigismund again. Or if you want to see him again, you must promise me that Ellen remains here. Here with me. Then I'll have her to myself. Tonight you must answer me that, Gunhild."

She didn't reflect. She said:

"Ellen can stay here."

And then Gunhild went off quickly and defiantly up the street. Ol-Kanelesa was taken aback. He had not expected to get that answer. Well, maybe he had expected that too. He had to test her. In a few hours he might perhaps have some use for what she had just told him. He was glad that Gunhild had answered as she had.

He changed the lamp over into his other hand and went quickly after her.

"Wait a little, Gunhild."

Gunhild stopped and turned towards him. She stood there erect and unyielding. And she looked him straight in the face.

"Now I want to be alone, Uncle. We have nothing more to talk about, we two."

"We have a great deal to talk about, now." His voice was strangely kind. "Now I know what I wanted to know."

"Uncle. I owed you much. You are a good father to me, you—but now I have repaid you. You demanded a high interest on what I owed you. No one could have demanded a higher one."

"Tomorrow you can have the interest. Then we will move our light up to your cottage."

"Ellen, do you mean?"

"Yes, it's she who has been my light now. When she's gone it'll be dark down in Elisabeth Cottage."

Gunhild could hear how difficult it was for him to say these words. She had never heard him speak so strangely before.

"You mustn't think about me now," he continued. "I'm old. And it's dawning on me that I shall soon be moving myself, too."

"But Uncle!"

"There's another Ellen waiting for me. She has waited a long time."

Gunhild went over to him and stroked his cheek with the back of her hand. His cheek was wet.

Early the next morning Ol-Kanelesa walked down the main street, dressed in yellow, tawed elkskin trousers and a blue tailjacket. Where was the sacristan going, all dressed up, and so early in the day?

Those who approached Ol-Kanelesa to ask him where he was going now were imperiously waved aside with his stick. It was clear he hadn't time to talk to anybody. Besides, he looked so serious that they didn't venture to be too forward with him. If he was in that frame of mind they could be exposing themselves to a stinging retort. In general, he had become more and more sharp of tongue with the years. He was almost dangerous.

No, Ol-Kanelesa was not always so gruff. When he came along leading little Ellen, Gunhild Finne's wee girl, he laughed and was in good humor—but if she wasn't with him, it was no longer advisable to let a straw come in his path.

At the pump he met the Works' managing director, Joachim Fredrik Daldorph. He was no less curious than the others. The great man placed himself with his gold-mounted stick in Ol-Kanelesa's path.

"May I ask where our sacristan is making for so early?"

"I'm going up to Mughøla to survey Endre Paasla's mine."

Mr. Daldorph didn't like that answer. He tried nevertheless to laugh. But he couldn't find a ready answer—the matter of surveying miner Endre Paalsen's mine shaft was a painful episode. The shaft had had to be surveyed and measurements taken twice, as the first survey had, notoriously, turned out to be completely wrong.

And, without raising his cap and without looking up at Director Daldorph, Ol-Kanelesa trudged on.

"I say, Ole," Daldorph called out. He had little desire to come off second best. "Who's going to help you with this, you can hardly do it yourself, can you?"

Ol-Kanelesa did an about-turn, went straight up to Daldorph, looked him straight in the face, and said with a wicked grin:

"I'd begun to think about getting Julie Bjelke to come."

Mr. Daldorph then raised his gold-mounted cane. "Watch your tongue, sacristan!"

After that the all-powerful director could stand no more stray shots—the affair of Miss von Bjelke and the Works was something Mr. Daldorph last of all wanted to hear talked about. Otherwise he was a sensible man. A capable mining man who never deliberately did wrong to anyone. He could quite well take a joke against himself without showing his teeth; but when it was a matter of the Works' honor and reputation—no. He wasn't going to put up with that.

Ol-Kanelesa now rushed in through the gateway of the manse.

Here his face became serious again. He stopped and breathed heavily. Today he was on an errand he would have preferred not to have had—he still didn't know how he was going to carry it out. He wanted most of all to turn back.

Slowly he went up the steep back stairs. This was his usual way. It also gave him the chance, before he went in to the pastor, to exchange a few words with the elder Miss Bjørnstrup who was still here helping. From this obliging lady he learnt how Sigismund had been since his last visit. Thus, Ol-Kanelesa never went in quite unprepared to the pastor.

Miss Bjørnstrup told him that the pastor had had a restless
night. She took her apron to her eyes and began to cry. The
housekeeper and she had lain awake almost the whole night
and had heard his Reverence praying aloud several times.
Now he was asleep—yes, it now looked as if peace had finally
descended on him.

"Then I'd best sit down and wait until his Reverence
awakes." Ol-Kanelesa looked round for a chair. "He must get
all the sleep he can. He's had a long night, I can see."

"Oh, he suffers terribly," the tender-hearted Miss Bjørnstrup
sobbed. "Do you know what he said, Ole?"

"No."

" 'Miss Bjørnstrup,' he said. 'Do you know who Nemesis is?'
'No, Mr. Sigismund,' I answered. 'You don't?' he said. 'Then I
prefer not to tell you who he is. You, who are so good, will
never get a visit from him.' Who is it, Ole?"

"Hm! It's retribution, that's what it is, Miss."

"How do you know that? Are you *so* learned?"

"I've only blundered my way through a few books."

"In dear departed Thomas von Westen's writings?"

"In them, too."

"But you intended to become a pastor yourself at that time,
didn't you? I heard it from your betrothed, Miss Ellen."

"God bless her!" was all Ol-Kanelesa said—at that moment
Sigismund called out from his bedroom:

"Is Ole Korneliusen out there?"

Ol-Kanelesa took off his cap. He grew pale as he stood
there. Sigismund's voice had taken on such an unpleasant
hollow sound.

And Ol-Kanelesa tiptoed quietly in.

"Good morning, Ole," Sigismund said and drew himself
up in bed. "Thank you for coming. Thank you! Thank you!"

He seized Ol-Kanelesa's hand and held it for a long time between both of his.

"Do you know what I did during the night, Ole?"

"No."

"I have prayed for David—David Finne; for his soul, I

mean. Don't you, too, believe that one can pray for a dead person? The Lord's boundless love can certainly include the departed—also those who, according to our ideas, did not enter into his glory. Our Lord and Saviour assuredly did not descend to the kingdom of the dead in order to increase their tortures, but to alleviate them."

Ol-Kanelesa stood bent over him. Sigismund's face shone with peace, happiness, victory.

"And I have also prayed for her—for Gunhild."

"Gunhild too?"

"I prayed that the light and the wondrous sun of grace might very soon dawn for her. She is still so young. She has quite certainly a long life before her. Ole, does Gunhild hate me?"

Ol-Kanelesa pursed his lips and shook his head. It seemed to him that this was the best answer he could give.

"Are you quite certain of it, Ole?"

"Yes."

"And do you have clear proofs of it?"

Ol-Kanelesa then began to tell him, slowly and with much detail, what had passed between them during the night. . . . Now he was wondering whether she might come up and speak with the pastor?

Sigismund lay for a while with his eyes closed. His face, which recently had shone with peace, once again took a sorrowing expression; suffering again came into it.

"I don't know, Ole," Sigismund said. "She will come in here in possession of her full health and in the beauty of her youth. And I—I lie here ill, marked by death. Don't you think we shall both be the losers in eternity if we see each other again? When we parted, we felt in spite of everything that we were one. If we see each other now, we will perhaps discover that time and the years have moved us far from each other."

Ol-Kanelesa withdrew his hand carefully.

Of course Sigismund was right. But would Gunhild understand this?

"No, Ole," Benjamin Sigismund said, and sat up in bed. "Two souls which once have been one will quickly find each other again. I want to see Gunhild. Yes, I want to see her, Ole Korneliusen."

The pastor is making a mistake here, Ol-Kanelesa thought. But he didn't want to discuss it now. Besides, he ought only to wish that it was him and not Sigismund who was mistaken. For other reasons, too, he preferred to get out of discussing these things. He had lived here now for almost two generations and formed some opinions—opinions which for *him* had acquired value. Why should he now, in his old age, destroy them?

"Help me up, Ole. These pains are plaguing me. Thank you! Thank you! Kari, bring a little warm water in here. No, its the pain in the left side—now, that was a bit better. Would you be so kind, Ole, to find my razor?"

And while Sigismund with great difficulty got his clothes on, Ol-Kanelesa stropped his razor. At intervals, he plucked a hair from his head and tested the edge on it—it was a poor razor.

"How happy I am that Gunhild wants to talk to me, Ole. Is she just as beautiful and wonderful?"

"Beautiful and wonderful?" Ol-Kanelesa repeated. "She's just about the same as people usually are."

He had never thought that Gunhild was—beautiful and wonderful. Wasn't that what Sigismund had called her? No, one could hardly say that Gunhild was that, nor anyone else either; yes, one! *She* was certainly one you could call both beautiful and wonderful. No, this wretched razor! The best thing would be to try spreading a little ash on the strop. Yes, now the edge was coming up. Wasn't that what he had thought, that ash would help?

"What do you think, Ole, do I look very ill?"

"Your Reverence could have looked worse."

He hadn't the heart to say what he thought. The truth was: the pastor looked fey. It was impossible that he could be long for this life.

"Thank you, Ole. Put the razor there. Thank you, Kari. Let me have the water over here by the bed."

The housekeeper dried her wet fingers on her skirt and then gave Ol-Kanelesa a furtive glance. He pretended not to see it.

"Will you ask Gunhild to come then, Ole Korneliusen? Give her my warmest greetings. And say that I am so happy that she wants to come."

"What time shall she come, then?"

"Now, at once—no, not just yet. Ask her to come when the clock in the church tower strikes ten."

Then it was Ol-Kanelesa who seized Sigismund's hand.

"You mustn't ask too much of each other, you and Gunhild. The world has been harsh with you both since you last met."

He put his cap on and left—as quietly as he had come.

In the cold half-darkness between the ancient timber walls out on the veranda, he stopped with bowed head and stared at the ground. Then he went a few steps down the stairs; but in the middle he stopped again. . . . He was not so certain that he would see Benjamin Sigismund again.

Ol-Kanelesa clutched his breast. When Sigismund was gone, it would be desolate and lonely here in Bergstaden. He had been a good friend; he couldn't remember a better—although there was a great difference between them in rank and station. He pondered a little, too, as to whether he ought not to go up to him again and thank him for their friendship. Tomorrow it might be too late. . . . He went up a step, but stopped again. He couldn't do it. It would probably only scare Benjamin. Then it was better to let it be. In a short time he would, anyway, meet his friend again. On the other side they would meet again. . . . He, Ol-Kanelesa, was an old man. He, too, would soon have to take his wanderer's staff in his hand and depart.

No smoke rose up from Ol-Kanelesa's smithy that day; the door was closed and the key taken out. Where was he then? He wasn't up at Elisabeth Cottage. Nor had anybody seen him in Bergstaden since early this morning when he was standing, dressed in his Sunday best, down at the pump talking to

Mr. Daldorph. Was he up at the pastor's? No. Miss Bjørnstrup could only say that he left there a little after the clock struck nine. But he hadn't looked well. He had been unusually pale.

About seven o'clock in the evening, a furnace minder, Jon Haraldsen Benz, had come with a load of hay on his back from his pasture up at the Hitter Lake. He had seen Ol-Kanelesa about midday walking quickly up the road over the sand banks. What had become of him, he couldn't say. He hadn't thought much about it.

                          In Benjamin Sigismund's study the resinous pine wood was burning with almost black flames.

Joachim Fredrik Daldorph, who was scarcely any friend of Benjamin Sigismund—that Swedish knight!—had one night in the autumn, without saying anything, sent two good loads of oily, phosphorescent pine of the finest sort up to the manse—it was mainly the result of an impulse on Mr. Daldorph's part. However, now he was ill this odd pastor was very welcome to this little gift. Here in Bergstaden, where almost everybody burned nothing but damp peat and birch from which there was little or no blaze, phosphorescent firewood was a rarity.

With Miss Bjørnstrup's help Sigismund had eventually found out who the donor was. Sigismund had then written a charming little letter to the director. He had the very same evening read the letter aloud to his cousin, Mrs. Dagmar Irgens. And moved to tears the beautiful lady had exclaimed: "In spite of everything, he's a great man, Joachim Fredrik." "Yes, perhaps he is," the director had answered, and threw the pastor's letter into the fire. "I know that there are certain women who like to think that." To this Mrs. Irgens had made no reply. . . . She just went on sitting there with bowed head, busily knitting a pair of mittens she had thought of giving her cousin on his birthday. He could use them on his many journeys to the mines in the coming winter.

. . . No other light was burning in Sigismund's study. He

sat fully dressed in his chair. He sat for long periods with
closed eyes and let the warmth from the hearth shine on his
pale face and cold hands. Gunhild sat on a stool—a little in
the shadows.

"Gunhild," he said. "Do you remember the last time we
two sat and talked to each other?"

"Yes, Benjamin."

"And you can now think of it without bitterness?"

"Yes, yes.

"How I love you—for that."

"And you, Benjamin, can you also think of it—without being
bitter."

"Can I?" He smiled as if in a dream. "There are no shadows
over that memory now. None, Gunhild."

And they went on sitting there, without saying anything—
for a long time.

They had sat there together for many hours now, but little
had been said between them. Where should they begin and
where should they end? And that which had been said had
been said by Benjamin. She had sat for so many years at the
spinning wheel and had been silent. She had forgotten to
speak. . . . She could only think and ponder. And be silent.

"Now I will try to walk to and fro in the room a little. Yes,
I am feeling better now. Today, I shall walk a little—tomorrow
a little more, the next day a little more still. Perhaps God wills
that I shall become quite fit?"

He stretched out his hand to her.

And again Benjamin Sigismund stood beside her. For the
first time for many years—many long years. . . . He put his arm
in hers. And, thus linked, they walked several times to and
fro between the window and the hearth.

And then he turned suddenly towards her. He took her head
between his hands and looked into her face.

"Oh, you mountain rose! How can you love me now—now,
when— Oh, you see yourself how I look."

"Benjamin." She leaned towards him. "If anybody found the

mountain rose lying in the street, they would spit on it and kick it out of the way."

He put his hand on her mouth, so that she could say no more. "Will you first answer my question, Gunhild?"

"Does it matter how anyone looks?" She said. "Aren't you what you are—however you look? If it's appearance it depends on, then I'll go. And then I'll never come back again, Benjamin."

"You are right, Gunhild. Certainly, you are right. You, too, are what you are, Gunhild."

"Are you tired, Benjamin?"

"No, no. I am not tired. No, I do not know. I only know that we have found each other again—we two lost creatures. And even if eternity sinks down between us, it cannot part us." And after a little he said: "How beautiful this day has been. All the days of sorrow, the hours of adversity, darkness, and fear are to be reckoned as nothing compared with the happy hours we have lived through today. How richly merciful God has been towards us two. Tomorrow we will go to church and thank him. And should my hour of death be postponed— let us say a few weeks—no, days—then you shall be my bride. The Reverend Mr. Holger can then marry us on the twenty-fifth Sunday after Trinity. I am quite certain that I shall live for a time yet—live so that we can be apportioned that happiness which we have been allotted."

He had tired himself with talking. He had to sit down again.

"Tomorrow when you come back, you will find me strong and many years younger. And then you can stay with me the whole day. Then we will only talk of our future, short or long, it stands in the hands of the Lord. How I look forward to your coming again tomorrow. You must come early, you promise that, don't you, Gunhild?"

"Yes. Yes."

"Tonight we shall not watch, we two. We shall go to bed, grateful and secure. Our night watches are at an end. . . . Even the fourth night watch is at an end."

"Yes, Benjamin."

"About midday your uncle, Ole Korneliusen, is also certain to come. He is a noble man. His thoughts have been with us today. I have felt it the whole time. He has certainly knelt somewhere or other and prayed for us. I have felt that too. I want to thank him for it."

Gunhild then said good night and left. Benjamin Sigismund went with her down to the door. He opened it wide so that she could see her way down the stairs.

She went down the stairs backwards—so as to see him as he stood there in the light of the fire. He was just as young and handsome now as on that first spring morning when she met him up by the church gate.

. . . That night a furious raging storm passed over the mountains and Bergstaden. People awoke about midnight with the north wind and driving snow howling in the chimneys and thrashing against the windows. Up in the churchyards there was a rending sound of old grave crosses being blown over. Tonight nature itself was obliterating and annihilating many a half-forgotten memory. Name boards were torn out and thrown amongst the grave mounds; grave stones were snowed up. But there were three crosses which the north wind couldn't master this time either, they were the three iron crosses Ol-Kanelesa had put up—the crosses over his brother's, Ellen von Westen Hammond's, and David Finne's graves. They went on standing.

During the most powerful gusts of wind there was a clinking sound from the big bell in the tower; a generation might pass between each time that happened. When it did happen, it seldom meant anything good.

And the men got out of bed and closed the dampers in the chimney breasts. Afterwards they lay there for a long time, listening to the storm before they got off to sleep again. But would there be reports of disasters after this? If this winter continued as it had begun it would be bad enough both for man and beast. True enough there had been peace and good harvests for a while now—but Poverty still sat grey, skinny, and shivering in many a home.

And as the night had been, so was the day too. The storm lifted a little in the grey of the dawn; then it began again with renewed rage. Walls and fences were lashed by the snow until the whole town lay completely white, snowdrifts hung in draperies out over the eaves; in the streets it was almost impassable.

Gunhild Finne was on her way down the main street. She had promised Benjamin to come early. She heard people calling and shouting in the driving snow—but she took no heed of it. She just went on. She hadn't any time to stop and talk to anybody.

She ran up the steep stairs in the manse. And it seemed as if her heart stood still in her breast. She didn't know why.

On the landing she met Miss Bjørnstrup. Her face was puffed up and tear stained.

"Mr. Sigismund is dead," she said.

She let herself down on a clothes' chest and sobbed into her apron.

Gunhild pushed past her and went in. There Miss Bjørnstrup and some others found her standing in front of the bed, staring fixedly down at the dead man.

Benjamin Sigismund lay as if he was asleep, with his hands folded over his chest. The housekeeper had found him in that position. His face expressed nothing but peace.

Gunhild was the only one who didn't cry. When they spoke to her, they got no answer. She didn't look up at them. She only looked at him, Benjamin.

About midday she went back up the main street again; the storm kept her hidden and threw a white, closely fitting cape over her shoulders. She could hardly be distinguished from the snow.

At Elisabeth Cottage six men were struggling, amongst them Jon Haraldsen Benz, to carry in the body of a frozen man through the narrow door; it was Ol-Kanelesa.

An ore wagoner from the Storvarts mine had found him sitting stiff and lifeless in a snowdrift at the north end of the Hitter Lake.

Gunhild was passing by. She heard little Ellen's frantic wailing from inside the cottage.

Now it was no longer snow that was falling; it was fire——

From Iceland

Fire and Ice:
Three Icelandic Plays,
with introductions by
Einar Haugen.
Jóhan Sigurjónsson, *The Wish*
(*Galdra-Loftur*), translated
by Einar Haugen.
Davíð Stefánsson, *The Golden
Gate* (*Gullna hliðið*),
translated by G. M. Gathorne-
Hardy. Agnar Thórðarson,
Atoms and Madams
(*Kjarnorka og kvenhylli*),
translated by Einar Haugen.
1967.

Gunnar Gunnarsson,
The Black Cliffs.
Svartfugl, translated from
the Danish by
Cecil Wood, with an introduction
by Richard N. Ringler. 1967.

Halldór Laxness,
World Light.
Heimsljós, translated by
Magnus Magnusson. 1969.

From Norway

Johan Falkberget,
The Fourth Night Watch.
Den fjerde nattevakt,
translated by
Ronald G. Popperwell. 1968.

Aksel Sandemose,
The Werewolf.
Varulven, translated by
Gustaf Lannestock, with an
introduction by
Harald S. Næss. 1966.

Tarjei Vesaas,
The Great Cycle.
Det store spelet,
translated by Elizabeth Rokkan,
with an introduction by
Harald S. Næss. 1967.

From Sweden

Tage Aurell,
*Rose of Jericho and
Other Stories.*
Berättelser, translated by
Martin Allwood, with an
introduction by
Eric O. Johannesson. 1968.

Karin Boye,
Kallocain.
Translated by
Gustaf Lannestock, with an
introduction by
Richard B. Vowles. 1966.

Peder Sjögren,
Bread of Love.
Kärlekens bröd, translated by
Richard B. Vowles. 1965.